SPECIAL MESSAGE TO READERS

This book is published under the auspices of

THE ULVERSCROFT FOUNDATION
(registered charity No. 264873 UK)

Established in 1972 to provide funds for research, diagnosis and treatment of eye diseases. Examples of contributions made are: —

A new Children's Assessment Unit at Moorfield's Hospital, London.

•

Twin operating theatres at the Western Ophthalmic Hospital, London.

•

A Chair of Ophthalmology at the University of Leicester.

•

The establishment of a Royal Australian College of Ophthalmologists "Fellowship".

You can help further the work of the Foundation by making a donation or leaving a legacy. Every contribution, no matter how small, is received with gratitude. Please write for details to:

THE ULVERSCROFT FOUNDATION,
The Green, Bradgate Road, Anstey,
Leicester LE7 7FU, England.
Telephone: (0116) 236 4325

In Australia write to:
THE ULVERSCROFT FOUNDATION,
c/o The Royal Australian College of
Ophthalmologists,
27, Commonwealth Street, Sydney,
N.S.W. 2010.

Kate Alexander is a prolific and successful author who has published short stories and novels, including *Voices of Song* and *Family Trees*, under three pseudonyms. She trained as a secretary and worked in Switzerland and Canada; on her return to England she was employed for many years in the steel industry before becoming a full-time writer. Her interests include drama, music, archaeology, history, walking and travel and she now lives in Surrey, in the town where she was born.

DAWN

Madeleine Ardingley is shocked to learn that her beloved father is a liar and a cheat. The innocent, convent-educated girl is swept into the Parisian demi-monde and finds it not to her liking, though it appears to her cousin, Lord Janus Chilcote, that she is very much her father's daughter. Two years later, Madeleine is forced to appeal to the charity of the family in England she barely knows. Her quiet dignity and gentle manners soon win their affections, but Janus is as cynical as ever. However, Madeleine is to discover that he is a truer friend than she had ever imagined . . .

Books by Kate Alexander
Published by The House of Ulverscroft:

PATHS OF PEACE
FRIENDS AND ENEMIES
FIELDS OF BATTLE
BRIGHT TOMORROWS
SONGS OF WAR
GREAT POSSESSIONS
THE SHINING COUNTRY
THE HOUSE OF HOPE
VOICES OF SONG
FAMILY TREES
LOVE AND DUTY

KATE ALEXANDER

DAWN

Complete and Unabridged

CHARNWOOD
Leicester

First published in Great Britain in 1981 by
Judy Piatkus (Publishers) Limited
London

First Charnwood Edition
published 1997
by arrangement with
Judy Piatkus (Publishers) Limited
London

The right of Kate Alexander to be identified as
the author of this work has been asserted by her
in accordance with the
Copyright, Designs and Patents Act, 1988

British Library CIP Data

Alexander, Kate
    Dawn.—Large print ed.—
    Charnwood library series
    1. Love stories
    2. Large type books
    I. Title
    823.9'14 [F]

    ISBN 0–7089–9050–9

Published by
F. A. Thorpe (Publishing) Ltd.
Anstey, Leicestershire
Set by Words & Graphics Ltd.
Anstey, Leicestershire
Printed and bound in Great Britain by
T. J. International Ltd., Padstow, Cornwall

This book is printed on acid-free paper

Le regret d'un instant te trouble et te dévore,
Tu dis que le passé te voile l'avenir:
Ne te plains pas d'hier; laisse venir l'aurore;
Ton âme est immortelle, et le temps va s'enfuir.

Lettre à M de Lamartine
Alfred de Musset

1

It was a wild day in March and the Channel ferry between Calais and Dover had been delayed; even the Age of Steam sometimes had to yield to the elements. The majority of the passengers who stumbled off her were only too thankful to find themselves on dry land once more, but there was at least one young lady who had not succumbed to the horrors of sea sickness. She had spent the greater part of the journey on deck, staring over the tumbling waves, wrapped impenetrably in a heavy, grey cloak with a deep hood, and oblivious to the stares of such passengers as felt themselves well enough to take an interest in their fellow human beings.

She continued to attract attention after she had disembarked, both from bustling travellers wishing to get past her and from more leisurely by-standers confident of obtaining rapid attention from the busy porters when they required it. Janus Ardingley, tenth Lord Chilcote, returning via Europe from a voyage to Egypt as a member of the unofficial entourage surrounding the Prince of Wales, who had spent the Channel crossing in the seclusion of a first class cabin, cast an idle eye over her and allowed his gaze to linger. A notable connoisseur of the female form, his experienced examination detected beneath the shabby cloak a figure both young and shapely. For all that, he would have spared her no more than a passing glance if a gust of wind had not caught the hood of her cloak and whipped it away from her head. He had been leaning negligently on the railing of the boat, in no great hurry to set foot on his native shore and willing to allow the crowd to disperse before making a leisurely descent of the gangway, but now he straightened up and looked at the girl with sharper attention. Not only had the sudden unveiling revealed a face of startling beauty, it was a face he knew.

His mind flew back to that one distasteful meeting in Paris with his late uncle, Francis Ardingley, and his daughter, Madeleine. He had gone, rigid with disgust, to Francis's lodgings in search of a young acquaintance who had been fool enough to allow himself to be inveigled into playing cards with Francis. The memory of the scene was vivid in his mind: the excited young man, a pigeon ripe for plucking, his Uncle Francis, smiling and genial, as well he might be with the pile of money already in front of him, and standing behind his chair, exquisite in a gown of yellow silk, the girl, Madeleine. He glanced down at her again as she stood on the quayside, his lips twisting in a sneer which had grown habitual with him. The face he now saw was altered in some subtle way. It was thinner, for one thing, and the change was becoming to her, revealing more clearly than before the fine bone structure beneath the flesh. It was older, too. He frowned suddenly. It was not so very long since he had played out that repugnant little scene and yet his recollection showed him a face lovely, but as yet unformed, retaining an almost childish plumpness about the cheeks and chin. For the first time something like a doubt of his own judgement came into his mind. Had she really been as young — so *very* young — as his memory now presented her to him?

She was still standing alone on the quayside. With sudden decision he tossed the cigar he had been smoking into the sea and made his way off the boat, as striking a figure in his way as his cousin Madeleine; taller than most of his fellow men, just as she was taller than most women, with the well-made figure of a natural athlete who, in spite of a physical handicap, excelled at most sports and indeed entered into them with a special recklessness born of an unstated requirement to overcome the misfortune of a weakness in his left arm and a curiously twisted hand resulting from a childhood fever. 'Claw' Chilcote men called him, and spoke with reluctant admiration of his notable feats of athleticism and, beneath their breath, of his equally notable conquests among the female sex. He was as dark as his beautiful cousin was fair and his naturally swarthy complexion had been recently tanned by his exposure to the Egyptian sun.

Madeleine felt his eyes upon her as he made his way across the littered stones and since she was expecting to be met, she turned to face him, expecting an almost-forgotten uncle and finding instead an only-too-well remembered cousin. He sketched an ironically courteous bow and she bent her head in acknowledgement in a gesture at once proud and submissive. It aroused in Janus Chilcote a feeling of amused irritation, not untouched by admiration. Just so did his finely-bred Arabian mare greet him, with that arching of the neck and lowering of the head which conveyed that, though she might be bridled, her spirit was far from broken. He sensed that the mare, for all her obedience to his commands, believed herself to be his superior and so, apparently, did this creature. His interest was aroused and he said less abruptly than he might otherwise have done: 'Good-day, cousin! I had not expected to see you in England.'

He could not remember that he had heard her speak before. It was intriguing to discover that she spoke her native tongue with a slight French accent.

'My father is dead,' she said. 'You knew that?'

'I had heard that the world had been relieved of his presence,' he drawled. 'Do you expect me to condole with you?'

She drew herself up and her eyes flashed, but all she said was: 'I am to live with my mother's family.'

Janus's mobile eyebrows flew up. 'You — in the Lorgan household? That should flutter the dovecotes. We shall be neighbours — on the rare occasions when I visit my Kentish home.'

'Are you going there now?'

He thought he detected a degree of anxiety in her question and the sneer on his lips intensified. 'No, cousin, you may rest easy.

4

I am going to London.' He hesitated and then asked reluctantly, 'Can I give you any assistance?'

She shook her head. 'My uncle is to meet me.'

Lord Chilcote looked round. 'Here he comes now,' he said. Again he hesitated, but Arthur Lorgan had seen him and he owed the fellow the modicum of politeness, so he waited until the older man had come up to his niece before bowing with the same half-mocking gesture he had bestowed on his cousin, and then sauntered away in the rapidly-dispersing crowd.

'I didn't know you were acquainted with Lord Chilcote!' Arthur Lorgan exclaimed, too surprised to greet his niece properly.

'We have met only once before,' Madeleine said. Arthur Lorgan was still looking at her strangely and so she added, as truthfully as she chose to speak at that time: 'He recognised me and came to ask if I required assistance.'

'I see.' Arthur Lorgan smiled. 'I must say I should not have recognised you myself if you had not been pointed out to me. You have changed a great deal since I last saw you as a little girl.'

He spoke as if in jest, but the truth was that he was filled with dismay. This beautiful, sad-eyed creature was quite different from the orphaned niece he had seen in his mind's eye. She was so tall, almost as tall as he was, and her looks were so striking. He cast a surreptitious look at her as he guided her away from the dock. Her carriage was noticeably good, which made her

5

seem all the taller, and her figure, as far as one could judge under that concealing cloak, was slender and graceful, but it was her colouring which was truly astounding. The piled masses of her hair were a true, rich gold — not red, but nothing like the delicate fairness of his own elder daughter — and her eyes were of a clear, light colour between blue and green. Aquamarine eyes, Arthur thought, and then pulled himself up sharply for being fanciful. One could not wonder that Lord Chilcote had remembered her; her face once seen was likely to remain stamped on a man's memory for many years to come. What was his wife going to make of her? It had not been easy to persuade Alice that it would be right to take this unknown girl into their household, and he knew his wife too well to imagine that the girl's looks would endear her to her aunt. Alice would do her duty, no doubt, but he was chillingly aware that Madeleine could have expected a far warmer welcome if she had been short, dark and rather plain.

Inland, the weather was not as turbulent as it was at the coast. Fitful gleams of sunshine lit up the Kentish hedgerows and tempted Phoebe and Bella Lorgan away from the lane where they had been taking their daily walk and into the adjoining woods in search of primroses, but a sudden flurry of raindrops took the girls by surprise and sent them running away from the scanty shelter of the still-bare trees, across the lane, through the gates of Bantock House and up the gravel drive.

Bella darted ahead while Phoebe, conscious

of her closer approach to womanhood, followed more sedately, her hands full of the flowers she had gathered. Seeing that her younger sister was making for the front entrance of Bantock House, she called out in her sweet, high voice, 'The side door, Bella, the side door!' But Bella paid no attention. Instead, she darted up the three broad steps which gave access to the imposing entrance to their home and set the bell pealing. By the time Phoebe had mounted the steps, the door had been opened by a smart man servant, with Fitton, the family butler, hovering in the background.

'Oh, Fitton!' Bella exclaimed unrepentantly. 'Did you think it was Papa? It's only us, sadly dirty and wet, I fear!'

'So I see, Miss Bella,' he replied, with a little severity in the look he turned on her. 'You had better let James take your pelisse — and you, too, Miss Phoebe.' He spoke more gently to Phoebe, for she was something of a favourite, and if she lacked the liveliness of her younger sister, she was a very pretty-behaved young lady and always ready with a word of thanks, such as she gave James now as he relieved her of her damp jacket.

One of the doors off the entrance hall opened and Mrs. Lorgan came out, the same look of expectancy on her face as Fitton had worn when he had approached the front door. It faded when she saw no-one there but her two daughters.

'Bella! Phoebe!' she exclaimed. 'To be sure it is by far too early for your father, but I thought . . . '

7

'I am sorry, Mama,' Phoebe apologised. 'We should have come in by the side way.'

'Oh, fiddle, it was raining too hard to go all round the house.' Bella interrupted.

Her mother frowned. 'That is a most inelegant expression and you look a sad pair of romps, the pair of you.' She said, 'I do not wonder at your want of conduct, Bella, though it is time you began to leave these childish ways behind, but I am surprised at you, Phoebe. Where have you been, may I ask, to return so muddy?'

'We ventured into Chauntry Woods, Mama, in search of primroses. See, are they not pretty? I mean to place them in our cousin's room, to welcome her.'

She held up the pale yellow flowers in an appealing gesture, aware that her words would not please her mother and hoping to divert her by the sight of the charming bouquet she had gathered.

'Chauntry Woods!' Mrs. Lorgan exclaimed. 'Phoebe, I am truly displeased with you! Surely you realise that you have been committing a trespass?'

'Oh, Mama!' Bella protested. 'Everyone goes into the woods, and I'm sure I do not know why we may not do the same. Lord Chilcote is never at home . . . '

'That is not the point,' her mother said. 'The woods are private. Besides, I'm told that the old tower in there is far from safe.'

'But we never went anywhere near the tower!' Bella exclaimed.

'Bella, I will not have you arguing with me,'

Mrs. Lorgan said, goaded into sharpness. 'Now, let it be understood, once and for all, you are not to go on to Lord Chilcote's land. And don't stand about here in your wet shoes. Go and change them — and your stockings, too!'

The two girls moved away obediently, Bella flushed and defiant, but Phoebe with tears in her eyes and her head bent over the offending primroses.

She raised her soft blue eyes to her mother's face as she passed her. 'I'm so sorry, Mama,' she whispered.

Mrs. Lorgan's face softened and, indeed, it would have required a harder heart than she possessed to withstand the charming sight her daughter presented, even with her eyes swimming in tears. How pretty the child had grown to be! Her complexion wanted brilliance perhaps, but her features were so regular and her expression so sweet, and her hair, arranged in soft ringlets, was just the colour of the primroses she held in her hand.

'Well, to be sure, it was very thoughtless,' she said indulgently. 'I look to you, you know, Phoebe, to check Bella. She is so headstrong!' She glanced round. Bella had already stomped up the stairs; Fitton and James had withdrawn. 'You must know, my dear, that we are not at all on good terms with Lord Chilcote. It's true that he is rarely at Laycott Manor, but if he should return home . . . it would cause your father grave embarrassment if any of his children offended Lord Chilcote. And then again, he is a man whose way of life . . . but, there, I must not enlarge on that subject. Suffice it to say he is not a person whose acquaintance I would desire you to make, and particularly not by means of an unauthorised trespass in his woods!'

'No, Mama!' Phoebe murmured, deeply impressed by these confidences, which marked, she felt, the adult standing she had only recently acquired. 'And may I place the flowers in my cousin's room?' she ventured to ask.

She regretted her question when she saw the frown reappear on her mother's face.

'Flowers in the bedroom!' Mrs. Lorgan said, with a hint of peevishness in her voice. 'Well, I suppose they can always be taken out at night. It is a kind thought.'

Taking this as consent, Phoebe made her escape. Her mother watched her fondly as she ascended the stairs. Next year, she thought, I must and will have a house in London. The child is so pretty, I will not have her throw herself away on some Kentish squire. The fact that she herself had married just such a Kentish squire and had been thought to have done remarkably well for herself was an idea that hardly touched the outer reaches of her mind. She was a little woman, approaching forty, but still with the remnants of good looks about her, with soft, pale hair, like her elder daughter's, a little faded now, but she still thought, and sometimes said, that dear Phoebe reminded her forcibly of what she had been herself at seventeen, although, apart from the pretty fair hair, the truth was that it was the stout, determined Bella who more closely resembled her mother.

She went back to the drawing room and glanced at the clock. For a moment she considered ringing the bell and ordering her afternoon tea to be served immediately, but it would appear in any case in a quarter of an hour and it was scarcely worth upsetting the kitchen routine for such a trivial span of time. The rain had set in in earnest and the fitful wind sent it pattering against the window. Mrs. Lorgan drew her chair a little nearer to the glowing coal fire and cast a thought towards the discomfort her husband must be experiencing on his journey from Dover. She would be glad to see him back once more, even though his return would also mean the arrival of one whose addition to Bantock House she anticipated with a feeling of unease she could not put into words.

Madeleine Ardingley, the cousin for whom Phoebe had gathered primroses, was the only child of Arthur Lorgan's sister, Margaret. Margaret Lorgan had made a foolish, improvident marriage; indeed, she had so far forgotten what was due to her family and upbringing as to elope with the profligate younger son of their neighbour, Lord Chilcote, for which neither family had ever forgiven her. Lord Chilcote, riddled with pride, had been outraged by his son's alliance with a girl whose antecedents had been of the lowliest, for all the family's present affluence, and he had expressed himself in terms which had led to a breach between the families which had not been healed to this day. Subsequent revelations, hushed up though they were, that Captain The Honourable Francis Ardingley had been honourable in title only, and had made his abrupt departure not so much because of his ineradicable passion for his neighbour's daughter as because of an imminent scandal involving a charge of cheating at cards and a request to resign his commission, had only added fuel to the quarrel, since they had allowed Margaret's father to reply to Lord Chilcote's animadversions with charges as wounding as they were true.

The truant couple fled to France and there remained. If Francis Ardingley hoped to achieve more than the company of pretty Margaret by his hurried marriage, he was disappointed. Her father, remarking caustically that he had not toiled and moiled all his life to provide his son-in-law with betting money, removed her name from his Will. A small income of some hundred pounds a year was assured to her, but he never during the remainder of his hard life advanced her another penny.

Lord Chilcote, wounded as much in his pride as in his affections, was equally unyielding. He was never heard to refer to his second son again and the news, conveyed to him by an old friend braver than most of his contemporaries, that Francis had become the father of a baby girl was received in quelling silence. The affair was generally held to have shortened his life. Not long after the child, Madeleine, had seen the light of day her paternal grandfather succumbed to an inflammation of the lungs and joined the seven previous Barons in the family vault.

Francis ventured to write to his brother on this occasion, expressing his regrets and hinting at a wish to make his peace with his family. Since he coupled this with complaints about the mounting expense of supporting a wife and child, the new Lord Chilcote correctly interpreted his desire for a reconciliation as being more pecuniary than filial. He sent him a draft on his Bank with a pithily-worded message to the effect that he would be obliged if his brother would refrain from approaching him again.

After this there was a long period when nothing was heard of the exiles. When Mr. Lorgan died no-one supposed that his demise had been influenced by the loss of his daughter. Only Arthur Lorgan knew that not long before his end his father had spoken Margaret's name in tones of unmistakable regret. It influenced him to make enquiries for his lost sister and even, when he discovered that she was living in Dieppe, to pay a visit to her and her little girl, by then a pretty child of six. The intervening years had not dealt gently with Margaret Lorgan. She had faded into a fretful, complaining woman with indifferent health and a sense of indignation at the way the world had treated her. She was fiercely loyal to Francis and defended his absence in Paris on the grounds that it was necessary for him to resort to the capital from time to time to raise money. Questioned about the means he employed to do this she returned only vague answers. Possibly she did not know, possibly — as Arthur suspected — she chose not to know. He returned to England full of unease and was only slightly reassured to receive a letter from his sister a few weeks later, written in the gayest of spirits, and saying that Francis had been blessed with good fortune and Margaret and the child were leaving their lodgings in Dieppe to join him in Paris. Arthur doubled the income paid to Margaret but since, like his father, he had a marked reluctance to wasting good money, and since his own young family was increasing, he made no further gestures towards her.

Two years later the news of Margaret's death was conveyed to him in a flowerily-worded epistle from Francis. Arthur, having won a reluctant agreement from his wife, wrote offering to take his niece into his own family, but Francis replied even more wordily that nothing would induce him to be parted from the sole pledge of his late wife's affection for him. He would, however, he said, be grateful if the income Margaret had enjoyed could continue to be paid to him in order to allow him to rear her child in some semblance of the station to which her birth entitled her. To this request Arthur acceded, wondering cynically as he did so how much of the cash would actually be spent for the benefit of the child.

Little further news filtered through from France. Once or twice Arthur heard secondhand reports of Francis having been seen in Paris. Nothing was ever said of the little girl. She was almost forgotten, thankfully by Mrs. Lorgan, with an occasional twinge of conscience by

Arthur. As for her father's family, they continued to treat her existence with the most complete indifference. When the ninth Lord Chilcote followed his father into the family vault it was Arthur who wondered whether anyone had notified Francis of his brother's demise; it was doubtful whether the idea even occurred to the new Lord Chilcote, who could have had little acquaintance with his uncle and who was, in any case, reputed to be a cold, hard man, intent on leading a life of dissolute recklessness, and unlikely to pay much attention to family ties.

It came as a bolt from the blue to receive from Madeleine in February 1869 a stiffly-worded letter conveying the news of Francis's death some months earlier, coupled with an appeal for assistance. There was a note of desperation behind her stilted words which alarmed Arthur. On making enquiries he discovered that Francis had long since disposed of his rights to his English funds in return for a cash settlement, and the income Arthur had believed himself to be paying for the benefit of his niece had been passing to quite other hands. The girl was, therefore, unless Francis had made provision for her, which seemed unlikely, quite destitute. She asked for nothing more than funds to pay for her passage to England and perhaps an introduction to some respectable family who might employ her to teach French, but this, of course, was unthinkable. On this occasion Arthur left his wife with little to say. His sister's child, now a girl of nineteen, must be received into their own family. If she was to teach French, let it be to her cousins. Alice Lorgan acquiesced, but with the liveliest apprehension.

Arthur, with an anxious eye to the various business interests which kept him occupied in England, had suggested advertising for a respectable Englishwoman journeying to France who might bring his young niece back with her on her return journey. Failing that, he made a halfhearted offer to go himself to Paris to fetch her. Madeleine had refused both suggestions. She felt herself, she wrote, to be fully capable of managing the journey to England, although she admitted that she would be grateful to be met on arrival. This in itself aroused Alice Lorgan's uneasy suspicions. So young and yet so ready to travel alone! It argued either a lack of sensibility amounting to dullness, or else a sophistication far beyond what was desirable from a mere nineteen years. She herself had never set foot out of England; had never, indeed, undertaken any journey unaccompanied and could scarcely imagine what it must be like to be put to the trouble of purchasing tickets and conveying luggage, and to be exposed to the jostling of a crowd of fellow travellers without the protection of a male companion. She was only thankful, although to be sure it was asking a great deal of him and not at all convenient, that Arthur should have gone to Dover to meet his niece in person. It would have presented such a very off appearance to have her drive up to the door totally unaccompanied.

Dusk had fallen by the time Arthur Lorgan's carriage drew away from the outskirts of Dover.

He had made conscientious efforts to sustain a conversation, but had not succeeded in eliciting much response from Madeleine. She answered his questions about her journey politely, but volunteered little information except in reply to a direct question. It was not that she was shy, he thought. Indeed, she possessed a degree of self-possession beyond her years, so that he found himself addressing her not as a near contemporary of his own daughters, but rather as a mature young woman. It was not until he remarked that England must inevitably seem like a foreign country to her that she turned her great, grave eyes on him and said, with more animation than she had previously displayed:

'Yes, and it distesses me that it should be so. It has been described to me so often that I thought it would seem familiar, but I was mistaken. I stood on the deck of the boat and the cliffs of Dover came towards me on the horizon — tall and white, just as Papa described them — and they were strange to me. Even some of the people who have spoken to me I have found difficult to understand.'

'I dare say some of the sailors may have been very broad in their speech,' Arthur Lorgan remarked. He smiled as he added: 'You have a little French accent yourself, you know.'

To his distress, her eyes filled with tears. 'Is it really so? Papa never remarked on it.'

'He had lived many years in France,' Mr. Lorgan pointed out. 'He probably didn't notice it.'

'He always insisted that I was English,'

Madeleine said sadly. 'But I think I am a foreigner in both countries.'

She turned her head away and gazed out at the darkening countryside and Mr. Lorgan was not sorry to let the conversation lapse for a time. The calm way she brought her father's name into the conversation surprised and confused him. It had not previously occurred to him that he would have to grow accustomed to hearing Francis Ardingley spoken of, still less that he might hear him referred to with some degree of affection. And yet, the unrelieved mourning worn by his niece, her gravity and, above all, the sadness in her eyes, argued a deeply-felt loss and made him admit, with a faintly irritated reluctance, that Francis might have been a better father than he had been son or husband.

Madeleine, watching with unseeing eyes the passing fields and hedges, was equally glad to fall silent. She felt herself unequal to the response her newly-discovered uncle seemed to require of her. She guessed that she might have endeared herself to him by a little display of animation, by exclaiming over the strangeness of her native country, by showing some curiosity about his family, but she felt the effort to be beyond her for the time being. She had been profoundly shaken by her encounter with Lord Chilcote, the last person she had expected to greet her on arrival in England, and the most unwelcome. In Madeleine's mind, as in his, their last meeting remained a vivid memory. A memory from which she shrank with something approaching horror: the first intimation she had

18

received that the life to which she had at that time only recently been introduced by her wonderful, delightful father — a life so packed with delights that it seemed a continual round of laughter and pleasure — might have another, darker side. All the unhappiness she had since experienced seemed to have begun with that one acrimonious interview and, illogically, she held her cousin to blame although, in her juster moments, she knew that it was not his bitter words, not even his contempt for herself and Francis, which caused her such deep distress; it was her father's failure to defend himself against his nephew's accusations.

She started when Mr. Lorgan addressed her again, although his words were innocuous enough.

'I am sorry that we should have provided such poor weather for your first day in England,' he said with what he felt himself to be somewhat forced jocularity.

Madeleine tore her mind away from the unhappy reverie into which she had fallen. Habits of politeness had been deeply inculcated in her and she felt it a duty to respond, now that she had recovered her balance, to the effort Mr. Lorgan was making to engage her attention.

'But it is entirely what I expected!' she said. 'It is well known in France that always it rains in England!'

Arthur Lorgan found himself smiling as much at the French twist she gave to her sentences and the charm of her pretty accent as at the slightly teasing note in her voice.

'Not *always*,' he protested. 'It is only March, after all, and we have a saying, you know, that March comes in like a lion . . . '

'And goes out like a lamb!' she finished for him. 'Oh, yes, yes! I can remember Mama saying that. How strange that I should recall it after all these years! And speaking of lambs, should there not be lambs in the fields now? And apple blossom? I am expecting apple blossom!'

'You shall have it!' Arthur said, as if it were a gift in his power to bestow. 'The orchards of Kent are famous. Kent has been called the Garden of England, you know.'

'So I have come to live in a garden! That pleases me! At my convent I liked very much to help Soeur Angélique to tend the garden, particularly the herb garden.'

'At your convent!' Arthur exclaimed blankly.

'But yes! Papa placed me with the nuns after Mama died, you know.'

'No, I didn't know,' Arthur said. 'You were educated by these nuns then?'

'Yes, until I was seventeen. Then Papa took me to be his hostess at the time of the Great Exhibition.' She forced herself to speak calmly, but once again she was swept by a wave of desperate nostalgia for those happy, brilliant days after her quiet years in the convent.

'His hostess! At seventeen!' Arthur Lorgan exclaimed.

'Yes, I was perhaps too young,' Madeleine agreed with a faint smile. 'At the time I felt myself quite equal to the task — and, indeed,

I managed very well. Now, I wonder at my confidence.'

'It is little more than two years ago,' Mr. Lorgan pointed out, smiling to himself at what he felt to be an unconscious betrayal of her youth.

But Madeleine repeated 'Two years!' in a tone of voice which made him remember uneasily what those years had brought her. The death of a father, a descent into poverty, and now a strange life in a country she had never seen. He did not at that time want to be drawn into a discussion of how Madeleine had lived since the loss of her father, so he returned to the subject which had taken him by surprise when she had spoken of it.

'When you say your father placed you in a convent, do you mean that you became a full-time boarder?' he asked.

'Oh, yes! Except that sometimes Papa took me out for a holiday, but not very often because he had many other things to attend to. You might say, in effect, that the convent was my home.'

'For nine years!'

'For nine years,' she agreed. 'I was very happy.' A shadow crossed her face. 'Very happy,' she repeated.

'Are you . . . I wonder I did not think of it before, but it never occurred to me . . . did you become a Roman Catholic?'

'No; I wished it very much, but the Church would not receive me without Papa's consent and he preferred that I should remain a Protestant.' Again that curious shadow crossed

21

her face. 'Now — it does not seem so important as it did when I was a child.'

The little spurt of animation she had produced for him was waning. It had grown too dark for him to see her face, but he thought she sounded tired.

'You must be very fatigued after your journey,' he remarked. 'Poor child! We shall soon be home now.'

There was a short silence and then Madeleine said in a low voice: 'Is it to be truly my home? You know I asked for no more than an opportunity to establish myself in England. Am I to live in your family?'

'Indeed you are!' Arthur found her hand and pressed it warmly. 'From today it shall be as if I had three daughters.'

2

The bedchamber in which Madeleine found herself when she was at last alone in Bantock House was large enough and comfortable enough to make her feel that she was indeed regarded in the light of a daughter of the house. To Madeleine, who had known apartments of noble proportions furnished in the first style of elegance, it might appear a little provincial and over-decorated, but she had also been acquainted with a degree of squalor which she shuddered to recollect, and so she looked with a sort of fatigued thankfulness at this room, with its pink roses climbing a trellis in a determined way all over the walls, the turkey red carpet, the high comfortable bed covered with a white counterpane, the dark, highly-polished furniture, and stretched out her hands gratefully to the warmth of the fire burning in the grate.

There was a tap at the door and Madeleine called: '*Entrez!*' before it came to her that she was in England now and might not be understood, but the door opened and her cousin Phoebe came in, with her shy, sweet smile and a little blush of bashfulness as she looked up at her tall new cousin.

'Mama has asked me to tell you not to make any alteration in your dress tonight,' she said. 'Dinner will be served directly.'

'I will do no more than wash my face and

hands and tidy my hair,' Madeleine said, with a quick glance in the dressing table looking glass. 'I have time for that?'

'Oh, yes! Jane will bring you some hot water.'

She hesitated, her errand completed, but wishing by some additional word or gesture to extend to Madeleine an individual welcome which she had been too shy to voice on her first arrival. By a happy accident Madeleine's eye fell on the blue china bowl filled with primroses which had been placed on her wash-stand. She moved towards it and touched the flowers with delicate fingers.

'How pretty they are! *Les primavères!*' She turned with a smile to Phoebe. 'You will think me very stupid, but I have quite forgotten what they are called in English.'

'Primroses.' Phoebe flushed with pleasure that her welcoming posy had been noticed. 'Bella and I gathered them for you this afternoon in Chauntry Woods.'

'Oh, that was kind!' Madeleine's eyes narrowed in concentration. 'Chauntry Woods! That is a name I have heard before. It is a part of my family's land, is it not? My other family, I mean. And there are some ancient ruins in the wood — is it not so?'

'There is an old tower in the woods,' Phoebe agreed. She shivered suddenly. 'A horrid place! Mama says it is unsafe. We are forbidden to go there.'

There was another tap at the door and a neat, red-cheeked maid came in, carrying a tall jug of hot water.

'If you please, miss, do you need any assistance?' she asked, obviously repeating a rehearsed speech.

Madeleine shook her head with a smile and would have spoken, but the maid hurried on, 'Madam says I'm to unpack for you while you are at dinner.'

'Oh, but I can . . . ' Madeleine began, and then she pulled herself up. The sparsity of her wardrobe would be known soon enough, there could be little gain in hiding it from the servants for this one night. 'Thank you, I shall be grateful for your help. Perhaps you will open the small bag and find my brush and comb for me now?'

'Yes, miss.'

Madeleine put up her hands and began taking the pins from her hair and Phoebe said, 'I will go. Do you know how to find your way down to the dining room when you are ready?'

Madeleine nodded and smiled and Phoebe went away, while Jane remained to watch in awed admiration as the great shining mass of Madeleine's hair fell about her shoulders.

It was a difficult evening for all of them. Bella was responsible for most of the conversation at dinner. For once Mrs. Lorgan did nothing to curb her younger daughter's chatter and Bella, who still suffered the ignominy of being banished to the schoolroom when there was company, made the most of the excitement of this small occasion. Mrs. Lorgan herself was markedly silent, although she fidgeted in her chair in a fretful way from time to time. Her reaction to her first meeting with Madeleine had been much as her husband had anticipated. The girl's remarkable beauty had induced in Alice Lorgan an irritation of the mind which showed itself in a constant flutter of nervous movement. She was not jealous, not for herself, but there could be no doubt that Madeleine's looks overshadowed Phoebe's demure prettiness and every time Alice Lorgan was forced to make the comparison she grew more dissatisfied with this new entrant to her household. It was all the more annoying that the girl's demeanour could not be faulted. She was quiet, expressing her gratitude simply, but it seemed sincerely, and sat looking sad and tired and distant until Alice Lorgan could have screamed with nervous vexation. It was a relief when Madeleine at last admitted her fatigue and asked permission to retire to bed.

It came as no surprise to Mrs. Lorgan to learn the next day that her husband's niece was not only penniless but had scarcely a rag to her back. She was indebted to her younger daughter for this information.

'Mama!' Bella exclaimed, round-eyed with astonishment. 'Do you know, our cousin has only two gowns, but her night-dresses are made of *silk*!'

She waited hopefully for her mother's reaction. Bella liked a little drama and was not above creating it by making the most of such snippets of news as came her way. But on this occasion she was disappointed. True, her mother looked disapproving and pursed up her mouth in a way Bella recognised as betokening displeasure, but although Mrs. Lorgan might have discussed the implications of this information exhaustively with a contemporary, she had no intention of indulging a fifteen-year-old girl in the same way. Instead, she vented some of her ill-humour by remarking sharply, 'I suppose you have been gossiping with the servants again, Bella! I have spoken to you about this before. It is not at all the thing and Jane is quite forward enough without your encouraging her. I should prefer to hear you practising your new piece on the piano rather than indulging in idle chatter.'

Bella pouted, but she knew better than to cross her mother in this mood and a few minutes later she could be heard picking an inexpert way through one of Mr. Mendelssohn's *Songs Without Words*.

Mrs. Lorgan sought out Madeleine and Phoebe, who were sewing together in the back parlour where the light was good. Madeleine had accepted without demur the suggestion that she should employ herself with some plain sewing for the poor, but when Mrs. Lorgan entered the room Phoebe looked up and exclaimed impulsively: 'Mama, only see how exquisitely cousin Madeleine sews! She says the nuns taught her.'

'No doubt,' Mrs. Lorgan said, giving no more than a cursory glance at the almost invisible stitches. She examined Madeleine herself more critically. Her black gown was plain in the extreme, relieved only by a narrow edging of lace at the neck. She wore no jewellery, no ornaments of any description, but her hair was an adornment in itself and she managed it well, coiling it up in a becoming knot which was an older and more sophisticated style than Phoebe's soft curls.

Mrs. Lorgan found her own sewing and sat down with the two girls, but she only played with her needle and thread.

'How long is it since your father died, Madeleine?' she asked abruptly.

'It was a year last November,' Madeleine said, bending her head over the plain seam she was sewing.

'As long as that! You might perhaps think of lightening your mourning now.'

Madeleine agreed quietly, but she had a very good idea of what Mrs. Lorgan was coming to and so she added: 'Unfortunately, I have only one other gown and that, too, is black.'

Mrs. Lorgan snapped off a length of thread with unnecessary vigour. 'You must surely have had other gowns before your sad bereavement,' she said. 'Could they not have been preserved against the day when you might want them?'

'I sold them,' Madeleine said.

'Sold them!' Mrs. Lorgan exclaimed. A spot of colour appeared on her cheeks. 'It seems a sadly improvident thing to have done, to me.'

'I was hungry,' Madeleine said. Her voice was even, but a spark of indignation had awakened in her or she would not have given such a stark reply even though Mrs. Lorgan's complacency grated on her almost as much as her own faint hauteur irritated the older woman.

Phoebe's sewing lay unregarded in her lap and

she was staring at her cousin in horror.

'How dreadful!' she said in a shocked whisper. 'To be so hungry as to sell your clothes for food!'

Mrs. Lorgan was regretting that she had ever begun this conversation, especially in front of her soft-hearted daughter.

'You managed to keep your silk nightdresses, I understand,' she said.

'Some things I had to keep, even against my will,' Madeleine said. She gave her aunt a quick glance and added with a disingenuousness that was lost on Mrs. Lorgan, 'Worn lingerie is less easy to sell than Worth gowns.'

'Worth!' Phoebe exclaimed. 'Oh, cousin Madeleine, did your gowns really come from Worth?'

Madeleine looked at her with a slight smile, 'Some of them,' she said.

'But I don't understand,' Phoebe said. 'If your Papa could afford to buy your gowns from Monsieur Worth, why were you so poor when he died?'

Madeleine's smile twisted into a rueful little grimace. 'Because Papa could *not* afford to dress me at Worth,' she said. She gave her aunt a very straight look. 'For one brief period of my life I was much indulged. I was too young then to understand that Papa's extravagance was at the expense of other people. I have learnt better since. Give me credit for one thing, madame — I left no debts behind me. I sold everything Papa owned — his clothes, his fine boots and shoes, his watch, his rings, his gold-topped cane.

When I found myself destitute, I sold my own possessions.'

For once Mrs. Lorgan was disconcerted. She had not expected this uncompromising recital when she had brought up the subject of Madeleine's wardrobe, still less had she intended that it should be revealed in front of Phoebe, whose gentle heart was obviously touched by Madeleine's story.

'I wonder you did not apply to your uncle sooner,' she said.

Madeleine hesitated. 'I thought I could support myself,' she said. 'I was wrong.'

'Did you have to *work*?' Phoebe asked in awe.

'I tried,' Madeleine said. A curious look of grief passed over her face. 'I did try,' she repeated.

Mrs. Lorgan fidgeted nervously with her neglected sewing. 'I can see that you will have to be provided with a gown or two,' she said in a more conciliatory voice. 'I will speak to your uncle.'

Madeleine bent her head in the proud, submissive gesture which was characteristic of her, but as soon as she could she escaped from the sewing room and out into the garden. The storm of the previous evening had blown itself out and the weather had reverted to its pattern of alternate sunshine and shadow, although it was far from warm. The shrubbery, however, provided walks which were sheltered and dry under foot and Madeleine pulled a woollen shawl round her shoulders — like a peasant woman, she thought scornfully — and paced about its winding paths until the agitation induced by her aunt's questioning had been subdued.

She paused by a bush of winter jasmine and stared at its delicate, starry flowers with unseeing eyes. It was hard — harder than she had realised it would be — to be an object of charity to these kind, complacent people. If she had not known the alternative she would have chafed against it more openly than she now dared to do. But Madeleine did know the alternative and standing in Arthur Lorgan's tidy, unimaginative garden with the solid comfort of her mother's old home behind her, she renewed the resolve she had taken when she had finally decided to appeal for help to her English relations: to conform in every way to their standards, to be dutiful, and submissive and, if possible, helpful. As to the future, it must take care of itself. Sufficient for the time being that she was fed and housed and, above all, protected. The shudder which went through Madeleine had nothing to do with the cold little wind which rustled through the rhododendron leaves. She huddled her shawl more closely round her shoulders and turned towards the house.

Madeleine was already aware that there were other Lorgan children besides the two girls: Edward, who was away at school, had been mentioned the previous evening, and little Harry, who was still in the nursery.

'We had another little sister, too,' Phoebe had told her that morning as they sat over their sewing. 'Dear little Maria, she came between

Edward and Harry, but she was taken from us when she was only five years old.'

For a moment Madeleine had looked blank and then she had understood Phoebe's meaning and had murmured: 'How sad!' in a politely regretful voice, but try as she would she could feel no particular interest in a cousin who had died without Madeleine having been aware of her existence. She wondered dispassionately whether her own troubles had so deadened her sensibilities that she could no longer participate in the grief of other people. It was a disquieting thought and she was glad when Phoebe had passed on to another subject and she could dismiss it from her mind.

It was Harry who was the next cousin to introduce himself to her, and that most forcibly. He came careering round the corner of the house as Madeleine walked towards it, puffing and shrieking and moving his small arms like pistons, so that it was obvious to anyone with the smallest degree of imagination that here was no small boy, but a railway train — and an express train at that, judging by the speed at which he was moving. The sight of an unknown young lady, dressed all in black, with wonderful golden hair, brought him to a sudden, unscheduled halt. He looked at Madeleine with large, steady eyes.

'Who you?' he demanded.

No-one had told Madeleine that Harry was barely three years old. For a moment she stood quite still, frozen into unnatural immobility, and then she answered slowly and gravely: 'I am

Madeleine. Are you my cousin Harry?'

Harry had not come across this cousin word before and he gave it some consideration before he answered tersely, 'Yes.'

He continued to stand looking at her with his searching, unwavering stare until she asked, 'Do you like to play at trains?'

Harry was smitten by sudden shyness. He took a step backwards. 'Yes,' he said again, and would have turned and run away, but at that moment his nurse discovered his whereabouts and came after him, out of breath and annoyed.

'There you are, you naughty boy!' she exclaimed. 'What do you mean by running out like that? You'll catch your death of cold!' She caught sight of Madeleine and stopped short. 'I beg your pardon, Miss,' she said awkwardly. 'Master Harry gave me the slip. I hope he hasn't been a nuisance.'

'Not at all,' Madeleine said in her prettily accented English. 'But you are right, the child should not stand around in this cold wind without his jacket. Come, Harry, back into the warm.'

She smiled and opened the side door through which she had made her escape to the shrubbery and Harry and the nurse followed her. They left her at the foot of the stairs and she heard Harry demand, as he stomped up the stairs, 'Who that pretty lady?' to which the nurse, conscious that she was overheard, replied: 'That's your cousin Madeleine, Master Harry,' and Harry's further interested question, 'What thing is cousin?'

Madeleine was still smiling at his quaintness

33

as she crossed the wide hall and, her uncle happening to come out of his study at that moment, he was able to remark in a pleased voice, 'I am glad to see you looking a little happier this morning, my dear. Have you recovered from the fatigue of your journey?'

'I am entirely recovered, I thank you, monsieur,' Madeleine replied.

'Good, good! But you must call me Uncle Arthur, not 'monsieur'.'

'Yes, Uncle Arthur,' Madeleine repeated obediently.

'That's better! In that case, I'd like to have a talk with you. Suppose you come and sit down with me now and have a little chat.'

He opened the door he had just closed once more and Madeleine entered the study. With a gesture of his hand Arthur Lorgan suggested a seat to her, but he himself sat down behind his desk and the 'little chat' at once took on the air of a formal interview. Madeleine sat down with all her customary composure, but there was a tautness in her bearing which had not been present a few minutes earlier. Deliberately, she folded her hands in her lap and resisted an inclination to grip them tightly together.

'Mrs. Lorgan has been telling me of the unfortunate straits to which you were reduced before leaving France,' Arthur Lorgan began, pleasantly enough.

Madeleine bent her head in acquiescence and made no other reply. He found himself curiously intimidated by her silence and the steady regard of her strange, haunted eyes.

'You did endeavour to find employment, I understand?' Arthur went on.

'Yes.'

'But you were not successful?'

'On the contrary, I held for a short time two positions.'

'And they were?'

'First I was employed in the salon of a milliner.'

'You mean, you made hats for a living?' Arthur Lorgan demanded in a startled voice.

'By no means,' Madeleine said with a slight smile. 'I had not the necessary skill. I sold the hats.'

'A shop girl!' Arthur Lorgan sounded so affronted that Madeleine smiled again, a little twisted smile with a touch of cynicism in it.

'You might call me so, although I do not think Madame Hortense would like to hear such a description applied to one of her young ladies. It was *un établissement de plus haute classe.*'

'Even so . . . it was hardly suitable for a girl of your birth and education.'

'No, I was ill-suited to it, as Madame Hortense came to realise.'

'She might well do so! What decided you against continuing in her employ?'

For the first time Madeleine's eyes failed to meet his. She looked down at her clasped hands and said slowly, as if she were seeking the right words: 'I was dismissed. In such a position one is much exposed to . . . to the *galanteries* of the gentlemen who come to the salon. I . . . it was better that I should go.'

'I should think so indeed!' Arthur Lorgan looked horrified, and all the more so since he had never entered a milliner's shop in his life and could scarcely imagine what a man would do in such an establishment.

'Of course, you are a very pretty girl,' he said awkwardly. 'This Madame Hortense should have had the sense to keep you out of the way when these men were about. I'm sure you did nothing that warranted her dismissing you.'

There was just the faintest question behind his last remark and again that curious little smile played across Madeleine's lips.

'You mistake the matter, monsieur,' she said drily. 'Madame Hortense was angry because I did *not* allow the advances of these . . . gentlemen. She had thought that they would come frequently to see me and permit their wives to order many hats and this would be good for business, you understand. But I would not at all permit this and so she did not think it of value to keep me.'

'You appal me,' Arthur Lorgan said truthfully. He rubbed a harassed hand across his forehead. 'A girl of your age should know nothing of such things.'

'No? Perhaps it is better that one should know. I was very ignorant and it was not good for me.'

Arthur looked down and began to fiddle with a brass letter-opener which lay on his desk. 'Perhaps it would be better if you did not talk about this to anyone,' he said awkwardly. 'It would distress your aunt and, of course, one would not want the girls to hear of such experiences.'

It was as well that he did not see the look of weary tolerance Madeleine directed towards him. 'I shall respect the innocence of my cousins,' she said, with an irony that was wasted on him.

'Yes, well . . . the purity of a young girl is such a precious thing, once smirched by worldly knowledge it is gone for ever . . . and Phoebe, in particular, has a sensitivity . . . I suppose in France they regard these things differently.'

'On the contrary, young girls in France are most strictly guarded. Young girls of family, that is. They believe that it is the English who have too much freedom.'

'Oh, really? Of course, your own case was somewhat out of the ordinary . . . ' It occurred to him that this remark was not entirely felicitous and he hurried on, 'At least your next situation was entirely respectable, was it not?'

The hands Madeleine had been keeping carefully folded in her lap gripped together so hard that the knuckles showed white.

'I underwent a period of great hardship,' she said. 'But later, yes, when I became the governess of the Bécaud children, it was a household of the most impeccable virtue.'

Again there was an undercurrent of something like irony in her voice which Arthur Lorgan failed to catch.

'It was a pity you had to leave them,' he suggested. 'Although, of course, we are very pleased to have you here,' he added hastily.

Deliberately, Madeleine unclasped her tell-tale hands and laid them one on top of the other in her lap once more.

'Madame Bécaud decided her daughters' education should be continued by a French-woman,' she said with a smooth finality which entirely deceived Arthur Lorgan.

'And that was when you wrote to me?' he asked.

'I despaired of finding another situation in France,' Madeleine said. 'And I could not again face being alone and without money in Paris.' She paused and then added in a low voice: 'I do not think anyone has known poverty who has not been poor in Paris.'

'Well, of course, any big city . . . your father is much to blame for leaving you in such a situation.'

'Possibly.'

'Not possibly — certainly! However, you are my sister's child as well as his and my intention is that you should take your place amongst us on that basis. I dare say that there may be little things you can do to help Mrs. Lorgan . . . '

'I shall be most happy to do so.'

'I don't intend you should become a household drudge, you understand! But it did occur to us that a little French conversation with Phoebe and Bella each day would be no hardship to you.'

'On the contrary, it would be a pleasure.'

'Good! As to the subjects you discuss . . . '

'I will be discreet,' Madeleine interrupted him. 'I have no wish myself, you understand, to revive unhappy memories.'

'No, quite! Then I think there is no more for me to say to you at the present time.' He stood up. 'Mrs. Lorgan will talk to you about clothes and so on,' he said vaguely. 'I believe she thinks it necessary . . . she means to employ a local dressmaker to fit you out in a becoming fashion.'

'I fear this will be a great expense to you,' Madeleine said, rising in her turn.

'No, no! I can't have my niece looking shabby, can I? If I am to have an extra daughter I must do the thing properly.'

He gave her a beaming smile and Madeleine responded by dropping him a small curtsey. Arthur felt a small glow of satisfaction at his own benevolence. It was some time later that it occurred to him that in spite of the readiness and apparent frankness of her replies, he had not, apart from that one unfortunate revelation about the milliner's shop, learnt a great deal about his niece's life in France, and at the back of his mind, unacknowledged and unrecognised, there was a regret, a faint irritation, that he had had to learn about Madame Hortense and the role she had designed for Madeleine.

It was too much to expect that he would keep the story to himself. He might not want Madeleine to discuss it with her aunt, but he was not capable of concealing his disquiet from Mrs. Lorgan. He told himself that it was necessary for her to be on her guard in case an unwary word from Madeleine might lead to awkward questions from Bella or Phoebe, but the truth was that he sought to unload some of his uneasiness by sharing it with his wife.

'She seems to have behaved just as she ought,' he said defensively, in the privacy of their bedroom that night, warned by the look on his wife's face that he had made a mistake in not respecting Madeleine's confidences.

'It's no more than I expected,' Mrs. Lorgan replied heavily. 'A girl with those kind of looks, alone in the world . . . one can only be thankful that it was no worse, with the example she had in front of her all her life.'

'Her convent education must have given her strong moral principles,' Arthur Lorgan ventured to suggest.

Mrs. Lorgan pulled the strings of her nightcap together with vicious force and winced as they bit into the soft flesh below her chin.

'Roman principles!' she said scornfully. 'I shall get the Vicar to examine her to make sure she has a proper understanding of religion.' A thoughtful look passed over her face. 'I doubt whether she has been confirmed. She can go to the Vicarage with Bella.'

Madeleine received the news that she was to join Bella's confirmation class with the same grave acquiescence that she showed towards all the plans Mrs. Lorgan put forward for her future. Bella was the more excited of the two. The classes she had found dull took on a fresh interest when she heard that she was to share them with Madeleine, particularly since they were allowed to walk to the Vicarage alone and this gave her a rare opportunity to have Madeleine to herself without Phoebe's restraining influence, and to ply her with questions which her more sensitive sister would have condemned as intrusive. They had already run into this difficulty during the French conversation periods Madeleine had conscientiously instituted each day. Phoebe would have been content to read aloud from one of the books approved by the governess who had started their French lessons and to follow it up with a plodding discussion; Bella demanded more interesting fare — details of Madeleine's life in France and anecdotes about the Emperor and Empress. Madeleine responded, up to a point. She told of the Tuileries, lit by a thousand candles night after night for balls and receptions, the Place du Carrousel packed with carriages as the *haute monde* struggled to arrive at the Palace.

'Were you presented?' Bella asked breathlessly.

Madeleine hesitated. 'I did not have that honour,' she said.

'But you saw the Emperor and Empress?'

'Frequently. The Empress drives every afternoon in the Bois de Bologne with an escort of the Cents Gardes. I have often seen her. And, of course, I have been at the theatre and the Opera when they were present.'

'Is she really as beautiful as they say?'

'Very beautiful,' Madeleine agreed. 'And always most beautifully dressed.'

'Our own Queen hardly ever appears in public since the death of the Prince Consort,' Phoebe explained.

'So London Society is very dull — except

for the Prince of Wales' set,' Bella added, with a worldly-wise air which brought a spark of amusement to her cousin's eyes.

'I believe the Prince is sometimes a visitor to Paris,' Phoebe said, seduced against her better judgement into joining in this heady talk of high society.

'Yes, he has a great love of France,' Madeleine agreed. 'He told me I was fortunate to have been brought up as a French-woman because the French alone understand *la douceur de vivre*.'

'He *told* you?' Both girls spoke at once, staring at Madeleine with wide, astonished eyes.

'You've *met* the Prince of Wales?' Phoebe asked in an awed voice. It was obvious that the Emperor and Empress of France counted for nothing compared with this.

'Only once,' Madeleine said. 'I was dining in a restaurant with Papa . . . '

'Dining in a *restaurant*!' Bella exclaimed, even more impressed, and fortunately unaware, as Madeleine had been herself at the time, that it was unusual for young ladies of quality to dine in that restaurant, even accompanied by their fathers.

'The Prince was acquainted with some of our party and he asked for me to be presented to him.'

'I expect it was because he thought you were pretty,' Bella said.

With belated discretion Madeleine refrained from repeating the fulsome compliments which his well-dined Royal Highness had showered upon her.

'Yes,' she said, with a dryness which was lost on her admiring cousins. 'I expect it was.' She picked up the book which had been lying neglected on the table. 'Were we not to have read La Fontaine this morning? And how does it happen that we have begun to speak English instead of French?'

Bella pouted. 'You're as strict as any schoolmistress,' she complained, but she took the book and began reading aloud in stumbling, heavily-accented French, which Madeleine did her best to correct. It was as well that they were so innocently occupied, since they were interrupted a few minutes later by Mrs. Lorgan.

She listened for a moment or two and then said, 'That is very nice, Bella, but it will do for this morning. Miss Hershaw is here to give Madeleine the first fitting for a new gown and I don't wish her time to be wasted.' She turned to Madeleine with something less than her customary assurance. 'It occurred to me that I had one or two gowns laid by which might very well be adapted to your requirements. To be sure, you are taller than I am, but you are not so full in the figure, and skirts are not as wide as they were. I think Miss Hershaw will contrive very well. She's quite a clever little woman.'

'It seems to me a most practical idea,' Madeleine replied. She went off to her bedchamber, where the dressmaker was waiting for her, and made a swift assessment of the dresses which were to be unpicked and adapted to her slender form, but if Mrs. Lorgan was

43

relieved by her niece's ready acceptance of her economical idea, Lottie Hershaw found her less tractable. Madeleine had very precise ideas of what was becoming and fashionable and, having been accustomed to the standards of Parisian seamstresses, she was not prepared to lower her sights to accommodate a village dressmaker. The black and white shepherd's plaid would do very well, the grey watered silk even better, but the bodices must fit precisely, the sleeves must be cut just so, and the fullness of the skirt must be taken to the back now that the full crinoline was so *démodé*.

'Hoity-toity!' Miss Hershaw remarked in the housekeeper's room when she descended for her mid-day meal. 'Her ladyship knows what she wants and means to have it, that's for sure. Not but what I was pleased enough to hear what she had to tell me about the Paris modes,' she added grudgingly. 'But you'd never take her for a poor relation, which is what she *is*, when all's said and done.'

'She's an Ardingley,' the housekeeper said portentously. 'Blood will tell. Ladyship you call her, and ladyship she is in all but name. But you'd know more about that than I do, Miss Hershaw.'

Lottie Hershaw, who had lived in the village all her life, agreed with a certain amount of complacency.

'It just came to me while you were speaking, Mrs. Blackett,' she said. 'Who she reminds me of. The old Lord. Not the present one's father, but her grandfather it would be. She's got just his way of carrying her head, and something of his colouring too, though he was more of a redhead than she is. Of course, I don't remember him all that well,' she added hastily. 'Me being only a slip of a girl when he died.'

'That was before my time,' Mrs. Blackett remarked. 'A little more apple tart, Miss Hershaw? Let me press you to a little more apple tart?'

'Well, I won't say no,' Lottie Hershaw agreed.

'I never really knew the ins and outs of how her parents came to go off the way they did,' Mrs. Blackett said casually, helping Lottie Hershaw liberally to an apple tart oozing with sugar and juice.

'Oh, that was a terrible thing!' the dressmaker exclaimed, and settled to a highly enjoyable half hour of gossip and exclamation, at the end of which both women agreed that Miss Madeleine Ardingley had been lucky indeed to end up in the safe haven of the Lorgan household.

'Though, as I said before, blood will tell,' Mrs. Blackett pronounced finally. 'Bad as well as good. Breeding she may have, looks she's certainly got, but it's to be hoped she doesn't take after her father in behaviour — nor her mother either, running off in that wicked way.'

Miss Hershaw was not the only person to remark on Madeleine's likeness to her paternal grandfather. Walking back from the Vicarage with Bella after the first of the classes in religious instruction she had agreed so readily, and with such inward irony, to accept, the two girls were passed by a pony and trap driven by

45

a stout, elderly lady with a mass of untidy grey hair imperfectly controlled under an outmoded straw bonnet. She gave them a piercing look as she drove by and turned her head for a second searching stare after she had passed them, then she pulled up and waited for the two girls to draw level with her.

'You, girl!' she called imperatively to Madeleine. 'Your name Ardingley?'

'Yes, madame,' Madeleine said, with an enquiring look at her.

'Thought so. Madeleine, isn't it, or some such outlandish name?' She held out a hand in a shabby grey glove. 'I'm your Aunt Gertrude.'

In total bewilderment Madeleine put out her hand and received a hearty shake. 'My aunt?' she asked.

'Great aunt by marriage,' the older woman explained. 'I married your father's uncle, Tom Ardingley. Died years ago. Don't suppose Francis ever mentioned him.'

'No, I don't think he did,' Madeleine agreed.

She looked at this unknown relation and found that she was being inspected by sharp grey eyes, as shrewd as they were kind.

'Knew who you were as soon as I set eyes on you,' Mrs. Ardingley said in her abrupt fashion. 'Got a great look of the old lord about you. Your grandfather, I mean. Got his temper too, have you?'

'I hope not,' Madeleine said.

Gertrude Ardingley chuckled. 'Francis put you against him, did he? Ah well, he had a lot to try him. Neither of his sons turned out well. Robert

46

was a fool, and Francis . . . but you know all about Francis.'

Madeleine returned no reply to this and she was again subjected to a long, searching look before her Great Aunt Gertrude gathered up the reins and prepared to move on.

'I make my home at Laycott Manor now,' she said. 'You must come and visit me.'

Madeleine's eyebrows rose. 'I doubt whether that will be possible,' she said.

'Why not? You're an Ardingley. Only right you should see where you come from.' She frowned in sudden understanding. 'Think the Lorgans might object? Probably right. I tell you what, I'll call on Mrs. Lorgan. I don't do the social round these days. Never was much in my line. But this feud is ridiculous now that everyone concerned in it is dead. High time it was forgotten.' She turned her piercing regard on Bella. 'You one of the Lorgan girls?' Bella, stricken to silence for once by this formidable old lady, dropped a schoolgirl curtsey. 'Tell your mother I'll call on her.'

She drove off and left the two girls equally bewildered by the force of her personality and her forthright manner of speech.

47

3

London in April was still a little thin of company, particularly since the Prince and Princess of Wales were prolonging their trip abroad.

'And who can blame them?' Mr. Charles Carford remarked, encountering Lord Chilcote in Bond Street. 'Ghastly weather in England, dull company, scarcely a pretty woman to be seen. Can't think why we don't all go and live somewhere else. What was Egypt like, old chap?'

'An interesting country; I'm glad to have seen it. And warm, which was pleasant in the middle of the winter.' A smile of reminiscent amusement lit up Lord Chilcote's face. 'The Prince was a little stunned by all the magnificence. The Khedive housed him and the Princess in the Esbekiah Palace — solid silver beds and furniture of beaten gold! It made Marlborough House look like a country cottage. Edward assured me their bedroom was not an inch under a hundred and forty feet long and illuminated fountains played in the gardens all night.'

'Did you share in all this luxury, old chap?'

'Not to that extent, but when we went up the Nile we travelled in gold and blue steamers and all six of them towed a barge full of provisions — useful provisions, like several thousand bottles of champagne! We didn't exactly rough it. I took my leave when they returned to Cairo and came straight home. Come and dine with me this evening, Charlie, and I'll tell you all about it.'

'Can't,' Charlie Carford said regretfully. 'Promised to a French chap called Henri de Cavaillon. Over here from Paris with an introduction to m'mother. Desperate nuisance, but I promised to do the pretty, show him the sights, give him a bite to eat n'that. Might take him on to the Alhambra or some such thing.' He was visited by a flash of inspiration. 'Come and join us.'

Janus Chilcote hesitated, but no other plans for the evening occurred to him and so he agreed to meet Charlie and his new acquaintance at the Café Royal at seven o'clock for dinner, followed by a visit to a theatre or music hall. He anticipated no great amusement out of the evening, but it was a way of passing the time and Charlie was quite right in designating London as dull.

The Frenchman proved to be sufficiently entertaining to wile away the dinner hour quite successfully, but Janus Chilcote stiffened when he mentioned a previous acquaintance with another member of the Ardingley family.

'Your uncle, I believe, Lord Chilcote,' he said in his precise, careful English. 'Mr. Francis Ardingley.'

Charlie Carford, embarking unwisely on a second brandy, gave a hoot of laughter. 'The black sheep!' he exclaimed. 'You won't endear yourself to Janus by claiming him as a friend, old chap.'

'He lived somewhat on the fringes of society,' Henri said, in apparent surprise. 'But he was received. Am I to understand that he was not acceptable in England?'

'He left the country under something of a cloud and lived abroad for reasons of economy,' said Janus, dismissing a misspent lifetime in one brief sentence. 'Did you know him well?'

Henri de Cavaillon appeared to hesitate. 'Quite well,' he said. 'But a friendship of the boulevards, you understand. We were not intimate.'

Lord Chilcote was watching him under lowered eyelids. 'Even so, you must have known that his way of life was not at all the thing,' he said.

Henri shrugged. 'As to that, we are none of us angels,' he said easily. 'Monsieur Ardingley was a pleasant companion for an occasional hour or so. His way of life was something one does not enquire into. The man is dead, let him rest and his reputation also.'

'Quite.' Lord Chilcote did not remove his steady gaze from the other man's face. Henri de Cavaillon looked down at the stem of the wine glass he was twisting between his fingers. He was a man of about thirty, compactly built and pleasing to look at. By inclination he was a Parisian, but by birth he was a man of the south and the warm brown tint of his skin and liquid dark eyes betrayed his origin. He smiled easily, white teeth gleaming against his dark skin, and women found an irresistible allure in his caressing manner, with its hint of languor and passion beneath the wordly aplomb. He was well liked by his fellow men, too, for his easy *bonhomie* and apparent good nature. Only cynical eyes like Lord Chilcote's detected in the first, faint blurring of his features, a touch of petulance about the mouth, the evidence of a self indulgence, ruthlessly pursued, which would one day turn him into a gross old man.

'One wonders what has become of the daughter,' he said casually, without looking up.

Janus's eyes narrowed and an unpleasant smile played at the corners of his mouth. 'Ah! My beautiful cousin Madeleine! You had an interest there, did you?'

Henri de Cavaillon looked up from his contemplation of his wineglass, a sudden flash in his eyes. 'An interest, yes, inevitably,' he said. 'She was, as you have said, very beautiful. I repeat, one wonders what has become of her.'

'She is in England,' Janus Chilcote said, still watching him. 'Living with her mother's family.'

Henri's tongue showed for a moment, moistening his full red lips. 'I am glad to hear it,' he said. 'She is not residing in London?'

'No, she is living close to my own estates in Kent. It would be inadvisable,' he added smoothly, 'for you to approach her.'

'The daughter of an old friend . . . ' Henri began, but Lord Chilcote interrupted him. 'Her regrettable father is best forgotten. By herself as well as the rest of the world. Her present decent obscurity will serve very well. I repeat, I would prefer you to leave her alone. Unless, that is, you contemplate marriage?'

'Marriage!' Henri de Cavaillon's head jerked up and he flushed as he met the other man's sardonic eyes.

'No, I thought not,' Lord Chilcote said.

'You never told me you had a beautiful cousin,' Charlie Carford said reproachfully.

'I scarcely know the girl,' Janus Chilcote said indifferently. 'We have only met twice.' He paused; it occurred to him that it was curious how deeply imprinted on his mind the image of Madeleine Ardingley had become in two brief meetings. He dismissed the thought impatiently and went on, 'Nevertheless, she is an Ardingley. I take a certain interest in her welfare.'

Charlie gave one of his sudden hoots of laughter. 'First time I ever knew you to play the part of a family man,' he commented.

Janus acknowledged the truth of this with a twist of his lips that was not quite a smile. 'Monsieur de Cavaillon understands my concern, I'm sure,' he said.

Again his eyes met and held those of the Frenchman. Henri de Cavaillon shrugged with an assumption of indifference. 'You exaggerate my interest, my lord,' he said.

'I hope so,' Lord Chilcote said softly. He took a thin gold watch out of his pocket and glanced at it. 'Do you really care to see one of our London Music Halls? If so, we should leave.'

The talk drifted to a discussion of the rival merits of various theatres, in which Charlie

Carford took the lead, and for the remainder of the evening Henri de Cavaillon exerted himself to be agreeable, although his efforts appeared to be wasted as far as Lord Chilcote was concerned. With Charlie he was more successful.

'Not a bad sort of chap,' was Charlie's version at the end of the evening after they had dropped Henri de Cavaillon at his hotel and were sauntering back towards Grosvenor Square. 'Talks a lot,' he admitted. 'But that's French for you.' He cocked an interested eye at Lord Chilcote. 'What made you take him in dislike, old fellow?'

Lord Chilcote's eyebrows rose in a manner which would have quelled most people, but Charlie was made of more resilient stuff, especially when well fortified by the brandy and soda he had imbibed before taking leave of Henri de Cavaillon. 'No use looking at *me* as if I'd just wriggled out from under a cabbage leaf,' he said. '*I* don't give a jot for your filthy temper.'

A touch of amusement lightened Lord Chilcote's swarthy features. 'I know you don't,' he admitted. 'It must be what I like in you. It can't be your conversation.'

'Not a clever cove, never was,' Charlie agreed. 'But I do know when you've taken an aversion to someone. Very polite, an' all that, but you've been walking round the Frenchman all evening like a stiff-legged dog spoilin' for a fight.'

Janus Chilcote hesitated. 'Damned if I know,' he said. 'Except . . . he revived memories of an old scandal I don't particularly want brought up again.'

'You didn't like him being a friend of that uncle of yours in Paris,' Charlie said shrewdly.

'No,' Janus agreed.

'And the way you warned him off the beautiful cousin was dashed rude, if you ask me.'

'Monsieur de Cavaillon understood me,' Janus said.

'So did I understand you,' Charlie retorted. 'If you'd talked to me like that I'd . . . I'd have planted you a facer!'

Janus Chilcote grinned. 'No you wouldn't, Charlie,' he said. 'You've too much regard for your own skin. Are you coming in for a nightcap?'

Charlie shook his head. 'Going to have an early night, recruit my strength,' he explained.

'It's past two o'clock already,' Janus pointed out.

'First time this week I've been in bed before six,' Charlie said with simple pride.

As he admitted so frankly himself, Charlie's intellectual attainments were not great, but he had a certain innate shrewdness and it struck him as a curious thing that for all his lack of warmth towards the Frenchman, Lord Chilcote appeared to be cultivating his acquaintance in the days that followed their first meeting.

'Funny thing is,' Charlie said. 'He seems to take quite an interest in you, too.'

They were playing billiards at Charlie's club and had the room to themselves. Lord Chilcote looked at the green baize table with narrowed eyes, his attention apparently given to nothing more than the position of the balls.

'What makes you say that?' he asked idly.

'He was asking questions at Mrs. Beauchamp's *soirée* yesterday — what an affair that was, some female screeching her head off and a Hungarian chap in a velvet jacket thumping the life out of the grand piano. Quite right not to go, old chap, though Mrs. B said she expected you. Spoke quite sharply about it; said it was all of a piece, you never did what was expected of you. Mentioned Laycott Manor, said you never went near it, it was probably crumbling to bits for want of attention . . . '

'It isn't,' Lord Chilcote said. He bent over the table with his cue carefully balanced and sighted along it. It was a pose which displayed his distorted hand to its worst advantage, but he appeared oblivious to it and it was such a familiar sight to Charlie Carford that he ignored it. For a few moments there was no sound in the room but the click and thud of the billiard balls as they ran across the table in precisely the way Lord Chilcote had intended. Charlie groaned.

'I wish I had your eye,' he said. 'I don't know why I play with you, the result is always a foregone conclusion. Anyway, as I was saying, de Cavaillon seemed mighty interested in the old ancestral home an' all that. Wanted to know all about it, where it was and so on.'

Lord Chilcote's lip curled scornfully. 'The man's a fool,' he said.

'What makes you say that? Seems a knowing sort of cove to me.'

55

'Because he could find out all he wanted to know from Burke's Peerage without betraying his interest.'

'French,' Charlie pointed out. 'Probably never heard of Burke's. Besides, funny thing to do, looking up your friends in the Peerage.'

'That's what it is for,' Lord Chilcote pointed out.

Charlie looked surprised. 'Suppose it is,' he said. 'Never thought of it before.'

'Is de Cavaillon coming to your mother's dinner tonight?' Lord Chilcote asked.

'Bound to be,' Charlie said. He took his turn at the billiard table and looked vaguely pleased at the result. 'How's that? Not bad, eh? Er, don't want to push you into doing anything you don't like, old chap, but I hope you don't mean to cry off tonight? The thing is, m'mother gets devilish upset if anything happens to disarrange her table.'

'Don't worry, I shall be there,' Lord Chilcote assured him.

He was as good as his word and since Mrs. Carford had had the forethought to place him between a dashing young lady about to embark on her fourth Season and a certain Mrs. Embury, with whom Lord Chilcote was reputed to be somewhat intimately acquainted, he was tolerably well amused. Henri de Cavaillon, as Charlie had anticipated, was also present, voluble, charming and an obvious asset to any hostess. He seemed equally popular with the men and scored quite a hit after the ladies had withdrawn with a risqué story skilfully translated into English with just sufficient strangeness of phrase to make it additionally funny.

'You really must be congratulated on your command of English,' Janus Chilcote remarked. 'No doubt you had a good teacher?'

'Several,' Henri de Cavaillon said, twisting in his chair to look at him. 'Some of them very charming and their method of instruction quite delightful.'

There was a general laugh. The port was circulating for the second time and there was a spirit of conviviality in the atmosphere. Someone remarked that bed had always been the best place to acquire a foreign language and the talk drifted away to an anecdote about a bizarre experience in Turkey. Under cover of the general conversation Lord Chilcote enquired,

'Do you intend to stay much longer in London?'

'No, I must return to Paris very soon,' Henri de Cavaillon replied. 'Next week, I think.'

'How do you travel? From Dover?'

'Yes.'

'Didn't I hear you say you meant to leave early and spend a little time exploring Kent?' Charlie joined in.

Henri de Cavaillon hesitated, a faint look of vexation passing across his face. 'I did have some such intention,' he admitted.

'Really?' Lord Chilcote said. 'In that case, will you do me the honour of being my guest? I am going to Laycott on Monday. Why not accompany me and I will see you safely on your way when you are ready to leave.'

The eyes of the two men met. Lord Chilcote was smiling faintly. Henri de Cavaillon shrugged. 'Until you spoke my plans were uncertain,' he said. 'But since you invite me I can only thank you and accept.'

Charlie had listened to this exchange with open-mouthed astonishment. 'Blest if I know what you're up to, old chap,' he confided to Janus later. 'What will you do with de Cavaillon in the country?'

'Keep an eye on him,' Lord Chilcote said. He saw that Charlie was looking puzzled and added, 'Don't bother your head about it, Charlie. I know what I'm about and I must in any case have gone to Laycott soon. It's an age since I was last there.'

'It must be,' Charlie agreed. 'What do they do when you pay them one of your rare visits — kill the fatted calf?'

'No,' said Lord Chilcote with a smile that was at once cynical and full of self mockery. 'They lock up their daughters.'

Beautiful Laycott, for all the neglect of its owner, was still tended with care and affection. Lord Chilcote might not wish to live there himself, but he was shrewd enough to employ an excellent steward and the presence of Mrs. Gertrude Ardingley ensured that the house was kept in reasonable order, while the gardens, to which she devoted herself, were superb.

She explained her obsession with gardening to Madeleine when she finally managed to obtain a visit from her great-niece. It had not been easy. Encountering Madeleine a second time at the

Vicarage gate she enquired whether Madeleine had told Mrs. Lorgan that she had been invited to visit Laycott.

'Yes, but it is a little difficult, madame,' Madeleine said hesitantly. 'My aunt says that I may not pay calls without her, and she does not visit at Laycott.'

'Stuff and nonsense!' Mrs. Ardingley said. 'I'm your aunt, too, aren't I? By marriage, at any rate. If I ask you to come and see me I can't see any reason why you should be prevented.' She paused to think about it. 'I suppose you can't very well come without Mrs. Lorgan's permission,' she admitted. 'Awkward for you, I see that. I said I'd call on the woman and I will. I'd have done it before if I hadn't been taken up with the herbaceous borders.'

She was as good as her word and Mrs. Lorgan was stunned into unaccustomed silence when she received a visit from a woman who might, if she had chosen, been the local great lady.

'For, quite apart from marrying Mr. Thomas Ardingley, she is astonishingly well connected,' Mrs. Lorgan told Madeleine after Mrs. Ardingley had taken her departure. 'Not that you would think it to look at her, so shabby as she is, and that weatherbeaten face, and her hands! Quite brown, and covered in scratches.'

'She had been tying up the climbing roses over a pergola,' Madeleine explained with a tiny quiver of amusement in her voice. The meeting between her aunt and great-aunt had awoken in her a sense of humour she had believed totally stifled. They had had so little

59

in common — the comfortable, well-dressed, but inescapably *bourgeoise* wife of a man whose father had made his money in trade, and the untidy, forthright aristocrat who saw no reason why she should not indulge the whim of taking an interest in her unknown great-niece and rode roughshod over the conventional hesitations of Mrs. Lorgan. All the embarrassment had been on Mrs. Lorgan's side; Mrs. Ardingley had seen nothing to be embarrassed about. The fact that this was the first ceremonial visit to be exchanged between their two houses since the disastrous elopement of Madeleine's parents troubled her not at all. She ignored the intervening years and behaved as if it were entirely normal for her to be sitting in Mrs. Lorgan's drawing room in her old grey mantle and atrocious bonnet, drinking tea and devouring fairy cake with a gusto which even Bella could not equal.

'Calceolarias!' she exclaimed, to Mrs. Lorgan's total bewilderment. 'I saw that fool Williams working in your garden as I came up the drive. I asked him what he was intending to plant in the beds under your windows and he said calceolarias! I never could abide them and they'll be a disaster against this red brick. I'd tell him to think again if I were you. The man never was a gardener — no eye for what's fitting.'

'We've found him very hardworking and conscientious,' Mrs. Lorgan said. 'He keeps the garden in excellent order.'

Mrs. Ardingley gave her a piercing look. 'Ah, well, if you're satisfied, I'll say no more. Of course, it may be that you like calceolarias,' she added generously.

'I like a nice splash of colour,' Mrs. Lorgan said defensively.

Mrs. Ardingley gave a crack of laughter. 'You'll get it,' she said. 'Now, what I'm really here to say is when is this great-niece of mine going to be allowed to come and see me?'

'I will, of course, bring Madeleine to return your call,' Mrs. Lorgan said with reluctant politeness, but Mrs. Ardingley was not satisfied.

'No, I don't want a formal fifteen minutes with you and me making most of the conversation,' she said. 'I want to get to know the girl. Send her over for the day next Wednesday. Shall I send the carriage for her?'

'That will not be necessary, we shall send Madeleine in our own carriage,' Mrs. Lorgan said, taking instant exception to the implication that the Lorgan household might require assistance in eking out its means of transport.

'Good. I don't use Janus' horses more than I can help, even though he gives me the use of his stable and wouldn't care if I had a four-horse travelling coach out every day — wouldn't know, in fact, the neglectful wretch. The old pony is my own and I drive myself wherever I go. Travelling under my own steam, I call it. One pony steam power, what do you think of that, young lady?'

The last question was addressed to Bella, who had been listening with avid interest to the forthright Mrs. Ardingley's conversation. Bella had no right to be in the drawing room at all and it was symptomatic of the disorder into which her mother had been thrown by Mrs. Ardingley's call that she had omitted to send her away until it was too late, and Bella was not the girl to oblige her mother by making a discreet exit. She sat tight and drank in every word. In response to Mrs. Ardingley's question she answered readily:

'I would very much like to have a pony and trap and go around on my own and be independent.'

'Bella!' Mrs. Lorgan exclaimed, but Mrs. Ardingley said: 'Quite right, quite right! Girls are too hedged about these days. Pretty ninnyhammers, most of them. There'll be a swing of the pendulum in the opposite direction, you mark my words.'

She turned her piercing eyes on Madeleine. 'You're very quiet, niece! Do you want to come and visit me?'

'Very much,' Madeleine said. She met her great-aunt's regard steadily. 'I want to see Laycott.'

Mrs. Ardingley nodded. 'Quite right. You ought to see it. Beautiful place. Gardens aren't at their best just now, but they're coming along, coming along. Come over at about ten o'clock on Wednesday and I'll send you home around five.'

'My husband . . . ' Mrs. Lorgan said weakly.

'You don't have to get permission from Mr. Lorgan to send Miss Madeleine to see her family home, do you?' Mrs. Ardingley asked scornfully. 'You and I can settle it between us, surely, madam? Now that we've agreed that it is right that she should come . . . '

Mrs. Lorgan could not remember agreeing anything of the sort, but she could not find a way of saying so, and Mrs. Ardingley concluded: 'Nothing left to do but settle the time, which I've just done. Wednesday at ten.'

She got up to go and Madeleine rose also. Their eyes met. There was a distinct twinkle in Mrs. Ardingley's and just for a second her eyelid twitched in something that might almost have been a wink. Madeleine was forced to look down to conceal her amused recognition of the fact that Mrs. Ardingley had deliberately exaggerated her bluntness in order to dispose of any objections Mrs. Lorgan might make to sending her niece to Laycott unaccompanied.

It was the beginning of a friendship as unexpected as it was welcome to Madeleine. Apart from that first day, when she spent several hours at Laycott, she did not see a great deal of her great-aunt, but it was a curious comfort to know that she was there and to know that, provided she could escape Mrs. Lorgan's vigilance, she was at liberty to wander at will in the grounds of Laycott Manor.

'Come through the woods. I'll give you a key to the gate in the hedge,' Mrs. Ardingley said. 'Bring your cousins — if they will come. It will make an object for a walk for you and there's usually something to see. The daffodils will be at their best in about a week's time. I've put a few hundred under the trees on the west side of the house, naturalised them, you know. Not a great one for formal beds. Calceolarias! Huh!'

It was obvious that to Mrs. Ardingley, Laycott meant the gardens. The house, a beautifully-proportioned mansion of mellow brick, built in the reign of Queen Anne, was to her merely the back-drop to the effects her zeal and imagination produced in the grounds. She worked prodigiously, not merely supervising, but seizing a spade or fork and digging herself, weeding, planting, trimming; out in all weathers, atrociously dressed and as far as Madeleine could judge, blissfully happy.

'Never had any children,' she confided on Madeleine's first visit. 'One still-born son. Never any more. Then I lost my Tom. Didn't fancy another husband. Tom was a good soul, not so cross-grained as most of the Ardingleys. I missed him, didn't know what to do with myself. Tried travelling, but it didn't answer. Fetched up here quite by chance really after a bad journey from France when I couldn't face going straight on to London. Janus was here, for once, and I talked to him about some of the gardens I'd seen in France and Italy. Told him the gardens of Laycott were a disgrace. He suggested I should stay on and put them in order. Gave me a free hand, not to mention the money which, to tell you the truth, was none too plentiful with me. Been here ever since. Don't think he minds. In fact, I sometimes think he might be quite fond of me, in his own peculiar fashion. You don't know him, do you?'

Madeleine felt her face stiffen. 'We have met — twice,' she said.

Mrs. Ardingley looked at her shrewdly. 'You didn't like him,' she said. 'Can't say I blame you.' She sighed suddenly. 'Poor boy, poor boy. He had a hard childhood. Not that that excuses the way he's grown up, but he's been good to me and I think more kindly of him than most people.'

Madeleine was silent. Try as she would, she could harbour no kind thoughts about her absent cousin. The memory of his strong, harsh face was still vivid in her mind, and always with an expression on it that seemed to mock her. It had been hard enough to bear at their first meeting, when she had been totally innocent and bewildered by his scathing denunciation of herself and her father; it was, she found, even more painful to remember their second encounter. Brief as it had been, she had a strange feeling that, alone amongst her new acquaintances, Lord Chilcote's cynical, indifferent eyes had succeeded in piercing the carefully-composed facade she had so painfully built up, seeing right through to the wild disorder that lay beneath, the agony of regret and heartbreak she bore with stoic resignation, believing herself to be beyond hope or salvation.

It was this deep and secret remorse which coloured all her intercourse with her newly-acquired relations. It made her meek where it was more in her nature to be proud, grateful for small kindnesses which she would once have expected as her right, and anxious to please, in a way her father would have despised. But it also inhibited her from the openness which would have allowed her to form a truly affectionate relationship with her mother's family. She had so much to conceal! The effort of always being on her guard made her seem stiff and cold. Almost unconsciously it irritated Mrs. Lorgan and she spoke grumblingly to her husband of her niece's 'airs and graces' when what she really meant was that, although Madeleine behaved with conscious humility, she kept always that little air of withdrawal which Mrs. Lorgan mistakenly attributed to pride. Pride it was, of a sort, but not pride of race, as Mrs. Lorgan thought — 'Too good for us, although she's little better than a pauper' — but the fierce pride of a lonely, vulnerable creature driven to secretiveness as a last resort against the worst the world could do to her.

The only people with whom Madeleine felt herself able to relax were her Great Aunt Gertrude — unconventional, indifferent to the strictures of society, and almost totally uninterested in Madeleine's former life — and her small cousin Harry. With Harry, Madeleine would play for hours at a time, gravely treating him as a person in his own right and listening with absorbed interest to his accounts of having met 'an interesting little snail' in the garden which his sisters would have treated as a joke. She taught him French nursery rhymes and soon Harry, with the unsullied ear of the very young child, could speak of '*les petits bateaux, qui vont sur l'eau*' with a purity of accent his sisters would never acquire. It was a friendship which bewildered Mrs. Lorgan, but she could not disapprove of it, and once when Harry, coming into the drawing room to say goodnight, placed two plump little arms round Madeleine's neck and gave her a wet and noisy kiss on the cheek, Mrs. Lorgan thought that she detected tears in the girl's eyes. It was a betrayal of feeling which did her no harm with Mrs. Lorgan; emotional display was something she understood, and if Madeleine had thrown herself into her aunt's arms on arrival at Bantock House with sobs and protestations of gratitude her success would have been assured.

For all the caution with which she moved in her new environment, there were times when Madeleine felt stifled and had to escape. It was this necessity which made the freedom to walk in Chauntry Woods and the gardens of Laycott Manor so welcome to her. The daffodils were as lovely as Mrs. Ardingley had promised they would be and as the warmer days of April advanced Madeleine began to escape more and more often for the pleasure of walking among them, usually alone, since Mrs. Lorgan was still uneasy about allowing Phoebe and Bella on to Lord Chilcote's estate. She did not realise how often her niece, when she believed her to be decorously strolling in the shrubbery or harmlessly employed on an errand to the village, had seized the opportunity of leaving the confines of the Lorgan grounds to enter the woods and gardens on the far side of the lane.

It was on such an impulsive expedition that, quite unaware of his unannounced arrival at Laycott Manor, she encountered Lord Chilcote.

She had no right to be outside the gardens of Bantock House, but Phoebe was painstakingly washing her mother's cherished china ornaments from the drawing room, Bella was doing her piano practice. Harry was confined to the nursery by a cold in the head, and Mrs. Lorgan was shut up with her housekeeper. She had spoken sharply to Madeleine about some imagined neglect of the small domestic duties assigned to her and it had taken all Madeleine's hard-won control to bite back the hasty retort that rose to her lips. As soon as she was free, she threw her shawl round her shoulders and ran down the drive, hot rebellion in her heart combining with an urgent need to escape from the confines of an environment which sometimes seemed to be stifling her.

There were stiff bushes of holly near the edge of Chauntry Woods, their berries withered but their dark leaves newly washed by the Spring showers. Farther in there were hawthorn trees, their pink and white blossom beginning to show, and then the beeches Madeleine particularly loved, with their smooth grey trunks and the sharp green of their new leaves, and underneath them the first bluebells. Her hasty steps slowed and she stopped to look at the haze of blue just beginning to show beneath the trees. Her mood of rebellion began to subside; she even managed a rueful smile as she realised how trivial her disagreement with her aunt had been.

There was a path through the woods and it had once been of some importance. It led steadily upwards towards the knoll on which stood the remains of an ancient tower, all that remained of a chapel which had once stood on the site. It was an object of superstitious awe in the village. Bella had repeated some of the more unlikely stories of mysterious organ music and figures in monks' habits to Madeleine, but nothing could persuade Madeleine to regard it with anything more than natural curiosity.

'Not monks, Bella!' she had protested. 'It was never part of a monastery. Just a very old church, which fell into disuse when the first Laycott Manor was pulled down and rebuilt on its present site. My father spoke of it often. He used to go birds nesting there when he was a boy. In fact, he had an accident there, climbing on the walls. A piece of the masonry broke away and he fell and broke his arm, and as soon as his arm had healed his father beat him for disobedience because he was forbidden to go there. He thought it was very unfair because his brother, who was with him but stayed on the ground, was not beaten and did not have the pain of a broken arm either.'

Madeleine thought of this conversation as she passed the crumbling old tower and smiled to herself. Just recently she had begun to find it possible to think of her father without the pain which usually accompanied her memories of him. It was not unpleasant, she found, to think of him as a young boy, indignant at what he believed to be an injustice.

The path plunged downhill again after the tower and ran straight on to the outskirts of the village, but Madeleine turned aside, felt in her pocket for the key, unlocked the gate in the hedge and let herself in to the gardens of Laycott Manor.

It was a particularly lovely Spring day after a week of almost continuous rain. With the capriciousness of the English climate, the air was suddenly balmy. Everything was newly washed; the grass was an intense vibrant green, the sky a pellucid blue, the clouds soft billows of white which bore no relation to the sodden grey which had hung overhead in the preceding days. Mrs. Ardingley's daffodils, a little past their prime now, still tossed their heads in the breeze and birds darted busily from bush to tree, distracted by family worries. In defiance of all Mrs. Lorgan's conventions, Madeleine wore neither hat nor gloves. She lifted her face to the sunlight and gloried in the warmth.

'Charming', a voice said behind her. She spun round and found herself facing Lord Chilcote.

'One can hardly accuse a relation of trespassing, I suppose,' he said. 'But have you any right to be here, cousin?'

'Aunt Gertrude gave me a key,' Madeleine said. It was as much of an excuse as she felt called upon to give him.

'A dear soul, but lacking in discrimination,' he said.

She flushed at this and he found himself thinking that the sudden colour in her face was not unbecoming. She had improved in appearance since he last saw her, had lost that somewhat haggard look that had curiously haunted his mind. They confronted one another, he faintly smiling, she taut with resentment and humiliation at having been caught unawares on his domain.

'I didn't know you were expected,' she said.

'I wasn't. The house is in a turmoil, rather like an ants' nest which has been disturbed. I came out to escape. May I ask if *you* are expected?'

'No. I didn't intend to go as far as the house. Aunt Gertrude gave me permission to walk in the gardens, but of course I will not come here while you are at home.'

He did not like that and a quick frown appeared on his face. 'Have the Lorgans no gardens of their own?' he asked impatiently.

'Oh, yes! But it is so beautiful here.' A tiny smile hovered on her lips for a moment. 'At Bantock House the gardener is planting out calceolarias and I . . . ' she made a swift expressive movement of her hand towards the expanse of golden, dancing flowers all round them — ' . . . I prefer daffodils.'

'One of Aunt Gertrude's happier fancies,' he agreed. For a moment there was a feeling of sympathy between them. He was wearing rough country tweeds and gaiters and he carried a gun in the crook of his arm, negligently supported by his damaged hand. He looked less formidable than he had at their previous meetings. Something of Madeleine's hostility began to fade and she said haltingly: 'Sometimes — like you — I need to escape.'

She thought that he understood her, but the slight rapport they had established was dissipated as if it had never been by his next remark.

71

'I brought an old friend of yours down with me,' he said abruptly. 'Henri de Cavaillon.' He was watching her closely, anticipating that her reaction would confirm the suspicion he had already formed about her former relation with de Cavaillon but he was not prepared for the effect the Frenchman's name produced on her. All the delicate colour he had remarked, which so much improved her appearance, drained away from her face. He took an instinctive step forward, fearing that she was about to faint, and came to an abrupt halt when she shrank away from him. The eyes she fixed on his face were dilated almost to blackness with shock and something that looked like horror.

'Henri?' she said. '*Here*? You brought him *here*?'

Janus shrugged. 'He claimed acquaintance with you. I believed that he meant to seek you out without my assistance. For all I knew you might have been pleased to see him.'

'No,' Madeleine said. 'I shall not be pleased to see him.' She spread her hands in a curiously fatalistic little gesture. 'So it begins again,' she said. Her head drooped as she turned away from him and, not for the first time, he was assaulted by a strange pity for her. It was a weakness which made him angry and he spoke more roughly than he intended.

'What fault did you commit, Madeleine, that makes you fear him so much?'

She thought that he was taunting her and she turned again to face him, her head held high once more.

'Do you think I shall confess myself to *you*?' she asked scornfully. 'No! I will tell you nothing. Ask your friend de Cavaillon.'

She left him, standing amongst his wealth of daffodils, all their golden beauty tarnished for her now by the corruption of Henri de Cavaillon's presence at Laycott Manor, and although Janus made a movement as if he would have followed her, he thought better of it and let her go.

4

Madeleine made her way through the woods, almost without knowing where she was going, only aware of an urgent necessity to put as much space as possible between herself and Laycott Manor. Bantock House, which had at times seemed to enclose her in an atmosphere which was almost too stifling, now resumed the aspect of the refuge it had seemed to her when she had first arrived in England. She had almost gained the top of the incline which led up to the ancient tower when Henry de Cavaillon stepped out from amongst the trees.

'*Bonjour, ma belle,*' he said softly. Like Lord Chilcote, he was dressed for shooting. He too carried a gun and a couple of dead rabbits dangled limply from his other hand.

Madeleine stood as if turned to stone and this appeared to amuse him. He propped his gun against the old stone wall of the tower and laid the rabbits on the ground. A whisper of ancient dust slithered down from the stones high above and was lost in the grass, too small a warning to be heeded by either of the two who confronted one another in the clearing. Smiling to himself, Henri stepped forward, took Madeleine's hand in his and pressed it formally to his lips. When he let it go there was a smear of blood on it, blood from the rabbits he had shot. Madeleine looked at her hand as if it were something belonging to another person and then instinctively wiped it against the skirt of her dress. Her silence and stillness appeared to irritate Henri de Cavaillon. With an exclamation of impatience, he took her roughly into his arms and kissed her unresponsive lips. Again her passivity defeated him. He let her go as abruptly as he had taken hold of her.

'There was a time when you were not so cold, *mignonne*,' he remarked.

'There was a time when I believed I loved you,' Madeleine responsed quietly.

'You *did* love me,' Henri insisted. 'With, as I recall, some passion.'

Madeleine ignored this. 'Why are you here?' she asked. There was a weariness in her voice which betrayed the fact that she knew quite well what his response would be.

'I came to find you — what else?'

'Even though you know that I no longer have any love for you? Indeed, I think I hate you.'

A little flame awoke in Henri de Cavaillon's eyes. 'It adds a certain spice to a *liaison* that might otherwise have begun to tire me,' he said. 'Come back to Paris with me, Madeleine.'

'No.'

'So uncompromising? We must talk about it, I think.'

'I have nothing to say to you.'

'And I have little to say to you, except that I still want you. But to your so respectable English family I might say — oh, so much!'

A look of weary distaste passed over her face. 'What satisfaction does it give you to destroy my

75

happiness?' she asked. 'Believe me, no matter what may happen I shall not return to you. Can't you accept that and leave me in peace?'

The glitter in his eyes intensified. 'Twice you have run away from me,' he said. 'It is time for you to be punished a little, I think. But I will be kind — come back to Paris and everything shall be as it was before. You shall have your fine apartment, your maid, your beautiful clothes, your jewels . . . do you know, it was the fact that you took none of these things with you when you left that made me determined to get you back again? You intrigue me, *ma mie*. Never before have I had a mistress who was so unmercenary! To engage yourself as a governess instead of profiting by my generosity, that was unique! And then to escape again, across the sea. It is a challenge, you must see that. To subdue a creature with so much spirit in her is something quite apart from taking the usual run of complacent whores.'

Her eyes flashed, but she controlled the indignation which rose in her, knowing that his taunt was deliberate and an angry reaction would please him. She turned away, not deigning to reply, but he caught her arm and pulled her back again.

'Not so quickly, *cherie*. I have not yet finished.'

'I have nothing more to say,' Madeleine said. His grip on her arm tightened painfully, but she bore it in silence, refusing to gratify him by an admission that he was hurting her. It was only when he began pulling her towards him that she said quickly: 'Lord Chilcote is within calling distance.'

'Then call,' Henri de Cavaillon said. Her continued silence made him laugh softly. 'No? I thought not. Come, *ma belle*, let us be friends. Kiss me, Madeleine. Let me see that you have not forgotten the arts I taught you.'

'No!' He had her fast now and she fought desperately, abandoning the pretence of coolness, intent only on escape, and forgetting in her panic that the cold impassivity she had first adopted was a far more effective tactic than a resistance which only inflamed him.

He drew back with an oath as she raked his cheek with her nails and she broke free, but only momentarily. As she turned to flee he caught at her skirt and she lost her balance and fell back against him. He seized hold of her and lifted her in his arms.

'Inside the tower, I think, my Madeleine,' he said. 'And you shall learn once again what it is to be loved by Henri de Cavaillon.'

The doorway to the tower had long since mouldered, but the arch still stood. He carried her inside, paying no attention to the long shudders that ran through her. The roof was open to the sky, but the walls still curved round the circle they had enclosed for centuries affording, in spite of their crumbling state, some measure of protection and privacy. A block of stone lay near the middle of the circle, the roots of a clump of valerian which had grown in its crevices still showing white and living, but again the warning went unheeded. As he set her down, breathing heavily from his exertions and the excitement she had aroused in him, Madeleine swung her arm with all her remaining strength in a wild, haphazard blow. It caught Henri in a sensitive spot at the angle of his jaw, he winced and his hold slackened. Again Madeleine broke away from him and darted towards the doorway. She had little hope of escaping from him, but her eye fell on the gun he had left propped against the wall by the opening. She seized it and turned to face him.

'Stand still,' she commanded. 'One step nearer and I will shoot.'

Inside the tower Henri de Cavaillon halted. He did not really believe her threat, but he recognised the note of hysteria in her voice and he realised that advertently or inadvertently she might indeed pull the trigger. It was necessary to proceed with caution. With an effort he forced himself into calmness. He was even smiling as he said: 'Oh, come, *ma belle*! You will not really shoot your Henri?'

He took a tentative step forward and Madeleine jerked the muzzle of the gun towards him. But she had said that she would shoot if he moved a step nearer, and she had not fulfilled her threat. Encouraged, Henri relaxed into a semblance of goodhumour. 'Put down the gun,' he coaxed. 'It shall be as you wish. I will not harm you. Did you really think I would force you against your will?'

With a confident smile on his lips he began to move towards her. Madeleine stared at him with dilated eyes and then her finger moved convulsively on the trigger. She shot blindly, literally blindly since she closed her eyes at the moment of discharge. The noise reverberated round the ancient chamber, a wood pigeon clattered into the sky in alarm, and then there was an ominous silence.

Madeleine opened her eyes. Henri de Cavaillon still stood in front of her and now he was openly laughing.

'But to miss me!' he exclaimed. 'To miss me at that range! *Ma belle*, I do not think your heart was in it.'

To Madeleine's disordered imagination it seemed as though the walls were swaying. Henri was only a step or two away and she was powerless to resist him further. And then the air was ·full of noise and choking dust. Already unsafe, further weakened by recent rains, peppered by shot, shaken by the detonation of the gun, the whole of the wall on the far side of the tower collapsed inwards. The first stones hit the ground by Henri and he turned, not realising what was happening, to see where they had come from. The wall seemed to lift above him, inexorable as a giant wave, and then it crashed downwards and engulfed him. All that remained standing was the arch of the doorway under which Madeleine stood and a jagged line of stone on either side.

When Janus arrived, running through the trees towards the source of the shock which had made the earth tremble beneath his feet, Madeleine was crouching on the ground outside the ring of fallen masonry. Instinctively she had retreated, but she was incapable of withdrawing further, or of turning her eyes away from the place where Henri de Cavaillon lay buried. When Janus bent over her she did not seem to be aware of him, even when he spoke to her.

He took hold of her shoulder and repeated his question: 'Madeleine, are you hurt?'

She turned her head and looked up at him with blank, uncomprehending eyes, and he repeated his question urgently in French. She slowly shook her head. Through parched lips, dry with the taste of ancient dust, she whispered: 'Henri . . . ' She turned her head again towards the fallen chapel. Janus Chilcote followed the direction of her fixed, shocked gaze.

'He's in there?'

When she responded with another slight movement of her head he straightened up and stared with equal horror at the tumbled stones.

'Dear God!' He went up to the remaining arch and stared inside. It was inconceivable that anyone buried beneath that weight of stone should still be alive. He turned back to Madeleine and helped her to her feet. She began to tremble violently as the first numbing effect of shock wore off.

'We must get him out,' she said. 'Together we could lift the stones . . . ' She took a step forward, but Janus restrained her.

'No,' he said. 'We cannot hope to move that weight — and I'm afraid he must be dead, poor devil.'

It was not quite true. It might have been

possible for their combined strength to lift the burden of stones, but he dreaded what they would find beneath, and she had borne enough.

'I'll get help,' he said. 'But there can be no doubt that it is too late to save de Cavaillon.'

His mind was already running through the complications this appalling accident was likely to cause. Was it necessary for Henri de Cavaillon's former relations with his cousin to come to light? It would cause a scandal and serve no useful purpose.

'He was your lover?' he asked abruptly.

'Yes.' The brief acknowledgement was only what he had expected, but his mouth twisted wryly at it all the same.

'He wanted me to go back to him,' Madeleine went on in a low voice. 'I made him angry. He carried me into the tower, but I hit him and got away. Then I fired the gun . . . '

'You *what*?' Janus picked up the gun from where it had lain disregarded on the grass and broke it open. 'Madeleine, did you shoot him? Before the walls collapsed, had you already . . . wounded him?'

'No. I did not hit him. I did not mean to hit him. It was only to frighten him . . . to make him leave me alone. He laughed at me because I missed him . . . and then . . . then I do not know what happened. There was a great noise, and he was *gone*!'

Janus stood for a moment in frowning thought. At last he asked, 'Madeleine, does anyone know where you are?'

81

'No. I came without permission.'

He gave her a long considering look. 'Could you manage to keep quiet about what has happened here today?' She stared at him and he went on: 'If no-one knows your whereabouts it need never be known that you were present when Henri was killed. Your former connection with him need not be revealed. But it all depends on your self control. If you feel you cannot conceal your natural shock at the horror you have witnessed then tell me now. It will be better to be frank at the outset than to have it come out later.'

'I am well practised in the art of concealment,' Madeleine said bitterly. 'What is one more deception amongst so many?'

'Then if you think you can carry it off, go quickly before you are missed. And remember this — Henri de Cavaillon claimed acquaintance with you and your father. When he is spoken of you must steel yourself to hear his death discussed incessantly. It will be a burning topic in this backwater for many weeks to come — and then you had better admit that you knew him. A slight acquaintance, someone you recollect having met in your father's lifetime, no more than that. Understand?'

She bent her head in that proud gesture of acknowledgment he remembered so well and he was struck by the pallor of her face. 'Can you get back to Bantock House on your own?' he asked. 'You look . . . I realise this has been an ordeal for you, but it will be best if you go alone, provided you don't swoon on the way.'

Madeleine took a deep breath. 'I shall not swoon,' she said. 'I can manage. I am . . . grateful to you.'

'You owe me no gratitude. Fool that I am, I brought Henri de Cavaillon down on you.' He hesitated. 'I would ask you to believe that I meant it for the best,' he said stiffly. 'Go now.'

In the days that followed Madeleine had ample opportunity to appreciate the accuracy of Lord Chilcote's warning of the sensation the death of Henri de Cavaillon would cause in the restricted neighbourhood of Laycott. It was discussed exhaustively and with relish, all the more so because of a vague feeling of relief that the tragedy had befallen a stranger, and a foreigner at that, for whom no particular grief need be felt.

In the Lorgan household Madeleine was spared some of the gossip, partly because her two cousins were forbidden to speak of it and partly because she herself was stricken down by a mysterious illness which attacked her during dinner on the evening of Henri's death when she was seized by a fit of trembling so violent that she was unable to lift her spoon to her mouth to drink her soup. Mrs. Lorgan spoke of 'a severe chill' and made an oblique reference to the folly of venturing out of doors with no covering for the head and no better protection than an old wool shawl. Madeleine was packed off to bed and visited by the doctor the following morning. Since he could find little the matter with her he confirmed Mrs. Lorgan's diagnosis and advised rest, warmth and a light, sustaining diet for a couple of days.

'A somewhat highly strung young woman,' he remarked to Mrs. Lorgan. 'But essentially in good health, I would say. Nothing of an infectious nature about her present ailment, you need have no apprehension on that score. As you say, these young creatures will venture out without adequate covering and it takes a chill or two like this to teach them prudence. I'll send you up a draught for Miss Madeleine to take and I have no doubt she will be up and about again before the end of the week.'

It was true that Madeleine recovered from her apparent illness, but she did not quite regain the look of health she had begun to acquire before she met Henri de Cavaillon in Lord Chilcote's woods. She lost weight and the haunted look returned to her eyes.

'I shouldn't wonder if she turned out to be consumptive,' Lottie Hershaw remarked, exasperated at having to take in the waist of a dress she had believed finished.

'Oh, don't say that, Miss Hershaw!' Mrs. Blackett cried. 'No, it's my belief she's been crossed in love or some such thing. She doesn't eat enough to keep a sparrow alive and she's got that moping look about her. You mark my words, there's a man behind it somewhere.'

'I have heard she knew that Frenchman that got himself killed,' Lottie Hershaw said thoughtfully.

'Oh, what a dreadful thing that was! A young man in the prime of life, I understand.'

'I saw him in the village with his lordship,' Lottie said. 'Handsome, I'd call him. Frenchified, but very good looking.'

'He never came here,' Mrs. Blackett said positively. 'And Miss Madeleine only spoke of him as if she knew him very slightly. I don't think there can have been anything in it.'

Regretfully the two women abandoned the idea of a tragic romance and turned to the more fruitful subject of the inquest which had been held the previous day.

'They say Lord Chilcote was reprimanded for not fencing the old tower off,' Mrs. Blackett said.

'So he was,' Lottie agreed. 'He took it better than you might expect. Said he regretted it. Accidental death they brought in. Well, all that could be expected really.'

'And what about the funeral? When's that to be, do you know?'

'He's not going to be buried in this country at all. His mother's coming over to fetch the body back for burial in France,' Lottie said with a certain amount of triumph at her inside knowledge.

'Poor woman, what an ordeal!' Mrs. Blackett exclaimed. 'There must be plenty of money in the family then. A pity there *wasn't* any connection with Miss Madeleine; she's not one who'll ever settle down with a poor man to my way of thinking.'

'As to that, it seems to me the Vicar's been growing rather particular in his attentions,' Lottie said.

'No! Well, Miss Hershaw, you do surprise me. That'll put poor little Miss Phoebe's nose right out of joint.'

If Phoebe had suspected that her shy admiration for their bachelor Vicar was not only well known to her mother, but also the subject of gossip amongst the servants she would have been mortified to the depths of her being, but so tentative was the affair, so nebulous this first stirring of an attraction towards a member of the opposite sex, that she had scarcely admitted it to herself, and would not have believed it possible that anyone else could have detected it, still less that Mrs. Lorgan had had it in mind to nip it in the bud by providing a counter-attraction when she had despatched Madeleine on a course of religious instruction. Mr. Nugent was very nice in his way, ran Mrs. Lorgan's thoughts; it was a good living and he was said to have a small private income to supplement it, but she had no intention of allowing her elder daughter to throw herself away on a country Vicar before she had seen anything of the world. It would have been different if Mr. Nugent had shown an interest in preferment; a future Bishop would have been quite acceptable; but the man had no ambition. He had been heard to remark that a small country parish was his ideal and he hoped never to stir from it, and in so saying lost all hope of an ally in Mrs. Lorgan in any pretensions he might form to her daughter's hand. He would do very well for Madeleine, in Mrs. Lorgan's opinion. Indeed, she felt it to be a matter for congratulation that there should be such an eligible bachelor in their immediate neighbourhood and she was pleased with herself for taking pains to promote the match. It was not every indigent young woman who had an aunt with her interests so much at heart. If it occurred to her that Madeleine would make a somewhat exotic mistress of a country vicarage, she dismissed the thought almost immediately. Miss Madeleine would have to cut her coat to suit her cloth. She would be doing very well for herself if Mr. Nugent could be brought to proposal point. He was invited to dinner and Madeleine wore the grey silk gown converted from Mrs. Lorgan's ample crinoline and looked very well in it, since this was before the mysterious malady which turned her back into the hollow-cheeked, silent creature she had been on first arrival at Bantock House. Mr. Nugent was obviously struck by her beauty and since, in Mrs. Lorgan's view, anyone foolish enough to be content with a country parish, would probably also be foolish enough to marry a penniless girl, she was well content with the progress of her campaign.

Only Phoebe guessed the full extent of the Vicar's admiration for her cousin. He had always found her sympathetic and to a certain extent he confided in her. Nothing explicit was said, but she found that he liked to speak of Madeleine to her, praising the seriousness of her mind and the modesty of her demeanour.

'A modesty which is all the more admirable since it must be admitted that she is a remarkably beautiful young lady,' he said. 'I am often reminded of Miss Ardingley — you will think me fanciful, I'm afraid — when I look at the angels on the church roof.'

It cost Phoebe a small pang, but she had to admit that there was a likeness to Madeleine in the carved wooden heads which decorated the church — the pure, uplifted profile, the streaming gilded hair, even the look of profound, inward contemplation, all belonged to Madeleine.

She repeated this conversation to Madeleine, bending her head over her sewing, her face half hidden by her forward swinging hair.

'An angel!' Madeleine said in a startled voice.

'I thought it was a very pretty compliment,' Phoebe said.

'Perhaps, but Mr. Nugent should have better employment for his thoughts in church.'

'I think he admires you very much,' Phoebe said, still without looking up. 'Suppose . . . suppose he were to propose marriage to you, would you accept him?'

'Marriage! But no, it is unthinkable!'

'I don't see why,' Phoebe said, sufficiently encouraged by Madeleine's horrified reaction to probe a little further. 'He is very well liked and I am sure he would make a nice, kind husband.'

'But not for me,' Madeleine said emphatically. 'No, no! Marriage to a priest . . . I could not contemplate it.'

'But it is perfectly permissible in the Church of England,' Phoebe pointed out.

'You mistake me,' Madeleine interrupted her.

'I am quite aware that Mr. Nugent is free to marry if he so wishes, but I am also sure that I would not be a suitable wife for him. I hope you are mistaken in your belief that he is thinking of me in that way — a man does not necessarily contemplate marriage merely because he admires a woman's appearance, you know, especially a man of sense like Mr. Nugent — but whether it is so or not, I cannot return his regard and I shall certainly not marry him.'

'I think he will be disappointed,' Phoebe said.

'I am sorry for it,' Madeleine replied quietly. 'But I am glad you have put me on my guard. I will take some pains not to appear to encourage him in future.'

Now that the idea had been suggested to her, she could see that it might very well be true. The thought had been so far from her mind that she had been blind to the meaning of Mr. Nugent's small compliments and admiring glances. She had found him sympathetic and had even, remembering the simple relief she had found as a child in confessing herself to the anonymous ear of the convent priest, contemplated the possibility of sharing with him the burden of secrets she carried. That idea must now be abandoned. She let it go with regret. She longed, with all the force of a passionate nature, for someone with whom she could share the regrets which darkened her days and the dreams which haunted her nights. Only one other possibility suggested itself to her and that was her cousin, Lord Chilcote. The fact that he had no illusions about her, that he knew of the part she had played in Henri de Cavaillon's death, made him the only person with whom she would have felt free to discuss the past and the shadow it cast over her future. She found herself thinking of him constantly. The memory of his dark, strong features was vividly before her whenever her mind turned, as it so often did, to the horror of Henri de Cavaillon's death. He had been concerned for her, there in the woods. She found that strange, but the knowledge that he shared the secret of her presence when the tower collapsed was curiously comforting. And he alone of her English family knew of her connection with the dead man. He had found the knowledge distasteful, but he had not been shocked. It would take a great deal to shock Lord Chilcote. She could talk to him, if only she had the opportunity, but she could not go to Laycott Manor while he was at home unless he specifically invited her, and nothing could be more unlikely than that he would visit Bantock House.

She moved through her days in miserable suspense, dependent on snippets of gossip from the servants for news of the sensation Henri de Cavaillon's death had caused. She heard of the inquest, but had very little idea of what this entailed, and when she tried to enlighten her ignorance, received a sharp reproof from Mrs. Lorgan for indulging in morbid curiosity. She understood that it implied an enquiry into the circumstances of the accident, but, perhaps fortunately, it did not occur to her that her cousin was putting himself in a somewhat invidious position by suppressing all mention of her presence. Nor did it occur to her that he, too, was seeking for a way to communicate with her without drawing suspicion on her, still less that her white, shocked face haunted his mind as insistently as the events of that nightmare day obsessed her own.

She had thought it unlikely that he would visit Bantock House, but in the end that is what he was driven to do. He preceded his visit by a careful note addressed to Mr. Lorgan, asking whether it would be convenient if he called that afternoon.

'Lord Chilcote wants to come here!' Mrs. Lorgan exclaimed when her husband communicated the contents of this letter to her.

'My dear Arthur, will you agree to see him?'

'I have already done so. How could I refuse? Particularly since it may be to Madeleine's advantage. He says he hopes to have the opportunity of seeing her as well.'

'Not alone,' Mrs. Lorgan said swiftly.

'Certainly I would prefer to be present and I hardly think Lord Chilcote will wish to exclude me. I imagine we owe this visit to the favourable impression Mrs. Ardingley has already gained of her and if, as I hope, there may be some financial gain to Madeleine in this recognition by her father's family then he would do better to discuss it with me rather than with a green girl.'

Mrs. Lorgan digested this in silence. It would, of course, be all to the good if her husband were to be relieved of some of the burden of the addition to his family, and if a settlement, however small, were made on Madeleine it would make it a great deal easier to find her a suitable husband, but there was something just a little galling about the interest the Ardingleys were taking in her. The open hostility which had existed between the two families at the time of the elopement had long since dissipated, but it had been replaced by a cold indifference which had often irked Mrs. Lorgan, and it was hard to owe the recognition belatedly bestowed by Mrs. Ardingley and Lord Chilcote to the arrival at Bantock House of a penniless girl from France.

In the event, Arthur Lorgan found it impossible not to accede to Lord Chilcote's request to be allowed to speak to Madeleine alone. He made it seem so much a matter of course that Henry Lorgan's little speech of apologetic refusal died on his lips.

'There was something he wanted to say to her about her father,' he excused himself to his wife. 'Naturally I did not wish to intrude . . . '

It did not by any means suit Mrs. Lorgan's ideas of propriety for a nineteen-year-old girl to have a solitary interview with a man almost unknown to her aunt, except by his singularly lurid reputation, but she was mollified by the remainder of her husband's news.

'He will settle £5,000 on her,' Arthur Lorgan said. 'It is more than I expected; indeed, I feel it to be generous.'

'Generous indeed!' Alice Lorgan said. 'Five

thousand pounds! The girl will be quite an heiress.'

'It is considerably less than our own girls will have,' Arthur Lorgan pointed out. 'But I could not have done a tenth as much for Madeleine without detracting from the portions of our own dear children, and we agreed before she came that that would not be right.'

It occurred to neither of them that the size of the gift Lord Chilcote had decided to bestow on his cousin had been cynically calculated by him. It would not have been politic to make the girl richer than her maternal cousins, but five thousand pounds should be sufficient to provide her with a degree of independence, lift the slur of being a poor relation, and possibly provide a marriage portion, without giving rise to jealousy.

He did not waste time discussing money with Madeleine when they were alone together. She tried haltingly to express her gratitude for his wholly unexpected generosity, but he cut her short.

'We shall not have long before we are interrupted,' he said. 'Mrs. Lorgan is probably having a spasm at the thought of your being without a chaperone.' He frowned as he looked at her. 'You look ill,' he said in his abrupt fashion.

'I have been unwell,' Madeleine admitted. A fleeting look of mockery passed across her face. 'It is supposed to have been caused by going out of doors without a hat.'

'I see. There have been no other . . . repercussions?'

'None. And you, have you encountered any difficulties?'

'No. The inquest passed off without incident, except that there is one more black mark against me.'

'I am sorry.'

He shrugged. 'It is of no importance — and the censure was not entirely unjustified.' There was a small silence and then he said: 'Madame de Cavaillon is staying with me at Laycott Manor. She wishes her son to be buried in France. As soon as the formalities are completed she will return with . . . '

Again he hesitated and Madeleine completed his sentence: 'With his body.'

'Yes.' He observed her increasing pallor and said with suppressed violence, 'Don't look like that! Good God, did you love him so much?'

His vehemence surprised her. 'No,' she said. 'I did not love him at all. Once perhaps . . . but it seems remote now and it did not last long.'

'How in the name of heaven did you come to put yourself so much in his power?'

'I think, to comprehend that you must understand something of my life in France,' Madeleine said. 'After Mama died I was placed in a convent and I remained there for nine years. The nuns were very good and I was happy, but it was not a place in which one gained much worldly knowledge. My ideas of life were gathered secondhand from the talk of the other girls. My father, too, was somewhat given to fantasy. Up to a point my education was excellent, but what it prepared me for was marriage. An early, advantageous marriage was the aim of every girl in the school. Indeed, two girls of my own age were betrothed before they finished their final year. It was what I expected for myself. All my life I had been told that I belonged to the English aristocracy. I knew that there had been a quarrel, but it was all very romantic and the few details I was able to pass on to my friends made me something of a heroine in the convent. I was like a Princess in exile. All that was required was the appropriate Prince to come and restore me to my rightful place.'

'With your father following in your triumphant wake?'

'I have told you my ideas were not very realistic. And Papa was the last person to disillusion me. When at last he took me to live with him the fairy story perpetuated itself. It happened to be a time when money was plentiful with him. I was fêted, spoiled . . . so happy that it never occurred to me that it was strange that none of the young men who paid me so much attention displayed any serious intentions towards me. If I thought about it at all I supposed that Papa had warned them off, saving me for a suitor who was worthy of me. You must remember that I was only seventeen.'

'The first time I met you . . . '

Madeleine interrupted him. 'That is a painful memory. I had not realised . . . I accepted that men gambled. It was incomprehensible, but exciting. That the money Papa and I spent so heedlessly came from foolish young men who faced ruin because of his activities never crossed my mind. The remarks you made that evening caused the first tarnishing of the image I had formed of Papa, of myself, of our life.' She looked down. 'You said — or, at least, implied, that I had acted as an attraction to bring these young men to our apartment, but it was not true. I mean, I did not *consciously* entice them to play cards with Papa.'

'I believe you,' Janus said swiftly. 'Though how you can have been so blind . . . '

'I was blind indeed,' Madeleine agreed sadly. 'And then Papa died and all my castles in the air fell to the ground. Suddenly there was no money and I soon found there were no friends either.'

'Why did you not come to England at that time?'

'I had not yet lost my pride. My English family had been represented to me as monsters, hardhearted and rapacious, and I still believed myself to be a little superior to the common run of men and women. I would earn my living, my worth would be recognised, Prince Charming would still come and rescue me.'

'My poor child, you were certainly living in a fairy tale!'

'So I came to realise after I was introduced to Madame Hortense,' Madeleine said.

She was watching him closely and she saw the involuntary movement of recognition he made when she spoke that name. 'Ah, you are acquainted with Madame and her establishment!

I thought perhaps you might be. I have no need then to explain why my employment did not last very long.'

'I am relieved to hear it,' Janus Chilcote said drily. 'Was that where you met de Cavaillon?'

'No, I was already acquainted with Henri. He had been not exactly a suitor, but certainly an admirer, for some months. I liked him well enough to be flattered by his flowers and compliments, no more than that. He was absent from Paris when Papa died, but on his return he sought me out. By that time I had sunk to a level of poverty I think you would have difficulty in comprehending.' She shivered at the memory and went on in a flat, unemotional voice: 'I was living in one room at the top of a house in a poor district. I had to carry all my water up from the courtyard. Do you know how difficult it is to keep clean when you have nothing but cold water you must fetch yourself? There were rats in the roof, and cockroaches everywhere. I existed by taking in sewing, finishing off garments for a dressmaker, but I earned very little. I was always hungry and almost always cold. As soon as it grew dark I would barricade myself in my room with the bed across the door because there was no lock and it was not safe . . . my landlord would come and try the door when his wife was not at home. Henri took me away from that.'

'You must have suspected his motives.'

'It would not be true to say that I did not,' Madeleine said in a low voice. 'But I was past caring. Better to give myself to a young, goodlooking man who swore that he loved me than to be raped on the stairs by a fat, lice-ridden old drunkard.'

'As bad as that?' Janus asked.

'I escaped once by soaking him in a bucket of water. I had reached the point where I was afraid to go out. Henri was all kindness, all consideration — at first. He even made me believe that if he could overcome the opposition of his family we would be married. Even so, I knew within a very short time that I had made a terrible mistake.'

'Nothing like a full stomach for restoring morality,' Lord Chilcote remarked.

'You say that as if it were a joke, but I tell you it is true! For all my disillusionment, it was many weeks before I allowed myself to admit that it would have been better to have starved than to become the mistress of Henri de Cavaillon.'

'He treated you badly?'

'*Au contraire*! He treated me extremely well, so long as I did everything he wanted, but he was jaded, you see; the novelty of having a new, young mistress wore off and he required something more to stimulate him.' She pressed a trembling hand across her face. 'I was pitifully innocent and it pleased him to destroy that innocence. I cannot tell you of the degradation to which he subjected me. And he talked about my father, gave me details of his life which it was not right that I should know. He even said that I was fulfilling the role he had always intended for me, that he had meant to sell me to the highest bidder.'

'I don't believe it,' Lord Chilcote said.

'Don't you?' she looked at him with so much wistful hope in her eyes that he saw that the idea had taken hold of her mind and been a source of additional anguish. It made him say with all the conviction he could muster, 'Your father was as much of a dreamer as you were and his ideas of his standing were as high, if not higher. I can well believe that he looked to you to make an advantageous match, but anything else would have been an affront to his idea of what was due to him.'

'You may be right. It would be a comfort to think so. Henri was . . . very convincing.'

'And so you brought yourself to leave him.'

There was a long pause. Madeleine seemed lost in thought, her face withdrawn and expressionless. 'Yes,' she said at last. 'The time came when I had to go, but I had grown cunning. I wanted nothing from Henri de Cavaillon, but I could not face a return to the poverty from which he had taken me. I dissembled a little longer. I answered an advertisement for a governess. I pretended to be a young widow, I forged references and I obtained the post. It would have answered very well. Madame Bécaud was also a widow, with two little daughters. There was no man in the family, which made her readier to admit me than some other ladies to whom I had applied in the past.'

She did not elaborate on this, but Lord Chilcote could readily imagine that prudent wives and mothers of young sons would be reluctant to admit a governess with Madeleine's looks into their household.

'She was very strict — I think there is an expression, straightlaced — is that correct?'

'Quite correct.' He found her serious enquiry touching.

'She was satisfied with me. I liked the little girls and they were easy to teach. It seemed that things would go well. And then Henri found me.'

'That was unfortunate.'

'It was not a matter of fortune at all; he knew where I was. He had placed me in an apartment with a maid to look after me. It never occurred to me that one of her duties was to spy on me. She read my letters. He already knew before I left that I had engaged myself as a governess to Madame Bécaud. It amused him to let me go and then to call me back again. He sent one of his actress friends to call on Madame. She told her all about me — that I had been kept by a man before I went to her, that I was not a widow, that I had worked for Madame Hortense. She exaggerated, of course, made it all sound worse than it was. She played her part very well, better than any role she ever had on the stage. She and Henri thought it was a great joke. Madame Bécaud was appalled. I was dismissed, but she was a just woman. I was given a month's wages, and on that and on the little I had saved I managed to live until my uncle arranged for my passage to England. Henri had forgotten that I still had that escape open to me.'

'And then I invited him down here — I find it difficult to forgive myself for that. But he would have found you without my help. I guessed something of all this and I thought it better to know what was happening.'

He got up and moved restlessly about the room. Her story had moved him to an unaccustomed compassion. He had little family feeling, but he was aware of a vague guilt over his past indifference to the fate of his uncle's child. When he had heard of Francis's death he had given no more than a passing thought to the girl he had left behind him. He had assumed that any child of Francis's would be more than capable of looking after herself, but how wrong he had been.

His regretful, half angry, reverie was interrupted by the entrance of Mrs. Lorgan, unable any longer to bear the suspense of knowing that her niece was shut up alone with a man she regarded as totally without scruples or morals. Lord Chilcote bore with her nervous twitterings with as much tolerance as he could muster, but she thought him abrupt and ill-mannered when he took his leave only a few minutes after she had entered the room. It irked him to make his farewells to Madeleine under the eye of her aunt; there was so much he might have said, but he was forced to choose his words carefully and in the end all he said, holding her cold hand in his, was: 'You have been unhappy, but that is over now. Let the past go. There is no reason why it should cast a shadow over your life in England.'

She gave him no answer but a half-smile and a slight shake of her head. He stood looking at her for a moment and then, to Mrs. Lorgan's fascinated surprise, he raised her hand to his lips.

'Quite Continental!' she commented acidly after he had gone. 'I suppose he thought it was what you were used to, though to my mind it shows a familiarity . . . however, let that go. You were not very polite, Madeleine. I expected to hear some words of gratitude from you for Lord Chilcote's extraordinary generosity. Five thousand pounds! You are indeed a fortunate girl.'

'I had already expressed my gratitude,' Madeleine said. 'We had been speaking of other things.'

'To be sure you had, and that was very good advice Lord Chilcote gave you. It is time you gave up these moping ways. With the better weather approaching we shall do more entertaining than has been possible in the winter and I look to you to play a full part. Nothing very formal, of course, just a quiet party or two to introduce Phoebe to a few people before we go to London next year.'

There was a half-formed hope at the back of her mind that she might succeed in getting Madeleine married and off her hands before Phoebe's debut in the Spring and she began to form busy plans to bring her to the notice of such unmarried men as the neighbourhood afforded in addition to Mr. Nugent; eligible men, not necessarily young, but not of sufficient importance to form part of her ambitions for her elder daughter. She felt a pleasant glow of benevolence towards her niece. Matters were arranging themselves very nicely, very nicely indeed.

While Madeleine could not immediately obey Lord Chilcote's injunction to forget the past, she did on the night following her talk with him sleep with a quiet mind for the first time since the tragedy of Henri de Cavaillon's death, and it was impossible not to feel satisfaction at her newly-improved circumstances. No longer wholly dependant on the generosity of her uncle, she was conscious of a new and welcome feeling of liberty. Strangely, this made her more willing to comply when Mrs. Lorgan insisted that she had fully recovered from her brief illness and could accompany Bella to the Vicarage for the last of her pre-confirmation classes. It no longer mattered that Mr. Nugent looked on her with admiration. She would treat him with coolness, but if he was not discouraged and insisted on proposing to her then she felt that she would be free to refuse him without incurring the reproaches this would have called down on her from Mrs. Lorgan when such a refusal might have left her a pensioner of her mother's family for the rest of her life.

As she had feared, the Vicar did not appear to notice her quiet withdrawal, or at any rate he did not attribute it to its right cause. Indeed, there was something in his manner which hinted at a secret understanding of her sudden access of maidenly reserve and he pressed her hand on parting in a way she thought unbecoming. Madeleine sighed briefly to herself as she and Bella walked down the garden path. It was going to be difficult and her sweet cousin Phoebe was going to be hurt. It was a pity that her aunt's wordly ambitions had seen fit to discourage a match between Phoebe and Mr. Nugent; in Madeleine's eyes they were well suited to one another.

At Laycott Manor that morning a small crisis had been caused by the desire expressed by Madame de Cavaillon to drive out to take the air. The pony and trap used by Mrs. Ardingley was hardly a fitting vehicle. Fortunately, the barouche which had belonged to the late Lady Chilcote, long unused but meticulously cared for by an under-worked coachman, was found to be in good order and a pair of quiet horses was provided which carried Mrs. Ardingley and the bereaved mother along the lanes in a decorous manner. Since Madame de Cavaillon spoke no English and Mrs. Ardingley's French was of the sturdy British variety which consisted of basic sentences atrociously pronounced in a clear, carrying voice, there was little conversation between them. Mrs. Ardingley, with her mind fixed longingly on a bed of hyacinths, blue, pink and white, just coming into bloom, was bored. As they turned into the village street her face brightened at the sight of Madeleine and Bella walking away from the Vicarage.

'*Cette jeune fille là est Mademoiselle Ardingley*,' she said laboriously. '*Elle parle français.*' She poked the coachman in the back. 'Pull up, John.' She leaned out of the carriage and signalled to the two girls. Madeleine, guessing that the other woman in the carriage must be Henri's mother, moved reluctantly towards them, but it was impossible to avoid the meeting. She heard Mrs. Ardingley effecting the introduction and bent her head in acknowledgement. When she looked up she found Madame de Cavaillon looking at her intently. The two women, both dressed in deepest black, confronted one another in silence for a long moment and then Madame de Cavaillon said, '*Mademoiselle, je vous ai déjà vue. A Paris, n'est-ce pas?*'

'*C'est bien possible, madame,*' Madeleine said, contriving with an effort to keep her voice steady. '*J'ai longtemps habité à Paris.*'

'*Je le sais. Une après-midi, dans le Bois de Boulogne, on m'a indiqué qui vous etiez. Je ne me trompe pas, j'en suis sûre. Et je me demande pourquoi vous êtes ici, vous la maitresse de mon fils, dans le village où il est mort.*' Her eyes flickered over Madeleine's black gown. '*Et en deuil!*' she exclaimed in a tone of bitter offence.

'*Je porte le deuil de mon père,*' Madeleine said quietly. '*Quant au reste, je n'admets rien. Je suis venue en Angleterre afin de demeurer dans la famille de ma mère, c'est tout.*'

Madame de Cavaillon drew back. '*Partons, je vous prie,*' she demanded to Mrs. Ardingley. '*Je ne veux plus parler avec cette fille-là!*'

The carriage drew away with Mrs. Ardingley almost totally bewildered. That there had been

105

some cause for disagreement between the two women she understood; she was not at all sure that she wished to know the cause of it. Something to do with the dead son, that was obvious, and Madeleine had lived in Paris and had presumably known him. She would have preferred to have left it at that, but Madame de Cavaillon insisted on enlightening her in words which a child with a rudimentary knowledge of the language could have followed. Mrs. Ardingley looked troubled and tried to feel shocked, but the truth was she was quite unable to share Madame de Cavaillon's sense of outrage at having been introduced to her dead son's mistress. She had no intention of spreading the story any further, and she did her best to put it out of her mind.

Not so Bella. With her quick ear and well-developed sense of drama she had followed the exchange of rapid French, but she could not quite believe that she had properly understood what she thought Madame de Cavaillon had said.

'Madeleine, what was it that French lady said to you?' she asked as they resumed their walk homewards.

'She asked me why I was in mourning and I said it was for my father,' Madeleine said in a steady voice.

'No, before that. About living in Paris or something.'

'She thought we had met before and I said it was possible because I had lived in Paris a long time.'

It was not quite enough to satisfy Bella. She hesitated to put the indelicate question that trembled on the tip of her tongue, but she was far from finished with the subject. She let it go for the time being and Madeleine allowed herself to hope that the French lessons she had given her cousin had not enabled her to comprehend the full implications of Madame de Cavaillon's contemptuous dismissal of her.

It was a shortlived hope. Bella honestly troubled by what she had heard, and quite incapable of keeping it to herself, confided in her sister. She described the meeting and added: 'The French lady was angry with Madeleine. Phoebe, she called her '*la maitresse de mon fils.*' What do you think she meant?'

Phoebe stared at her, her eyes widening in horror. A burning blush spread over her face. 'You must be mistaken,' she said hurriedly.

'No, that was what she said,' Bella insisted. 'It means 'my son's mistress', doesn't it? I don't understand. How could she call our cousin that? A mistress is someone who lives with a man without being married to him, isn't she? But Madeleine is not wicked, she is just like us.'

Phoebe's blush had subsided and she was very pale. She put both hands over her ears. 'Don't speak about it,' she said. 'Bella, did you ask Madeleine for an explanation?'

'Not about that,' Bella admitted. 'I wanted to, but somehow I could not speak of it to her.'

'But someone must,' Phoebe said. 'Out of justice to Madeleine, if nothing else. You may have mistaken the matter entirely.'

'I didn't,' Bella said obstinately.

'I cannot do it,' Phoebe went on. 'Bella, I think we must tell Mama.'

'No!' Bella said in horror. 'Phoebe, I *couldn't*. She will be so angry.'

'I will speak to her,' Phoebe said resolutely. 'I feel it to be a duty.'

Before her resolution could fail she sought out her mother and repeated the gist of her conversation with Bella, her eyes fixed on the floor and the colour in her cheeks fluctuating wildly. When she had finished she stole a look at her mother. Mrs. Lorgan's face was rigid and she was sitting so still that Phoebe was frightened. At last Mrs. Lorgan stirred and caught her daughter's anxious eyes.

'I will speak to Madeleine,' she said. 'I dare say Bella has got it quite wrong. They were speaking French, you say. She could perfectly well have misheard a totally innocent remark. You were right to come to me, but now you are to put it out of your head. I forbid you to speak of it to anyone, including Bella, except to tell her what I have said.'

'Yes, Mama,' breathed Phoebe and slipped thankfully away, leaving her mother to her bitter reflections, all her happy plans for the future in ruins. Not for one moment did she doubt the truth of Madame de Cavaillon's accusation. It accorded all too well with her instinctive recoil as soon as she had set eyes on this girl who was too beautiful for her own good. The girl was ruined and unless she could be instantly removed from their vicinity she might bring her cousins down with her.

5

Lord Chilcote, returning to Laycott manor after escorting Madame de Cavaillon to France, was fatigued and out of temper. In common courtesy he had felt obliged to lend the bereaved mother his support. He had remained for the funeral, the day after their arrival in France, and had taken the first available Channel crossing back as soon as he could decently get away. The journey had involved long hours of travel in trying circumstances, not made any easier by the nagging worry that Madame de Cavaillon's meeting with Madeleine, about which she had complained vociferously, was going to involve the girl in yet further difficulties. The discovery of a note from Arthur Lorgan requesting permission to call on him on his return did nothing to improve his mood, and the subsequent interview exacerbated his uncertain temper still further.

'I thought it right to inform you of the arrangements I have made for Madeleine, in view of the interest you have recently taken in her welfare,' Mr. Lorgan said with what Lord Chilcote deemed to be unnecessary portentousness. 'Naturally I can no longer allow her to live in my own home.'

Janus Chilcote stirred restlessly in his chair, but he said nothing. In the light of the revelations Mr. Lorgan had already conveyed to him in a hushed voice, he knew that it would serve no useful purpose to say that for all he could see Madeleine might just as well remain where she was, nor did he think it expedient to reveal that the story was not new to him. He listened in silence, scowling heavily as Mr. Lorgan continued:

'For the time being my own dear girls have been sent to stay with my wife's mother. She has had to be let into the secret, naturally, but she lives a very retired life and I do not think we need fear that it will spread any further through her. Fortunately, I have many connections with charitable institutions of various sorts and I have been able to locate a most suitable establishment where my poor, unhappy niece can be placed.'

Lord Chilcote leaned back in his chair and looked at him in dawning wonder, but he still said nothing and Mr. Lorgan, somewhat intimidated by that fixed, dark look, hurried on nervously, 'There is a house on the outskirts of Dover, run somewhat on the lines of a small, private hotel, by a lady for whom I have the highest regard. She has under her guardianship some half dozen girls in the same distressing circumstances as Madeleine and I can assure you that nothing could be more fortunate than that she should have a vacancy at this time.'

He ended on a defensive note, for the look of derision on Lord Chilcote's swarthy face warned him that his lordship by no means shared his thankfulness at finding such a suitable hiding place for Madeleine.

'Good God, man!' Janus exclaimed. 'You're

not seriously proposing to put my cousin into a Home for Fallen Women?'

'Since you put it like that, yes, I suppose you may say that that is my proposal,' Arthur Lorgan said stiffly.

Lord Chilcote got to his feet and took a turn about the room.

'What does Madeleine have to say about this?' he asked over his shoulder.

Arthur Lorgan hesitated. 'She asked to be allowed to carry out her first intention when she applied to me for help, to take a post as a governess,' he admitted. 'But that is out of the question.'

'It's not an ideal solution, but better than this prison you design for her,' Janus Chilcote said.

'I could not reconcile it with my conscience to allow her to become an instructress of young children,' Arthur Lorgan said, ignoring the reference to a prison, and closing his ears even more resolutely to the imprecation Lord Chilcote muttered under his breath.

Janus resumed his restless perambulation of the room. 'It won't answer,' he said abruptly. 'Think, man, think! For a few months, yes — possibly even a year or two — but is she to remain in this institution of yours for the rest of her life? Believe me, I understand Miss Madeleine's temperament better than you do. She may appear acquiescent, but she has the pride of the devil and she will rebel against the sort of regime you are trying to impose on her. She'll abscond and God knows what will become of her.'

'She is still a minor,' Mr. Lorgan said. 'And as her guardian I have the right to insist on obedience.'

'Who appointed you her guardian?' Janus enquired. 'She is an Ardingley and I am the head of her family. I might, if I chose, constitute myself her guardian. Come to that, I might have her made a Ward of Court.'

Since Mr. Lorgan was by no means sure what this entailed, he was momentarily nonplussed. 'I am sorry you do not approve my proposal,' he said, trying not to let his rising annoyance get the better of him. 'Have you any alternative to suggest?'

Lord Chilcote spent some moments in frowning thought. At last — 'Let her come here,' he said.

'*Here?*' Arthur Lorgan exclaimed in total disbelief. 'To Laycott Manor?'

'Why not? The place is big enough, in all conscience. I am rarely at home, as you know, and when I am I imagine my great aunt must be a sufficient chaperone. I doubt if Madeleine will corrupt her morals — or mine!' He watched in sardonic amusement the struggle which was visibly taking place in Arthur Lorgan and went on softly: 'You are thinking that association with me will do nothing to enhance Madeleine's reputation, and no doubt you are right. On the other hand, once you place her in that Bridewell of yours and it becomes known, as it will be, she is lost indeed. What could be more fitting than that she should come to live in her father's old home? You can visit her or not, just as you choose. Considering the lack of intercourse there has been between our two houses over the last twenty years, no-one will think it strange if you abstain.'

'I shall consider it a duty to enquire about Madeleine from time to time,' Arthur Lorgan said. With an effort he nerved himself to speak the other thought that was in his mind. 'Your lordship has spoken quite openly of your own reputation . . . '

'Or lack of it,' Janus said cheerfully.

'You cannot blame me, therefore, for admitting that some doubt arises in my mind about your motives in admitting so young and lovely a girl to your house.'

For a moment he quailed before the blazing anger in the other man's face, and then Janus relaxed. He even laughed softly. 'You may rest easy, Mr. Lorgan,' he said. 'On this occasion I am acting out of pure benevolence, and perhaps a little family pride. I leave for London tomorrow. You may send Madeleine to Laycott Manor with an untroubled conscience.'

And so it was arranged. Mrs. Gertrude Ardingley raised no objection. 'Not the first girl who's made a bit of a mistake,' she said. 'At my age it no longer seems particularly important. I dare say we shall rub along together quite well. I like the girl, got a bit of spirit about her for all she seems so quiet. *I* shan't talk to her about the past. No point. What's done is done.'

Having delivered herself of this opinion she proceeded to put the matter out of her mind and Madeleine found herself received into an easy

114

going, somewhat haphazard household, where she had a freedom she had never known before. At the time of her arrival she had retreated into her accustomed state of withdrawn, proud isolation, but once installed at Laycott Manor she began to relax. She had the strange sensation of putting down roots. It was as though she had come home. The place had been described to her so often that it seemed familiar, and the atmosphere at Laycott Manor was infinitely more congenial than Bantock House had ever been.

Inevitably, the servants knew that there was more behind her sudden change of residence than a simple invitation to visit her father's home, but the reason for her fall from favour at Bantock House was not known. There had been 'ructions' and the Lorgans were displeased with her, that was all that the most assiduous enquirers could discover. Somewhat to their disappointment, it appeared that the trouble could not on this occasion be laid at Lord Chilcote's door. As far as anyone was aware, he had scarcely set eyes on his beautiful cousin before her arrival at Laycott Manor, and so little interest did he take in her that he left for London as soon as she was installed and remained away for several weeks.

In the weeks before Janus Chilcote, to his own intense private annoyance, felt himself obliged to return to Laycott Manor on business connected with an imminent bye-election in the neighbourhood, Madeleine blossomed in the glorious summer sunshine, revelling in her new-found freedom. At Laycott Manor no-one knew or cared if she chose to walk in the gardens without hat or gloves, she could come and go as she pleased. She found the library and read for long hours without being scolded for idleness. Touching the piano with tentative fingers she found it sadly out of tune. She mentioned it to her great-aunt and was told with mild surprise to tell Matchett to get the thing tuned if she wanted to play. It was the first request she had ventured to make to her cousin's steward and she was secretly astonished to find that he accepted it as an order to be carried out immediately. She visited the stables and learnt that Janus went in for breeding horses, but when she was asked if she would care to ride she shook her head with a smile, and continued to make her explorations on foot. She rarely ventured outside the grounds of Laycott Manor, but since these were extensive this was no hardship. There was only one area into which she never penetrated, and that was Chauntry Woods. To her the memory of Henri de Cavaillon's death was still a recurring nightmare and the crumbling tower a thing of menacing horror.

A few days after her arrival at Laycott Manor she came down to breakfast to find an envelope by the side of her plate. Inside were five golden sovereigns and a brief note from her cousin. It began without any preliminary.

I have instructed Mr. Matchett to make this payment to you on the first day of each month. The remainder of the interest on your money will accumulate for you unless you require it,

116

in which case please ask him to advance it to you.

It concluded with his initials *J. C.*, nothing more. Looking at that curt, businesslike message and at the small fortune in golden coins, Madeleine's eyes filled with tears. It was the first English money she had ever handled and to her it represented a thoughtfulness which Janus Chilcote would have been amazed to have attributed to him.

She tried to thank him when he found himself forced to return to Laycott Manor, but he cut her short.

'It's no more than I had already arranged to do for you.'

'But that was before you had the expense of feeding and housing me,' Madeleine pointed out in all seriousness.

'My dear child!' He looked amused. 'I am quite a rich man and the expense of keeping you is negligible.'

'Truly?' She glanced round her doubtfully. 'If, as you say, you are rich, why is your house so . . . so . . . ' She paused, searching for the right word and realising too late that what she wished to say might sound rude.

'Shabby?' he supplied without offence. 'I suppose it is. One grows accustomed. I no longer notice. The structure is sound and that has been all that concerned me.' He walked over to the long window of the drawing room where this conversation was taking place and shook out one of the curtains. 'Somewhat faded,' he admitted.

117

'I only wondered if you would permit me to embroider some new seats for the chairs,' Madeleine said hurriedly.

'Why not? That one, I see, is quite frayed. Aunt Gertrude has probably not noticed, she is too obsessed with the garden. Embroider chair covers by all means if it will amuse you.'

'It will give me great pleasure,' Madeleine said.

'Will it? You must be finding life tedious if you can look upon that as a great pleasure. How *have* you been passing the time? They tell me you don't ride.'

'No,' Madeleine admitted. 'At least, I do, but only for show. Very quiet horses at a very slow pace, not really riding, you know.'

'I can imagine,' Janus said. 'You'd better learn.'

'I have no suitable clothes,' Madeleine said, somewhat overwhelmed by this rapid plan for her amusement.

He looked at her thoughtfully. 'My mother was a tall, slim woman,' he said. 'I dare say her riding habit is put away somewhere upstairs. Nothing ever seems to get thrown away in this household. It will hardly be in the latest fashion, but it will do until we discover whether you are a horsewoman or not.'

Madeleine's eyes sparkled and he thought how much the flush of pleasure on her face became her. She was looking better than when he had last seen her, some at least of the strain of her life had been lifted and she moved about Laycott Manor with an assurance which had been lacking at Bantock House. He regretted having to return again so soon after his recent visit, knowing that his presence in the house with his beautiful cousin was likely to be misconstrued, but since there was no help for it he took pains to treat their enforced proximity in a matter of fact manner designed to disarm suspicion. He did not even supervise her riding lessons beyond suggesting which horse might be suitable and giving his groom some curt instructions, but it was inevitable that they should meet at the stables and he was able to observe the progress she made on horseback.

'Soames tells me you are a most promising pupil,' he remarked one day. He had just dismounted from the big black stallion he frequently rode for visiting farms across country, when Madeleine and the groom came clattering into the yard. Janus put up his hands to help her dismount and she jumped lightly to the ground with a hand on his shoulder. The late Lady Chilcote's riding habit, severely cut on classic lines, was not as outmoded as an ordinary gown would have been. It was a little loose around the waist and hips, but apart from that it fitted Madeleine to perfection and its plain uncluttered line was more becoming to her than anything he had previously seen her wearing.

She went to her horse's head, patting him gently and murmuring to him. 'I enjoy my rides immensely,' she said. 'And dear old Pompey carries me to perfection.'

'He reminds me forcibly of a wooden rocking horse I had in the nursery as a child,' Janus remarked. 'When you have made a little more progress we might find you something rather livelier. Have you met Alisha, the love of my life?'

'Indeed I have,' Madeleine said, following him to the stall where his beautiful Arab mare peered out at him. 'She is a very lovely lady.'

'She thinks I'm neglecting her,' Janus said.

The mare, her cream-coloured coat gleaming almost golden in the sunshine, butted him reproachfully with her head and Madeleine thought as she watched him laugh and pet her that she had never seen him appear to better advantage.

She was still thinking about it as they walked back to the house together, remembering the admiring way the groom had talked about his way with horses.

'He seems to understand all their ways by instinct, you might say,' Soames had said. 'And he's a first class rider, which at one time we didn't think would be possible.'

It was no part of Madeleine's policy to gossip with Janus's servants, but Soames was obviously an old and valued friend and so she allowed herself to look at him enquiringly, inviting an explanation of this remark.

'On account of his illness,' Soames explained. 'At one time it seemed like he would be paralysed all down one side, but thank God it wasn't so bad and in the end there was just the weakness in his arm and that poor old hand of his. I thought it might've affected his balance and, of course, the feel on the reins isn't what it ought to be, but he was up in the saddle as soon as he was able and he worked out a way of getting over the difficulties. It cost him something, but he was always full of spunk. I've thought sometimes the fever might have left him a lot worse off if he hadn't fought back the way he did.'

'I didn't realise he had been so ill,' Madeleine admitted. 'It must have been a terrible anxiety to his parents.'

There was no reply to this and, glancing at Soames, she saw that his face wore its most wooden expression. 'Her ladyship took it hard,' he said at last. 'Very hard indeed. It made her quite ill and she had to go away and, of course, where her ladyship went his lordship followed. So that's how I come to see so much of Master Janus — Lord Chilcote, I *should* say — while he was ill, me being a sort of friend, you might say, having known him from the cradle.'

By tacit consent they let the subject rest there, but Madeleine was deeply troubled by this unexpected insight into her cousin's childhood. She had a vision of him, a lonely, courageous, sick little boy, fighting against a disability which must have bewildered him, and without, it seemed, the loving support of his parents to help him. There was a portrait of his mother at the top of the great staircase at Laycott Manor. Madeleine had not greatly admired it, thinking that the artist had given the beautiful, pale face beneath its pile of black hair, too remote an expression, but now it occurred to her that he might have portrayed all too accurately a discontented, coldhearted woman staring bleakly into a loveless future.

Her troubled thoughts were interrupted when Lord Chilcote remarked abruptly, 'I shall be having guests to dinner on Tuesday — our prospective Member of Parliament and a few of the men who are supporting him.'

He held the heavy door at the rear of Laycott Manor open for her and Madeleine glanced up at him as she passed through. 'You wish me to dine separately?' she asked.

'Certainly not! I would like you to join us for dinner, and Aunt Gertrude, too, of course, but after that we will not intrude on you.'

'Will . . . will my Uncle Arthur be one of the guests?' Madeleine asked.

Lord Chilcote smiled. 'No. Arthur Lorgan and I support opposing parties. I am a Liberal and he is a Conservative.'

'I know nothing of English politics,' Madeleine said.

'Excellent! You can ask our guests to instruct you. That should keep the conversation going.'

He had spoken in jest, but he was amused to find that Madeleine took him at his word. He was not quite sure why he was surprised by the success of that small dinner party of local dignitaries, perhaps it was because he himself had looked upon it as a necessary duty which was likely to provide a boring evening. Instead, there was a sparkle in the air which he realised derived almost exclusively from Madeleine's skill in the social arts. She looked lovely, but that went without saying; what came as a surprise was her ability to direct the conversation. His experienced eye detected the hand of a village dressmaker in her grey silk gown, but she wore it with such an air that it might equally well have come from Paris. Her diffidence dropped away from her and she conversed with easy assurance. Her look of absorption as she listened to involved explanations of the Parliamentary system was acutely flattering and the comparisons she made with French politics, if not very profound, were sufficiently intelligent to be taken seriously by men of good sense. They approved of her and she blossomed in this atmosphere of masculine admiration, an atmosphere to which she had been accustomed and which, quite unconsciously, she had missed since her father's death.

'By Jove, Miss Ardingley, you'll make a splendid political hostess one of these days!' one of the men remarked when they all rose to their feet as Madeleine and Mrs. Ardingley prepared to leave them. She only smiled and shook her head, but to Janus Chilcote's watchful eyes it seemed as though a shadow crossed her face. He glanced at his aunt, splendid, if old fashioned, in black velvet and pearls, and saw her frown and then remember herself and dismiss her worried look with a smile. It brought home to him as nothing else had done how far he was from solving the problem of Madeleine's future. He had substituted a more acceptable home for the one Arthur Lorgan had proposed for her, but was it any less a prison? Marriage was the obvious answer, and if she became acceptable to local society there would surely be no lack of applicants. The barrier was likely to arise from Madeleine herself. She would never marry anyone who did not know the truth about her and it would be the devil of a job deciding whether a suitor could be trusted with such a story — trusted not to cry off, and trusted to keep it to himself.

Pushing the port decanter absently away from him, and paying scant heed to the conversation around him, Janus reflected that it would be a sad loss if all that beauty and capacity for deep emotion were condemned to a life of spinsterhood mewed up in Laycott Manor. Madeleine Ardingley belonged in the world, it was her natural milieu. The man who had seen her as a political hostess had put his finger on a talent which would only be realised if she were allowed to take her place in society — and how was that to be achieved? She had been a decided asset at his dinner table tonight, even in that countrified gown, but she would undoubtedly profit from a spell in the capital, if only it could be arranged. There was a burst of laughter from the other men and he came to himself with a start, hurriedly recalling his wandering thoughts and realising, a little blankly, that on no pretext whatsoever could he make any arrangements for his cousin Madeleine to visit London. He had provided a home for her in the depths of rural Kent and there, it seemed, she must stay.

The problem of her future was something that occupied his mind a great deal during the days that followed his dinner party, particularly after he had received a visit from the local vicar. Mr. Nugent had applied in vain to the Lorgans for an explanation of Madeleine's sudden change of residence. Now, with considerable courage, he seized the opportunity of speaking to Lord Chilcote. The interview gave him little satisfaction, but after listening in silence to his stumbling words, Lord Chilcote suddenly stood up, saying, 'If I understand you correctly, you contemplate making Miss Ardingley an offer of marriage. I doubt whether your suit will be successful, but it must be made to Madeleine herself — I have no authority over her. I will send her in to you.'

He went out of the room, leaving poor Mr. Nugent, who had only intended proceeding to this point if his enquiries about the reason behind Madeleine's departure from Bantock House proved satisfactory, to mop his brow and try to assemble a speech which would combine an earnest assurance of love with a necessity to be assured that the prospective wife of a clergyman of the Church of England was a woman of unblemished character.

He need not have worried; Madeleine refused his tentative proposal with kindness but in terms that gave him no hope of any change of mind. It was gracefully done, almost too gracefully, so that he began to feel a little nettled at being dismissed so easily, and he ventured to say:

'Leaving aside my disappointed hopes, there is one subject on which I feel I must speak to you as one who could, until recently, term himself your spiritual adviser. Your continued residence under the roof of a man whose character is universally condemned . . . '

Madeleine stood up. 'I must remind you that you are speaking of my own close relative,' she said. 'And one, moreover, who has shown me great kindness. I respect your scruples, but I cannot share them, Mr. Nugent. I wish you good-day.'

He was shown out and a few minutes later Janus came back into the room. 'Have you dismissed your suitor?' he asked.

'Of course. Did you expect anything else?'

'No; one hardly sees you as the wife of a country vicar. Poor devil, he is very much in love — although I think he had qualms about actually making you his wife.' He looked at her averted face and added: 'I hear young Thomas, who dined here the other night, called to see you and you refused to see him.'

'Yes, for the same reason as I tried to avoid a meeting with Mr. Nugent. He showed some preference for me and I thought it better to give him no encouragement.'

The frown on Lord Chilcote's face was deep enough to be called a scowl. 'What the devil am I to do with you?' he asked.

'Nothing,' Madeleine said. 'I am happy enough as I am.'

But for how long, he wondered; how long before she woke up to a realisation of the empty years that lay ahead of her? It was impossible, he found, to keep up the elaborate precautions he had taken at first against being thrown into her company, although he still

126

took care not to give rise to unnecessary gossip. The August weather was warm, even sultry. In the gardens the bell flowers swayed above clove-scented pinks, the heavy-headed roses dropped crimson petals on the grass as Madeleine brushed by them, the sweetness of the great white bushes of philadelphus mingled with the creamy honeysuckle cascading over the warm brick walls. The trees had lost their springtime delicacy and the foliage was heavy, dark and still. They rode together, through woodlands for the sake of coolness, always accompanied by Soames, his face expressionless, but his eyes watchful. In other circumstances Soames would have taken odds against Lord Chilcote wanting an escort when he disappeared into a wood with a beautiful girl. There was something strange about his insistence on Soames going along whenever he went riding with his cousin, whatever the conventions demanded; conventions had been something to be flouted in the past.

He was still more surprised by an encounter they had with Madeleine's little cousin Harry. They had been on a visit to a farm on the estate. Lord Chilcote had arranged to meet his agent there to discuss a disputed boundary, and since Madeleine and Soames had been going in much the same direction, had issued a curt, almost unwilling, invitation to her to join him. She had dismounted at the farm and while he was conducting his business she had visited the dairy and drunk a cool glass of milk, trying to make conversation with the farmer's wife and daughters, but finding it a little difficult to discover any common ground with them. Their way on their return lay through the village and their progress gave rise to some curious looks, which Madeleine bore with her head held high and a slightly increased colour, and which Lord Chilcote appeared not to notice. Their progress was brought to an abrupt halt by a small figure darting into the road, waving excitedly and calling, 'Cous'n Mad'lin, cous'n Mad'lin!'

It was fortunate that Madeleine was still riding placid Pompey. 'Harry, *chéri*, be careful of the horses!' she cried.

Seeing that she intended to dismount, Soames moved round to assist her, while Lord Chilcote stayed where he was.

'Mad'lin, why have you gone away? Nobody don't talk French with me any more,' Harry said.

Madeleine crouched down on a level with him, heedless of her riding habit sweeping the dusty road. She ignored his first question. 'Have you forgotten all I taught you?' she asked.

'No, I can still say '*Un, deux, trois, j'irai dans les bois*'.' He looked past her. 'Can I have a ride on your horse?'

Madeleine straightened up. 'Oh, darling, I don't think so,' she said. 'I'm not a good enough rider — suppose I should let you fall?'

'I won't fall off,' Harry promised. 'Please, cous'n Mad'lin?'

Madeleine glanced at Soames, holding their two horses, but it was not Soames who offered to give Harry his wish. 'Give him up to me,

Joe,' Lord Chilcote said.

Suppressing a surprise at least as great as Madeleine felt, Soames picked up the small compact figure and helped Harry to scramble up in front of Janus, a sight which caused his nurse, emerging from the village shop, almost to faint in horror.

'Right,' Janus said. 'Just to the end of the street and back, understand? Hold tight and don't wriggle about.'

Harry, recognising the voice of unshakeable authority, desisted from his attempts to goad the horse into action by kicking with his small heels.

'Yes,' he said. 'Giddee-up, gee-gee!' a form of address which surprised Black Prince very much indeed. He stared with undisguised interest at Janus's hands on the reins. 'Why you got that funny hand?' he asked.

'I had an illness which made it go twisted,' Lord Chilcote said.

'Does it hurt?'

'No.'

Harry abandoned a subject which held no further interest for him. 'Can your horse go faster than any other horse in the world?'

'Not quite.'

'Shall we make him gallop?'

'No.'

'Why not?'

'Because the ground's too hard, it will hurt his legs.'

'Can he jump big, tall fences?'

'If I ask him to.'

'Does he understand you?'

'Tolerably well.'

They reached the end of the village street and turned back to where Soames, Madeleine and the agitated nurse were waiting for them. 'That lady is my cous'n Mad'lin,' Harry told Janus.

'Yes, I know; she is my cousin, too.'

This was rather more than Harry could understand. 'You're not *my* cous'n,' he said doubtfully.

'No.'

'Cous'ns isn't old people like you,' Harry said. He turned his head to look up into the dark, harsh face above him. 'I 'spect you're her uncle!' he concluded triumphantly.

Janus shook with silent laughter and his face was still full of amusement as he came up to the little group who were waiting for them. 'Take him down, Joe,' he said. He hauled Harry unceremoniously into the air and handed him over. Soames lowered the small boy to the ground and he went charging off without a backward look.

'Mary, Mary, did you see me? I can ride a horse!' he called to his nurse.

'Indeed I did see you, and what your mother is going to say when you come home smelling of the stables I'm sure I don't know.' She glanced back at Lord Chilcote, immobile on his big, black horse. 'Did you say thank you to his lordship?'

Harry stopped in mid-flight and turned round. 'Thank you very much, lordship,' he said conscientiously.

Janus lifted one hand in casual salute, but still he did not move and Soames, looking up curiously after he had helped Madeleine to remount, caught on his face a glimpse of a hunger which gave him quite a jolt; in all his long dealings with his lordship it had never before occurred to Soames that he might want children, and if he really felt like that why the dickens didn't he get married and have half a dozen?

'I am discovering the joys of domesticity,' Janus remarked that evening when Madeleine played the piano for him and Mrs. Ardingley after the three of them had dined together.

It was the kind of remark Madeleine never knew how to take from him. It was said with a twisted smile, full of self-mockery, and yet he had seemed well enough amused as they had talked at the table, and he had listened to her music with real attention. Yet now, meeting her eyes across the shining top of the piano, he got up with a muttered excuse and left them, and when he had gone it seemed quiet and a little dull with only her aunt for company.

'When does Cousin Janus mean to return to London?' she asked Mrs. Ardingley.

'At the end of the week, I understand,' Mrs. Ardingley replied. 'The shooting parties will be starting soon and he is such a fine shot that he is in great demand. And I know that he is attending a reception at Marlborough House on Monday.'

'How splendid!'

Mrs. Ardingley shrugged. 'I suppose so, if you

care for that kind of thing. Janus seems to. At least, he never misses the Season, though he always complains of being intolerably bored. Affectation, if you ask me.'

Madeleine thought wistfully of the balls, the theatres, the concerts which presumably made up the London Season and was ashamed of her hankering after gaiety. I am never satisfied, she thought in horror. I could not be better placed than I am at Laycott Manor and only a week or two ago I thought I would never ask for more than this, and yet already I am . . . not bored, no not bored, but restless, dissatisfied, almost resentful because Cousin Janus is going away and leaving me behind.

She very much feared that Janus had guessed something of her state of mind and that he was displeased by it, which was not surprising when he had given her so much; she had no right to be dissatisfied. He avoided her company and spoke to her more curtly than had been his custom. She accepted the implied reproof and in her turn drew back from the intimacy which had begun to form between them. Since this was precisely the effect Janus had intended to achieve, though not for the reason Madeleine thought, it was illogical of him to feel regret at her dignified withdrawal.

Janus, at least, had no doubt about his own symptoms. He had allowed his eyes to linger once too often on his beautiful cousin, with results he attributed to too many celibate weeks confined to a limited country society with only one girl worth a second look. The sooner he

132

returned to the metropolis and the solace that was available to him there the better it would be for his peace of mind. The vivacious Mrs. Embury, with whom he had recently enjoyed a discreet liaison, would no doubt welcome him back, and he would quench the fire that threatened to burn him in her ample charms. Had she grown recently a little *too* opulent? He found himself thinking of her fleshy shoulders and voluptuous bosom with something like distaste, but he told himself obstinately that Charlotte would serve his purpose very well. At least she understood the rules of the game and would expect neither fidelity nor false expressions of undying affection from him. In the meantime, he would manage very well by just keeping out of Madeleine's way.

But Lord Chilcote left one factor out of his assessment of the relationship between himself and Madeleine, or perhaps he deliberately closed his mind to it. He was dealing not with an unawakened girl, whose innocence would have protected her from all knowledge of his desire for her, but with a young woman who had lived for months with a practised sensualist. However much his later excesses might have revolted Madeleine, Henri de Cavaillon had begun by revealing to her the delights of her body. Disgust, and a growing fear of him, had driven Madeleine to a point where she believed that she would never again be able to accept a similar relationship with any man, but in this she mistook herself. As her strained nerves relaxed in the congenial atmosphere of

Laycott Manor her senses began to reassert themselves and she turned, as naturally as the flower towards the sun, to the man who had already played such a decisive role in her life. With all his faults of temper and conduct, Janus Chilcote had always possessed a powerful attraction for women, an attraction of which he was perfectly well aware and used callously to get what he wanted, although he observed certain private rules, not apparent to an outsider, which confined his depredations to women who understood very well what they were about. The disability of his twisted hand counted for nothing compared with the promise implied by that long, lean body, the flexible mouth with its mocking smile, and the enigmatic glance of his dark eyes; there were even some women who declared that the strangeness of his touch gave an added fascination to his embraces. The delicately perceptive feminine antennae which Madeleine did not even recognise that she possessed, probed the atmosphere surrounding this intensely masculine man and fed back to her the subconscious knowledge that between Janus and herself there was an affinity which had nothing to do with their family ties. With an inner excitement she attributed to vanity, she had rediscovered the pleasure of dressing up in a silk gown and being admired and, quite unconsciously, she displayed herself to advantage. She did not intend to be enticing, it was an instinct she did not know herself well enough to suppress, and since Janus had himself well in hand it fretted her to receive so little response from him.

The restlessness which had begun to afflict her on the evening when she had heard that Janus was going away spread to her night-time hours. She began to dream again, terrible dreams in which Henri de Cavaillon pursued her and she fled from him down endless corridors to an abyss where the walls fell in and crushed her. Several times she started up in bed and awoke disorientated and trembling, only slowly returning to a realisation of her surroundings, until the night came when, in a strange, hallucinatory state, she fled from the horror which pursued her and did not know where her flight was taking her.

Her bedchamber opened on to a corridor, at the end of which was a half-glazed door leading out on to a wide terrace which ran the whole length of that side of the house. The door should have been bolted, but the servants had grown careless in the long months when the door remained unused and had forgotten it. Lord Chilcote, mounting the stairs long after everyone else had gone to bed, saw a flutter of white at the end of the corridor and heard the door crash shut. He cupped his hand round the flame of the candle he was carrying as it flickered in the sudden draught and peered into the darkness. Had he really seen something or was it only the curtain blowing in a gust of air? What ever it was, the door had certainly opened and shut and it had no business to be undone at that hour of the night.

He stepped out on to the terrace at the

moment when the cold night air and the chill of stone beneath her bare feet brought Madeleine out of her dream. Dazed and bewildered, she stared around her, not knowing where she was or how she had got there. She looked behind her and saw the tall figure of a man in the doorway, his face lit from below by the wavering light of a candle. With a moan of fear she put out a hand to ward him off and then crumpled to the ground unconscious.

6

Madeleine came to herself as Lord Chilcote carried her back to her room. She struggled feebly in his arms and he said: 'Be still! You are quite safe now.'

'Janus?' she asked.

'Yes, of course. Don't talk.'

Obediently, she subsided and he felt the tension go out of her. It was oddly moving, that instant relaxation when she realised who held her. He carried her into the bedroom and put her down on the bed. She shivered as he let her go and he said, 'Cover yourself up. I don't wonder you are cold. How did you come to run out in nothing but that thin nightgown? One would think the house was on fire!'

'I was dreaming,' Madeleine explained haltingly. 'I don't know how I came to be on the terrace. I woke up and did not know where I was, and then I saw you — it was you, wasn't it? — and I thought he had caught me at last!'

'He? De Cavaillon?'

'Yes, Henri. In my dream I run away from him, and tonight I suppose I truly ran, not knowing what I was doing.'

Janus sat down on the edge of her bed. The light was so dim that he could scarcely see her, only a darker shape against the white of her pillows. 'How long has this been going on?' he asked.

'It was very bad at first after . . . after Henri died. When I came here it stopped, then during this last week the dreams came back again, worse than ever.' Her voice faltered. 'Even from the grave he pursues me,' she said.

'That is melodramatic nonsense! Henri de Cavaillon is dead and buried and it is only your disordered imagination which recreates him. You suffered a severe shock when he died and it was only natural that it should prey on your mind. Possibly there has been some minor upset to your health recently which has started the disturbance up again.' He stood up. 'I will get you something to help you sleep.'

He returned in a few minutes with a freshly kindled candle and a wine glass containing a liquid which Madeleine looked at doubtfully. 'What is it?' she asked.

'A few drops of laudanum. Drink it down.'

She obeyed him and lay back on her pillows again. Janus moved his candle so that the light did not shine on her face, then he sat down on the bed again, and took her hand in his. 'Close your eyes,' he commanded. 'I am going to sit with you until you are properly asleep.'

Madeleine gave him a long, questioning look, but she could read nothing in his face beyond a certain impatience. 'You are kind,' she said. 'So much more kind than you seem. Janus . . . '

Her voice trailed away and her eyes closed. Her hand clasped his warmly, but in a few minutes her grasp slackened. She was deeply asleep. Lord Chilcote disengaged his hand and sat looking at her; the bright, tumbled hair, the pure curve of her cheek, one round, bare shoulder. He leaned down until his mouth brushed her shoulder and he felt beneath his lips the texture of the skin which he already knew to be finer and more silken than the nightdress which imperfectly concealed it. Madeleine sighed and moved her head on the pillow and he straightened up and got to his feet in one swift shamed movement. Infamous to have taken advantage of her helpless state, and who could tell what reaction might be set up in her unconscious mind by even the most gentle of caresses? He picked up the empty glass with a wry twist of his lips. Much more of this and he would be having recourse to the laudanum bottle himself.

Lord Chilcote's kindness was not noticeably in evidence the next morning. Madeleine slept late after her disturbed night and was not aware of the prevailing climate, but word went swiftly round amongst the servants that his lordship was in the devil of a mood, and they moved about their duties cautiously, taking care not to cross him. Madeleine woke reluctantly, still heavy with the drug he had administered to her, and clinging hazily to a feeling of happiness which seemed to have come to her in her sleep. She lay for a while, blinking sleepily in the morning light, trying to account for this unusual sensation. As the events of the night came back to her she felt her face grow hot. She sat up in bed, pressing her hands to her cheeks, overcome by shame. She had behaved so foolishly, running out into the night, and

Janus had come and rescued her, but that was not why she had woken up happy, of course it was not. She pushed to the back of her mind the memory of strong arms which had felt like a refuge. Even more rigorously she suppressed the recollection that she had been wearing only one of the silk nightdresses Henri de Cavaillon had bestowed on her and which she had still not replaced.

She swung her legs out of bed and set the bell pealing for the maid who had been allotted to her. She would take nothing but tea and a slice of bread and butter, she announced, and then she would go riding.

In the well-cut, but voluminous, habit which had belonged to Lady Chilcote she walked down to the stables. Soames was not expecting her, but it was of no importance; she had more confidence on horseback now and if he were otherwise occupied one of the lads could go with her. Janus was in the stableyard, just leading Alisha out of her box. He was in his shirtsleeves, his illhumour forgotten as he coaxed the lovely mare over the cobblestones. He laughed and gently chided her as she threw up her head and made a little dancing sideways movement.

'Come, now, my lovely; no need to be frightened!'

'Reckon she's bashful,' one of the watching grooms remarked. He caught sight of Madeleine and touched his peaked cap, suddenly looking awkward. Janus glanced over his shoulder and the black mood snapped down on him again.

140

He relinquished the horse. 'Take her round to the paddock,' he said curtly. He moved towards Madeleine, waiting uncertainly with the skirt of her riding habit looped over her arm.

'You'll have to go away,' he said. 'You're embarrassing the men.'

'I don't understand,' she said.

'We're taking the mare to the stallion, my dear.' His eyebrows rose in exaggerated enquiry. 'You are acquainted with the process, I believe?'

A deep wave of colour swept over her face. Without answering him, she turned away. He accompanied her for a few steps, through the brick archway which concealed the stables from the house. 'Alisha may require a little coaxing,' he said. 'Being a virgin.'

The sound of his jeering laugh, pursuing her as she fled back to the house, seemed to ring in her ears for the rest of the day. They did not meet again until the evening and then they found themselves alone together in the drawing room, waiting for Mrs. Ardingley, who was a little late for dinner. Madeleine picked up her embroider frame and set a few stitches, obstinately determined not to speak to him. Janus glanced at her bent head and his lips set in a thin, straight line, but after a brief struggle with himself he said, with an attempt at lightness: 'Is that one of the chair covers you promised me?'

'Yes.' She spread out the gold-coloured silk and he exclaimed: 'But that is exquisite!'

He touched the delicate fabric and was visited by an all too vivid recollection of the last time he

141

had felt silk beneath his hands as he carried her back to her bedroom. He drew a deep breath. 'I should not have spoken to you as I did this morning,' he said. 'Forgive me.'

Madeleine was startled, not having expected him to refer to the incident again, still less to offer her an apology.

'I am returning to London tomorrow. God knows when we shall meet again,' Janus went on. 'Before I go, tell me I am forgiven.'

The door was opening. She murmured hurriedly: 'Yes . . . yes . . . I will forget about it.'

'You are too generous.' He gave her his wry, twisted smile and went to offer his great aunt his arm to the dinner table.

For all the lightening of the atmosphere, the conversation at dinner was desultory and they separated very soon afterwards. Mrs. Ardingley remarked that the unseasonably sultry weather had given her a headache and she was retiring early. Madeleine, with an unacknowledged reluctance to be left to a tête-à-tête evening with her cousin, followed her example, and Lord Chilcote withdrew to the library, taking the brandy with him. He sat for longer than he had intended, just as he had the night before, vaguely aware of the mutter of thunder in the distance, until he was roused by a sudden clap almost overhead. He stood up and grimaced as he staggered slightly. It was time to go to bed. He tilted the brandy bottle and estimated the amount he had drunk. Decidedly time to go to bed. He went over and pulled back the heavy

142

curtains and looked out. A flash of lightning lit up the garden and then the rain, dashing against the window, obscured it again.

He had drunk enough to make it necessary for his movements to be unusually deliberate and he was glad that he had told his valet not to wait up for him, but his preparations for bed sobered him and after he had plunged his face in a bowl of water he felt tolerably sure that no-one could call him drunk. The storm was raging in earnest by this time, peal after peal of thunder followed by blinding flashes of lightning, and the rain was falling with torrential force. Janus paused in the act of towelling his head dry as an ear-shattering clap of thunder burst overhead. Somewhere a door banged and he thought he heard a cry. Without pausing to consider that the maids were probably having hysterics together in their attic bedrooms, he seized his dressing gown and covered his nakedness. Madeleine! If the girl ran out in this downpour she would be soaked to the skin in less than a minute!

His impetuous thought carried him down the corridor to her room and he entered without the formality of knocking. Madeleine was standing by the side of her bed. She had got up and re-lit the branch of candles on her dressing table and was about to get back into bed, to wait with wide, frightened eyes for the storm to subside.

Janus came to an abrupt halt half way across the room. Behind him the heavy door swung to and clicked shut. 'I heard a cry,' he said. 'I thought . . . I am sorry, I should not have burst in on you like this. Are you . . . are you all right?'

Madeleine nodded. 'I am wide awake,' she said. 'I shall not run out in *this*, I can assure you.' There was another reverberating crash and she flinched and shivered, crossing her arms over her breast with her fingers pressed nervously into the flesh of her upper arms. Janus took one slow step forward and then another. The echoes of that roll of thunder were still pealing round the sky when a second explosion shattered the air. Madeleine flung her arms wide in a wild, panic-stricken gesture. 'Janus, I am frightened,' she said.

His arms closed round her and she hid her face against his shoulder, recapturing for a few minutes the illusion of safety she had known the night before. His hands moved gently, soothing her fears, and she stood submissively until gradually it came to her that these were the hands of a lover. He sensed the moment when the realisation struck home to her and waited for the recoil that must surely come, but she still stood perfectly still in the circle of his arms. She lifted her head and put her hands on his shoulders, holding herself a little way away from him so that she could look up into his face. He bore that strange, searching look for as long as he could and then he pulled her close again. He caught up a handful of the warm, silken hair that streamed down her back and, twisting it up into a thick rope, lifted it to his lips.

'Send me away,' he said in a low voice.

She moved her head, mutely protesting, and

again he said: 'I can't bring myself to go from you unless you send me.'

Her reply was no louder than the breath which fanned his cheek. 'Stay.'

He drew a deep, unsteady breath and closed his eyes, searching blindly until he found her mouth, starving for his kisses with a hunger that matched his own, and then it was only a step to the bed that had been waiting for them.

Exquisitely matched, they drove one another to the utmost reaches of ecstatic abandon, until at last, invaded by the delicious languor of complete fulfilment, Madeleine slowly returned to herself and opened her eyes. Beside her, Janus sighed deeply once, then he turned his head against her breast and slept. By the light of the candles they had forgotten to extinquish, guttering on the far side of the room, their wavering light reflected in the looking glass, she saw his face, curiously young, the harsh lines of the day all wiped out. A smile just lifted the corners of her mouth. She touched the damp fronds of hair at the nape of his neck with gentle, wondering fingers, full of tenderness for him. Her eyelids drooped and she too slept.

Janus was the first to wake in the chill, grey dawn. He disengaged himself from her clinging arms and slipped out of bed. He found the dressing gown which had fallen unheeded to the floor and shrugged it on, still watching Madeleine as she slept. She sensed that he had gone and moved in her sleep, seeking him again. He thought that she would awaken but, finding the warm spot where he had just lain, she was satisfied and sank back into deep slumber again. Janus stood watching her for a moment longer, his expression unreadable, then he turned away, let himself silently out of the room and crept back to his own bed before the servants began to stir.

They did not meet again until the middle of the morning. Lord Chilcote rode out early, ostensibly to inspect the damage caused by the storm, an attention to duty which met with surprised but favourable comment amongst his tenants, coming on a day when he was supposed to be leaving for the pleasures of London. He returned mud-splashed and silent, and sought out Madeleine without stopping to change his boots and riding breeches. She looked up as he entered the room, then she put her sewing on one side, folded her hands carefully in her lap and waited for him to speak. Their eyes met briefly and then he turned away and looked out of the window, his fingers playing restlessly with the gilded cord that held back the curtains.

'I have lived up to my reputation beyond anyone's expectations,' he said over his shoulder.

She was conscious of a sudden compassion for him. She had not known what to expect from this meeting, dreading to be met with a light, careless word, or an air of jocular conspiracy. It was a relief to read his grim face and to know that he was as troubled as she was by what they had done.

'The blame is at least half mine,' she said quickly. 'You offered me a choice.'

'Would I have gone if you had said the word?

I wonder. I was a little drunk, you know.'

'Oh, no!' she protested swiftly. 'You were sober enough. You knew what you were doing, as I did. We are equals in this, let us not offer one another excuses.'

He left the golden tassel swinging and turned to face her.

'I have ridden miles this morning, thinking about the situation we have created,' he said quietly. 'I wondered how you would greet me when we met; perhaps with tears and reproaches, perhaps coquettishly, sure now of your power over me.' He gave a strange little laugh. 'I should have known better. What ever else you are, my Madeleine, you are not commonplace.'

'Do you wish me to go away?' she asked.

'Go away? No! Where would you go?'

'There must be a cottage somewhere . . . ' her voice trailed away. 'You cannot keep me here to be your mistress, I will not consent to that,' she said more firmly. 'If I am to remain at Laycott Manor, then it must be as we were before . . . before last night. It must never happen again.'

'Do you think that is possible?' He moved towards her and took her hand in his. She thought that he would kiss it as he had once before, but instead he undid the half dozen little buttons at the cuff of her dress and ran his finger slowly over the soft skin of her forearm. Every nerve in her body jumped in response.

'You see?' he said with his eyes fixed on her face. 'If I came to you again tonight, Madeleine, would you refuse me?'

She answered him with stark honesty. 'No.'

'No,' he agreed. 'But you are right; we cannot carry on a clandestine liaison here, nor can I take you away with me. There is another solution.' There was an infinitesimal pause and then he said, 'Marry me.'

She jerked her hand away from the loose clasp in which he was still holding it. '*Marry* you! No, that is not possible.'

'Why not?'

The colour flamed in her face and receded, leaving her paler than before. 'You know why not. I am not chaste.'

'My dear girl, neither am I!'

'Ah, you know what I mean. You must marry a girl like my cousin Phoebe — pure, untouched.'

'A shrinking virgin? Hardly my style and I should be sorry for the unfortunate girl.'

He thought he had silenced her, but she said in a low voice: 'There is still something I have not told you about my life with Henri.'

He flung up his hand in a distasteful gesture. 'Spare me your reminiscences. I do not wish to hear them.'

'No, this must be said.' She got up and, as he had done earlier, went to stare out of the window at the grey, drizzling day which had succeeded the previous night's storm. 'I was to have had a child.'

He looked at her rigid back with mingled compassion and impatience. 'What happened?'

'Henri did not wish it. He got one of his women to give me a draught to take.'

'And it was successful?'

She spread her hands in an eloquent gesture. 'As you see.'

'In the circumstances . . . perhaps it was for the best,' he said gently.

'Perhaps . . . no, it was cowardice,' she said with sudden energy. 'If I had had the child, Henri must have given me some support. Or, if not, if I had appealed to Mr. Lorgan, or even to you, would you have seen me and my baby starve? No! I tell you in every situation there is always a moment when it possible to say yes or no — as there was when I went to live with Henri, as there was when I swallowed that evil potion, as there was last night — and always, it seems, I take the wrong path.'

'Is it not possible that if you became my wife you might feel that you have turned your feet on to the right path?'

Her head was bent, her face completely hidden from him. 'I killed my child and the father of my child,' she said in a low voice. 'How can I ever hope to be forgiven?'

'You exaggerate — ridiculously so, in my opinion,' he said with a roughness that concealed the pity he felt for her. 'You had a religious upbringing, didn't you? Were you not taught that repentance brings forgiveness?'

'Yes — and I have bitterly repented.'

'Then it is time you forgave yourself. Come, can you not swallow me as a husband?'

She turned back towards him and looked up into his face with searching eyes.

'Is that what you truly want?' she asked.

Again there was a tiny, tell-tale pause and then he said, 'I must have married sometime, and God knows who would have me! I am rich, well-born, titled, but let me tell you that even the most ambitious of matchmaking mamas would think twice before surrendering a daughter to me. I shall be the devil of a husband.'

Still she did not answer him and he asked, speaking with sudden constraint, 'This doesn't bother you, does it?' He held up his maimed hand and she said with genuine surprise: 'Oh, no! I never think about it.'

His mouth twisted in his familiar, mocking smile. 'My mother screamed when I touched her,' he remarked. She sensed the bitter hurt that lay behind those light words and something of the bravado which had sent him searching for woman after woman who had not shrunk from his touch.

'I will marry you,' she said abruptly.

'Good.' He displayed neither surprise nor elation at her decision. 'I have given some thought as to how it is to be done. I shall go straight away and see Arthur Lorgan.'

'Do I need his consent?'

'I'm damned if I know, but it will be as well to secure it. There is bound to be talk, but I will do what I can to minimise it. If you are given away by your uncle it will lend an air of respectability to our union. I shall go to London, as I had planned, and obtain a special licence. Can you be ready by this time next week?'

'So soon?'

'Better a precipitate marriage than a

conventional engagement and the pretence of a premature birth.'

'I had not thought of that,' she said blankly.

'No? It could be so, but we will not wait to find out. I shall come back next week, bringing Charlie Carford to act as my best man. He's a fool, but a kindhearted fool, and I can rely on him to put the best of interpretations on our eccentricity and spread his story all over London. I shall take you back to London with me as soon as we are married.'

'Shall I be received?' Madeleine asked.

'In Society? That is the intention behind all these careful plans. A lot depends on Aunt Gertrude. If she will present you, you will be safely launched.'

'Present me to the Queen? Could she?'

'Certainly. Aunt Gertrude, my dear, was in attendance at Court in her younger days and I believe the Queen still has a fondness for her.'

'She might feel it was cheating to take a woman like me to Court.'

'She would be presenting my lawful wife,' Janus said with sudden hauteur. 'I am not one of Her Majesty's favourite subjects; she distrusts my influence on her son; but she will not refuse to receive you on that account. Our marriage cermony will wipe out the past — for both of us.'

'Will you tell Aunt Gertrude?'

'Yes, say nothing until I get back from seeing Arthur Lorgan. I will break the news to her myself.' He looked at her worried face with another of his wry smiles. 'Don't look

151

so downcast. Who knows, we might even be happy!'

He left her and she sat down on the nearest chair, conscious suddenly of an enormous fatigue and an empty feeling of desolation. She tried to tell herself that she had been infinitely more fortunate than she deserved, but she found her mind concentrating solely on the omissions in the dialogue between herself and Janus. He had not said that he loved her; he had not asked if she loved him; and his strange proposal had included no word of endearment and no caress.

7

'Janus Chilcote is to be married!' The news flew round the small section of London which was interested in such news. Clerks in the City, shop assistants in Oxford Street, porters in Covent Garden, cabbies in Mayfair, sweeps, housemaids, postmen, grooms and knife-grinders remained unmoved by the news; amongst his own small circle it caused a sensation. The German-born Duchess of Manchester, friend to the Prince and Princess of Wales, mistress to Lord Hartington and the *bête-noire* of the widowed Queen, put into words the query which was in everyone's mind: 'An unknown girl! Has she trapped him?'

Mrs. Embury, to whom she put the question and who was perfectly well aware that the Duchess knew of her own interest in Lord Chilcote, although neither of them would have dreamed of referring to it, replied with a shrug of her shoulders. 'One would hardly imagine so. Lord Chilcote is the last person to be coerced into any action which was not in accordance with his own wishes. From the way he spoke to me about her . . . '

'You had the news from his own lips?' the Duchess enquired in a tone of sympathetic interest which made Mrs. Embury grit her teeth. 'Oh, certainly!' she said in an airy way. 'We are such old friends, you know. As I was about to say, the girl is his cousin. He spoke of her as if they had been acquainted for some time, but he has only recently come to know her well.'

'A love match then?'

'I suppose one might call it so. There can hardly be any other consideration. Francis Ardingley's daughter! She must be penniless.'

'An undesirable match in every possible way,' the Duchess agreed. 'One awaits her arrival in town with interest. She must be something quite out of the common way to have persuaded our bad Lord Chilcote into matrimony.'

Mrs. Carford, mother of the prospective best man at this strange union, was seriously put out. 'Bringing her back to London immediately after the ceremony!' she exclaimed when her son told her the news. 'No honeymoon, no period of decent seclusion! Really, it has a most peculiar appearance. Am I expected to call on her? I shall hardly know how to go on!'

In Mrs. Porter's discreet establishment in Berkeley Street the news was greeted with hoots of laughter and the girls took ribald bets on the length of time Lord Chilcote might be expected to remain faithful to his new wife. 'I'll bet my bottom dollar we haven't seen the last of him!' Betty Markham exclaimed. 'He'll be back.' She was a little older than the majority of Mrs. Porter's girls, very sure of herself in her lush maturity. 'He'll soon be up to his old larks, you mark my words! Not but what he hasn't calmed down compared to what he used to be like,' she added thoughtfully. 'I knew him when he first hit the town. Wild! My word, he was wild! Of course, he was Janus Ardingley then, the Honourable Janus Ardingley; and then his Pa died and he inherited the title.' She picked up the newspaper which had excited their hilarity. 'He's put it in the paper, all right and proper, so I suppose there's no mistake. 'Miss Madeleine Ardingley, daughter of the late Hon. Francis Ardingley' — that would make her his cousin, I take it.'

The French girl, fair and languid, took the paper out of her hands. 'Madeleine Ardingley!' she said thoughtfully. A strange little smile appeared on her lips. 'Madeleine Ardingley!' she repeated, but the other girls had already lost interest and her preoccupation with the unexpected announcement went unremarked.

In the village of Laycott the news caused equal stupefaction. 'You could have knocked me down with a feather,' Lottie Hershaw assured her crony, Mrs. Blackett, after she had been summoned to Laycott Manor and given hurried instructions to concoct a suitable wedding gown. 'Cream satin, she's going to wear, and very nice too, although I won't be able to put the work into it that I would have liked, there's not the time. Who would have thought it when I was making Mrs. Lorgan's gowns over for her only the other day?'

'We all thought there was something afoot when she went off to the Manor so sudden,' Mrs. Blackett remarked. 'Very strange, that was.' She looked down and fidgeted with the lacy edge of the tablecloth in Lottie Hershaw's parlour, where she was taking tea. 'You will have had occasion to take her measurements afresh for the wedding gown, I suppose, Miss Hershaw?' she suggested.

The eyes of the two women met. 'I won't pretend I don't understand you, Mrs. Blackett,' Lottie said slowly. 'But on this occasion I would say *no*. I did run the tape measure over her, just to be on the safe side, you know, but there wasn't an inch of difference. No, I don't think she's caught him that way.'

'Of course, she's a lovely girl,' Mrs. Blackett said generously. 'And there's something about her . . .'

'Oh, she'll make a fine-looking ladyship, there's no doubt about that,' Lottie agreed. 'And his lordship seems to think a lot of her. I'll tell you one thing, Mrs. Blackett, she's wearing the biggest hoop of diamonds on her left hand that I ever saw in all my born days!'

The ring which had excited Lottie's admiration had been delivered by special messenger two days after Lord Chilcote's return to London. It was accompanied by one of his brief, scrawled notes: *You had better wear this, it will look better — JC.* Not exactly a loverlike message, Madeleine thought to herself, looking at that uncompromising line of black script, but the ring itself took her breath away. She slipped it on her finger. It was a little loose, though not dangerously so, but it felt strange and heavy on her finger. She sought out her great-aunt and held out her hand a little hesitantly. 'Janus has sent me a betrothal ring,' she said.

156

Gertrude Ardingley took the girl's slim hand in her own and stared at the magnificent stones with something like disbelief. 'Doing the thing in style,' was all she said, but she cast a sudden curious look up at Madeleine's face and instead of letting go of her hand she kept it in her own and drew Madeleine down to sit beside her.

'I was startled out of my wits when Janus told me he was to marry you,' she said in her abrupt fashion. 'So much so that I haven't spoken to you about it — except to wish you happy, which of course I do. None of my business, of course, but are you sure you are doing the right thing?'

'No,' Madeleine said. 'But Janus has refused to listen to all my objections.' She made a helpless gesture with her free hand. 'I know only too well that I am not a suitable wife for him, but he insists that we are to be married.'

'Oh, him!' Mrs. Ardingley said. 'Janus can look after himself. It's not him I'm worried about, it's you! Think you can stomach married life with him, do you?'

'Yes,' Madeleine said. 'It is true that I am a little afraid, but that is because I do not yet properly understand what will be required of me. My only wish is to please him.'

'Oh, dear!' Mrs. Ardingley said. 'Yes, I was afraid of that. Now you listen to me, my girl, don't you go making yourself a doormat for him to wipe his feet on! A little healthy opposition is just what Janus needs. He's in love with you, I suppose, otherwise he wouldn't be rushing you into this precipitate marriage, but if you want his respect you'll have to earn it — and you won't do that by giving in to him all along the line. There've been too many women ready to do that in the past, and he's ended up despising them. Stand up for yourself! Speak your mind when necessary and don't let him shake you out of it.'

'There may be something in what you say,' Madeleine admitted. 'But to me it seems that all the giving is on Janus's side. I have so little to offer him, except that he finds me beautiful. We . . . know a great deal about one another. I think we can make a life together.'

'It could be the making of Janus,' Mrs. Ardingley said slowly. She looked at her lovely niece a little helplessly. 'I've given you what advice I can, I don't know what more I can say, except . . . be kind. He's a hard man and not the husband I would fancy for any daughter of mine, but there have been few people in his life who have given him any sort of affection. You may do very well together — two burnt children — but by the same token, you have more power to hurt one another than most. You know too well where the old wounds lie!' She looked down at her workworn hands. 'You'll be mistress of Laycott Manor now,' she said gruffly. 'I suppose you'll be wanting me to leave?'

'Leave? No!' Madeleine said. 'I have no such thought in my head. This is your home! I am sure Janus feels the same. Besides, I think he means us to live in London for much of the year. Laycott will still need you.'

'Can't say I like the idea of looking for another

house,' Mrs. Ardingley admitted. 'If Janus is agreeable, I'd be pleased to stay on. Will you like living in London, do you think? Ghastly place, you know. Can't stand it myself.'

'I don't know,' Madeleine admitted. 'It is one of the things I am nervous about. I know so little of London society and I have no-one to instruct me.'

'No use looking to me,' Mrs. Ardingley said. 'I did a stint at Court in my younger days, but I can't say I enjoyed it. Quite out of touch now. Janus should be able to set you right about how to go on. At least he will be up to date with all the latest scandals!' She felt in the capacious pocket of her skirt and fetched out a packet wrapped in crumpled tissue paper. 'Not much I can give you by way of a wedding present,' she said. 'Thought you might like this.'

Madeleine unwrapped the untidy little parcel and lifted out with reverential fingers a length of exquisite rosepoint lace.

'It's good stuff,' Mrs. Ardingley said. 'Italian. Been in my family for years.'

'It's quite the most beautiful lace I have ever seen,' Madeleine said. 'Aunt Gertrude, are you *sure*? About giving it to me, I mean? It must be an heirloom of your family.'

'It's my own personal property,' Mrs. Ardingley said obstinately. 'To tell you the truth, I wore it for my own wedding. They made it into a sort of panel down the front of my dress. Can't say I liked the effect, but my mother insisted.'

Thanks to this rich gift, and another one equally unexpected, the bride presented a very creditable appearance on her wedding day. The plainness of her cream satin gown was relieved by the fine lace which she wore as a veil, and by the long rope of pearls which she wore twisted twice round her throat. The pearls had been handed to her by the bridegroom when, contrary to all convention, they met on the morning of the wedding. Janus and his best man had come straight down from London and he had thrown the servants into a twitter by walking into Laycott Manor and demanding to see Madeleine. She came to him, still wearing the old grey gown she had put on that morning, probably for the last time.

Janus looked her over thoughtfully. 'You aren't going to church in that, I hope?' he asked.

Madeleine shook her head. 'I am going to be quite resplendent in cream satin,' she said, with a small, ironic smile. 'And Aunt Gertrude has given me some wonderful lace.'

'Good of her. Here — these are for you. My grandmother — your grandmother, too, now I come to think of it — left them to me to be given to my bride on her wedding day.'

He watched as she opened the rubbed, leather case, but when she took the long, lustrous rope in her hands and looked up at him with all her dazzled pleasure in her eyes, a cynical smile twisted his lips. She took an impulsive step towards him, but Janus moved away. 'Save your kisses,' he said, 'I have no use for love that comes out of a jewel case.'

It was a rebuff that quenched all the delight

Madeleine had taken in this unexpected gift, but it did not prevent her wearing the pearls to church, proudly and a little defiantly. It was a curious ceremony. The bridegroom performed his part with an air of careless indifference, but the bride shook visibly throughout the service, and the hand Janus took in his was icy cold. He glanced down at her, his eyes suddenly keen and searching, and she looked up with a pitiful little smile on her lips. His face softened and he spoke his pledge to her without taking his eyes from her face. A faint colour appeared in her pale cheeks for the first time since they had met that morning. Somewhere in the pews behind them Mrs. Ardingley blew her nose vigorously, but Mrs. Lorgan, speechless with chagrin as she watched her penniless niece marrying a man of wealth, position and title, found nothing touching in the scene in front of her. She had not wished to be present, but for once she had been overridden by her husband. Whatever arguments Janus had chosen to employ with Arthur Lorgan, they had worked powerfully on him. He would have liked to have had Madeleine back in Bantock House for the night before her wedding so that it might be said that she had been married from the house of her uncle, but Mrs. Lorgan had refused to receive her. He had given in over that, but he had insisted that she should be present in church and that she should accompany the bridal party back to Laycott Manor for a short time after the ceremony. Mrs. Lorgan, sipping champagne and darting curious looks about her at the shabby

161

splendours of a house she had never entered before, managed to bring herself to offer a few words of felicitation to the girl she now saw as a designing hussy. Looking down into her aunt's angry eyes, Madeleine had no doubt about the value to be placed on her congratulatory words. It was a relief to turn to Charlie Carford, who looked at her with open admiration.

'I'll tell you frankly, Lady Chilcote,' he said. 'I couldn't think what had come over old Janus when he told me he was to be married. I understand it now, by Jove! Don't blame him at all. Perfectly right to snap you up before anyone else got a look in. Only way of making sure of you!'

It was a very flattering way of looking at their hurried marriage. Madeleine blushed and laughed and shook her head at him, but it was reassuring to find that one of Janus's oldest friends was prepared to treat her with such easy friendliness.

'You are the first person to call me by my new title, Mr. Carford,' she said. 'It sounds so strange!'

'Have to get used to it,' Charlie pointed out. 'After all, what else are we to call you?'

In the easy going society she had moved in with her father she might have invited him to call her by her Christian name, but she guessed that in England such a gesture would be considered premature and a little fast, and so she moved away with a smile on her lips and went to join Janus.

'You are looking a little happier,' he remarked,

observing her smile and and her flushed cheeks.

'Mr. Carford has been saying some very kind things,' Madeleine said.

'Be careful — poor Charlie is extremely susceptible!' Janus said with an amused glance at his friend on the other side of the room. His eyes went back to her face. 'But if he has been telling you that you look quite lovely, then he spoke no more than the truth,' he said deliberately, and smiled as the colour rose even higher in her cheeks.

This little exchange did not go unremarked. As Janus had intended, Charlie Carford was despatched back to London that same evening to report that Lord Chilcote was madly in love with the most beautiful girl he had ever set eyes on, that the marriage apparently had the blessing of her maternal relations and of Mrs. Gertrude Ardingley, who might have dropped out of Society but was still a person to be reckoned with, and the only reason for the marriage taking place so swiftly and so privately was Janus Chilcote's well-known disregard for convention.

Mrs. Carford had only one question: 'Is the girl a lady?'

'Oh, certainly!' her son replied, looking shocked. He hesitated. 'The mother's family smells of the shop a bit,' he admitted. 'But I think Janus means to cut that connection. They didn't seem any too friendly — not exactly his type, you know.'

Since Arthur and Alice Lorgan showed no disposition to linger at Laycott Manor,

Madeleine and Janus were left to a somewhat uneasy threesome with their great-aunt that evening. After dinner, Madeleine went to the piano. At the end of a Chopin nocturne Mrs. Ardingley got up.

'Champagne in the middle of the afternoon always gives me a headache,' she remarked. 'I shall take myself off to bed.'

Janus got up, a glint of malicious amusement in his eye, and went to open the door for her. 'I think that was meant to be a piece of monumental tact on Aunt Gertrude's part,' he remarked as he moved back into the room.

Madeleine was still at the piano and he went and stood behind her. She played a few notes with fingers that were suddenly uncertain on the keys. Her left hand felt strange, burdened now not only by the magnificent diamond ring, but also by a wide band of gold. Janus's fingers touched the nape of her neck. 'Shall we follow her example and go to bed?' he asked.

'It's still very early,' Madeleine said, not looking round.

'Who's to remark on that, except the servants? And, after all, it is the reason why we married one another,' Janus said softly.

Madeleine's downbent head hid the sudden desolation in her eyes. She stood up, the gleaming satin of her gown golden in the light of the branch of candles which stood on top of the piano.

'Are you still occupying the same room?' Janus asked.

'Yes,' she said. 'It did not seem worth making

any change since we are to leave for London so soon.'

'Then go up and I will come to you — if I may?'

She moved away without answering and he repeated, 'Madeleine, I said 'if I may'?' He looked down into her shadowed face and added with false concern, 'I do hope you haven't got a headache too?'

'No,' Madeleine said. 'And of course you may come.' With bitter irony she added: 'You know the way, don't you?'

She had not recovered from this exchange when Janus entered her room. She had been brushing her hair, but she got up from the dressing table and stood facing him. He looked her over and then asked: 'Did you get that nightgown when you were living with de Cavaillon?'

'Yes, I kept two to wear because I had no others.'

'It's a very seductive garment, but get rid of it. We shall manage better if you keep no reminders of that period in your life.'

'I agree,' she said quietly. 'I will see to it as soon as we are settled in London.'

Janus stood looking at her, his hands in the pockets of his long dressing gown. 'There is one thing I want to make clear to you now, at the start of our married life,' he said. 'I demand fidelity. You may think that strange. I have strayed often enough in other men's fields, God knows! In spite of that, I would find it intolerable to receive such treatment from my own wife. Remember this, because I shall not say it again.'

After such a start it was not surprising that he found Madeleine stiff and awkward in his arms. He drew away from her and raised himself on his elbow and looked down at her. 'Come, now, my lady,' he said with a touch of impatience. 'This is no time to start being coy with me.'

Madeleine had a wild desire to burst into tears, but she managed to control herself. 'Everything seems so strange,' she said helplessly.

He laughed and lay down again by her side, holding her loosely. 'The married state is something of a novelty to both of us,' he agreed. 'However, we shall have to try to grow accustomed to our shackles.'

He made no attempt to resume the lovemaking from which she had recoiled, but lay quietly by her side, only occasionally touching her forehead with his lips.

'I don't think your Aunt Lorgan liked seeing you marry me,' he remarked.

'I imagine she resents what she thinks of as my great position,' Madeleine agreed. 'She is very ambitious for her own daughters.'

'She surely doesn't imagine I would ever have given one of them a thought? How many are there, any way?'

'Two — Phoebe, who is very pretty and well behaved, and Bella, who is more like her mother. And then there are two boys — Edward, who is still at school, and little Harry.'

Janus chuckled. 'Yes, I remember Harry. I liked that little rascal. By the way, they tell me

166

that we can hope for a foal from Alisha.'

'That's good news,' Madeleine agreed.

He continued in this vein, chatting lightly of matters connected with Laycott, and if he smiled to himself in the darkness as he felt her beginning to relax against him, Madeleine was not aware of it. His gentleness surprised her, but when at last she slipped her arms round his neck and returned his kisses with a fervour born as much of gratitude as desire, he began to make love to her with all the wild fierceness he had shown the first time they had lain together. Two memories remained with Madeleine at the end of that long night, and one of them almost cancelled out the other. The first was that for all his apparent harshness, Janus had shown himself capable of patience and a most delicate understanding. The other was that he had spoken of their marriage vows as shackles.

The new Lady Chilcote was introduced to her London household just two days after her wedding. Since the servants at Laycott Manor remained permanently in the country, all those in London were strangers to her. With outward composure she acknowledged the introduction to Mr. and Mrs. Hawkes, butler and housekeeper, and smiled faintly at James and Thomas, footmen. Her first impression of the house in Grosvenor Square was that it was gloomy. Laycott Manor, for all its shabbiness, was a house full of light. The London house was far more elegantly furnished, but it seemed dark even on that bright autumnal day. Madeleine hesitantly expressed this opinion when Janus asked her what she thought of her new home.

'Make any changes you see fit,' he said carelessly. 'I have already instructed Hawkes and his wife that from now on they take their orders from you. But I suggest that before you turn the house inside out you look to your own furbishing — you are in dire need of some new gowns. I doubt whether you will receive many callers for a week or two, so use that time to collect a new wardrobe.' He gave her an unexpectedly mischievous grin. 'I can give you the names of some very good dressmakers.'

'And no doubt they are used to sending their bills to you?' Madeleine suggested.

'They are, but it will be thought unbecoming for you to be aware of it. In any case, I have no intention of paying your bills. I shall make you an allowance which I think you will find adequate and you can pay them yourself.'

The allowance he gave her was, indeed, more than adequate for any expenditure Madeleine thought herself likely to make, but she had learnt better than to try to thank him for his generosity. Janus, for some reason, did not like to be thanked.

Household expenditure, he made it clear, was entirely his affair and all bills would go to him as they had before he married. He was a little surprised to find that the first bill he was called upon to pay was for work on the servants' bedrooms, just as Mrs. Hawkes had been startled to be told that Lady Chilcote required to see them.

'I wish to see the entire house,' Madeleine

said. 'Right from the top to the bottom. Not today; I think it is only right that the servants should be given notice of my intention to enter their rooms.'

Mrs. Hawkes blinked. 'Yes, my lady,' she said woodenly. 'Does your ladyship wish to see the cellars?'

Madeleine smiled. 'I think I will draw the line at the cellars,' she said. 'But everything else I wish to see.'

Her faint air of hauteur stood her in good stead during exchanges like this. Her behaviour might be eccentric, but Mrs. Hawkes was far from despising her for it, as she might have done if it had been carried off with less assurance.

'I tell you what, Lil,' Mr. Hawkes remarked thoughtfully to his wife. 'There might be a little bit in this for you and me if we play our cards right. Have a word with the shopkeepers, why don't you?'

'Her ladyship is doing all the ordering herself,' Mrs. Hawkes said. 'And she wants to see the bills.'

'She's a fly one,' Hawkes said admiringly.

'The only thing we'll get out of it is a new mattress,' Mrs. Hawkes said. 'I had to smile, though I did think it a liberty, when she felt our bed and said, 'Don't you find this rather lumpy, Mrs. Hawkes?' '

'Which it is,' Hawkes put in.

'You'd never take her for a green girl, which she *is*, when all's said and done,' Mrs. Hawkes went on. 'I don't know what his lordship is going to say when he finds he's laying out his

169

blunt for new eiderdowns for the maids, I'm sure.' She sniffed. 'It's difficult enough to get the lazy little sluts out of bed now — there'll be no shifting them after this!'

Having classified her new mistress as somewhat soft on the subject of the lower orders, it came as a shock to Mrs. Hawkes to discover that in return for the new comforts Madeleine expected a far higher standard of housekeeping than had been evident at Chilcote House when she arrived to take up residence. The house was by no means neglected, but Janus did not have a woman's eye for the minor details and during his long bachelorhood a certain carelessness had crept in. Madeleine's thorough inspection had revealed these shortcomings to her and she took an early opportunity of pointing them out to Mrs. Hawkes. Untried she might be, but Madeleine had grown up in a convent where the long, shining corridors glowed with hard polishing and the walls were whitewashed by the nuns with their own hands once a year. She would tolerate no lower standards in her own house, now that she had one that she could call truly her own.

Janus, returning home one afternoon from lunching at his Club, paused in the hall to consider a large copper bowl filled with white chrysanthemums.

'Her ladyship ordered it to be placed there,' Hawkes murmured.

'Charming,' Janus remarked idly.

The following week he discovered that the dark red plush curtains in the dining room had been replaced by a soft pink damask which picked up one of the colours in the Aubusson carpet which had been moved into that room from the drawing room. He raised his eyebrows slightly on being informed that he would be required to pay for a new carpet for the drawing room.

'I went to the warehouse this morning and chose it and it will be delivered tomorrow,' Madeleine told him. 'I hope you will like it.'

'Your taste is impeccable, if expensive,' Janus remarked drily. 'I trust that you are not neglecting your own needs in dealing with those of the house?'

'No, indeed! My first new gowns were delivered today. I shall wear one of them to show you this evening.'

'So you are now ready for callers?'

'Yes,' Madeleine agreed. A faint crease appeared between her brows, 'Janus, no-one *has* called here yet. Why is that?'

'I understand they are staying away out of delicacy,' he replied. 'You are supposed to be still overcome by maidenly shame at the loss of your virginity. I am not sure how long this state of affairs is supposed to last, but I doubt whether the general curiosity to see you will allow the ladies to hold out much longer.'

It was such speeches as this which reduced Madeleine to stricken silence. Her relations with Janus since their wedding seemed to have fallen into a pattern which she feared would never be broken. She saw little of him during the daytime and, if she had not busied herself about the household matters which had proved unexpectedly absorbing, she might have been very lost and lonely. Nor did she always see him at night. They occupied separate rooms and although Janus had access to her room by a communicating door, he did not always use it. Madeleine found herself thinking wistfully that they might have reached a better understanding if they had been forced by poorer circumstances to sleep together in the same bed every night. As it was, when Janus visited her it was because he intended making love to her and he wasted little time in conversation.

She sat, a little disconsolately, in her refurbished drawing room the following afternoon, wearing one of her new gowns, admiring her new carpet, and wishing that someone would come to relieve her boredom. When Hawkes came in carrying a note on a salver she looked up hopefully.

'A young person has called,' Hawkes said in a tone of voice which showed plainly that he had no great opinion of the young person in question. 'A young French person,' he added.

'A woman?' Madeleine asked, puzzled by his manner. He inclined his head in a stately manner. 'What is her name?'

'Ma'm'selle Soubise,' Hawkes replied.

Madeleine shook her head. 'I know no-one of that name,' she said.

'So I thought, my lady,' Hawkes agreed. 'However, the young woman desired me to give you this message.' He offered Madeleine the salver and she took the folded sheet of paper and opened it out. There was very little writing on the sheet of paper, just an address, but it drove the colour out of Madeleine's cheeks. Only long habits of dissimulation enabled her to keep control over herself. After no more than the briefest of pauses, she said in a steady voice: 'I will see Mademoiselle Soubise, Hawkes. Bring her in here.'

After he had left the room she unfolded the sheet of paper again and looked at it — *Appartement 2, 36 Boulevard des Italiens* was all it said — the address of the apartment where she had lived with Henri de Cavaillon as his mistress.

8

Madeleine rose to her feet when Hawkes announced her visitor. She had dreaded to see one of Henri's actress friends enter the room, but this girl was quite unknown to her. She was a pretty young woman, a little on the thin side for current tastes perhaps, but the slimness of her waist added elegance to her figure, and the faint hollows in her cheeks set off her high cheekbones. She had a quantity of fair hair, elaborately dressed in curls at the back of the head, and very large pale eyes of a flat, opaque blue, which betrayed nothing of what she was thinking. She was smartly dressed, a little too smartly, just on the acceptable side of flashiness. Her little jacket was of scarlet velvet, nipped in tightly to the waist and fluted out behind over a cascade of flounces in black and white striped taffeta, and her small, forward-tilting hat was decorated with a bunch of cherries. It was a striking outfit, designed to catch the eye. Madeleine had no doubt why the butler had been hesitant about admitting this theatrical-looking young woman to her drawing room.

Madeleine found that she was being looked over with an interest that verged on the impertinent. The two women could hardly have been a greater contrast to one another, even though there was a superficial resemblance between them, a matter of colouring and type rather than a real likeness. Now that Madeleine had what seemed to her almost unlimited funds at her disposal she was able to indulge her own taste in dress, and her appearance was one of extreme refinement. Her gown, newly-delivered and in the first style of elegance, was of olive green marocain with no trimming but a narrow velvet ribbon in the same dull green and a square yoke of thick, creamy lace. It set off her lovely colouring, more vivid than the slightly faded fairness of her visitor, and heightened now under the other woman's frank appraisal. There was a sparkle of annoyance in her eyes and she raised her chin in an unconsciously haughty gesture as she asked: 'You wished to see me?'

'*Parlons français*,' the other girl replied. She continued in the same language, 'It will be better for us not to speak English, we run less risk of being overheard.' She looked round the imposing room. 'You have done very well for yourself, haven't you?' she asked.

'Please tell me what your business is with me,' Madeleine said. She sat down and indicated the chair opposite her with a gesture that made the other girl say with something of a snap, 'Quite the little princess, aren't we?'

'Will you please tell me who you are and what you want,' Madeleine repeated.

'I should think that was fairly obvious. I am Jeanne Soubise — that is my real name — but I am known as Maxine De Lisle.'

Somewhere in the recesses of Madeleine's mind a memory stirred. She frowned, trying

175

to recollect where she had heard that name before.

'You recognised that address I sent in to you, didn't you?' Jeanne Soubise asked. She waited for a reply, but when she received none she went on, 'I was your predecessor at the Boulevard des Italiens.'

'You mean you lived in the same apartment?' Madeleine asked.

'I mean that Henri de Cavaillon kept me there before he put you in my place.'

'I think you are mistaken, mademoiselle,' Madeleine said in a pitiful attempt to brazen the matter out.

The other girl laughed. 'I think I am not!' she said. 'I not only know your name, I saw you in Paris, and I remember you, yes I remember you very well indeed — my lady.'

'It is true that I once resided at the address you have mentioned,' Madeleine said. 'As for anything else, I totally deny it. In any case, the flat had been empty for some months before I took up residence.'

'*Took up residence!*' Jeanne repeated. 'I like that, it has a very dignified sound to it. Before you became Henri de Cavaillon's kept woman, you mean. But you are right about one thing, he had turned me out some time before he took up with you.' She gave a short, hard laugh. 'I committed the fault you managed to avoid, you see. I had a child.'

All the lovely colour drained out of Madeleine's face. 'He abandoned you because of that?' she asked in a horrified whisper.

176

Jeanne shrugged. 'He gave me a few hundred francs for my lying-in,' she admitted. 'Nothing more. I was a fool. I kept quiet about the baby until it was too late to do anything about it. Henri was away, visiting his family in the South, and I greeted him with the news on his return. I thought he would be pleased, that it would bind him to me. I could hardly have been more mistaken.'

'But the child, did he give you no help in maintaining it?' Madeleine asked.

'Not a *sou*.' Her eyes flickered to Madeleine's appalled face. 'I had a hard time of it, I can tell you.'

'What has happened to the child?' Madeleine asked.

'I left her with my mother in Paris.'

'It was a little girl?'

'Yes. I called her Véronique. God alone knows what will become of her. If my dear old mother brings her up the same way she did me I suppose the poor little bastard will follow the same road.'

Madeleine found herself unable to speak. Her own words to Janus returned to her — if she had had her own child surely Henri must have provided for it? But if Jeanne Soubise was to be believed, and Madeleine felt sure that she was speaking the truth, he would have thrown her off with all the callousness he had shown to this other girl, and what would have become of her then?

She roused herself to ask, 'What are you doing in London?'

177

'Making a living as best I can,' Jeanne answered. 'I was told that French girls could do well for themselves in London, and it was true up to a point. I got taken into quite a good house, but I am growing tired of the life and my health has not been of the best lately.' She laid her hand on her chest in an unconsciously betraying gesture and for a moment a look of fear showed in her face.

'But what do you *do*?' Madeleine asked.

The other girl stared at her. 'I'm a whore, my dear, what else?' she said.

'Oh, no!' A burning blush swept over Madeleine's face.

Observing it, Jeanne remarked bitterly: 'We can't all find rich lords to dote on us, you know.'

'But surely there was *something* else you could do?' Madeleine protested.

'Nothing that paid so well,' Jeanne said brutally.

She paused, but Madeleine could find nothing to say. She was contemplating with horror the possibility that she too might have to come to such a pass if she had had no English relations to fall back on. But no, she thought, she could never, never have brought herself to lead the life Jeanne had chosen.

'No need to look so disapproving,' Jeanne said in a grumbling tone. 'What have I done that you haven't, except that you have been lucky enough to sell youself to a man who has put a ring on your finger — you and every other high-born lady who marries for money and position. And

178

if some of them kept their bargains better, me and my sort would be out of business!'

Madeleine shook her head, knowing that there was a vast difference between herself and Jeanne Soubise, but unable at that time to enter into an argument on the subject.

'What do you want from me?' she asked.

Jeanne smiled. 'I don't imagine you would like your new husband to know about your life in Paris?' she suggested.

Madeleine got to her feet in one swift movement. 'Lord Chilcote knows everything there is to know about my past life,' she said. 'If this is an attempt at blackmail I am afraid you have come to the wrong place, mademoiselle.'

'Blackmail!' Jeanne's assumption of indignation hid her annoyance at this unwelcome news. Smoothly, she abandoned her first, and easiest, plan and switched to the second one she had prepared against such a contingency. 'I had no such idea in my head,' she said untruthfully. 'What I require is something quite different. I would like to apply for the position of lady's maid.'

'*My* maid?' Madeleine asked, not quite believing her ears.

'Certainly. Before I had the misfortune to fall in with Henri de Cavaillon I was, in fact, maid to his sister.'

Madeleine fixed her eyes on the other girl's face. 'He . . . he seduced you?' she asked almost inaudibly.

Jeanne's large, pale eyes gave nothing away. She had called her meeting with Henri de

179

Cavaillon a misfortune, but the truth was she had looked upon it as the culmination of a career she had embarked on in her early teens, interrupted only briefly by occasional spells in domestic employment. She had entered into her liaison with him in triumph, had extracted every penny she could from him, and had been furious when her own miscalculation of the effect parenthood would have on him had resulted in the ending of one of the most enjoyable and profitable periods of her life. However, if Madeleine Ardingley wanted her to be an ill-treated innocent, then that was the role Jeanne was perfectly prepared to assume.

'Alas, yes,' she sighed.

'I cannot possibly employ you,' Madeleine said. She betrayed her agitation by walking restlessly about the room. 'It would be an embarrassment to both of us. I . . . I apologise for suspecting you of wishing to blackmail me, and if you will allow it I am prepared to help you to return to France. Surely there you can find some suitable employment?'

No doubt, but it was by no means what Jeanne had in mind. 'It would be difficult, without references,' she said smoothly.

Since Madeleine knew this to be true from her own experience, she was silenced. 'To have you here, in the house, knowing about me and Henri, it would be a great embarrassment,' she said in a low voice.

'I am discreet,' Jeanne said. 'I shall not gossip to the other servants, nor to anyone else.'

Again there was a long silence. Jeanne hid

180

her impatience and waited. This interview was not following quite the lines she had envisaged. She had expected to meet either with tears and entreaties from a weak, pretty woman who had entrapped a rake into marrying her, or else a bold schemer who would be prepared to enter into a bargain with Jeanne as a price for her silence. All the same, the idea of becoming Lady Chilcote's maid was not without attractions. She was beautiful and in the past she had allowed herself to be swayed by her passion for Henri de Cavaillon. Lord Chilcote's reputation was well known; it was unlikely that he would remain faithful to his lovely wife and once he began to neglect her she would surely turn to other men. Jeanne had no illusions about the morals of the set Lord Chilcote frequented. She did not doubt that there would be messages to be taken, assignations to be made, bribes to be collected from lovers and would-be lovers. She would make a tidy sum and then return to France.

'You truly wish to reform your life?' Madeleine asked. She turned her great, grave eyes on Jeanne and for once Jeanne had difficulty in sustaining the gaze of another woman, but she replied with the greatest readiness, 'Indeed, I do! Employ me, I beg you. I will serve you faithfully.'

There was another pause and Jeanne said with sudden passion, 'What right have you to deny me the chance to start afresh, you who have made such a fine marriage and are safe for life?'

'It is true,' Madeleine acknowledged. 'If there

had been someone to help me in this way in France . . . ' she broke off and stood, lost in thought, while Jeanne fidgeted nervously on her seat.

'Could you divorce yourself completely from your . . . your present friends?' Madeleine asked.

'Oh, yes! They don't even know my real name, and I shall tell them I am going back to France,' Jeanne answered readily, all the more readily because this was what Mrs. Porter had already recommended her to do. There had been hints that she was losing her attraction, she was too thin and the cough which troubled her annoyed the customers. The shadow of a dreadful spectre hovered for a moment on the fringes of Jeanne's consciousness and was hurriedly dismissed.

'Are you properly qualified to be a lady's maid?' Madeleine asked in a low voice.

'I am very good,' Jeanne replied. She looked Madeleine over and added reluctantly: 'You need little assistance in the way of beautifying, and I can certainly look after your clothes as well as anyone.'

'Your own style of dress is a little . . . ' Madeleine hesitated, not wishing to give offence, but very sure that scarlet velvet would not be acceptable in Mrs. Hawkes' eyes, even for off duty wear.

'Fast,' Jeanne supplied without rancour. 'Well, what do you expect? Don't worry, I will tone it down a bit to suit my position.'

She was already talking as if it were a foregone conclusion that Madeleine would take her on. Madeleine tried to consider the matter dispassionately, but she was full of horror at the thought that this — *this* — was what she might have come to if her circumstances had been the same as Jeanne's. How desperately she herself had pleaded against her dismissal by Madame Bécaud — and how unavailing it had been. If she had had a lever to use, such as Jeanne possessed against her, would she not have used it to obtain respectable employment? She had forged her own references, it seemed to her that the least she could do was to provide Jeanne with the chance to obtain a genuine recommendation.

'If I took you on it would have to be for a trial period, perhaps for three months to begin with,' she said.

'I would agree to that.'

'You would have to be very careful in your behaviour. There must be no scandals amongst the men servants.'

Jeanne sniffed. 'Certainly not! I have been used to something a bit better than that,' she said.

'And your manner to me must not cause comment. Even when we are alone, even if we speak French to one another, you must remember that you are my maid.'

'Yes, miladi,' Jeanne replied submissively. She glanced under her thick, fair lashes at her new employer. 'Will you tell Lord Chilcote about me?' she asked softly.

There was a long silence while Madeleine considered this. Janus had said, and truly, that they would do better without any reminders of her past life. He had taken exception to a nightdress, what would he say to a maid who knew all about her? She thought that he would not tolerate it and she had no doubt that if he so wished he could pack Jeanne off to France whether she wished it or not. With sad honesty Madeleine acknowledged that if he did so it would be a relief to her. She had no real wish to have Jeanne Soubise in her house, and yet that was unfair. She had longed for help herself in similar circumstances and it had been bitter to find that there was no help to be had. How could she refuse the request of her fellow victim and how could she call in the help of a husband who would be ruthless in getting rid of this threat to her peace of mind?

'I shall not tell Lord Chilcote your story,' Madeleine said.

The flat blue eyes betrayed neither surprise nor satisfaction, but inwardly Jeanne exulted. The first deception. It had begun.

As was only to be expected, the sudden introduction into the household of a new maid for Lady Chilcote caused some comment. Hawkes, in particular, was scandalised by the way Jeanne had obtained the position. 'Came to the front door as bold as brass!' he said. 'Asked for Lady Chilcote as if she'd known her all her life!' He shook his head. 'I only hope her ladyship hasn't been taken in,' he said ominously.

Mrs. Hawkes raised the question of references and Madeleine replied, 'I was acquainted with

Jeanne's former employer in France. I think she will give satisfaction. I have made it clear that she is only on three months' trial.' The finality with which she said this silenced Mrs. Hawkes, although she joined her husband in shaking her head over her employer's foolhardiness in private.

To Madeleine's relief, Jeanne appeared for work soberly dressed in black and her manner was quietly respectful, even when they were alone. With her fellow servants she was somewhat aloof, an attitude which, strangely enough, did her no disservice in their eyes. A top-flight lady's maid was expected to be a superior being. She seemed to know her business and, apart from being foreign and thinking herself above the rest of them, they could find little fault with her.

For all the ease with which she had slipped into the establishment, however, Madeleine found her presence a constant strain, nor did she like the deception she was practising on Janus. Perhaps it was only her imagination which made her feel that her manner towards him had become more constrained since Jeanne had come to look after her, but it was certain that she could not respond with any spontaneity if he chanced to come into her room while Jeanne was still there. She was acutely conscious of the other woman's listening ears, and even Janus's more lighthearted remarks got nothing but a perfunctory smile from Madeleine until after Jeanne had gone out of the room. Worst of all, the reminder of her life with Henri which Jeanne represented brought back the nightmares from which she had suffered before her marriage. They never attacked her on the nights when Janus came to her, but when she slept alone she woke frightened and shaking, shivering with fear of the hands that clutched for her from the grave.

She awoke one night in such a state and sat up in bed, looking fearfully round the darkened room, then she slipped out of bed and re-lit the oil lamp, with fingers that trembled. The bright, steady light reassured her and she got back into bed again, resolving to turn it out once more as soon as her mind had freed itself from the horrid recollection of her dream, but the line of light underneath the connecting door had attracted Janus's attention and he came in to see what was the matter.

'I had a bad dream,' Madeleine said uncertainly.

'Again? I thought that had stopped since our marriage,' he said with a frown. 'Are you all right? Can I get you anything?'

She shook her head. With every fibre of her being she longed for the reassurance of his presence and yet she could not bring herself to ask him to stay. To seem to be importuning him — that would be unbearable! Janus turned away and she thought he was going to leave her, but he merely closed the door, turned down the lamp and came back to her bedside. 'Move over, my dear,' he said. 'If we are going to be wakeful, we may as well be wakeful together.'

She clung to him in an agony of gratitude until he said casually, 'I suppose this French maid of yours hasn't got anything to do with your nightmares coming back again?'

Madeleine felt herself stiffen. 'How do you mean?' she asked in a voice she tried to keep as offhand as his own.

'I notice you always speak French to her. I wondered whether perhaps it might have revived memories which had begun to fade.'

'Oh . . . I see. I suppose it is possible,' she said.

'In that case, perhaps you should get rid of her.'

'I couldn't do that!' Madeleine protested. 'I mean, it would be so unfair to send her away for something that is not her fault.'

'A month's wages would take care of that,' Janus said.

'She is quite a good maid, and she has been here for such a short time. I think I should keep her — at least until the end of the three months' trial I promised her.'

'As you wish,' he said.

Reassured that he had not suggested parting with Jeanne out of any suspicion of her connection with her life in Paris, Madeleine thankfully relaxed. She was weary after her disturbed nights and under Janus's gently caressing hands she began to drift into a pleasant state of torpor.

'It is very nice, being married to you,' she murmured, not really knowing what she was saying.

'I am glad you think so,' Janus said politely. Her heavy eyelids closed. 'Are you going to sleep?' he asked, but the only reply he received was an incoherent little mutter. 'My powers must be waning,' he remarked, but he did not sound as if he particularly minded, and she fell into a deep sleep with the sound of his soft laughter in her ears.

She awoke the next morning more deeply contented than she had ever been after his most passionate lovemaking. It was almost worth suffering a horrible nightmare to have Janus so kind and considerate towards her. By this time she loved him with quiet desperation, determined never to burden him with the knowledge of her love, since that was not what he appeared to want, and yet longing to give expression to it and for him to love her in the same way. His passion for her showed no signs of diminishing, but there were few occasions such as the quiet minutes they had spent together that night. He used her, she sometimes thought despairingly, in much the same way as Henri de Cavaillon had used her, because he worshipped her beauty and found satisfaction in her body, but there were few signs that he regarded her as a companion, although they had begun to go about together. Madeleine had received her first callers, rapidly followed by her first invitations. When she commented in all innocence to Janus that Mrs. Carford and Mrs. Embury had been particularly kind there was an infinitesimal pause before Janus said deliberately: 'Be a little careful of Charlotte Embury's friendship. I was her lover before our marriage.'

'Not now?' The question slipped out before

Madeleine could stop it.

Janus's eyebrows rose in almost comical astonishment. 'You flatter me!' he said. 'I am not superhuman. Besides . . . compare her with yourself. A farthing candle to the sun, my dear!'

It was carelessly said and he walked out of the room immediately he had spoken. He would perhaps have been surprised, he might even have been touched, to have seen the effect of this offhand compliment on his beautiful wife. She did not care that Charlotte Embury had been her husband's mistress in the past; the only thing that mattered was that the liaison had come to an end and that he had said that he preferred Madeleine. Mrs. Ardingley's warnings against making herself a doormat for Janus to walk on were forgotten. Madeleine had progressed far beyond that stage: all her actions were bent towards the necessity to please him.

For all that, her love was put to a severe test only two nights later, when he showed her a very different side to his character. They were invited to a ball, the first London ball Madeleine had attended. The Prince of Wales was to be present, though not the Princess, who was expecting to be confined very shortly. Madeleine dressed for it in a happy glow of anticipation. Everything seemed to promise well; she was young and in love, and even if she had reservations about the nature of Janus's love for her, she could not complain that her husband was inattentive. She was newly launched on an exciting new life and everyone had been unexpectedly kind to this unknown girl, so that she was able to look forward to the evening in the knowledge that she would find at least some friends in the ballroom. Her looks were enhanced by her excitement — and she had a most successful new gown to wear — a concoction of white tulle over pale green satin ornamented by white flowers and trails of dark green leaves.

'I think they are meant to be water lilies,' she said seriously, in answer to a question from Janus when he came to her room to see if she was ready.

'Charming,' he said. 'This watery look is becoming to you. You have something of a mermaid air about you; I can imagine you ruling over a kingdom under the sea.' He lounged against the back of her chair, watching her reflection in the glass as she fastened her pearls around her neck. 'A princess of the waves,' he murmured. His eyes rested on her gleaming shoulders, rising out of a foam of white tulle. 'Or Venus,' he added. Their eyes met in the mirror and Madeleine blushed, deliciously conscious of the force of his desire for her.

'W-we must go,' she said, suddenly aware, as she was so often these days, that Jeanne was still there, waiting to be dismissed. 'Thank you, that will be all,' she said and, as always, was conscious of a feeling of relief as the maid left the room.

Janus picked up the dark green velvet wrap she had left draped over the end of the bed and put it round Madeleine's shoulders and suddenly, lulled into a false sense of security by the new warmth she felt between them, Madeleine found the courage to bring up a subject which had been on her mind for some time. The pearls she wore were lovely, but apart from her two rings, they were the only jewellery she owned. She had all the other appurtenances of a rich woman — her fine house, her servants, her carriage and pair, her box at the Opera, her extensive wardrobe — and she had purchased one or two trinkets for herself, but in spite of her ample allowance she did not have the funds at her command which would enable her to purchase the sort of jewels which were considered appropriate to her rank. It was a matter which had only recently become apparent to her, and she owed the knowledge that the simplicity of her toilet had caused comment to a honey-sweet hint from Mrs. Embury; but the information which caused her to broach the subject to Janus came from Charlie Carford's mother, and it was this which made her believe, wrongly as it turned out, that there would be no harm in speaking to him about it.

Mrs. Carford had thought the flowers Madeleine wore in her hair when she went to dine at the Carford mansion quite charming. 'But it would be proper for you to wear a jewelled pin to fasten them, or something of that sort,' she had said, intending to be helpful. 'And the Prince will certainly expect to see you in a tiara on more formal occasions. He is such a stickler for the proper mode of dress, you know. Has

Lord Chilcote not handed over his mother's jewels to you?'

Madeleine had shaken her head and Mrs. Carford went on: 'Men don't think of these things. She had some quite remarkable pieces. I dare say they are sitting in a bank vault — and what use is that to anyone? Remind him about them, dear Lady Chilcote.'

And so Madeleine, very happily wearing her splendid pearls, but conscious that for a grand ball at which the Prince of Wales was to be present she might be thought to be a little under-dressed, looked up at her husband and said: 'The pearls are well suited to my 'watery look', aren't they? Janus, are there any other jewels I should have? Mrs. Carford says that your mother was quite famous for her splendid jewellery and she asked me if you had passed it on to me.' Her voice faltered. Warned by the darkening of his face that this was a subject that would have been better left alone, she subsided into dismayed silence.

'You will have to make do with what you have,' he said. 'I sold my mother's jewels.'

'I didn't mean to offend you,' Madeleine said unhappily.

He looked at her with the unpleasant sneer she had not seen on his lips in recent weeks. 'Only a short time ago you were overwhelmed by what I had given you. Have you been corrupted so soon?'

'No! It is the custom for ladies to wear diamonds in their hair. Mrs. Carford suggested that there were family jewels lying unused in a

192

safe. It seemed only sensible to remind you of them. I was not asking you to buy jewellery for me.'

'Just as well, for I should most certainly refuse. I do not care to pay the price my father was forced to give for something which was his by right.'

Remembering the cold, proud face in the portrait of the late Lady Chilcote which stood at the top of the stairs in Laycott Manor, Madeleine guessed at his meaning and shivered. Janus's insolent gaze wandered over her as she stood reflected in the looking glass, brilliantly illuminated by the lamplight. 'Content yourself, my dear,' he drawled. 'It is your beauty unadorned which holds me in thrall.'

It was an unpropitious start to an evening which turned into a disaster. They dined alone in almost unbroken silence and left for the ball at a fashionably late hour. As Janus, outwardly attentive to her comfort, assisted Madeleine out of the carriage, he nipped her fingers unkindly between his own. 'Smile!' he said in a savage undertone. 'I won't have you sulking because I have refused you a few tawdry gee-gaws!'

For once he had gone too far. Burning with indignation, Madeleine lifted up her head and swept into the house, her colour high, her eyes sparkling magnificently. It was the injustice of Janus's accusation which she most bitterly resented. She had had no mercenary motive in mentioning the jewels to him and she was certainly not sulking! He must surely be aware as he looked round the splendid scene in front of them that she was the only woman of her standing in the room who was wearing nothing but pearls by way of ornament. She did not care for herself. Indeed, she preferred their soft glow to the harder sparkle of diamonds. It was only because she was anxious to be a credit to him that she had raised the subject at all. For the moment she shut out of her mind the knowledge of the deep love she believed she had come to feel for him. There was room for nothing but a biting anger. He had chosen to class her with a woman who had placed a high price on her favours: she — who had given him so lavishly everything he had desired of her, who had had no thought but to please him. She looked round the crowded ball room with a sense of anticipation which had nothing in common with the pleasure with which she had looked forward to this event earlier in the evening. There was plenty of scope here for a wife who wished to be revenged on her husband. Janus had shown himself to be unworthy of her unceasing efforts to please him, now let him beware.

9

In one sense the evening was a triumph for Madeleine. She had been much admired by the few people who had already made her acquaintance, but it had been thought that she lacked animation. Inhibited by her fears of doing the wrong thing, she had sometimes seemed a little stiff, but on the occasion of the Marchmounts' ball she displayed a vivacity which added an extra dimension to her beauty.

It was a brilliant scene, and one which Madeleine, for all her knowledge of the café life of Paris, had not experienced before. The throng of people twisted and twirled on the shining floor of the ballroom under the myriad lights of the crystal chandeliers in a constantly shifting kaleidoscope of colour. The billowing gowns of the ladies in pale, bright colours contrasted with the black and white and occasional gay uniforms of their partners; the scent of flowers mingled with their perfumes; there was a constant murmur of music in the air combined with the subdued roar of many voices and the laughter of young people and the soft shuffle of their feet over the dance floor.

'You will dance first with me,' Janus said. It was an order and in spite of her resentment at his tone, Madeleine did not care to provoke the scene which would inevitably have ensued if she had refused to comply. They had completed only one turn of the room when the music stopped. Everyone turned towards the staircase and the orchestra broke into the National Anthem as the Prince of Wales came down the stairs. He passed close to Madeleine and Janus and she sank into a profound curtsey, her eyes on the floor. His Royal Highness stopped. 'What's this I hear about you, Chilcote?' he enquired. 'They tell me you've married the most beautiful girl in London. Is it true?'

'Your Royal Highness may judge for yourself,' Janus said. 'May I present the new Lady Chilcote to you, sir?'

He drew Madeleine forward and once again she made her curtsey. The Prince took her hand in his. 'For once rumour spoke the truth,' he said. 'My felicitations, Chilcote.'

'Thank you, sir.' Janus would have stepped back, but the Prince still kept Madeleine's hand in his. 'What do you say, Lady Chilcote, shall I steal you from this fellow and complete the dance with you?'

'It will be an honour, your Highness,' Madeleine murmured, not daring to look at Janus.

'I don't think Chilcote thinks so,' the Prince remarked. 'But I can see I shall look for a dance in vain unless I seize my opportunity now.'

The music started again, an insinuating waltz, and Madeleine and the Prince took the floor, in solitary state for the first few bars, and then rapidly joined by the other dancers, while interested eyes sought through the crowd to keep watch on this intriguing pair.

The Prince was growing a little stout, but he was light on his feet and an experienced dancer. 'Lady Chilcote, I have the strangest feeling that this is not the first time we have met,' he said. 'Am I right? Have I had the pleasure of seeing you before?'

For a moment Madeleine thought of denying it, then with a recklessness born of her feeling that nothing was of any importance since Janus had such scant regard for her, she looked up into his face with a conspiratorial smile and said: 'You are quite right, sir, but I had hoped that you might not have remembered the occasion. You see, until this year I lived in France with my father, who had somewhat . . . Bohemian ideas. A year or two ago, when I was a very young girl, he took me with him one evening to the Maison d'Or. Your Highness was also dining there. Not . . . ' her eyes lifted mischievously to his face and then her long lashes veiled them demurely, ' . . . not in the public restaurant,' she said in a bland tone of voice which made him chuckle. 'You saw me when you passed through the public rooms. You asked my name and I was, in fact, presented to you.'

'And why, may I ask, do you hope that I had forgotten such a pleasant occasion?'

'I should not have been there,' Madeleine said. 'It was not the right milieu for a well-brought up young lady of seventeen. I think I would not like London Society to be aware of our former meeting.'

Again he chuckled. He was shrewd enough to guess that there was rather more to her story than met the eye, but he was famous for his indulgence to pretty women and not averse to sharing a secret with this new beauty. 'Tell me, Lady Chilcote,' he said. 'On this occasion — which I have, of course, already completely forgotten — was I alone?'

Again Madeleine lifted her eyes to his face, smiling in a way which made him tighten his hold on her slim waist. 'I believe Mademoiselle Hortense Schneider, the actress, was also dining at the same address that evening,' she said. 'But like your Royal Highness, my memory has faded to the point where I really can't remember whether I saw her in your company or not.'

The Prince threw back his head and laughed aloud, much to the interest of the onlookers. 'I understand you,' he said. 'Your memory will remain bad as long as mine does, is that it? Blackmail, Lady Chilcote, blackmail! You really mustn't blackmail your Prince, you know. I shall have to think of a suitable punishment for you.'

The music came to an end and once again Madeleine sank into her profound, graceful curtsey. 'I am already punished, sir,' she said. 'My dance with you is over.'

Her success was assured. Where the Prince of Wales had shown himself to be pleased — and he insisted on a second dance with her later in the evening — lesser mortals were not likely to find fault. Madeleine went from one partner to the next, with scarcely time to draw breath between dances and no time at all to consider the effect this behaviour was having on her husband. To be sure, there were one or two carping remarks, at least one of them unfortunately made in Janus's hearing. 'With the Mordaunt case hanging over his head, you would think the Prince would be a little wary of entangling himself with young married women,' a young Guards officer in blazing scarlet remarked to a companion.

'Oh well, everyone knows Lady Mordaunt is off her rocker, poor little woman,' the other man said tolerantly. 'Dare say the Prince will brush out of it all right and tight even if he does get called to court. Charles Mordaunt is a fool in my opinion, washing his dirty linen in public.'

Their talk drifted to a discussion of this scandal which had had fashionable society holding its breath for months, wondering whether the heir to the throne really would be required to give evidence in a particularly unsavoury divorce case, and they did not speak again of his new predilection for Madeleine's society, and remained unaware of the murderous hatred they had aroused in her husband's breast towards chattering fools who gossiped about his wife.

While it would not be true to say that the excitement of the evening caused Madeleine to forget the bad terms on which she stood with Janus, it did soften her mood to the extent where she would have been prepared to listen to an apology if he had deigned to offer one. But Janus was far from apologising. He had lashed himself into a state of barely-controlled fury by the time the Prince of Wales left the party and they were free to go home. In this state of mind he saw Madeleine's triumphant progress and glowing looks as proof that he had married an incorrigible coquette, thriving on flattery and avid for conquest and if, at the back of his mind, he knew that he did her less than justice, Madeleine's deliberate courting of admiration that evening was not designed to make him more rational. He resolutely stifled the voice of reason and concentrated on the fact that she had not found time to dance once with her husband, except for that one short turn round the floor which had been interrupted by royalty. He would have been nauseated by the suggestion that what ailed him was old-fashioned jealousy, but it was nevertheless true that the sight of Madeleine spinning in apparent pleasure in one pair of arms after another eventually drove him out of the ballroom altogether. It also never occurred to him that even his own wife could not dance with him unless he asked her, nor that Madeleine was waiting in vain for some sign from him that he had recognised the unreasonable nature of his behaviour earlier in the evening, and that when it did not come she smiled with all the more determination on the partners who surrounded her.

She was dismayed to realise when they eventually left the ball that Janus's mood had, if anything, hardened still further. They scarcely spoke during the short drive home.

'I shall go straight up to bed,' Madeleine said

as soon as they entered the house. 'Oh, I am so tired!'

Janus said nothing, following her up the stairs as if he too intended to retire immediately, but when she opened the door of her room, to her surprise he followed her inside. Jeanne was sitting by the fire, waiting for her mistress to return and nodding with weariness over some sewing.

'You need not wait,' Janus said curtly. 'Lady Chilcote will not require you tonight.'

She gave him a resentful look as she left the room, thinking that if either of them had thought of this earlier she might have been spared a long, tiresome wait, but relieved that she could at last seek her bed and escape from the dragging weariness that had made her life a burden since she entered Madeleine's service.

'You should not have sent Jeanne away; I need her to unfasten this gown,' Madeleine said. She glanced at him warily, a little unnerved by the look on his face.

'Don't worry, you will find me as skilful as any lady's maid,' Janus said.

'I . . . I have already told you that I am tired,' Madeleine said.

'Of course — the excuse of the reluctant wife throughout the ages!' His eyes were glittering strangely as he confronted her. 'You have spent a very enjoyable evening displaying yourself to other men, now it is time for you to remember that you have a husband, and one, moreover, who doesn't take kindly to being treated as if he were some tame lap dog.' He spun her round and began to undo the fastenings of her delicate gown with fingers which were not quite as deft as he had boasted. 'Hold still, my dear, you won't get away from me, and I have no wish to hurt you.'

'Haven't you?' Madeleine said bitterly. She jerked herself away from him and began taking the pins from her hair, shaking it about her bare shoulders. With rapid, careless hands she began to throw off her remaining clothes. 'Very well, if this is all you want of me, come to my bed and I will pay the dues you feel are owing to you. Why not? I have been well educated in the art of pleasing. But I will tell you this, after tonight I will have no respect left for you. Almost I had come to believe you capable of kindness, of feeling, but now I know you are as much a monster as any other man I have ever known.' She paused, and then with an angry sob she said the unforgivable words, 'You are exactly the same as Henri de Cavaillon!'

He caught her by the shoulders and drew her towards him, the look on his face so murderous that she held her breath in fear, then with a movement so violent that she lost her balance and fell full length on the floor against the side of the bed, he flung her from him. Half dazed by the force with which she had fallen, Madeleine heard his rapid footsteps cross the floor and then the sound of the door between their rooms crashing to. He had left her and she lay crouched on the floor in despairing tears until finally, cold and shivering, she crept into her solitary bed.

For ten days the quarrel between them continued, for ten days of freezing courtesy in public and a total lack of communication in private, they held out against one another, both conscious of having been to some extent in the wrong and both too proud to admit it. The breach might have widened still further if Madeleine had not had to look to Janus for assistance in a most difficult social problem.

Her friendship with the Prince of Wales had flourished in the days following the Marchmounts' ball. Since they moved in the same circle it was inevitable that they should meet at the soirées and receptions which crowded the calendar and he always had a smile and a genial word for the charming wife of his old friend, Lord Chilcote. There could be no doubt that he admired her, he made no secret of it, and at first Madeleine saw no harm in the discreet encouragement she gave him. But the day arrived when she felt vaguely alarmed at the warmth in his eyes as he made his way towards her, and when he said, in a confidential undertone, 'May I give myself the pleasure of calling on you one day soon, Lady Chilcote? Perhaps tomorrow afternoon?' she knew that the time had come to put a little check on his mounting ardour.

She smiled and replied: 'Of course. Lord Chilcote and I will be delighted to receive you at any time, sir.' She glanced round and was fortunate enough to catch Janus's eye. He responded to the appeal in her look and came to join them.

'We may have the honour of a visit from his Royal Highness tomorrow afternoon, my lord. I have been telling him how pleased we shall be,' Madeleine said, with a quick look up into his face.

Janus smiled and bowed, secretly amused by the flash of chagrin in the Prince's eyes. They knew, all three of them, that his intention had been to find Madeleine alone, that he had hoped to further his flirtation with her, and that the husbands of ladies in whom the Prince of Wales had displayed an interest were supposed to make themselves scarce if he chose to spend an afternoon of dalliance in the drawing room.

'I shall make a point of being at home,' Janus said politely.

'Of course, we know that your time is not entirely your own, sir,' Madeleine added. 'But if you should find yourself free we shall be delighted to see you at Chilcote House.'

They waited the following afternoon, Madeleine in the drawing room, a little on edge, Janus in the library, apparently oblivious to the tension the projected visit had aroused. At four o'clock a charming bouquet of flowers was delivered for Lady Chilcote, together with a little note.

Dear Lady Chilcote,

I am so sorry that I have been prevented from calling on you this afternoon. I look forward to seeing you and Lord Chilcote at Marlborough House when I return from Scotland.

Albert Edward

She took the note, with her bouquet of white roses and pink carnations, into the library and handed it to Janus without a word. He read it and laughed. 'Poor old Bertie, I feel quite sorry for him,' he said. He glanced at his silent wife. 'There goes your chance of being a royal mistress,' he said.

'It doesn't happen to be one of my ambitions,' she said and moved towards the door with her head held high. His voice stopped her as she put her hand on the door knob. 'Madeleine!' She turned and waited. 'You handled it very well,' Janus said. She bent her head in the proud gesture which awoke memories of their early meetings and left him without another word.

Lord Chilcote attended a debate at the House of Lords that evening and Madeleine went to a piano recital given by a young protégé of Mrs. Carford's, and then retired to bed at an earier hour than she had achieved for some nights. She was sitting up in bed, propped up on her pillows, reading a novel — anything to avoid thinking about Janus behind that obstinately closed door between their rooms — when the door she had been trying to ignore opened and Janus came in, his hands in the pockets of his long silk dressing gown. He did not look at Madeleine, but came to a halt at the foot of her bed. One of his hands clasped the carved wooden bed post with such force that his knuckles showed white beneath the skin.

Still without looking at his wife, he said abruptly: 'Did I hurt you?'

She did not pretend to misunderstand him,

nor did she feel inclined to spare him. 'Yes,' she said.

'I am sorry.' The words came out as if they would have choked him. 'I have a devil in me sometimes.' He began to walk about the room. 'You knew that before you married me,' he flung at her over his shoulder, almost accusingly.

'I set out to provoke you that evening,' Madeleine said.

His perambulation about the room stopped and he came and stood by the side of her bed. 'You succeeded,' he said drily. There was a long pause; neither of them was prepared to go any further in admitting a fault. 'Am I forgiven?' Janus asked at last.

Madeleine nodded reluctantly. 'I must forgive you,' she said. 'How else can we go on living together?'

The hopes of Jeanne Soubise had been raised to the highest pitch of expectation by the news that the Prince of Wales had been sending flowers to Madeleine. At last, it seemed, her weeks of patient waiting were about to be rewarded. Dazzling visions of royal patronage passed across her mind's eye. For the first time she looked at Madeleine with something approaching approval. She was flying high indeed, and Jeanne was moved to congratulate her on this notable conquest.

Madeleine had become insensibly so accustomed to the unobtrusive service Jeanne gave her in the well-acted role of the typical lady's maid that this reminder of the other woman's real place in her life came as an unpleasant shock. In

206

her most quelling manner she said, 'The Prince has been most kind, but you must not think that one small bouquet means anything more than a gesture of friendship to myself and my husband.'

Jeanne laughed. 'I don't think your husband has much part in it!' she said.

'On the contrary, he has everything to do with it,' Madeleine said with that deceptive quietness which led Jeanne to believe that she could be easily handled. 'It is gratifying to know that one is admired by a prince, but the Prince of Wales is far too great a gentleman to go beyond the bounds of what would be pleasing to me.'

Jeanne stared at her, struggling to understand her meaning. 'You can't mean to turn him down,' she said at last.

'You might, in effect, say that I have already done so,' Madeleine replied. 'The Prince understands — and I should like you to understand too — that under no circumstances will I receive him unless Lord Chilcote is also present.'

'You fool!' The hoarse whisper burst out of Jeanne. All the coarseness she had suppressed since coming to live in Madeleine's house rose to the surface; even her expression changed as her fury overcame her. In a stream of Parisian argot which Madeleine barely understood she poured out her reproaches for the folly which threw away the opportunity of a lifetime. Since Madeleine had no idea of the ways in which Jeanne had proposed to supplement her wages and make her fortune, she did not fully comprehend the depths of the other woman's disappointment, but as she listened a cold rage began to possess her.

'That is enough!' she said sharply. 'I think you forgot yourself, Jeanne. I have employed you as my maid for no other reason than to allow you to re-establish yourself. You are not here to judge my conduct — especially since it seems to be my virtue which displeases you! If you wish to do so you are perfectly at liberty to leave my employ. I will give you the best reference I can in the circumstances, whatever money is due to you and a little assistance towards your passage to France.'

Jeanne subsided, muttering angrily, but she had no mind to depart for France, to be at best a pensioner on her mother until some other prospect loomed on the horizon, and so she swallowed her rancour and grudgingly gave Madeleine the apology she seemed to think was due to her. Once again Madeleine found herself trapped by her compassion for this girl who had suffered as she had done at the hands of Henri de Cavaillon. She would have been justified in sending Jeanne straight out of her house without a minute's notice after the way she had spoken to her. Most mistresses would not have hesitated, but Madeleine sighed and agreed to allow the lapse to be forgotten, even though it would have been an unspeakable relief to have seen the back of Jeanne Soubise. Perhaps because she was a little ashamed of the distaste she felt for the other girl, she forced herself to be more forgiving than she would have been to anyone else, and once again her forbearance was seen as weakness.

As for Jeanne, she seethed with indignation. Almost she felt she had been taken into Madeleine's employ on false pretences. It was a bitter blow to discover that her calculations had been so wrong — and if Madeleine could withstand a potential offer from the Prince of Wales she was not likely to succumb to any other man. The only reason Jeanne, with her faulty moral sense, could see for Madeleine's curious adherence to the strict path of virtue, was that she must be in love with her husband, a piece of sentimentality for which Jeanne had little time, although the man was not without his attraction. Pondering on this, it came to her that there might be yet another way of making her fortune in the Chilcote household, and one which would provide a rich revenge on Madeleine for having lifted herself to a level Jeanne could never hope to reach. Lord Chilcote had a notoriously wandering eye and all was not well between him and his beautiful wife. Jeanne was well aware that there had been some sort of quarrel, and although it seemed to have been patched up, the atmosphere was strained. They were not on the terms they had been a few weeks ago. She was a goodlooking girl herself and she knew to a nicety how to tease a man into taking notice of her. It would be a real pleasure to enjoy a secret liaison with Janus Chilcote and to laugh up her sleeve at the girl she still always called in her mind Madeleine Ardingley.

Only one thing gave her pause and that

was the lack of tangible assets with which Lord Chilcote had rewarded his wife's fidelity. Jeanne frowned to herself over this. She was not prepared to give herself for nothing. She discounted the house and standard of living that Madeleine enjoyed. To her what counted was the sort of goods which could be turned into hard cash at a moment's notice, and Madeleine was singularly lacking in these. And yet Lord Chilcote had the reputation of being carelessly, even wantonly, generous to his light loves. Jeanne decided that it must be yet another example of Madeleine's mismanagement of her advantages. Jeanne would not make any such mistake, trust her for that!

Her nature was sanguine. To have thought of the scheme was to see it in execution and brought to a successful conclusion. That she might fail did not for the moment enter into her calculations. It gave a lift to her spirits to have this ploy in hand, it did something to alleviate the boredom of her life — and Jeanne was finding life in service very boring indeed. The truth was that she was missing the life to which she had become accustomed at Mrs. Porter's; the lazy, sluttish mornings, the company and coarse chit-chat of the other girls, the mounting excitement of the evening, the possibility of catching a rich prize. She let the more sordid aspects slip out of her mind and began to feel a sense of grievance at having made an exchange which so far had been so little to her benefit.

She studied Lord Chilcote surreptitiously as

soon as she got the chance. He was looking moody, and somewhat abstracted; not, in Jeanne's opinion, at all like a happy bridegroom. She began to put her plan into operation. First, he had to be made aware of her, and Jeanne thought she knew just how to catch his interest. But, for all her cunning, she was not a clever girl, and her tactics were by no means as subtle as she imagined. Janus Chilcote had had too many lures thrown out to him in the past not to recognise the nature of this approach. He was surprised, with just a touch of sardonic amusement. Apart from the passing suspicion that contact with Jeanne might have been responsible for the return of Madeleine's bad dreams he had not given his wife's maid a second thought. As far as he was concerned she was a piece of the furniture, to such an extent that he had not even recognised his wife's embarrassment when Jeanne occasionally overheard remarks which were not intended for any ears but Madeleine's. To find this disregarded object suddenly putting herself forward for his appraisal made him smile to himself once or twice, but then he began to find it annoying. He had never involved his own servants in his intrigues; he had no intention of beginning with his wife's maid, and he found the insinuating way in which Jeanne brushed against him, quite unnecessarily, as she went past, a source of irritation. A few weeks ago he would not have hesitated to have told Madeleine that she must get rid of the girl, and no inhibitions about explaining why. Now, Madeleine had retreated behind the impenetrable wall of glass which had surrounded her when they first met and he found that he dared not disturb the precarious balance of their relationship by making such a complaint about her maid.

Janus was in a curious frame of mind. He had married Madeleine for the straightforward reason that he wanted her more than he had ever wanted any woman before and there seemed to be no other way of establishing himself in her bed. From the standpoint of his cynical experience, he had expected that his passion would wane. It showed no signs of doing so, but its character had undergone a subtle change. He had overlooked the inconvenient compassion he had felt for her before their marriage, had thought of it as no more than a passing weakness. Yet now, when his physical desire for her was abundantly satisfied — except that it seemed it could never be satisfied — he had begun to feel this same weakness in an even more acute form. It mattered to him that Madeleine should be happy; he had suffered more than he would have believed possible when his own conduct had separated them; he felt a ridiculous anxiety on the rare occasions when she complained of some minor ailment. Above all, he had reluctantly begun to reassess his understanding of Madeleine's own character. He was too deeply and bitterly disillusioned to accept immediately that he had had too low an opinion of her, but it gradually began to be borne in on him that this might be the case. He had thought he was marrying a beautiful, proud and passionate creature, easily swayed by her senses; an ornament to his house, but not requiring any serious consideration outside the social scene and the turbulent bed. He was not now quite sure that this judgement had been correct. Jeanne Soubise, if she had but known it, had little chance of interesting him in her tawdry wares. Janus, a little dazzled and not quite daring to believe that it could be true, was contemplating the possibility that he had, almost accidentally, acquired sovereign rights over a vein of pure gold.

Unfortunately, his fear of being proved wrong made him more awkward in his dealings with Madeleine than he had ever been with any woman before, and more alert to anything in her behaviour which would seem to prove that she was not what he longed for her to be. He watched her suspiciously, to such an extent that she in turn became more withdrawn, even resentful of what she took for unreasonable jealousy. Far from drawing them together, the uncomfortable emotion Janus felt within himself, and which Madeleine shared but had for some time been at pains to conceal, drove them further apart.

It baffled Jeanne that at first she aroused so little interest in Lord Chilcote, not so much because she had an exaggerated idea of her own attractions as because she had believed him to be a man unable to resist sexual temptation. She grew angry and her anger made her careless in her dealings with Madeleine. She had always played her role very carefully indeed, but now

213

she allowed herself to be betrayed into small acts of negligence and her manner of speech was no longer exaggeratedly respectful, as it had been in their early days together.

Madeleine still had her eyes fixed longingly on the day when she would be free of Jeanne Soubise. Three months she had promised her and that period was nearing its end. She reminded Jeanne of this one day when they were alone in Madeleine's bedroom. It was the middle of the afternoon; Madeleine had been driving in the Park and now she had sent for Jeanne to help her out of the gown she had been wearing into a looser and more comfortable tea gown. It was an enchanting concoction of coffee-coloured chiffon and lace. Jeanne handled it resentfully. More and more she was coming to feel that it was unfair that Madeleine should have these exquisite gowns while she was confined to black alpaca. A steel hook scratched against the delicate skin of Madeleine's shoulder and she murmured a protest.

'*Je te fais mal?*' Jeanne asked. '*Je suis desolée!*'

Her tone was so loaded with sarcasm that Madeleine looked up quickly with a frown.

'*Pourquoi restes-tu avec moi?*' she asked. '*Tu es malheureuse, je le sais. Retourne en France, je te prie!*'

'*Non!*'

'*Les trois mois de notre contrat sont presque finis —* ' Madeleine began, but Jeanne interrupted her with a harsh laugh.

'*Je ne veux pas partir après trois mois seulement. Non, c'est trop tôt. Je resterai en Angleterre chez toi plus longtemps que cela.*'

'*Mais, pourquoi? Je ne le comprends pas.*'

'*Tu comprends bien pourquoi j'ai besoin d'argent.*'

Madeleine subsided with a sigh. She did indeed understand why Jeanne had need of money, what was beyond her comprehension was why the other girl would not allow her to pay her off and be quit of a job which was obviously giving her little satisfaction.

It occurred to neither of them that they might be overheard since it was unusual for Janus to be in the house at that time of day, let alone in his room, but on this occasion he had returned to obtain some papers he wanted to read before he went to a meeting of a company in which he had an interest. He had left them the previous night by the side of his bed and as he stood idly glancing through them to make sure that everything he required was there he could hear the sound of voices in Madeleine's room through the door which had been left slightly ajar by the maid who had cleaned the rooms that morning. He moved a little closer, with his eyes still fixed on the papers in his hand, but with the thought in his mind that it might be rather pleasant to get Madeleine to give him tea before he did anything else.

Something in the quality of the voices next door brought him to a halt. He heard Jeanne's angry laugh and her deliberate insolence, he heard Madeleine's patient reply and her dismay

215

at Jeanne's announcement that she intended staying for longer than the period of three months which they had apparently agreed between them. Above all, he heard and understood the implications of the use of the familiar '*tu*' which Jeanne had begun and Madeleine had unthinkingly continued in their conversation. The use of that form of speech between mistress and maid implied a degree of intimacy totally at variance with what he had understood to be their lack of previous acquaintance. It might, just possibly, have been permitted from an old and valued retainer; from a newly-acquired maid it was a shocking piece of familiarity. He stood, so near that he could have put out a hand and touched the door, trying to comprehend the meaning of this unexpected revelation, and slowly it began to be borne on him that there must have been a previous connection between Jeanne Soubise and Madeleine. He remembered that he had been slightly surprised when the young girl who had accompanied Madeleine to London from Laycott Manor had been discarded in favour of this newcomer. It was not unreasonable for Madeleine to want the best possible maid, but it had not been like her to be so capricious with a youngster who had been eager to learn.

They must have known one another in Paris, but at what period of Madeleine's previous life? From the nature of Jeanne's recent advances to him he knew that she could not be a woman of good character and this made it only too likely that she belonged to the time after Francis's

216

death since, for all his carelessness, he seemed to have taken some care of his young daughter during his lifetime, and it seemed to Janus all too likely that Jeanne Soubise had known his wife while she was living with Henri de Cavaillon. Otherwise, why had Madeleine not admitted their previous acquaintance to him? He had believed that there had been complete frankness between them on that subject at least: it seemed that he had been mistaken. For some reason Madeleine had not chosen to take him into her confidence. She must have known that he would not allow her to receive into his household anyone who had been associated with Henri de Cavaillon. It was almost incredible that she herself should have wished to do so — unless she had been forced into it by some hold that Jeanne Soubise had over her. What secret was there between them?

He moved away from the door without betraying his presence and as he thought over the implications of this wholly unexpected revelation he became possessed by a terrible, slow anger. Not the sudden flare up of rage which had so often betrayed him in the past into actions which he afterwards regretted, but a corroding bitterness which hurt him more than he was prepared to admit. Madeleine was deceiving him. For whatever reason, she had deliberately concealed an acquaintance, perhaps even a friendship, with a girl for whom he had formed the lowest of opinions. What hold did Jeanne Soubise have over her? What secret did they share which allowed the maid to address the mistress as if she were her sister?

He tested Madeleine out that evening. In the most casual manner he asked, 'You haven't had any nightmares recently, have you?'

'No, thank goodness,' Madeleine said, quite unaware of the purpose of his enquiry.

'I must have been mistaken in blaming your French maid,' Janus went on. 'Is she giving satisfaction? Are you keeping her on after her three months' trial?'

'Yes, she will be staying,' Madeleine said. He was watching her closely but unobtrusively and he did not miss the shadow which passed over her face. She did not want to keep the girl on, and yet it seemed she must. Why?

He threw in the question which was the real purpose of this conversation. 'Did you know her before in France?'

Under his carefully veiled scrutiny the telltale colour rose in Madeleine's cheeks and then subsided, leaving her paler than she had been before. She could not meet his eyes, even though the answer she gave him was strictly truthful, if disingenuous. 'No, I had never seen her before she applied for the post.'

He did not believe her, but for the moment he decided not to challenge this flat statement. Although he did not acknowledge it to himself, he had no wish to push her into further deceit. Instead, he turned his attention to Jeanne, not a difficult matter since she still showed every disposition to put herself in his way. Her tactics were so obvious that he felt nothing but scorn for them. Glancing in at Madeleine's door the next day he caught Jeanne, her foot on a chair, adjusting her garter with a fine display of calf and thigh in a black silk stocking. Had she known he was there? He was sure that she had. She let down her skirt with a flash of white petticoat, but her confusion was only assumed. She looked him boldly in the face and smiled, touching her hair into place as she watched him. He looked at her for a moment through narrowed eyes and then he caught hold of her round her waist, pulled her against him and kissed her on the lips. Her response told him all he needed to know about Jeanne Soubise. The catlike way she rubbed herself against him, her flickering, practised tongue, awoke a faint echo of lust in him, but his strongest feeling was of disgust. So short a time ago he had amused himself with women like Jeanne; now there was nothing he wanted from her but confirmation of the suspicion he harboured against his wife. He put her away from him and she laughed up into his face with triumphant relief that at last one of her schemes seemed to be achieving success.

'I give you good time, *cheri*,' she whispered in her imperfect English, using the phrases she had picked up from the girls with whom she had associated. 'You want Jeanne, hm?'

He bit back the impulse to reply with an emphatic negative. He did not want Jeanne, but he did want the information he believed she could give him.

'Perhaps,' he said. He kissed her again, and a more perceptive woman might have shuddered at the cold calculation behind the caress. 'Tell me,' he said in her ear as he released her. 'How well did you know my wife in Paris?'

Jeanne drew back, uneasy and suspicious at this unexpected question, but a moment's reflection showed her that here was a way she might get back at Madeleine for the humiliation she had endured in having to pretend to be her maid when, if she had had her rights, she might have been equally well-established, with a house and servants of her own.

'I knew her well,' she answered readily. 'But very well indeed! She does not wish that you should know this, you understand. I am in London — 'ow do you say — down on my luck, is it not? And I appeal to 'er and she say come to my house and be my maid.' She shrugged. 'It is not what I wish, but I come.'

'Did you . . . did you know a man called Henri de Cavaillon in Paris?'

'But yes! Madeleine and I, both of us, we shared his bed,' Jeanne answered with the greatest enthusiasm.

The vision of a monstrous threesome passed through Janus's mind, although he knew that was not what Jeanne had really meant. He put her away from him with a roughness that surprised her. He was consumed with anger. The thought of this promiscuous little slut claiming friendship with his wife, knowing all her secrets, calling her by her Christian name, was so nauseating that he shook with the force of his revulsion. And Madeleine had lied to him. Beyond his anger he was conscious of a desolation which threatened to hurt him in a way he had thought he could never be hurt. If she had lied about this, what other untruths had she told him. Was that lovely, graceful façade, that appearance of good behaviour, no more than a sham? He could not believe it. The thought came into his mind that he did not want to believe it and he was appalled to realise that, whatever her faults, he did not want to part with Madeleine. To lose her, for any reason, would be intolerable.

Jeanne was still waiting for further advances from him. When he continued to stand, apparently lost in thought, without taking any further notice of her, she was puzzled. A tentative caress elicited no response. Without another word, he turned and left her. It was odd behaviour, but she was not displeased with the progress she had made. Had it perhaps been a mistake to claim a previous knowledge of Madeleine? It had seemed to anger him and it had certainly disturbed his amorous mood, but on the whole she did not regret it.

She was in high spirits that evening as she assisted Madeleine with her preparations for a reception at the French Embassy, and Madeleine attributed her good humour to the promise she had extracted from her to be allowed to remain at Chilcote House after the three months' trial had ended. It had not been easy to agree, but Jeanne had found the key to Madeleine's generosity. She had spoken of her little daughter, spoken with assumed affection and regret for the way in which she was being brought up, and against that appeal Madeleine had no defence.

Her toilet completed, she stood up, exquisite as ever in black Chantilly lace over white satin. Jeanne fingered a fold of the delicate lace enviously, not so much because of its beauty as because of the amount it had cost. Lord Chilcote must be finding a wife an expensive item in his life when she chose to dress in this manner; it was to be hoped that he would be as generous, and in a more solid form, to the woman who had every intention of becoming his mistress.

Lord and Lady Chilcote dined in some state at Marlborough House and went on to the Embassy, where Madeleine had already been noticed for her elegance and perfect, bilingual French. She moved now in a circle of agreeable acquaintances, sure of her milieu and of her ability to cope with the demands of such an evening as this. Janus was very quiet, but then he so often was these days. She sighed inwardly for the brief period when they had seemed to be moving towards such close accord, but she would make no more moves towards him.

The only thing that roused him to anything like animation was when he introduced Madeleine to Mr. Gladstone. The Prime Minister had little time for the fashionable nonenities, but he was not impervious to Madeleine's grace and charm and unexpectedly he had some very kind words to say about Janus.

'I don't despair of persuading Lord Chilcote to take office one of these days,' he said.

Janus in Government? Madeleine looked at him with new interest. She already knew that he was far more punctilious about attending the House of Lords than she had expected from the accounts she had been given of his frippery life, and she had not forgotten the trouble he had taken with the Parliamentary candidate at Laycott, but it had not previously occurred to her that his services might actually be sought after by no less a person than the Prime Minister.

The withdrawn look had momentarily faded from Janus's face. He looked alert and almost pleased. 'You have plenty of eager young men looking for patronage, Prime Minister,' he said. 'I have no ambitions along those lines.'

'Have you not?' Mr. Gladstone's shrewd eyes surveyed him thoughtfully. 'I wonder why? You have a good brain and I suspect you enjoy exercising it. Give the matter some thought. I make no promises, of course, but you are still a young man, with time to make your mark on the world if you choose. If a junior appointment were to come along, suitable to your age and lack of experience, the Party might do worse than try you out.'

He bowed in his stiff way and moved away and Madeleine asked curiously, 'I don't properly understand the system, but would it interest you — to take a bigger part in Government?'

'I should have to serve my apprenticeship first,' Janus said. He grimaced. 'I am not sure I could stand that. For all that Mr. Gladstone classes me as a young man, I am a little too set in my ways to enjoy being at someone else's beck and call. Still . . . yes, he is right. I have sometimes thought about it.'

It was an agreeable moment of sympathy between them. Madeleine was interested and impressed. She even ventured to say, 'I have sometimes thought that, agreeable though it is, the life we have been leading since we came to London might not be entirely satisfying if it continued indefinitely.'

He looked at her for a moment in a peculiarly searching way. 'If you want employment, I dare say one of Aunt Gertrude's charitably-minded old friends could make use of you,' he said.

'Committees and sales of work,' Madeleine said, wrinkling her nose.

'Your ambitions run higher than that?' The sneering look was back on his face. 'Resign yourself, my dear. I doubt whether I shall ever reach the Cabinet. In the meantime, perhaps we should concentrate on keeping you occupied by setting up our nursery.'

Her face flamed. 'This is not the place to discuss such things,' she said.

She moved away from him, graceful and dignified, an obvious asset to any aspiring man, except that perhaps she was almost too goodlooking. Janus put his political ambitions on one side and spent the rest of the evening concentrating on forgetting that he had a wife who was still devastatingly attractive to him, but who had entered into a conspiracy with her maid from which he was excluded. Since this attempt at forgetfulness took the form of flirting desperately with every pretty woman with whom he came in contact and drinking far more than was his normal custom, he was in no mood to be reasonable when Madeleine became involved in a tiresome little contretemps with one of the young attachés who, intoxicated at finding himself alone with the lovely Lady Chilcote, attempted an embrace from which Madeleine emerged very flushed and angry.

They were not even completely shielded from the ballroom, since the place to which they had withdrawn was no more than a deep alcove filled with cool green ferns and miniature palm trees in great brass pots. It had seemed a delightful refuge from the heat and glitter of the ballroom and Madeleine had subsided gratefully on to the cushioned seat thoughtfully provided, and allowed young Raoul de Melincourt to fetch her a glass of iced champagne, even to take her fan and create a breeze to cool her hot cheeks, but when he suddenly leaned forward under the shadow of the overhanging palm, smoothed back a fold of black lace from her shoulder and planted a burning kiss on the bare flesh this manoeuvre revealed, she exclaimed in indignant protest and would have got up from her seat if he had not pushed her even further back against the cushions and tried to kiss her lips. She twisted her head away and, seizing the fan which he had let fall, dealt him a smart blow on the side of his head. Young Raoul winced and let her go. In the seconds that followed he regretted that Lady Chilcote's knowledge of the French language was quite so comprehensive

225

and idiomatic. Her condemnation of his conduct was scathing and uncompromising and he could only be thankful when her first anger subsided into icy disdain.

Scarlet-faced with shame at having so far offended against the rules of proper behaviour, the boy stammered an apology and, seeing his wretchedness, Madeleine could do nothing but say she forgave him. She wished she had not been so lenient when he tried to excuse himself on the grounds that he had been overcome by her beauty. He seized both her hands in his and bent his head over them. Madeleine looked down at the top of his sleek head with mingled compassion and impatience. He was very young and she could not bring herself to be hard on him. She leaned over him, chiding him softly and not reproving him when he passionately kissed her hands. She freed herself very gently and stood up. A pat to her hair and a tweak to her gown and she was ready to return to the ballroom, but as they emerged from their shadowy concealment the first person they encountered was Lord Chilcote. Madeleine would have preferred to have had more time to regain her composure before facing his perceptive scrutiny, but since there was no help for it she chose to carry the situation off with bravado. She laid her hand on his arm.

'If you are not dancing, will you be my partner, my lord?' she asked.

He bowed, his eyes going quickly from her face to that of the unhappy boy behind her.

He had a reasonably good idea of what had been happening, but that did not stop him from blaming Madeleine for putting herself in a position where this youngster had felt he might make advances to her, nor did it prevent a wave of blazing jealousy from sweeping over him. Raoul de Melincourt, meeting his black, contemptuous eyes, began to make hurried plans for a recall to Paris, and was relieved when Lord and Lady Chilcote moved away without anything further being said.

As they took the floor, Janus said in his most unpleasant drawl, 'You must learn to conduct your flirtations with more discretion, my dear. You were quite clearly visible through the ferns to anyone who cared to notice what you were up to. The first rule of the game is not to be found out, you know — I speak as one having experience.'

'He was just a silly boy,' Madeleine said. 'If I had known what he was going to do . . . '

'You would have taken him somewhere which offered better concealment?' Janus suggested.

'No!' She glanced round. 'Janus, don't quarrel with me here,' she begged.

'No, of course not,' he agreed. 'Smile, chatter, keep up appearances. We are all such good actors, we put the professionals to shame — and you, my pretty, are one of the best performers I have ever come across.'

His black mood persisted throughout the evening, and after they had returned home. He was torn by a conflict within himself which owed more than he would ever acknowledge

227

to a horrified admission of the importance Madeleine had come to assume in his life, an importance he had always sworn no woman would ever have for him. Part of him longed to go to her, to pour out his fears and suspicions and perhaps be reassured, but the other part regarded this desire as a shameful weakness, something which would only lead him into deeper subjugation and destroy such self respect as he still retained.

He dismissed his valet absentmindedly and stood, torn by indecision in a way that was unusual for him, and listening without realising it to the sounds of movement and voices in the next room. Unconsciously, he was waiting for the moment when Jeanne would leave Madeleine, and yet when it came he still could not bring himself to open the door and go through. A discreet tap at his own door made him start. When he opened it Jeanne stood outside in the corridor, an expectant smile on her face. Janus stared at her for a long, frowning minute and then a look of cynical resignation came over his face.

'Why not?' he said, without expecting an answer. Why not purchase half an hour's oblivion from the questions that tormented him? He held the door open wider and stepped back and Jeanne glided inside.

10

The life of Lord and Lady Chilcote continued in an apparent amity which deceived all but the most perceptive into thinking that it was a successful marriage, but when they went to Laycott for Christmas Mrs. Ardingley shook her head over the worldly smoothness of their manner towards one another and grieved for her hopes that his marriage might give her great-nephew's mind a more serious turn. She could make nothing of Madeleine, displaying with some ostentation the Russian sables which were her husband's Christmas gift, but unaccountably evasive when it seemed possible that the older woman might ask awkward questions about her married life.

The hunting season drew Janus away from London and for the first time they were separated, sometimes for weeks at a time, until in March Mrs. Ardingley reluctantly joined them for the purpose of presenting her great-niece at one of the Queen's infrequent Drawing Rooms. She thought the girl looked lovely, but remote, in dull lavender blue and silver, with her now famous pearls and the feathers on her head fastened by a jewelled aigrette she had purchased herself, since Janus still showed no signs of bestowing on her the jewels her rank demanded. She performed her part with grace and dignity, sweeping her curtsey to the dumpy, formidable Queen, who actually went so far as to greet Mrs. Ardingley as an old friend and ask her how she did. Gertrude Ardingley, in an iron-grey satin gown paid for by her great-nephew, looked unexpectedly magnificent, and perfectly at home. She had, after all, been brought up in Court circles and how ever little she thought of it, she could not quite escape her heritage. Several very august ladies were genuinely pleased to see her again and looked with new eyes on Lady Chilcote because she was sponsored by Mrs. Ardingley. At the beginning of the 1870 Season Madeleine found herself in an even more assured position than she had been the previous autumn, and when she allowed herself to be drawn, as Janus had once suggested, into taking an interest in various charities, she began to be spoken of with slightly puzzled approval in circles which could not reconcile her fashionable appearance and continuing friendship with the Prince and Princess of Wales with a serious interest in slum children and the working conditions of shop girls.

The Prince at this time was in bad odour. He had come out of the Mordaunt divorce case with what should have been an unsullied character, but the country at large was outraged by his involvement with a young married woman, however blameless it had turned out to be on this occasion, and at the beginning of March, when he had appeared in a box at the Olympic Theatre with the Duchess of Manchester and Oliver Montagu, he had been greeted by hissing and catcalls. He accepted his unpopularity philosophically, but he took note of the friends who stood by him at this difficult time, and Lord Chilcote and his beautiful wife were not the least amongst them.

In her personal life Madeleine struggled against a deep and bitter disappointment. She and Janus seemed to drift ever further apart. She was not entirely neglected, he came to her with spasmodic frequency, made love to her with urgent and almost silent concentration, and then left her. She remained unaware of his one act of infidelity with Jeanne and it had almost faded from his mind. He had yielded to the very worst of his instincts on that occasion and had afterwards recoiled from the memory of it. He would have been glad to have seen the last of Jeanne and had even tried to frame a request to Madeleine to get rid of her, only to realise that this was impossible, since it would inevitably lead to an accusation from Jeanne which it would be impossible for him to deny.

He had no idea of the importance that one night with him had assumed in Jeanne's eyes, nor how bitterly offended she was because it had never been repeated. He had paid her off — like any common prostitute, she thought, forgetting that that was a description which might with justice be applied to her — and had dismissed the matter from his mind. Once again her aspirations to become the reigning mistress of a rich man had been foiled and, since she knew very well that he had returned to Madeleine, she blamed her for the loss. Her secret rancour seemed to gnaw at her, she lost more weight, to an extent that was becoming noticeable, and the rather becoming high colour which had once given her cheeks a look of health began to take on the appearance of a hectic flush, especially in the evenings. Her tiredness increased and she took to swallowing bottles of a patent medicine which promised to restore energy and build up the debilitated. The only satisfaction she had at this time was in playing on Madeleine's credulity with stories of her little girl. She fortunately remembered the date of the child's birthday and extracted a generous present from Madeleine, ostensibly to buy a gift for her. She pretended to have had letters from her mother, that coarse and illiterate old peasant, with news of childish ailments which required the payment of doctors' bills. She wondered sometimes at Madeleine's gullibility, but her savings were growing and she had no compunction about drawing on this rich source of revenue as long as the vein held out.

The Season continued and the Chilcote *ménage* presented an unbroken front to the world. Across the Channel some curious manoeuvres were taking place, but the world at large remained unaware that the Spanish crown had been offered to a German Prince. Queen Victoria was asked for her opinion and, on the advice of her Foreign Secretary, declined to comment. The affair appeared to fall into abeyance, but under the surface there were rumblings which caused a curiously uneasy feeling on the European scene.

In April the Lorgans came to town, and Madeleine insisted on taking notice of them,

232

although Janus would have ignored an event in which he took absolutely no interest.

'Mr. Lorgan is still my mother's brother,' Madeleine said with the new obstinacy she used when she wished to withstand his wishes. 'And they did give me a home when I first came to England. If it had not been for them . . . ' Her voice trailed away, but the thought at the back of her mind was that if it had not been for the helping hand extended to her by Arthur Lorgan she might have found herself no better off than Jeanne. It was a possibility which contact with the Lorgans brought very much to the front of her mind and it made her more lenient with Jeanne than she would otherwise have been at this time. Jeanne was being tiresome, insolent in her manner and offhand in her attentions. Slowly Madeleine's resolution hardened: at the end of the Season Jeanne would have to go.

Mr. and Mrs. Lorgan and Phoebe were invited twice to Chilcote House, once to a large, crowded party and once to a more select dinner, and Lord and Lady Chilcote were seen once in their company at the theatre. After that, Janus called a halt and even Madeleine had to admit that their meetings had not been a success. The Lorgans bored her smart friends and she was wounded by the way pretty Phoebe seemed unable to look her in the face without blushing. They went their separate ways and little more was heard in the circles the Chilcotes frequented of Mrs. Lorgan's attempt to take London Society by storm.

In June Lord and Lady Chilcote were present

233

when the Prince of Wales was booed by the crowd as he drove down the race course at Ascot, only to be cheered at the end of the afternoon when it was believed that the horse which won the last race was one in which he had an interest. He took both demonstrations in his stride. 'You seem to be in a better humour now than you were earlier this afternoon, damn you!' he called out, and the crowd cheered him again, with cheerful inconsistency, rather pleased to have a Prince who damned their eyes with such geniality.

A few weeks later they were invited by the Duchess of Manchester to stay at Kimbolton Castle from Friday to Monday, an invitation not to be refused since the guest list had been given the approval of His Royal Highness. Janus, coming into the drawing room one afternoon, found Madeleine examining samples of silk for the new gown she had decided to commission for the occasion.

'Another new gown?' he queried idly.

'Am I too extravagant? I have never yet over-spent my allowance, at least not seriously — and it is rather a special occasion.'

'Why so? It is just another country house weekend, and you are surely sufficiently accustomed by this time to Bertie's exalted company not to have to buy a new gown every time you meet him.'

'It isn't that.' She hesitated, not sure whether to explain her reason for regarding this as a somewhat out of the ordinary event, but it was ridiculous that he should not know, and so she said, almost apologetically, 'It will be my twenty first birthday.'

'Really? I don't recall any celebration of your birthday at this time last year.'

'I didn't think it would be appropriate to mention it.'

He gave her a curious look. 'You are a strange creature,' he said. He began to play with the scraps of silk which lay scattered on the low table in front of her, finally picking up a scrap of fabric in a pale shade between green and blue and holding it out to her between his long fingers. 'Have that one,' he said. 'It will look wonderful with those eyes of yours.'

It was carelessly said and she thought no more about it, though she agreed with his choice and ordered the new gown to be made of the lustrous silk in the shade he had admired. She found that she was looking forward to this brief stay in the country, more for the sake of getting away from London, which was getting hot and stuffy as the summer advanced, than because of any amusement she expected to derive from the exalted company. After the weekend she and Janus were to spend only a few more days at Chilcote House and then she was going to Laycott Manor while he went north for the start of the grouse shooting season on the 12th August. Then there would be the partridge shooting on the 1st September, and the pheasant shooting on the 1st October, and sometimes she would accompany Janus and sometimes he would go alone. Then he would start hunting and in the Spring presumably the whole process would start again. It was not a prospect that excited her. She had heard nothing lately of any employment for Janus. He seemed content to spend his days in idleness, an idleness which was growing more and more irksome to her. It was not a subject she cared to raise with him, fearing that he might once again bring up the subject of their empty nursery, perhaps even taunt her with her barrenness. It was something she grieved over in private. She would not speak of it, but she had a secret fear that she would never conceive another child, and this was one of the reasons why she listened so wistfully, and responded so generously, to Jeanne's stories of her own little girl in Paris.

They arrived at Kimbolton in company with several other couples. The ladies in their travelling costumes and veiled hats, swooped on their hostess, soft cheeks touching, kissing the air and exclaiming in their high-pitched, well-bred voices on the fatigues of the journey, the pleasures of the journey, the slowness of the journey, the speed of the journey, according to temperament and humour. They disappeared to their rooms and reappeared for tea in delicate robes which pretended by their airy lightness and floating lines to allow them some degree of comfort. The Prince of Wales arrived and was greeted by a great fluttering of chiffons and laces as the ladies made their curtsies. He accepted a cup of tea and munched his way through several slices of heavy fruit cake before withdrawing with his host. A little more gossip, a few whispered confidences and the company dispersed to rest

236

for a little before changing their clothes once again for dinner.

Madeleine was dressed and almost ready to go down when Janus came to her room. With a brief jerk of his head he indicated to Jeanne that he wished her to leave them, a movement which would not have been necessary if she had been the well-trained lady's maid she pretended to be. He was carrying a large flat box in his hand. Madeleine, exquisite in the blue-green taffeta he himself had chosen, looked at him with wistful eyes, thinking how well his evening clothes became his tall, upright figure. He glanced at her and then looked away as if unwilling to meet her eyes.

'I have something for you,' he said. 'I suppose you could call it a birthday present.'

He put the flat box down on the dressing table and watched her with a curious, fixed intensity as she opened it. There was a long, long silence while Madeleine assimilated the magnificence of the gift her unpredictable husband had bestowed on her. After all the months when Janus had obstinately refused her any jewellery but the pearls which had belonged to their common grandmother, he had suddenly given in to a whim to make her a gift of overwhelming generosity, and now he was waiting to see how she received it. It took her breath away, and what particularly pleased her was that the splendid parure of aquamarines and diamonds had obviously been chosen with care to set off her special colouring. The pale, clear, bluey-green of the aquamarines was just the colour of her own eyes. The setting of gold and diamonds was a background to their intense yet elusive colour, like the water of a mountain pool newly melted from the snow fields. She took up the necklace and held it up in a great shining loop.

'Oh, Janus, it is beautiful, so beautiful!' she exclaimed. 'And the colour of my gown is exactly right! You chose that too — did you already have it in mind to make me this wonderful present?'

He nodded, his eyes fixed on her excited face. Madeleine picked up one of the earrings and fixed it into place, moving her head to admire the way the sparkle of the diamonds enhanced the clarity of the aquamarine in the middle of the setting. 'And bracelets, too!' she murmured. All the impulsive generosity of her nature, usually so rigorously suppressed, rushed to the surface. Their recent estrangement was forgotten. She got to her feet and turned to him, hands outstretched.

'Oh, Janus, I do love you so much!' she exclaimed.

Instinctively, he took a step backwards, a curious little smile on his lips. 'In all our months of married life, that is the first time you have ever said that,' he said. He gave a hard little laugh. 'I wonder why I never tried jewellery before? It is, after all, the traditional way to a woman's heart and of all men living I should have known its efficacy! So you love me, do you? It takes a very costly gift to make you say so, my dear.'

'It is not the jewels I value, beautiful though they are,' Madeleine said haltingly, horrified by the way her impulsive confession had been received. 'It is the thought you have taken for me, the fact that you have obviously chosen them with care.'

'In other words, you are pleased because I know what suits you?'

'No! You misunderstand me most profoundly if you think that,' Madeleine said quietly. 'If you do not wish to hear me say that I love you, will you not at least allow me to express my gratitude without trying to pick a quarrel with me?'

Again he looked at her with that strange little smile. 'You never put a foot wrong, do you?' he said. 'How fortunate I am to have such a wife; beautiful, courteous, astonishingly well behaved. No doubt you will be prepared to express your gratitude in a more tangible manner if I come to you later tonight? And I will come, you can be sure of that. You have become as necessary to me as his opium is to an addict. You love me, you say? I will make a confession, too: I cannot live without you and I will pay any price to keep you.'

The sound of the great gong sounding for dinner downstairs in the hall made them both start. Madeleine pressed both hands to her temples. 'I can't go down!' she said.

Lord Chilcote drew a deep breath. 'You must,' he said. 'We will continue this . . . conversation later.'

'Too much has been said already,' Madeleine said in a low voice.

'Complete your toilet and come down,' he said, and left her abruptly.

Madeleine stood looking at her reflection in the looking glass without really seeing herself, only the mocking glint of the exquisite jewellery. With fingers which were unexpectedly steady she removed the necklace and the one earring she had put on and laid them down on the dressing table. Then she went down to join the company assembling for the formal procession into the dining room.

Her appearance caused something of a sensation. On every other lady present great jewels glowed and sparkled — rubies, emeralds, sapphires, a famous rope of black pearls, Mrs. Embury's fire opals, Mrs. Carford's Russian tiara. Amongst that scintillating throng Madeleine was immediately noticeable, head, ears, arms and neck all bare, but it was too late for anyone to do more than stare and whisper. She laid her hand on her partner's arm and the line sauntered casually yet purposefully towards the dining room.

She had to endure a few barbed hints about the strangeness of her appearance when the ladies were alone after dinner, but since she chose not to appear to understand them her companions retired into baffled silence. It was not so easy to refuse an answer to the Prince of Wales when he came up to her, a frown marring the geniality of his expression, and said: 'What's this, Lady Chilcote; setting a new fashion?'

She curtsied without replying, at a loss to think what to say to him. Unthinkable to

240

reveal her quarrel with Janus, but what other excuse could she offer for appearing without the customary ornaments? It had been a mistake, she realised now, not to have twisted her pearl necklace round her throat before coming downstairs, but at the time she had been too distracted to think of this expedient.

'I take the trouble to dress correctly for these occasions,' the Prince was saying reproachfully. 'And I expect you ladies to follow my example.'

Janus appeared at her side. 'There was an unfortunate accident to Lady Chilcote's jewel case and rather than keep you waiting she came down as you see — somewhat unadorned, sir,' he said. He turned to Madeleine. 'I think you will find the lock has been repaired and the box can be opened now,' he said. 'I will come with you and make sure that you are able to turn yourself out in a fit manner for an evening with his Royal Highness.'

The hard line of his mouth and the glitter in his eyes contradicted the smoothness of his speech and the hand he put under her elbow was far from gentle as he propelled her up the stairs. Madeleine caught her foot in the long folds of her gown, gasped as his hold tightened painfully and he saved her from stumbling, and then lifted up her skirt with her other hand to prevent it happening again. Janus flung open the door of her room and thrust her inside.

The sight that met their eyes was unexpected and curiously shocking. Jeanne had seated herself at the dressing table and she had put on all the magnificent jewellery Janus had just bestowed on Madeleine. Against the black of her gown the aquamarines and diamonds blazed, the earrings dangled from her ears, and she had set on her head the delicate half circle of fine stones set in gold which should have been a foil to Madeleine's lovely hair. She got up and stood facing them, defiant and at bay. There was a high colour in her cheeks and her eyes glittered strangely, but in some peculiar way the perfection of the jewels made her face look haggard, and for the first time Madeleine was aware, at the back of her mind, of how much Jeanne had deteriorated in the few months since she had come to her employ. But this was a subject far from her thoughts at that moment. All the anger she had been ready to pour out on Janus, and all her growing distaste for Jeanne's continued presence in her life, came suddenly to the surface.

'How dare you touch my belongings!' she said in a whisper. 'How dare you presume to put on my jewels!'

She took a step forward and Jeanne backed against the dressingtable. Her own temper began to rise, joining with the burning sense of injustice from which she had been suffering for all the long weeks during which Janus had continued to ignore her.

'Why should I not wear fine jewels?' she asked. 'I have as much right to them as you! Why should you always come out on top? Why should you have the ring and the title, the house and the servants, all the money and jewels you want, when all he has ever given me is money — and a miserable pittance at that!'

Her rapid French almost defeated Janus, but he understood enough of what she was saying to feel a thrill of uneasiness. 'Be quiet,' he commanded.

'I will not be quiet,' Jeanne said in English. 'You 'ave not treat me well. You take me to your bed and then you throw me away and what you give me? Fifty pounds!'

'I considered it generous,' Janus said in his most indifferent drawl, but his eyes were watchful and he had gone very pale.

'I don't understand,' Madeleine said. She looked from one to another of them in mounting horror.

Jeanne reverted to French. 'It means that you and I attract the same men, *chérie*,' she said. 'Your husband has been sharing his favours between us — curious how history repeats itself, isn't it?'

'I don't believe it,' Madeleine said, but it was an automatic reaction and the gaze she turned on Janus unconsciously pleaded for reassurance. When he said nothing she drew herself up and asked with biblical simplicity: 'Is it true? Have you committed adultery with my maid?'

Janus glanced once at her white, strained face and then looked away. 'Yes,' he said. He heard the little gasp she gave and if they had been alone he might have gone on to say that it had only happened once, even to ask for her forgiveness, but Jeanne Soubise was standing by, her face alight with triumph, and he could not bring himself to plead his case in her presence.

He turned on her savagely. 'You will leave my employ immediately,' he said.

'In which capacity are you dismissing her?' Madeleine asked. 'If it is as your mistress then I admit your jurisdiction; if it is as my maid then I reserve the right to say when she shall go.'

She was trembling with the effort to hide the appalling hurt which had been dealt to her. Not only did Janus not love her, he had been deceiving her with her maid, dividing his attentions between them. She felt physically sick. The jewels still round Jeanne's neck danced and swam before her eyes. She turned on her in sudden fury. 'Take those things off at once and go to your room,' she said. 'I do not wish to see you again tonight. I will speak to you in the morning when I have decided what to do.'

Jeanne obeyed her sullenly. She was suddenly aware of having blundered. The momentary triumph over Madeleine had been sweet, but it had gained her nothing. She dropped the jewels on the dressing table with a metallic clatter and scuttled out of the room, banging the door behind her.

Madeleine and Janus were left confronting one another. Janus took a deep breath. 'Will you listen to my explanation?' he asked.

Madeleine shook her head. '*Qui s'excuse, s'accuse*,' she said. 'Let it go. It is a situation to which I presume I must accustom myself. I was warned before our marriage that you would not be faithful to me. It was a shock to find that you had chosen to betray me with my own maid, but already I am beginning to recover.'

The determined lightness of her tone made him grit his teeth and it was belied by the whiteness of her face and the way her hands trembled as she took up the splendid jewellery, item by item, and tried to fasten it into place.

'Madeleine, you must listen to me,' Janus said, his own voice not quite under control.

'Not now,' Madeleine said, her attention apparently fixed on the proper placing of her tiara. 'We mustn't keep the company waiting, must we?'

She turned to face him, regal and remote, as beautiful as he had known she would be when he had chosen the aquamarines to complement the unusual colour of her eyes, eyes which now were wide with shock and horror and a queer blind determination to carry on as if nothing had happened. He would have detained her, but she slipped out of the room with a rustle of taffeta, her head held high, and descended the stairs with all the assurance of a reigning beauty decked in the tribute to her charms.

All through the rest of the evening he watched her, his own nerves stretched to breaking point, and wondered at the self control which enabled her to play her part without betraying the painful scene that had been played out upstairs. She accepted compliments on her new magnificence with no more than a slight smile, while Janus himself writhed inwardly at the memory of the remarks he had made earlier when he had given her the jewels. He had known the words to be unjustified even as he had uttered them; what ever Madeleine's faults might be, she was not mercenary. There had been a painful sweetness in hearing her say that she loved him, but because of his doubts about her he had allowed himself to react with superficial cynicism and the recollection of it shamed him. He thought that he might be able to bring himself to admit as much, if he could only get Madeleine alone for long enough, and he waited impatiently for the long evening to end.

The ladies retired to bed and eventually he, too, was free to leave, but when he tried to enter Madeleine's room he discovered that for the first time in their married life she had locked her door against him. He was dismayed, and then angry, to such an extent that if he had been in his own home he might have tried to break the door open, but he retained sufficient command over himself to realise that it would not do to make a scene in this house, that to disturb the rest of the Prince of Wales because of a sordid quarrel with his wife would bring both of them into disrepute. He turned away, hoping furiously that Madeleine had not had the satisfaction of hearing him try the door. He told himself now that his intention had been to put things right with her, to admit the fault he had committed with Jeanne and to explain what he considered to be its trivial nature, to beg for an explanation of Jeanne's remarks about her association with Madeleine and Henri de Cavaillon, and to try for a reconciliation.

He was completely defeated by the action Madeleine took the next morning. Quite early, before most people were stirring, she sought out her hostess. She carried a sheet of paper in her hand and explained with a complete lack of truth and great conviction that she had heard that her great-aunt, Mrs. Gertrude Ardingley, had been taken ill.

'She begs me *not* to return to Laycott Manor,' Madeleine lied, her great candid eyes fixed on the Duchess's face. 'But she has been so good to me, I feel I must go to her. Will you forgive me? I shall insist on Lord Chilcote remaining behind with you, men are not the slightest use in illness, are they?'

The Duchess cast a savage thought towards the arrangement of her table for dinner that evening, but she smiled and agreed with everything Madeleine said, even commending her for her kind heart and hoping that Mrs. Ardingley would soon recover from the illness which seemed, so suddenly, to have struck her down. By the time Janus learned of his wife's imminent departure the carriage had been ordered for her and every one, it seemed, was aware that she was leaving. He caught her as she descended the stairs, gloved and veiled and ready to depart. He seized her wrist in an ungentle hand and pulled her into the library. Madeleine glanced round swiftly, but the room was quite empty.

'It seems I am the last to be told of your plans,' Janus said. 'I forbid you to leave this house.'

'You have no power to stop me,' Madeleine replied. She appeared calm, but inwardly she quailed before the depth of his displeasure.

Her apparent coolness infuriated Janus. 'You

are my wife,' he said. 'You will do what I say.'

'I am not your wife, nor have I ever been,' Madeleine replied bitterly. 'Oh, yes, the tie between us is legal, but I am as much your concubine as if you had never placed your ring on my finger. What you require of me can be just as easily obtained elsewhere, it seems. Do you expect me to share your favours with my maid? I form part of no man's seraglio, my lord. I will not tolerate it. Jeanne returns to Laycott Manor with me, from there she can travel to Dover and then to France.'

'Is your obligation to her so easily cancelled?' Janus asked, watching carefully for her reaction. He got nothing but a proud lift of her chin. Behind her veil her expression was unreadable.

'I owed her nothing, except in my own mind. I have been generous to Jeanne, and amply has she repaid me! I should have known that anyone associated with Henri de Cavaillon would be tainted by the same corruption. Was I not myself contaminated? Would I otherwise have fallen so easily into your arms?'

'You admit that you knew her in Paris?' Janus asked swiftly.

'No, I did not know her, but he did. Surely she has told you her story?'

He shook his head, confused by this hint that a different construction might be placed on her strange conspiracy with Jeanne from the one he had thought to be true.

'What motive did you have for taking Jeanne into your employ?' he asked abruptly.

She gave him a strange little smile as she moved towards the door. 'Have you ever heard of compassion?' she asked.

He did not understand this, but since she seemed about to leave him he asked, 'Is this parting of ours to be permanent?'

Madeleine turned back towards him. 'I don't know,' she said. 'At the moment you disgust me. I cannot bear to have you near me. Perhaps this will pass, I cannot tell.'

'I am sorry,' Janus said, but whether he was sorry for his own misdemeanour or whether he was sorry because he appeared to be losing her she could not tell.

Again that strange little smile passed across her lips. 'I have heard you say that before,' she said. 'It seemed to come more easily this time. Are we to live in an atmosphere in which you become accustomed to apologising to me? I do not think you would tolerate that — and neither would I.' She paused again. 'Give me a little time,' she said uncertainly.

He shrugged. 'As you wish,' he said indifferently. 'But be assured of one thing, my love. If you hold yourself away from me I shall not lead a celibate life. You run the risk of increasing your disgust rather than lessening it.'

There was a brief, unhappy silence between them and then he said abruptly, 'Get Jeanne off to France as soon as you can; I don't like the sound of the news from across the Channel.'

Madeleine was sufficiently surprised to pause in her movement towards the door. 'But I thought that the trouble between France and

249

Germany had all blown over,' she said.

'I wouldn't be too sure of that. The Prussians have created a magnificent fighting instrument, for what other reason than to use it? And the Emperor is obsessed by *la gloire*.'

She looked troubled, her mind momentarily diverted from her own unhappiness. He watched her for a moment, struggling against the impulse to seize her in his arms and demand that she stay with him, and then went on in the same curt, unconciliatory manner, 'I shall stay in London until the beginning of August and then fulfil my shooting engagement in Perthshire with the Manners. You, no doubt, will be fully occupied for the next few weeks in nursing Aunt Gertrude, though what illness you have contrived to drum up for a woman who enjoys the rudest health of anyone I have ever known is more than I can imagine. When I return from Scotland I shall come to Laycott Manor. Perhaps by that time . . . ' he paused and then said, not without difficulty, 'We might both contrive to swallow our pride.'

It was almost an attempt at reconciliation. For one brief moment Madeleine was tempted to go to him, to put her head down on his shoulder and to sob out her bitter hurt and her reproaches, but the moment passed. The door opened and a polite servant murmured that her ladyship's carriage was at the door. Without a backward look, Madeleine walked out of the room, out of the castle and, if she had but known it, out of her husband's life for many long and anguished months.

11

On the fifteenth of July 1870 France declared War on Prussia. The fears which Lord Chilcote had expressed to his wife had been only too well founded. In Great Britain, except amongst a few noted Francophiles, such as the Prince of Wales, the feeling was that the French had gone to war for frivolous reasons not worthy of the nineteenth century, while in both France and Germany the declaration gave rise to scenes of wild enthusiasm.

The French had felt themselves threatened by their old fear of 'encirclement' when Prince Leopold of Sigmaringen had been put forward as a candidate for the Spanish crown. Because of their violent reaction, his candidature had been withdrawn, but this did not satisfy the French Government. Urged on by his Foreign Secretary, the heavy-handed Duc de Gramont, the French Ambassador in Prussia pressed King Wilhelm for a guarantee that the Hohenzollern candidature would not be put forward again at some time in the future. The King refused to give any such undertaking, refused to receive the French Ambassador to discuss the matter further, and sent a telegram to his Chancellor, Count von Bismarck, setting out his version of what had transpired. Judiciously edited by Bismarck the contents of the King's telegram became public knowledge and, as the astute Bismarck had anticipated, Louis-Napoleon allowed himself the luxury of feeling insulted, threw caution to the winds and plunged his country into war on what the *Illustrated London News* called 'a mere point of etiquette'.

Although the French were blamed for going to war in the first place, it was widely believed that they must be the victors. The Prince of Wales was said to have told the Austrian Ambassador, Count Appanyi, while dining at the French Embassy, that Prussia would be taught a lesson at last, a remark which had to be denied when Count von Bernstoff, the Prussian Ambassador, complained of this partisanship on the part of a member of the Royal Family of a neutral Power. Only the more far-seeing understood the true gravity of this conflagration across the Channel which Mr. Gladstone described austerely as a 'stain on the whole face of society'.

The news troubled Madeleine more than anyone else at Laycott Manor. Mrs. Ardingley dismissed it as something of no great concern to an Englishwoman and went back to her own private war against the greenfly on her roses. She was more worried by Madeleine's solitary return to Laycott.

'Quarrelled with Janus?' she asked. 'I thought you would. Is it serious?'

'Yes, it is,' Madeleine admitted.

'Daresay it was his fault,' Mrs. Ardingley said. 'All the same, you will probably have to forgive him in the end. Can't live apart for ever, no sort of life for either of you.'

Madeleine's mouth set obstinately. 'Am I

always to be the one who forgives?' she asked in a low voice.

'Probably. No use to expect Janus to go down on his knees. Something else I want to say to you — that French maid of yours . . . '

Madeleine's head jerked up, and her eyes flashed, but Mrs. Ardingley did not notice these warning signs and she went on, 'The girl's ill. Are you sure she's fit to travel to France?'

'I didn't think about it,' Madeleine said, dismayed by the possibility of a setback to her plans for getting rid of Jeanne. She thought about it now, remembering the haggard look she had sometimes seen on Jeanne's face, her lackadaisical manner and disinclination for work. She had set this down to a silent refusal to serve her, but possibly Mrs. Ardingley was right and Jeanne was indeed unwell. The hideous possibility that she might be pregnant by Janus suddenly presented itself to Madeleine's mind. 'I will speak to her,' she said.

'I'd do more than that, if I were you,' Mrs. Ardingley said. 'I'd send for the doctor. I know what I think, but I'll not say anything until we hear his verdict. My own maid tells me the girl fainted in the Servants' Hall last night. Tired out by the journey, she said. Well, maybe, but I think there's more to it than that. Get Dr. Blakey in, and do it soon.'

The next time Madeleine saw Jeanne she looked at her with closer attention than she had done for some time and suddenly realised that she had actually been avoiding looking at the girl because the sight of her was so hateful.

253

It was true that Jeanne looked miserably unwell. She was thinner than ever and her enormous, expressionless eyes blazed in her wasted face.

'I am told you are ill,' Madeleine said, watching her carefully.

Jeanne shrugged. 'It is nothing,' she said. 'I was tired last night, and I have a little tightness of the chest which troubles me at times, nothing more.'

'Nothing more?' Madeleine asked with emphasis.

For a moment Jeanne looked puzzled, then she gave a derisive laugh. 'Your precious husband hasn't managed to get a child on either of us, if that is what you mean,' she said.

It was a relief, more of a relief than Madeleine wanted Jeanne to know, and she went on quickly, 'I have arranged for the local doctor to call and see you.'

'No!' Jeanne said. 'No, I don't want a doctor.'

There was a note of panic in her voice which Madeleine found difficult to understand at the time, but some comprehension of the fear which drove Jeanne to conceal her illness came to her when the doctor gave his verdict.

'I am sorry to say that your maid is very seriously ill,' Dr. Blakey said with a grave face.

'Consumption,' Mrs. Ardingley said. 'I thought as much. And far gone too, if I am not mistaken. I've seen it before. Poor child, poor child.'

'Very far gone,' Dr. Blakey agreed.

'She was to have travelled to Paris tomorrow,'

254

Madeleine said in a troubled voice. 'Is she fit to undertake the journey?'

The doctor shook his head emphatically. 'I don't think you understand, Lady Chilcote,' he said. 'There can be no question of allowing her to travel. In fact . . . ' he hesitated, reluctant to commit himself, but Mrs. Ardingley had no such scruples.

'The girl's dying,' she said. 'How long do you give her doctor?'

'I can hardly say, on the basis of one examination,' Dr. Blakey protested. 'But I must admit that my prognosis is not hopeful.'

'Three months, six months?'

'I doubt whether she can survive beyond the end of the year,' Dr. Blakey said quietly. He looked at Madeleine's white, appalled face with concern. 'I am sorry, Lady Chilcote, I am afraid this has been a shock to you.'

'I had no idea,' Madeleine whispered. 'How can I have been so blind? Does . . . does Jeanne know?'

'I have not told her in so many words,' the doctor said. 'In her heart, yes, I think she knows, but quite often in these cases there is a curious euphoria, a false hope which prevents the patient from admitting that her case is hopeless.'

'If she isn't to go to France, what are we to do with her?' Mrs. Ardingley asked practically.

'She is a source of possible infection if she remains here,' the doctor warned them. 'I can arrange for her to be nursed privately, or there are hospitals . . . '

'I will pay for her to be looked after,'

Madeleine said. She was deeply distressed. Almost it seemed as if this was yet another blow aimed at her by fate, another contrivance to make her feel guilty over the other girl's tragic life. The distinction between them grew ever more marked: Madeleine had so much, even if she was at present on bad terms with the person who had bestowed so many of her benefits on her, and now to be the one who retained her health while Jeanne, poor Jeanne, was stricken down; it was too horrible.

In this frame of mind she went to see Jeanne, ready to promise her almost anything that would in some way make amends for the difference in their fortunes. She was very careful in what she said to the girl, but she could not disguise the fact that the doctor did not consider Jeanne fit to return to Paris. Jeanne lay back against her pillows and raised a handkerchief to her eyes with a faltering hand. 'I fear I shall never see France again,' she said. 'How my mother will weep when she knows that I am not returning to her! And my little girl, what is to become of her?'

With a new insight, Madeleine saw through this hideous play-acting, but the fact that it came so much nearer the truth than Jeanne appeared to understand filled her with horror.

'I am sorry that you cannot go to your daughter,' she said. 'Especially now, with this terrible war — not that the fighting is likely to reach Paris, but one cannot help feeling anxious.'

'More than anxious, I am beside myself with

worry,' Jeanne said mendaciously. 'My little Véronique! If only I could hold her in my arms once more!'

'Something might be arranged,' Madeleine said slowly. 'Véronique is more than two years old and quite able to travel. Would your mother be willing to bring her to England if I made all the arrangements? It should surely be possible, even in time of war.'

Jeanne shook her head emphatically. The last thing she wanted was to be saddled with her ageing mother or, indeed, the child for whom she only occasionally felt a twinge of sentimental affection.

'Maman would never travel to England,' she said. 'No use even thinking about that. She is . . . she is not strong. Sometimes I am afraid she will die and my dear child will be left quite alone in the world with her mother unable to go to her. What will become of her?'

'I could go to Paris myself,' Madeleine said. 'It would take only a few days.'

'What about the fighting?' Jeanne said, taken completely by surprise by this unexpected suggestion.

'I am English,' Madeleine said. 'The war is nothing to do with me. Besides, I shall not go anywhere near the seat of war. Would Madame Soubise part with the child to me, do you think?'

'Well, of course she is very fond of her grandchild,' Jeanne said, knowing full well that, while it was probably true that *la Mère* Soubise had a rough and ready affection for the baby

257

in her care, she would part with her readily if the price was right, and might, indeed, already have done so. It gave her a malicious pleasure to think that she might be sending Madeleine off on a wild goose chase, and if she really did bring the child back to England it would be an additional hold over her, since she was just the sort of sentimental fool to be inveigled into parting with her cash for the little girl's upbringing. Another thought occurred to her.

'Shall you tell Janus where you are going?' she asked.

Madeleine winced at this casual use of her husband's Christian name, but she did not comment on it, a piece of forbearance which ought to have warned Jeanne that there was something unusual about the degree of consideration Madeleine was prepared to extend to her; but she was too taken up with her latest ploy to think about it.

'I shall tell no-one where I am going,' Madeleine said. 'It will take me a little while to make the necessary arrangements. It will not do to fail in any formalities. I am not sure what my situation is regarding a passport or whether any special permission is needed to visit a country which is at war. I may have to visit London and I cannot do that . . . just yet.'

She did not say so, but it was Janus's presence in London which prevented her from visiting the capital. If she did, where could she stay except at Chilcote House, and she had no intention of doing that until he had left for Scotland.

No more than the majority of her countrymen

did Madeleine doubt that the war in France would end in victory for the French, but almost from the first things went badly for the French Army. The Emperor arrived at Metz on the evening of the 28th July looking old and ill, with his head sunk on his breast, and issued an address to the Army which struck some oddly sombre notes amongst his injunctions to his soldiers to prove what the French Army could perform. 'You go to fight against one of the best armies in Europe . . . the war which is now commencing will be a long and severe one . . . ' Already the Emperor was aware that the army he had called into the field was neither as enormous nor as well equipped as he had been led to believe, and it was matched against a superb fighting machine, organised to the last detail by the ice-cold intellect of Count von Moltke.

On the 2nd August Louis-Napoleon captured Saarbrucken from the Germans and sent a telegraphic message to the Empress announcing that their fourteen-year-old son, the Prince Imperial, had received his baptism of fire, and had been admirably cool and in no way affected, even going so far as to keep a bullet which fell close to him as a keepsake. Paris was delirious with delight at the news, and Madeleine when she learnt of it felt emboldened to carry out her plan to make a quick visit to France to fetch Jeanne's infant daughter back to England. The news of the French defeats at Weissenburg, Wörth and Forbach which followed rapidly on their initial small success at Saarbrucken did nothing to deter her. As soon as she was sure that Janus had departed for Scotland for the 'glorious twelfth' on which grouse shooting commenced, she put her own arrangements in hand.

She travelled alone and told no-one but Jeanne where she was going. She went up to London, giving Mrs. Ardingley the impression that she would remain there for several days, and left from there, so that even her great aunt remained unaware of her true destination. Her journey was uneventful, since the railway lines to Paris were still available, and it was only on arrival that she was invaded by a feeling of unease. The train on which Madeleine had travelled from Calais had been singularly empty, but the Gare du Nord seethed with passengers seeking to leave the capital. She was jostled and pushed and became aware, as she had not been during the earlier stages of her journey, of how accustomed she had become to the comfort of travelling with a husband and servants to make the way easy for her.

She established herself in one of the hotels in the Rue Cambon, prudently choosing one of the more modest establishments, but without feeling the need to stint herself of reasonable comfort since she had brought a sizeable sum of money with her to cover the expenses of her journey. At the back of her mind she had the idea that Madame Soubise might, after all, be persuaded to accompany her to England; or, failing that, it might be necessary to engage a nurse to look after the little girl, and for this reason she had provided herself with more funds than she would otherwise have done.

When the proprietor of the hotel enquired about the length of her stay, Madeleine replied with the utmost confidence that she expected to remain for no more than three or four days.

'You are wise, miladi,' Monsieur Jaques remarked. 'Paris prepares itself for a siege, you understand. I would not myself choose to remain, but what would you? The hotel is my livelihood and one must stay and protect one's own.'

'Until today I had not realised matters were so serious,' Madeleine admitted. 'A siege! Surely that is impossible?'

'By no means! Already the workmen are cutting through the roads which lead through the fortifications into Paris, the trees in the Bois du Boulogne have been cut down and I myself have seen the horizon crimson with the flames of the fires which consume the trees of Fontainebleau. I tell you, miladi, it would be well for you to be gone from Paris within the week — and I say this against my own interest since my beautiful hotel is already half empty.'

'I am fatigued by my journey,' said Madeleine. 'Tomorrow I will put in hand the business which has brought me to Paris and I will certainly take your advice and complete it as quickly as possible.'

Having made this resolve she set out early the next morning for the address which Jeanne had given her, only to receive a setback. Madame

261

Soubise had removed from that address some months previously. It was news which surprised Madeleine, who had been under the impression that Jeanne was in frequent contact with her mother. She could not help remembering the money she had given Jeanne to send to Paris. If she was not aware of her mother's where-abouts what had happened to that money? All too probably it had remained in Jeanne's pocket. More than a little angry, Madeleine began making enquiries as patiently as she could about Madame Soubise's present address. It took her two days to track her down and when she did so she found that Madame Soubise was employed as the *concierge* of an apartment building on the Left Bank of the Seine.

She was a heavy woman in her early fifties, not as old and by no means as feeble as Jeanne's description had led Madeleine to believe. On the contrary, Madame Soubise was obviously strong and healthy, though not over-endowed with intelligence. It took some time for Madeleine's news of Jeanne's present predicament to penetrate her understanding. She had Jeanne's large, pale eyes and they betrayed little emotion when she learned that her daughter was ill and likely to die. Madeleine faltered over this and tried to soften what she had to say, but since Madame Soubise did not appear to understand her hints, she was forced to be explicit.

'So, my Jeanne will die in England, is that what you are trying to tell me?' Madame Soubise asked. 'Poor Jeanne! I told her it would do her no good, the life she led. Not that she did badly out of it at one time, but when all's said and done there's nothing like a husband and a steady income, eh, Madame?'

Madeleine sat in silence with her for a few minutes in the dark little room, giving on to the courtyard, from which she could, if she wished, watch the comings and goings of the tenants.

'I ought to have known better than to let her go off to England and leave me with the baby to keep,' Madame Soubise said at last. 'A fine expense it's been from first to last, and now I suppose I'm stuck with her for the rest of my life. It's hard, madame, you must admit it's hard.'

'Where is Véronique?' Madeleine asked. 'I want to talk to you about her. In fact, the reason I am here is to ask if you will allow me to take her back to England. Jeanne is anxious to see her again and I would be prepared, if you were agreeable, to support the child and see to her education.'

'I can't see what Jeanne wants with her,' Madame Soubise remarked. 'She's scarcely set eyes on Véronique since the day she was born — and a fine time she gave me over that, I can tell you! You'd think no-one had ever had a baby before! I'd buried three before Jeanne was born and I've lost count of the number I've helped into the world. My own daughter gave me more trouble than all the rest put together.' She gave Madeleine a cunning glance. 'Of course, I shall miss the little darling if you take her away from me, madame.'

'My first idea was that you should bring Véronique to England yourself,' Madeleine said. 'Me, leave France? Not likely!' Madame Soubise broke in. 'No, I shall stay here, even if the Prussians come. But I shall be lost without my little ray of sunshine.' There was a pause and then she hinted, 'Some little compensation for my loss would not be unreasonable, would it, madame?'

'No doubt we can reach a suitable arrangement,' Madeleine said with a coldness that warned Madame Soubise that the subject was best left alone for the time being.

She heaved herself to her feet. 'I'll get the little sweet,' she said. 'She was a mite fractious this morning, so I've left her in the bedroom.' She opened the door of the inner room and Madeleine caught a glimpse of a frowsty, unmade bed. 'Véronique, my little love! Véronique, my treasure! Come to your old Granny, then,' Madame Soubise called in tones of honey.

A small figure detached itself from amongst the tumbled bedclothes and slid, not without difficulty, down from the high bed and on to the floor. She took Madame Soubise's outstretched hand and was led up to Madeleine, wide-eyed and doubtful of this stranger, the thumb of her free hand in her mouth for comfort. Véronique Soubise was an elfin creature with her mother's fair curls and her father's dark brown eyes, small for her age, with the well-shaped hands and feet which Henri de Cavaillon had been proud of in himself, and a little face with a pointed chin, just now flushed and puffy. She was still in her nightgown and her feet were bare.

'She'll be a beauty when she grows up, don't you think, madame?' Madame Soubise asked.

'Quite possibly,' Madeleine said. She searched the little girl's face, but she could find no likeness to Henri de Cavaillon in her infant features beyond those large brown eyes, which were something of a relief after the vacuous deception she had found behind the flat blue gaze of Jeanne and her mother. The little girl buried her face in Madame Soubise's skirts and murmured fretfully.

'Is she unwell?' Madeleine asked.

'Oh, nothing to worry about,' Madame Soubise said easily. 'I'll give her a tisane and that'll put her to rights.'

The little girl pulled up her nightdress with a total disregard for modesty and scratched her small stomach. It was covered in spots.

'I would like a doctor to see her,' Madeleine said. 'I must be sure that she is fit to travel before we leave for England.'

Madame Soubise shrugged her ample shoulders. 'As you wish, madame,' she said indifferently. She stooped down and picked up the little girl. 'Perhaps the little one has eaten something which disagreed with her,' she said vaguely. 'The American doctor could tell us, no doubt, and Véronique likes him, don't you, *ma chère*? You like Doctor Anthony, don't you, my little cherub?'

Véronique rubbed her eyes with one chubby fist and then her head drooped again, but it appeared that she did have a liking for the American doctor, and when Madeleine learned that he had rooms on the third floor of the house, she volunteered to climb the stairs and ask him if he would come down to visit the child.

It did not surprise her to find that the stairs were none too clean, but when Dr. Richard Anthony opened his door to her she could see that the room behind him was bright and airy, with a certain neatness about it which predisposed her in favour of the young doctor. She explained her errand and he looked doubtful.

'The thing is, I'm not supposed to practise in France,' he said. 'I am qualified . . . ' a smile lit up his face. 'Just,' he admitted. 'I qualified in April in the States and I'm spending a year in Paris, attending a few lectures and demonstrations.' Again his face was illuminated by his infectious smile. 'Enjoying myself,' he said cheerfully. 'However, I don't suppose there'd be any harm in my taking a look at the little kid. Sweet little thing, isn't she? Hold on and I'll be right with you.'

Madeleine began to walk slowly down the stairs and in a few seconds he came clattering down behind her. He had put on the jacket which had been missing when he had opened the door to her and he was carrying a professional-looking bag. He was a prepossessing young man, tall and loose-limbed, and there was something about his easy manner and well cut, if negligently worn, clothes which made

Madeleine suspect money in his background; surely there could not be many newly-qualified young doctors who could afford to spend an additional year in Paris?

'Are you related to the Soubises?' Richard Anthony asked as he joined Madeleine on the stairs. He cast a puzzled look at her. Madeleine had chosen her most subdued clothes for this journey to Paris, but she no longer possessed garments such as the black gowns she had worn when she first arrived in England. Her brown travelling costume and cream silk blouse bore the unmistakable stamp of a first-class dressmaker, and her shining hair, delicate complexion and beautifully-tended hands were rare sights in the Allée Racine.

'No. Véronique is the daughter of my maid,' Madeleine replied briefly. She hesitated, but there was little to be gained by attempting to conceal her identity. 'I am Lady Chilcote,' she said.

'Wow, a real lady!' Dr. Anthony exclaimed. He sounded so deeply impressed that Madeleine was forced to laugh. 'Jeanne Soubise is very ill,' she went on. 'In fact, my own doctor thinks she cannot live for many months. It is her lungs, you see. She was distressed at the thought of her child remaining in France because of the war, so I have come to take Véronique back to England.'

'That's very good of you,' Richard Anthony said. He cast another curious glance at her. It was none of his business, but it seemed an act of quixotic generosity for a high-born lady to come

267

herself to carry her maid's child to safety.

It required only the most cursory examination by the young doctor for him to arrive at a verdict on Véronique's ailment. 'Measles,' he said laconically. He glanced up at Madeleine. 'I'm not sure of the French word for it,' he admitted.

'*La rougeloe*', she said.

He held the baby gently while he examined the inside of her mouth. 'She's already had it for a day or two, the rash on her poor little body is a secondary symptom,' he said. 'Poor little tyke, she's going to feel very sorry for herself for a day or two.'

'How long will it be before she is ready to travel?' Madeleine asked.

Dr. Anthony pursed his lips. 'Ten days, perhaps two weeks,' he said.

'I shall have to wait.'

'Can you afford to do that? You may find yourself trapped inside Paris, you know.'

'Surely not!' Madeleine protested. 'I am British; surely I shall be able to pass through the German lines, if it really comes to a siege? Are you leaving?'

'No, I'm planning to stay and see the fun,' Richard Anthony admitted. 'But it's a different proposition for me, being a man, and a doctor — I may be of some use.'

'Meaning I shall not be?' Madeleine asked, with a gleam of amusement as she observed his confusion.

'I guess that sounded pretty rude,' Richard Anthony admitted ruefully. 'I didn't mean it like that, m'am — er, Lady Chilcote.'

'I am more practical than I look,' Madeleine said. 'And to prove it I shall help to nurse little Véronique.'

'Have you had measles?'

'No,' Madeleine admitted.

'Then I think you should stay clear. Leave her to her grandmother.' He glanced at Madame Soubise, who obviously understood nothing of this exchange. 'She's a rough and ready character, but she has raised children and she knows what she's about.'

'Does she? She didn't seem to know what was the matter with the child before I insisted on calling you in,' Madeleine retorted.

Dr. Anthony smiled. 'I think she did, but she didn't want the expense and trouble of calling a doctor. She let you bring me downstairs because she knew I wouldn't charge her anything. She knows as well as I do that there is not a lot we can do for Véronique except keep her warm and quiet. The tisanes she brews will do the child no harm, in fact they might even be beneficial. Madame Soubise is a wily old peasant from Normandy; she won't spend a *sou* she can see a chance of putting in her pocket. If you are taking the child back to England is there nothing in it for Madame?'

'Quite possibly,' Madeleine admitted. 'We did just touch on the subject of compensation to her for the loss of her grandchild.'

'I'll bet you did! But that isn't to say she doesn't care for the child, in her own fashion. She'll look after her, don't you worry, especially

269

with you and me both keeping an eye on her.'

'I can come and see the child?'

'Certainly, but keep your distance.'

Madeleine turned to Madame Soubise and in her rapid, accentless French explained the situation to the older woman. Madame Soubise nodded. 'Certainly I know what to do for the little one,' she said. 'I will take care of her, madame, never fear.'

'I shall come and see her every day,' Madeleine said firmly. 'Now I must go.'

'May I escort you?' Richard Anthony asked.

Madeleine's smiling consent was given automatically. It piqued him just a little to feel that she had taken it for granted that he would offer to see her back to her hotel, but there was something about this exquisite stranger, with her mysterious interest in the obscure child of a Paris back street which intrigued him.

He found her a distrait companion on their journey back to Madeleine's hotel. For the first time Madeleine was a little afraid of what she was doing; not afraid of being caught up in the Franco-Prussian war, since she still believed that her nationality would be her passport out of the country, but afraid of Janus's reaction. Her original intention had been to make a swift sortie into France, lasting no more than a day or two, and to return with Jeanne's child to Laycott Manor before he had become aware of her mission, but if she were away for a matter of weeks her prolonged absence would be remarked, and the reason for it was not likely to find favour in his eyes. The possibility of a reconciliation between them receded even further. Everything she did seemed to widen the breach between them. With this on her mind, she responded to Richard Anthony's friendly overtures with an abstracted smile and answers given somewhat at random, but he did manage to establish that she would be visiting Véronique the following morning and he knew, without wishing to look too closely at his own motives, that he would be calling on Madame Soubise at the same time himself.

On the other side of the Channel Lord Chilcote had not been displaying his customary marksmanship and had had to endure a number of tiresome jokes about his sudden loss of skill. In his leisure moments his mind turned obstinately towards his absent wife, until one day it occurred to him that there was really nothing to stop him paying a visit to his own home in Kent. Madeleine might receive him coldly, but she could not object to his presence in a house which belonged to him. It was time they got things sorted out between them. He would go to Laycott Manor.

He arrived without warning and, apart from the servants, found no-one there to greet him but his greataunt.

'Where's Madeleine?' he demanded, a frown drawing his black eyebrows together.

'In London, or so I thought,' Mrs. Ardingley said.

'No, she's not — at least, she's not at Chilcote House. Did she say anything about paying a visit to anyone?'

Mrs. Ardingley shook her head. 'Now I come to think about it, she was a bit vague about her movements,' she said. 'None of my business so I didn't see any reason to cross-question her, but I must admit I rather expected her back before this, especially since she went quite alone, not even a maid to accompany her.'

'She's got rid of that French maid of hers then?' Janus asked with an air of indifference which concealed his anxiety to be assured that Jeanne was no longer going to be around to remind him of his own misdeeds.

'Jeanne?' Mrs. Ardingley shook her head emphatically. 'No, indeed, Jeanne has not been able to leave. She is far too ill to travel.'

She explained the nature and seriousness of Jeanne's illness, while Janus stood in apparent indecision, until at last he said in his curt way, 'I'll go and see her.'

He was shocked by the change he found in Jeanne, but he managed to conceal it and she greeted him with all her old coquettishness. He had to endure some minutes of suggestive talk until he could find an opportunity to ask the question which had brought him there. With deceptive casualness he enquired, 'Do you happen to know where my wife has gone?'

'To Paris,' Jeanne replied readily.

'To *Paris*? But that's madness! What on earth made her take it into her head to go to Paris at this time?'

She caught the note of real perturbation in his voice and the jealous dislike she had always felt for Madeleine flared up again.

'She 'as gone to fetch a child,' she said.

'Whose child?' He rapped out the question his face dark with angry suspicion.

'The child of Henri de Cavaillon,' Jeanne answered cautiously.

'That is impossible, the child was aborted,' Janus said, too shaken to be as much on his guard as he would normally have been with Jeanne.

A momentary flash of chagrin showed in Jeanne's expressionless eyes. That was a piece of information she would have liked to have had earlier. Now, she could see little use for it, but the news that Madeleine, too, had once been pregnant by her own former lover reinforced her malicious pleasure in misleading Janus.

'This child of which I speak 'as already three years *à peu près*,' she said.

'Three years old! A child conceived nearly four years ago! It isn't possible! Madeleine would barely have left her Convent, she was living with her father . . . ' His voice tailed away. He was remembering that Madeleine had admitted to knowing Henri de Cavaillon during her father's lifetime. All the same, surely there must be some mistake. He drew a deep breath. 'Let me understand you,' he said. 'Are you telling me that Madeleine has a child by Henri de Cavaillon living in France and that she has gone to Paris to fetch it?'

It was not in the least what Jeanne had set out to tell him when their interview began, but the misunderstanding which had sprung

273

up between them seemed too fortuitous to be thrown away now.

'Yes,' she answered with the greatest readiness.

Janus stood looking at her with such a black expression on his face that she began to feel alarm, but she had no need to worry, he was not even aware of being in the same room with her. Without another word he turned on his heel and walked out of the room.

Arriving back at Laycott Manor he gave curt orders for his bags to be repacked immediately. In response to an enquiry from his greataunt he said merely that he was returning to London.

'But where is Madeleine?' Mrs. Ardingley asked, bewildered by his air of barely suppressed fury.

'In Paris,' Janus said.

Mrs. Ardingley gave an exclamation of distress. 'Something must be done!' she said. 'She may be in danger! Are you going to fetch her back?'

The laugh this drew from him made her wince. 'No, I am not going to France to fetch back my dear wife,' Janus said. 'Let her rot there for all I care!'

12

The days in Paris passed all too slowly for Madeleine. Moving nostalgically about the city she had once known in such different circumstances, when it had seemed the epitome of civilised life, she noted with sadness and deep foreboding the preparations which were being made for the expected siege. She drove with Dr. Anthony to see the fortifications and found the sight of the activity there both reassuring and disquieting. Even more disturbing was the sight of the Bois de Boulogne, denuded of its trees and covered by a vast flock of sheep and oxen. August came to an end and vague rumours began to circulate about the town: there had been a wonderful victory; some disaster had overtaken the Prussian King; and then, later, a counter-rumour that it had all been a mistake, there had been no victory. The people rejoiced and then wept to find that their rejoicing had been premature. At last the truth was known: there had, indeed, been no victory but a most crushing defeat and the Emperor had surrendered his sword to the King of Prussia.

On the afternoon of the 4th September Madeleine, trying to get across the Seine to visit Véronique, made the mistake of attempting to do so by the Pont de la Concorde. She found herself caught up in a jubilant crowd, singing the Marseillaise and shouting 'A *bas l'Empereur, vive la République!*' She extricated herself with difficulty and eventually arrived at the Allée Racine shaken and distressed.

'Will it really make so much difference if a Republic is declared?' she asked Richard Anthony. 'Everyone seems to be rejoicing, and having lived so much of my life in France, I can understand this almost superstitious regard people have for the Republic, and yet . . . '

'Nothing can alter the fact that France has suffered a humiliating defeat,' he agreed.

'The Tuileries has been taken over by the people,' Madeleine said. 'The poor Empress! No-one seems to know what has become of her.' The memory of the last time she had seen Eugénie in a box at the theatre in a gown of ice-blue satin and tulle with diamond stars in her hair came into Madeleine's mind and her eyes filled with tears.

'She is safe,' Richard Anthony said. He hesitated. 'This must go no further, but I can tell you that she has taken refuge with one of my own fellow-countrymen, a dentist called Dr. Evans, and he will help her to get out of the country. He is an interesting fellow, I have been in touch with him a lot lately. After the Great Exhibition he bought up the American exhibit of medical equipment from the Civil War and he means to organise a field hospital to help deal with the wounded. I have volunteered to help him.'

'Wounded!' Madeleine said faintly. 'Oh no, no!'

'You must face the fact that if there is

276

an attack on Paris there must inevitably be wounded soldiers, and possibly even civilians,' Richard Anthony said. 'It is becoming imperative for you and Véronique to leave. In ordinary circumstances I would have preferred to keep her here for another week, but I think you should make your arrangements as fast as you possibly can.'

'Yes, of course, you are right,' Madeleine said. She put her hand to her head. 'I am sorry to seem so stupid. Coming through all that crowd was a strain — the excitement, the feeling of everything being upset — can you understand me when I say that I felt as if the whole world had gone mad?' Her voice faltered. 'I look upon France not as my second home, but as my first, yet now . . . I long for England.'

'You will see it soon,' Richard Anthony promised. 'You must rest before you attempt to go back to your hotel. I have to go out myself for an hour or so; if you would like to make use of my own apartment while I am away I shall be very happy to put it at your disposal.'

'I would be so grateful for that!' Madeleine said. 'I find these small rooms Madame Soubise occupies quite over-powering on such a warm day.'

He took her up to his big, airy room on the third floor and made sure she was comfortable in an armchair near an open window before he left her. Madeleine removed her hat and leaned back with a sigh of relief. 'That is so nice,' she said.

He looked at her thoughtfully, his professional

instinct overcoming his pleasure in her presence in his living quarters. She was flushed and heavy-eyed and there was something about the way her head drooped under its heavy load of hair that gave her an oddly pathetic air. He went out to the kitchen and returned a few minutes later carrying a tray.

'Tea,' he said. 'And I'd like you to take this powder to relieve your headache. Stay quietly where you are until you feel ready to leave. If you are still here when I return I will take you back to your hotel.'

He cut short her thanks and left her. To his regret he was gone longer than he had intended having, like Madeleine earlier in the afternoon, been delayed by the crowds of excited people roaming the streets. He expected to find her gone, but Madeleine was still in the big armchair, the tea tray forgotten by her side. She had fallen into a heavy sleep. Without waking her, Dr. Anthony took one of her hands lightly in his own. To his dismay it was burning hot. She started and turned a vague look on him.

'I fell asleep,' she said in a worried, confused way. 'My head hurts, and my throat. The light is so strong, it makes my eyes ache. I am sorry to be so tiresome; I must go, mustn't I?'

'No, I think you must stay where you are,' Dr. Anthony said with a grave face. 'Unless I am very much mistaken, you have taken Véronique's measles.'

The tears began to run down Madeleine's face. 'I must go home,' she said. 'What will Janus say? I must go back to England.'

278

'Dear Lady Chilcote, you shall go back to England,' Richard Anthony promised. 'Not just yet, but as soon as you are well again.'

'I don't want to be ill in a hotel.'

'No, as I have just said, you must stay here.' He thought deeply. 'The apartment below this one is vacant. The tenants left Paris last week. I think we should move you in there where I can keep an eye on you and Madame Soubise can help to nurse you.'

'I don't want Madame Soubise to nurse me,' Madeleine said, the weak tears still wet on her cheeks. 'I want to go home, I want to go home!'

He recognised this for what it was, the heartfelt but irrational cry of sickness. He made soothing, meaningless noises; there was no way in which he could give her her heart's desire and he had the gravest forebodings about the delay in her departure which her illness would entail.

Madeleine suffered severely for the next two weeks, but not so severely that she could not take note of the devoted care Richard Anthony lavished on her. She tried to thank him, but he would not listen.

'Good practice for me,' he said cheerfully. 'After all, I came to Paris to study medicine and though I must admit measles was not quite what I had in mind, every case is of interest. You have been a very good patient.'

'You have been a wonderful doctor,' Madeleine said. She had lost weight during her illness and her lovely face had a gaunt look about it, but once the fever had subsided and the dreadful irritation of the skin rash, she began to pick up and to feel more cheerful. 'How soon can I go home?' she asked.

'There may be a little difficulty about that,' Richard Anthony said. He tried to find some way of breaking the news to her gently, but the stark truth could not be avoided. 'Paris has shut her gates; the Prussians have occupied Versailles; we are cut off from the outside world.'

'But surely it is still possible for non-belligerents to pass through the lines?' Madeleine protested. 'I shall see the British Ambassador.' She spoke with unconscious hauteur, still sure of her right to go where she chose.

'The British Ambassador has already left,' Richard Anthony said.

For the first time Madeleine's belief in her ability to return to England faltered. She looked so stricken that he added hurriedly, 'I have heard that a party of British are planning to leave the city — or I should say to try to leave the city — in three days' time. I suggest you accompany them, if you are really determined to make the attempt.'

'With Véronique,' Madeleine said quickly. 'Having waited so long and suffered this tiresome illness on her behalf I am certainly not leaving without her.'

She persisted in this determination even though she found that the organisers of the British party had grave doubts whether a French child would be allowed to pass. There were mutterings amongst the little group that she was endangering the passage of the whole party, but Madeleine was not to be deterred. In the few weeks she had known her she had grown very fond of the little girl. Even when she had been unwell Véronique had been an endearing little creature; now that she was well she was enchanting — merry, affectionate, with an odd little air of independence about her as she trotted round the courtyard, always occupied on some childish ploy and often talking busily to herself. She adored Richard Anthony and, although he tried to hide it, he was her doting admirer, who could always be coaxed into giving her rides on his back and packets of sweets.

Because of his misgivings he insisted on accompanying Madeleine as far as he could on her journey out of the city. He also suggested that he should take charge of the sum of money Madeleine had promised to Madame Soubise.

'I'll hand it over when you are clear of Paris,' he said with brisk practicality. 'If you don't get away you may need all the money you can raise — and once it is handed over to *la mère* Soubise you won't see it back again.'

'That is the banker in you coming to the fore,' Madeleine said with a mischievous smile that chased away the worried expression her face usually wore in those days.

She had become the firmest of friends with the young American doctor and knew all about his family history. 'Dad's a banker, and as near to being a millionaire as makes no odds,' Richard had told her. 'He thinks I'm a mite eccentric, wanting to be a doctor, but he's let me have my way. My older brother is all set to follow him in the Bank, so he didn't put too much pressure on me.'

'If your father is so wealthy why have you chosen to live in this part of Paris?' Madeleine asked curiously. 'Your own apartment is quite agreeable . . . '

'It is now I've fixed it up, and having Lulu come in to look after me is a big bonus,' Richard said. He avoided looking at her. He was not quite sure whether Madeleine realised that Lulu, who cleaned and washed for him, also supplied other services with careless generosity and was a very good reason why a young man whose needs were so well catered for should choose to remain in a rather poor area of Paris. Madeleine, who had understood the situation from the first, suppressed a smile. She knew that in his eyes she was too much of a lady to be expected to have any knowledge of such arrangements and she guessed that it would upset him if she betrayed her awareness.

'I guess I was a bit naive when I first came to Paris,' Richard Anthony went on. 'It was my first trip to Europe, you see, and I had this idea of living the Bohemian life. I soon found I liked my comforts more than I had imagined! I've hit on a sort of compromise now and I've come to like it here. For one thing I can — or I should say I could before the war brought it to an end — avoid the social scene. Lady Chilcote, you have no idea how many matchmaking American mothers bring their daughters to Paris to find a husband! I am supposed to be here to work, not to play!'

'I can't say I have seen much evidence of work so far,' Madeleine said.

'Exceptional circumstances,' he said. 'Raging infection in the house.'

He spoke solemnly, but his eyes were dancing and when she laughed he joined in, tacitly admitting that he did not take his programme of work in Paris very seriously. Obviously he did not, otherwise how could he have been free every time Madeleine visited Véronique? How could he have spared the time for nursing her when she herself fell ill? Unconsciously, Madeleine thought of him as very young, although he was older than she was by some years. She thought him, as he had said himself, a little naive; certainly he lacked the worldly wisdom most of the men she knew wore like a second skin, but this was offset by his strong commonsense, as shown by his insistence on holding on to the money Madeleine would have handed to Madame Soubise. There was still a gangling boyishness about his long limbs, he wore his wavy brown hair a little longer than was fashionable, a relic of 'la vie Bohème' he had come to Paris to sample, and he affected a studied carelessness in his dress which amused Madeleine, who had heard a grumble or two from the oblinging Lulu on the subject of the laundry work his fastidiousness caused her. He had studied hard for his medical degree and took his profession seriously, and something about his firm mouth and keen grey eyes, as well as the compassion and skill he had shown in nursing Véronique and herself, gave Madeleine an inkling of the fine doctor he would one day become. In the meantime, this was his playtime, and even the war might have been specially arranged as a diversion for him, so pleased was he at the possibility of taking part in really exciting events.

He seemed more exotic to Madeleine than he ever realised, and for a reason which he would have had difficulty in understanding. As she came to know him better, to listen with absorbed interest to his account of his upbringing and home, Madeleine began to look on him with something like awe. Here, almost unique in her experience, was someone to whom nothing bad had ever happened. Friendly, gregarious — for all his avoidance of the matchmaking mamas — the child of parents in comfortable circumstances, who had a warm, uncomplicated affection for one another and for their children; enjoying splendid health; well-educated and with sufficient intelligence to make it easy for him to follow his chosen profession; goodlooking, with charming manners; and yet, with all these advantages, quite unspoilt, saved from complacency by sturdy commonsense and a genuine streak of altruism which gave him a desire to serve his fellow men.

'You have lived always in sunshine,' Madeleine said to him one day.

Richard looked puzzled. 'Plenty of rain and snow in Vermont,' he said.

She shook her head. 'I was not talking about the climate!'

'Oh, I see! Yes, of course I have been pretty lucky,' he said blithely, and she dropped the subject, realising that for all his acknowledgement of his good fortune he was far from understanding how wide a gulf there was between him and someone who had known what she felt to be the depths of poverty and degradation. It would be a pity if his happy view of life were ever to become clouded, she had a curious feeling that he ought to be protected from the harder knocks of life. And yet, if he were to suffer hardship would it perhaps broaden him, enlarge his understanding? One thing she was sure it would not do, and that was to sour him or make him bitter. Richard knew in the uttermost depths of his being that life was good, and nothing would ever entirely shake that belief, whereas Madeleine only had this conviction occasionally, and it seemed as fast as she built up a little edifice of faith and hope, something happened to bring it crashing to the ground again.

She looked back over her life — her early childhood, marred she now realised, by her mother's failing health and the tension between her and Madeleine's father; her convent girlhood in which she had always been a little apart, marked out by her different nationality and faith; her brief period of exciting happiness with her father — and even that she recognised now as having been too hectic, too brilliant; her descent into poverty; her liaison with Henri; her period with the Lorgans and the way the restrictions imposed on her had begun to chafe; her strange marriage when she had walked a tightrope between heartstopping happiness and despair. Looking back, the only times she could identify when she had been really happy with the deep, contented happiness Richard seemed to look upon as his right, were a few quiet periods in the convent, the time she had spent alone with her greataunt at Laycott Manor before Janus had begun to trouble her mind, and the short period during their marriage when she had believed that Janus might come to love her as she loved him.

And Janus, what of him? From the hints she had gleaned it would seem that his childhood had been disastrous, and it seemed to her now that he had emerged from it crippled in both mind and body. With a new insight she recognised that a large part of the trouble between them arose from his obstinate refusal to believe that it was possible to owe one's happiness to another human being. With the understanding she seemed to have gained since they had been apart she thought that if she had their time together again she would devote herself to convincing him that he could trust her. Janus trusted no-one, and in that context her deception over Jeanne's presence in their household had been calamitous. If she had the chance . . . but it seemed unlikely that she would have the chance, and it was yet another source of grief that she had perhaps already lost her best hope of attaining that elusive state of happiness Richard seemed to take for granted.

He was immensely attractive in his gaiety and easy outlook on life, and no woman could have resisted entirely the appeal of his warm, infectious smile. He was always in a hurry. Richard never descended the stairs less than three at a time; he was always to be seen, jacket flying open, just disappearing round a corner in pursuit of an elusive cab, running to an appointment for which he was already late; he was appallingly untidy, full of restless energy and unbounded interest in his fellows. Lulu, who had agreed to take care of Madeleine's flat as well as Richard's, spoke of his careless ways in mingled horror and admiration, but always with a laugh — most women smiled when Richard's name was mentioned. Lulu, cheerfully amoral, made no secret of her relations with him, something which Richard did not realise and which would have embarrassed him if he had known. Lulu's attitude was that Madeleine was obviously a woman of the world and understood these little arrangements; in any case, a young woman of her calibre, living alone, probably had a friend of her own somewhere. Madeleine did not encourage these communications and the day came when Lulu retired baffled from an attempt to win her confidence and after that they settled into a more formal mistress and maid relationship which Lulu accepted with a philosophical shrug of her shoulders.

Insensibly, Madeleine had come to look on him as something of a talisman. He was so sure that everything would turn out well eventually, that she was tempted to share his optimism, but on the day they left Paris his pleasant face was unusually serious and the cheerful insouciance which normally characterised him was missing. He drove with Madeleine and Véronique to the outpost at which the British party proposed to present itself for permission to leave the city. They got as far as the Pont de Neuilly and were halted. A long and acrimonious argument developed, until at last they succeeded in obtaining an audience with General Ducrot. He looked them over in exasperation and even when Madeleine, hurriedly chosen to speak for them because of her aristocratic connections, not to mention her youth and beauty, put forward their plea to go on, he shook his head.

'You don't seem to understand the situation,' he said. 'I sympathise with your desire to return to your native land — though why you have left it until this late date is beyond my understanding — but to venture beyond this point towards the Prussian lines is to court almost certain death. You will be shot, miladi, you and your fellow countrymen. A note of regret will be sent from the German Government to the British Government and who will be blamed? I will, for allowing you to put yourselves into such danger! Possibly at some later date it may be possible to make an arrangement, but as the situation stands at the moment I cannot take the responsibility of letting you pass.'

There was no-one else to whom they could appeal. Dispirited and dejected, they climbed back into the carriages which had brought them that far and turned their faces towards Paris once more.

'It was what you always expected, wasn't it?'

Madeleine asked Richard Anthony.

'I was afraid this would be the outcome,' he admitted. 'General Ducrot is quite right, of course, it would be a dangerous undertaking and, apart from that, I have heard it said that it is bad for morale for large numbers of foreigners to be seen leaving the city.'

He was driving Madeleine and Véronique himself in an open carriage he had hired. Véronique was enjoying this novel form of outing and had to be held back from leaning over the side to see the wheels go round. Automatically, Madeleine restrained her lively movements, while her mind grappled with this disaster.

'I shall move permanently into the apartment I have been occupying,' she said. 'It would not be reasonable to take Véronique away from her grandmother unless I were to leave Paris, but I shall wish to keep an eye on her. And you . . . '

She broke off. She had been about to say 'And you will be there,' but now she pulled herself up short of this unconscious betrayal of dependance on the young American.

'Yes, I shall be there,' Dr. Anthony agreed, apparently without noticing that she had not completed her sentence. 'I have been giving this matter of surviving in a siege some thought. I am going to give you back the money you meant for Madame Soubise and my advice is that you spend it on a stock of food, a very good supply of wood for the stove, and some warm clothing.'

'Do you think the siege will go on into the winter?' Madeleine asked, appalled by the thought.

'We are already in the third week of September,' Richard Anthony pointed out. 'Winter is not far off. My own belief is that this is going to be a much longer drawn-out affair than people are prepared to acknowledge. Everything has happened so fast, the Parisians have not really taken in the disaster which faces them, they still believe a miracle will happen and France will come out of this war victorious. Because of this, and because of the sense of shame people feel at the defeats the Prussians have inflicted on them, they will hold out to the bitter end.'

'You think France must be defeated at last?' Madeleine asked in a low voice.

'I can see no other help for it.'

'What are you going to do?'

'I have already told you that Dr. Evans is organising an American Ambulance — that's what they call a field hospital over here. I shall join him and help all I can.'

'At least there is something useful you can do,' Madeleine said. 'Do you need nurses? Could I join you?'

Richard Anthony hesitated. 'Do you have much experience of illness, Lady Chilcote?' he asked.

'No, none, except when my father died, and that was very sudden,' Madeleine admitted.

'And your nerves, I would say, are not of the strongest. Better keep clear.'

'I could be of use to you as an interpreter,' Madeleine suggested. 'Or, if you will not have me, perhaps someone else will make use of me.'

'There are other posts being fitted out — two by Mr. Wallace, the British millionaire,' Richard Anthony admitted. 'I guess if anyone is to have a claim on your services I would rather it was me. It's true my French is a bit shaky at times and it might be handy to have you around.'

Their return to the Allée Racine was received by Madame Soubise in grim silence. 'You should have gone while you had the chance, madame,' she said at last. 'No harm would have come to the child if she had travelled with a few spots on her belly.'

'You must blame me for that,' Dr. Anthony put in quickly. 'Perhaps I was over-cautious.' He turned an unhappy face towards Madeleine. 'It's at times like this that I realise my lack of experience,' he said. 'I thought too much about the possible complications and the spread of infection and not enough about what it would mean if your departure was delayed until it became impossible to leave. I feel pretty badly about this, Lady Chilcote.'

'You were not to know that I would catch the measles,' Madeleine said. She turned to Madame Soubise and began to make arrangements to take up permanent residence in the apartment on the second floor.

The mood in Paris had changed since Madeleine had last been able to go about the streets. There was a martial fever in the air.

Everywhere bands of men marched and drilled under the admiring gaze of their compatriots and the Mobiles from the provinces, in grey or blue blouses with red collars or improvised red badges on either arm, walked about admiring the sights and were themselves the subject of interested stares from the inhabitants. The general feeling was that the Prussians must fall back in dismay once they understood the spirit which animated Paris. Even the news that Strasbourg had fallen did not dampen the curious optimism, for still the guns outside Paris were silent and the full weight of the Prussian army had not been brought to bear against the beleaguered city.

One of the greatest deprivations was shortage of news from outside, although a novel method of sending news out of Paris was improvised, Madeleine, visiting the Right Bank on an errand for Richard Anthony, attempted to pass through the Place Saint Pierre Montmartre and was prevented from doing so by a considerable crowd of people, and a little boy told her importantly that they were waiting to watch 'the ascent'.

'Look, look, madame! It is going up!' he said, pointing with one grubby finger. A great red and white striped mushroom seemed to grow out of the ground; it wavered, lurched to one side and then rose steadily into the air, soaring over the crowd, over the buildings, and away into the distance. The first balloon-borne despatches had left Paris. Madeleine completed her errand and hurried home, bubbling with excitement.

'The Post Office say that we can send private

letters by balloon!' she said. 'Only on very thin paper, of course; they mustn't weigh more than three grammes, and they have to be left open, but it means I can write to my husband.'

'I am glad,' Richard Anthony said mechanically. He turned away, trying to suppress the pang of jealousy he felt at her obvious pleasure in this news. She so rarely referred to her absent husband that it had become easy for him to overlook her married state, even to wonder whether there was some estrangement between her and Lord Chilcote, but judging by her present excitement, that was not the case.

Madeleine wrote her letter, but she had no means of knowing by which balloon it was sent, nor whether the balloon survived its perilous journey. So many of them met with accidents or even fell into enemy hands, and she could not be sure that Janus would ever see the brief note she had sent him, but at least she had made the attempt and it eased her mind to feel that possibly her message was flying through the air towards him.

It came as a surprise to Richard Anthony to find that she had considerable organizational flair. He had set her to work to obtain some of the more mundane requirements of a military hospital and discovered that she started with considerable natural advantages. Her knowledge of the language and her intimate acquaintance with Paris were of obvious value, but so was her natural assumption of authority. Although he did not recognise it, she had all the Ardingley highhandedness when it came to getting what she wanted and this, combined with her great charm and beauty, made her a formidable ally.

'You know, I'd like you to meet my Dad,' he joked when she reported that she had successfully negotiated the purchase of a consignment of blankets. 'You drive as hard a bargain as he does.'

'And there is a wagonload of wood being delivered to Madame Soubise tomorrow,' Madeleine said triumphantly. 'Really, you know, I do think it was a mistake to burn all those trees when we are going to need the wood for fuel this winter.'

'They didn't have the benefit of your advice at the time,' Richard Anthony said gravely. 'The only difficulty now will be to prevent Madame Soubise selling off the logs at a profit.'

'Yes, I thought of that,' Madeleine said. 'So before she knew why I wanted it I rented the cellar from her. The wood will be stacked down there to keep it dry, together with anything else I think requires safekeeping. I have the only key and I shall keep a very strict tally of what is removed.'

'General Trochu should be told about you,' Richard said.

She laughed, pleased by his admiration and borne up by the common spirit of excitement. It was perhaps the last time either of them was able to treat the war with anything approaching lightheartedness.

On the 21st October the French Army made a great sortie out of Paris, not perhaps in the hope of dispersing the Prussian Army, but certainly to make them feel the precariousness of their position. The fighting was bitter and for the first time Richard Anthony found himself pressed into service. He came back the next day, his face grim.

'You asked me once whether I could use you as a nurse,' he said to Madeleine. 'And I refused you offer. Now I think I may have to change my mind. The French have been pushed back into Paris. There are hundreds of wounded.'

'Were you in the fighting?' Madeleine asked.

'I went up to the front yesterday evening with one of the ambulances.' He drew a deep breath. 'It was a terrible sight. Two lines of ambulances constantly moving, one advancing towards the battlefield, one passing it going the other way, returning to the city with the wounded and the dead.'

'And the Prussians?'

'They suffered too, but I think we had the worst of it.'

He had called in to see her on his way up to his own apartment, and now he sat slumped by the warmth of the closed stove, reluctant to move.

'Have you eaten?' Madeleine asked, worried by his immobility and the unusual grimness of his young face. He shook his head.

'I have some rabbit stew,' she said. 'It's very good.' It was not the moment to tell him that she had had to wait two hours in the market to obtain this one rabbit and that she had already shared it with Madame Soubise and Véronique, nor to mention that there would be nothing but horse flesh for them for the remainder of the week.

He ate the hot stew and the small piece of hard bread she was able to give him to go with it, and drank a glass of wine. 'At least there is no shortage of that,' he said with a wry twist of his lips. He looked up at Madeleine, concerned but composed as she watched him, and said 'You'll come with me tomorrow?' She nodded and the next day he took her to the American Ambulance and introduced her to Dr. Swinburne, the Chief Surgeon.

Madeleine had expected her usefulness to be limited at first, but she soon saw that there were tasks she could undertake and she began to move amongst the beds, talking quietly to the wounded men, helping to feed those who were helpless, taking names and addresses from those who wanted messages sent to their families, fetching and carrying for those who had a better knowledge of what was required, until when at last a doctor said to her brusquely, 'Here, hold this,' she took without flinching the bowl of blood and pus he held out to her and stood by while he examined the horrendous would he had uncovered. Her hands were shaking as she cleared away the mess, and she had to fight against a sensation of nausea, but she had passed the first test; she knew now that she could see a man's bowels exposed and subdue her sick horror in her desire to be of service to him.

Eight hours later she was so drained of strength that Richard Anthony took one look at her white, exhausted face and ordered her home. 'You are staying?' she asked.

'I still have work to do, but I shall be off duty in an hour or so. Go home, Madeleine — go home and light my fire for me. I shall be grateful for the warmth when I get in.'

It occurred to neither of them that for the first time he had addressed her by her Christian name, it arose so naturally out of the situation in which they found themselves.

'Yes, I have been cold all day,' Madeleine agreed. She looked round the bare tent, with its straight rows of narrow beds, heated only by a stove in a depression in the middle of the earth floor. 'Richard, can nothing better than this be arranged?'

He smiled. 'It looks pretty awful, I know, but believe me, it's the best arrangement. Dr. Swinburne is an expert and his belief is that the cold fresh air keeps infection at bay. I must say I am inclined to agree with him. There are cases of septicaemia at the hospital in the Grand Hotel, but so far we have none here — and gangrene, you know, is our great enemy when we are dealing with amputations and open wounds.'

Madeleine shuddered. 'I know so little,' she said.

'You have done very well,' he said gently. 'Now, go home — and that's an order.'

'I have already learnt the correct answer to that,' Madeleine said with a slight smile. 'Yes, doctor!'

13

News of the fighting was sent to London both by the carrier pigeon messages which left Paris and by the British newspaper reporters observing the action from the German side, and was read with deep concern by the British public, not least by the few people who were aware that Lady Chilcote was incarcerated in Paris. Only Charlie Carford had the courage to broach the subject to Lord Chilcote. When Janus left Laycott Manor in a white heat of fury and revulsion he had returned to London and embarked on a determined course of dissipation which made the people who had said hopefully that he had been vastly improved by his marriage shake their heads in regret, or in some cases, satisfaction. The leopard was not capable of changing his spots was the general verdict, and where was his lovely wife? Madeleine's whereabouts remained a mystery until Charlie enquired one day whether she would be joining Janus at Chilcote House.

'Nothing wrong, I hope?' he asked when he got nothing but a curt negative to this question.

'There is plenty wrong,' Janus replied. 'But I don't, if you will excuse me, propose to discuss my marital difficulties with you, Charlie.'

'No, no . . . no wish to pry, old chap,' Charlie said hastily. 'Just wondered what to say when people asked me where Lady Chilcote is, that's all. Staying down at Laycott Manor, I take it?'

'She's in Paris.'

'Paris! You can't be serious!'

'Perfectly serious.'

'But . . . dash it all, old man, I mean, that could be dangerous! Aren't you going over to fetch her out?'

'No. Why should I?'

'Well, seems obvious to me! She's your wife, got to look after her. How on earth did you come to let her go off to Paris?'

'My permission wasn't asked.'

'I see what it is,' Charlie said. 'You're miffed because Lady Chilcote went off without asking you first. Dashed silly thing to do, of course, but you can't hold that against her when her life may be in danger!'

'It's none of your business, Charlie.'

'Yes it is,' Charlie said with obstinate courage. 'I mean, very fond of Lady Chilcote.'

'Really?' Janus's black eyebrows rose in insolent surprise. 'How strange, you were one man I never suspected.'

'You know, you've got a damned nasty mind,' Charlie said, really stung. 'Nasty! Lady Chilcote never looked at any other man but you. Wouldn't even take any notice when old Bertie was throwing out lures to her. As for me, I never thought of her with anything but the greatest respect. Admiration, if you like, but respect too!'

'Oh, leave it alone, Charlie,' Lord Chilcote said, but Charlie was seriously upset and nothing less than a full apology would satisfy him. He got it, since anything was better than listening to him going on about the subject of Madeleine. Janus left him as soon as he could and continued his determined search for the oblivion that eluded him. Nothing could drive the memory of Madeleine from his mind for very long. He saw her in every tall, blonde woman who crossed his path, and yet nothing could equal the grace of her movements, the exquisite turn of her head when she looked back to smile at him. She haunted him, lovely and remote. Damnably remote. Had he ever really possessed her? Was it possible that they could have lived for so many months in apparent intimacy and she had concealed from him the fact that she had borne a child to Henri de Cavaillon, especially when she had spoken with apparent frankness of the abortion which she said had been forced on her. Perhaps she had thought he would draw the line at taking over a living child. Could she really have borne a child and remained so apparently untouched by the experience? The memory of her smooth, unmarked flesh was an enduring torment. When Charlie, alarmed by the accounts of the bitter fighting outside Paris, again raised the question of a rescue operation for Madeleine, the response he got was even fiercer and more negative than it had been the first time he had made the suggestion.

If Madeleine, immured in Paris, had no knowledge of her husband's almost demented pursuit of pleasure, she understood him well enough to guess his frame of mind. Like Charlie, she had cherished a hope that he might rescue her, but gradually she had come to the sad conclusion that he could not want her to return. Otherwise, with his connections and determination, there must surely be some way of getting her out. It was not easy, but people had left and she heard of their departure with a composure which concealed her hurt. She thought of him constantly, always with regret and often with resentment. She was ashamed of the way her body craved for him, even while her mind and fierce, hurt pride tried to suppress the memory of him.

She found an outlet for her starved affections in caring for the little Véronique when she had leisure from her new duties at the American Ambulance, teaching the little girl as she had once taught her small cousin Harry, except that to Véronique she taught the English nursery rhymes her own mother had sung to her when she was a child. Richard Anthony, coming home one day from an exhausting tour of duty, found the pair of them in Madeleine's room, both seated on the floor and playing with some painted wooden bricks Madeleine had bought for Véronique before wood became too precious to be made into play things. He heard her voice singing as he came up the stairs and paused to listen, then with a brief tap at the door, he went in. Madeleine looked up, a little confused at being caught in such a lowly posture, but smiling a welcome nevertheless, while Véronique immediately scrambled to her feet and held up her arms to 'M'sieur Anthony'. His silence surprised her, but he looked down at Madeleine and said in a low, moved voice: 'You don't know what it means to me, to come home and find this . . . this normality here.'

He stooped and picked up the little girl, who was clamouring for attention, and then held out his hand to assist Madeleine to her feet. She took his hand and clasped it warmly as she got up. Richard turned his head away and gave Véronique a kiss and she responded with a big, wet kiss from her warm little mouth in the middle of his cheek. He laughed, but in his heart he knew that it was not the child he longed to hold in his arms, but her companion.

In an effort to hide his emotion, he put the little girl down and squatted down in his turn on the floor. 'Have you been having a good game?' he asked.

'We have been playing at building houses,' Madeleine said.

'Have you? Look, Véronique, this was the game I liked to play with bricks when I was a little boy. You build up a tower, like this — high, high, as high as it will go — and then boom! down it crashes!'

There were delighted screams of excitement from Véronique, but something in the quality of the silence behind him made him turn his head enquiringly. Madeleine was staring at the fallen tower with dilated eyes. Richard scrambled to his feet. 'Is anything wrong?' he asked in concern.

'No . . . no, it's just that there has been so much destruction,' Madeleine said. 'I don't like to see it being re-enacted in play.'

He thought that she was referring to the

destruction of the war and he was instantly remorseful. 'It's time you were in bed, Véronique, *chérie*,' he said. 'I will take you back to *gran 'mère*.'

'Véronique has grown thinner,' he said when he returned.

'We have all grown thinner,' Madeleine said quietly. 'But it is hardest on the children. Madame Soubise has not been able to get any milk this week.'

'There is food to be had . . . of a sort,' Richard said.

'If you can afford it,' Madeleine replied. She did not tell him that she had that day made a very difficult decision. She now had little money left, and money was necessary if one was to eat in Paris. She had decided to sell her engagement ring. With the worldly wisdom she had learnt from bitter experience, she had not gone to a small, back street jeweller. Instead, she had dressed herself in the best of the clothes she had brought with her to Paris and had visited one of the most expensive jewellers in the town, now sadly lacking in customers except those on the same errand as herself. She had explained who she was and had offered her ring for sale on the understanding that if it could be sold at a profit the jeweller was free to part with it, but that if it remained in his hands on the almost unimaginable day when Paris would be relieved, then Lord Chilcote would undoubtedly redeem it for his wife. She had little faith in Lord Chilcote doing anything of the sort, but she was determined to strike the hardest bargain she could, and she was not dissatisfied with the sum she had obtained. In celebration, she had purchased a goose at the exorbitant price of thirty francs and now she was able to offer Richard Anthony a share in her feast.

'It's rumoured that there is to be another sortie,' he said abruptly as they sat over their meal.

'Will it be successful?' Madeleine asked in a low voice.

Their eyes met. 'I wish I could say yes,' Richard said. 'But now that Metz has fallen the whole might of the Prussian army is concentrated outside Paris. I'm afraid it can only be a repetition of the last fiasco.'

His fears proved all too well-founded. Again the French army fought hard and again they were repulsed, and the losses were fearful. Richard worked like a demon and Madeleine worked by his side, inured now to sights which would have sickened her only a few weeks earlier. Inevitably, they clung together. Always, when they were both free, they shared their frugal meals, and the life they created for themselves at the Allée Racine was something apart from the harsh demands of the reality outside, a delicate world of warmth and companionship, fragile as a bubble and shimmering with the same iridescent colours. They lavished attention on Véronique, seeing her not only as a hope for the future, but also as an outlet for their own frustrated affections: Richard, fathoms deep in love with this beautiful woman who shared some of his worst hours and yet was always able to create an illusion of civilisation, even graciousness, when they were alone together, and Madeleine, caught up in events more dreadful than she could ever have imagined, despairing of her future with her indifferent husband, and turning in relief to the man who gave her not only his unspoken admiration, but also something she had looked for in vain from Lord Chilcote, a share in his life's work.

Her work at the Ambulance brought her one encounter she would rather have been spared. She had been helping to serve a meagre meal to the soldiers who were sufficiently recovered to be able to eat, and she was engaged in scraping the plates and piling them together for washing up, when a voice behind her said: 'Surely I am not mistaken? No — it is Madeleine, Madeleine Ardingley!'

Madeleine turned slowly. This was something she had always feared as a result of her unexpectedly long sojourn in Paris, a meeting with someone who would recognise her from the time when she was kept by Henri de Cavaillon, but of all the people she recalled from that time the one she least wished to meet again was the actress who had exposed her to Madame Bécaud.

The other woman, a few years older than Madeleine, appeared not to notice the cold silence with which her greeting was received. To Madeleine it seemed incredible that someone who had served her such an ill turn should speak to her with apparent friendliness and expect to be treated the same way in return.

'What are you doing here, *chérie?*' the older woman asked. 'I thought you'd gone to England? Poor Henri was quite beside himself when he learned about it. He died — did you know? Also in England as it happens.'

'Yes, I knew,' Madeleine said.

'And you never went back to him? You were a fool, you know. Poor dear Henri, so generous and so devoted to you! All that trouble he went to to get you back! I still think about it. I could die laughing when I remember that woman's face — what was her name? — when I told her all about you!'

'You knew very little about me if you thought I would ever go back to Henri de Cavaillon after that,' Madeleine said.

'Oh, well, he had his funny ways, I suppose, but don't they all? What are you doing now, *chérie?*'

'Nursing.'

'Oh, of course — aren't we all? But I'm only here so as to be able to say I worked at the American Ambulance. I shan't stay more than a few days, then I'm off to one of the private houses which have been turned into hospitals. Much better than these draughty tents and not half the work to do. Why don't you come and join me? Much better chances than you have here, especially amongst the ones who are convalescing, if you see what I mean.'

'I am very well satisfied here,' Madeleine said through stiff lips.

'Well, aren't you lucky to be able to say so! It's more than I am, I can tell you. Have you got a friend these days?'

'I am married,' Madeleine said, understanding only too well the significance of her use of the word 'friend'.

'No! Congratulations, or is that the word? You can't have done very well for yourself if you have to work as a kitchen skivvy.'

'I am here from choice,' Madeleine said. She drew herself up. 'My recollection of our last meeting is not happy. It surprises me that you feel so little remorse for the part you played in denouncing me to Madame Bécaud. I cannot find it in my heart to forgive you and I do not wish to speak to you again.'

The other woman's face reddened; she stared at Madeleine with a mixture of chagrin and discomforture, then she tossed her head and turned away, muttering to herself as she departed. Madeleine bent over her pile of dishes with their unsavoury scraps of congealed food and felt her eyes filling with tears. Again she was interrupted, this time by Richard.

'We are going to have to fit in at least one, and possibly two, extra patients into each tent,' he said. 'Will you liaise with the Stores over the necessary supplies? You know what is needed . . . Madeleine, is anything wrong?'

'No, no. I'm sorry,' she said, trying to keep her face turned away from him.

He glanced round. It was impossible to be private with her there. Grasping her by the arm he draw her outside into the cold, dark evening. 'Now, tell me,' he commanded.

'It was only . . . only that I saw someone I

knew,' Madeleine faltered. It was a miserably inadequate explanation of her distress and she dreaded having to explain herself further, but to her mingled relief and shame he wholly misunderstood her meaning.

'My poor dear girl! How upsetting for you! Of course, with your long knowledge of Paris it was almost bound to happen. Is he one of the severely wounded?'

She felt obliged to try and disabuse him of this misapprehension. 'Not . . . not one of the wounded,' she said, but again he misunderstood and leaped to the assumption that she meant that the friend she had seen had been amongst the dead.

'My dear, my dear,' he murmured, and gathered her up against him in a warm, comforting clasp, not realising that it was his own kindness that made her weep still more bitterly, and not the loss of a friend.

She lifted her face, but he could only dimly make it out, a white blur in the dusk. Without realising it, he tightened his hold.

'Oh, Richard, you are so good,' Madeleine murmured brokenly. Her head drooped against his shoulder and he laid his hand gently on it, pressing it against him in an unconsciously tender gesture. They stood like that for a moment and then Madeleine whispered: 'Thank you. I am better now.'

'Sure?'

'Yes.' She raised her hand and touched him on the cheek, the tiniest pat of gratitude, but he seized her hand and pressed it against his lips.

Madeleine caught her breath. 'Richard?'

He raised his head and said her name in a hoarse, broken voice, 'Madeleine! Madeleine!'

Before she could recover from the surprise which filled her, he had found her lips and kissed her long and hard. Carried away by the force and unexpectedness of his passion, for a few long moments she acquiesced, and then she stirred restlessly in his arms, turning her head away from his questing lips, and said: 'No, Richard, no! I cannot, I must not . . . you forget that I am married!'

His grasp slackened, but he did not entirely let go of her. 'I don't forget it,' he said. 'Never. Madeleine, you must let me tell you . . . '

'No!' she interrupted him. 'Nothing more! If we are to go on being friends then this must be forgotten. I was too wrought up to know what I was doing and you are overtired . . . emotional . . . '

'No, I'm not,' he began, but again she stopped him.

'Let it go, Richard, please!' she said with a note of real command in her voice, and he subsided.

'You won't drop me because of this, will you?' he said.

'Of course not. As I have said, we are friends and there is no reason why that should not continue.'

She knew that she was being less than honest. What Richard felt for her was not friendship and she had been unforgiveably blind not to have seen it before; and what she felt for him was not merely friendship either. It was true that when she had clung to him it had been in a moment of distress, out of nothing more than a need for support and comfort, but that did not account for the strong warm tide that had swept through her at the height of his passionate kiss, leaving her weak and trembling, with the suspicion that if he had taken away his arms immediately she would not have been able to stand alone.

It was not easy to admit that, just as the lack of Henri's attentions had once driven her into Janus's bed (but, no, it was more than that, much more than that! her tired mind protested), so now her estrangement from her husband had rendered her susceptible to the love of this attractive young man. She turned away from the idea with loathing, refusing to admit that she could be open to temptation. It was not so; her liking for the young American had nothing physical in it, and that one disturbing moment had been born out of weakness, nothing more. She had been tired, shocked by her unexpected encounter with a figure from the past, a little faint; and when the memory of a long, hard body pressed against her own disturbed her mind it was Janus she was thinking of; Janus, not Richard.

She tried to resume their friendly relations as if nothing had happened, but she could not help being a little stiff and they were not as easy with one another as they had been before. Richard accepted it as no more than natural. He had a deep, inbred reverence for women, and Madeleine he almost worshipped. He did not find it strange that she should hold herself a little aloof from him now that she knew that he loved her. He accepted it humbly and did his best to keep his unruly emotions under control, and since he was a resilient young man he even managed to smile and seem as light-hearted as the times they were living in would allow, so that Madeleine let herself believe that the dangerous moment had passed and would not recur and she could enjoy Richard's company once more without troubling her conscience about the effect that their intimacy might have on both of them.

It took the death of Lulu finally to quench the laughter in Richard's eyes. The rumour that she had been hurt by a fragment of shell while on a risky scavenging hunt for potatoes after persuading the soldiers to let her pass outside the barricades flew through the *quartier*, but no-one knew how badly she had been hit. The story was told to Madeleine by the *blanchisseuse* and repeated by Madame Soubise as soon as she entered the courtyard and passed by the doorway of the *conciergerie*. It was another two hours before Richard came in and confirmed not only that it was true, but that the girl had died of her injuries.

'I was in time to see her,' he said, his young face haggard. 'She couldn't speak, but I held her hand and I think she knew I was there.' He turned away, unable to hide his distress.

'I am truly grieved,' Madeleine said gently. 'We shall all miss her very much indeed.'

'I shall miss her more than most,' Richard

said, driven to a confidence he would not normally have made. 'I . . . we were . . . '

'Yes, I know,' Madeleine said quickly, sparing him the embarrassment of spelling out his relationship with the dead girl.

Richard's face reddened. 'I didn't realise you knew. I suppose I might have guessed. Lulu had . . . no shame. It was one of the things one couldn't help liking about her. I was not . . . not really in love with her, I suppose, but I was very, very fond of her.'

Again his voice broke. Madeleine took his hand and pressed it in wordless sympathy. Still too overcome to guard his tongue, he said, 'I feel particularly badly because I sort of neglected her recently. I pretended that it was because I was over-worked, but it wasn't altogether true. Lulu guessed, I think, but she didn't *seem* to be hurt. Now, I feel I behaved heartlessly.'

Madeleine withdrew her hand, her heart beating uncomfortably fast. This was too close to a renewed declaration of his love for her to be encouraged.

'She took life very easily,' she said. 'Dear Lulu. She would be the last person to reproach you for any fancied neglect, particularly knowing how hard-pressed you are. We must remember her with kindness, as she would remember us.'

There was a brief pause and then Richard accepted her refusal to allow him to approach the subject of his feelings for her. With a muttered apology he left her and climbed the stairs to his own lonely apartment.

There was a new grimness about him after

312

that. The boy who had so charmed Madeleine when she had first known him had disappeared for ever. In his place there was a man deeply committed to the relief of suffering, who had lived to repent his careless anticipation of the 'excitement' of war. They rarely spoke about the hospital during the leisure hours they spent together. By common consent their talk turned to other, less demanding, subjects. Richard described his childhood in America and was amused by the way he could hold Madeleine enthralled with tales of the backwoods and prairies. She was more reticent than he realised when it came to reciprocating with stories of her younger days, but by careful editing she gave him a version of her convent girlhood which was as exotic to his ears as his stories of Red Indians were to hers. Of her life in England she never spoke and since the last thing he wanted to hear was talk about her husband he never enquired about that period in her life.

The weather became bitter, a terrible freezing winter which took its toll of the young children and the inadequately fed. Richard began to number civilians amongst his patients, fitting them in as best he could between bouts of duty at the American hospital, and sick with frustration at the little he could do for them without milk and vegetables and good, red meat, and fuel for their often squalid hovels. Inevitably the day came when he stumbled home, worn to the bone by fatigue and the nagging feeling of inadequacy, and broke down as he tried to explain to Madeleine what had kept him away from the house for eighteen hours at a stretch. His voice broke as he told her of the children who had died, the man whose leg he had not been able to save, the young woman who had given birth and whose baby could not hope to survive. He turned away, fighting for self control, and Madeleine, in an agony of compassion, went to him and put her arms round him.

'Richard, my dear, my dear,' she said. 'You have done too much, you are too tired to be rational. Yes, I know about the failures, but think of the people you have been able to help! Remember Pierre Bougainville and how triumphant you were when he was able to move his fingers after your operation; think of Marc Lemaître, who is walking thanks to you, on crutches I know, but alive and able to get around.'

He buried his face in her crown of golden hair. 'You are my one comfort,' he said. 'Madeleine, I love you. Beyond all hope or reason. If I had not had you to come to I think I would have gone out of my mind before this, from the sheer hopelessness of it all.'

She drew back, deeply troubled by this confession she had held at bay for so long. Her voice was faint as she reminded him yet again, 'I am married', but her eyes searched his face as she spoke, trying to find the answer not to his feelings, but her own.

'Yes, I know,' he agreed. 'There is no hope for me, is there?'

She did not answer and he took sudden fire from her silence. 'Madeleine, my darling, if you can feel even a tenth of what I feel for you, then I beg you to say so.'

His arms closed round her strongly, his fatigue forgotten, and she looked up into his face with searching, bewildered eyes, trying to discover the reason for her suddenly awakened desire to hold him and comfort him. He was Richard, her dear companion, the man she had come to admire and respect, but he was also an ardent young man, long limbed and goodlooking, with eager lips and arms which held her as she had not been held since the days, an interminable age ago, when Janus had sought her out. Her treacherous body stirred. Almost without volition her head tilted back, her lips half open, her eyelids drooping. It was a temptation no man could resist. Carried away on a tide of passion he had never hoped to satisfy, Richard Anthony kissed her wildly again and again, murmuring broken words of endearment. Madeleine herself caught fire from his ardour. She twisted her arms around his neck and returned his kisses, pressing herself against him, until at last when Richard said brokenly: 'Madeleine, please . . . please, darling, please . . . ' she committed herself to him with no more than a tiny movement of her head, assenting to his love without ever having said that she loved him in return, without even knowing whether it was true or not.

He fell into an exhausted slumber as soon

315

as they had made love, but Madeleine lay wakeful, staring into the dark, cradling him in her arms, while out of the past the memory came back to her of an arrogant voice which stated categorically, 'I demand fidelity.'

14

It was December before Janus received the letter Madeleine had written to him with such high hopes weeks earlier. The balloon to which it had been entrusted had been blown hundreds of miles off course, the bag of mail had been jettisoned and it had only been found by accident, but the letter was eventually delivered, water stained and almost illegible. It lay on his breakfast table and he looked at it with distaste, not realising at first what message this grimy piece of paper contained. His head was aching abominably, so much so that he wondered in a detached fashion whether he was at last succeeding in undermining his previously impervious constitution by the treatment to which he was subjecting it. The simplicity of the letter, when he eventually made it out, stabbed him to the heart. Every word of it breathed Madeleine to him, to such an extent that at the first reading he missed the implications of the message to Jeanne. He spread out the thin sheet and read it through again:

'My dear husband,

I am safe and well. I tried to leave Paris, but I was not allowed to pass. Please tell Jeanne that her little daughter is with me and I am taking as much care of her as I can. There is little I can write in a letter which must be left open, but I am sorry that we parted in anger. Please forgive me for coming to France without your knowledge, and allow me to call myself what I have always wished to be,

Your loving wife,
Madeleine'

'*Tell Jeanne that her daughter is with me . . .* '

Jeanne's daughter! He sat for a long time over his neglected breakfast table and then got up without tasting a morsel.

'Have the horses put to. I am leaving for Laycott within the hour,' he said as he crossed the hall.

He might have taken the train, but he chose to drive himself to his home in Kent and when he arrived he went straight to his great aunt, sitting disconsolately by the fire with nothing but her gardening journal and her dreams of the following summer to console her for the bitter weather.

'I've heard from Madeleine,' he said without any preliminaries.

'Thank God!' Mrs. Ardingley said, and meant it literally. 'How is the dear girl? Is she well?'

'She was when she wrote, but that was weeks ago. I want to see that maid of hers, and then I intend going over to France to see what I can do to get her out.'

Mrs. Ardingley shook her head. 'You are too late to see Jeanne,' she said quietly. 'Poor soul, she died two days ago.'

Janus took a turn about the room, unable to keep still in his fever of impatience to start on a journey which he knew now should have been undertaken weeks, if not months, earlier. 'Perhaps it's as well,' he said. 'I might have done her a mischief if I had met her face to face. I wanted to hear an admission from her own lips of the lies she told me about Madeleine, but after all what does it matter? I know now that they *were* lies.'

'What is your plan?' Gertrude Ardingley asked, her eyes fixed on his anguished face.

'I imagine I shall be able to get as far as the Prussian Head-quarters at Versailles. After that . . . it depends on who I can see and how much I can impress him. It's a pity I don't speak German.'

Mrs. Ardingley shook her head. 'You are going about it in quite the wrong way,' she said. 'A General conducting a war will have little time to spare for an importunate Englishman seeking his wife. You have powerful allies; use them!'

He paused in his restless perambulation about the room, struck by the extreme good sense of what she said. 'The Prince of Wales!' he said. 'If he wrote to King Wilhelm . . . '

'That's aiming a little high,' Mrs. Ardingley interrupted. 'But a note from His Royal Highness to his brother-in-law, the Crown Prince, that would undoubtedly have a beneficial effect.'

'You are absolutely right.' In an unusual gesture of affection, he bent over her and kissed her on the cheek. She put her hand over his and held it tightly for a moment. 'If all else fails, I will write to the Queen,' she said.

'Bringing up the big guns,' he said. 'Thank

you. Of course, if I manage to get the Germans to let me pass, I shall still have to deal with the French — they may not let me in!'

It took him days to obtain the letter he required from the Prince, who happened to be out of London, and to his fretting impatience the waiting seemed interminable, nor did he find his journey across France as easy as it would have been in peace time. Again, when he eventually reached Versailles and presented his letter to a Court official, he had to wait to know what the result of it would be. There was great activity at Versailles, messengers coming and going, troops constantly on the move, and the noise of gunfire incessantly in the air. To his surprise, Janus was received by the Crown Prince personally, a bearded, likeable man who showed the utmost sympathy with Lord Chilcote's desire to seek out his wife.

'But you have chosen a bad time to make your request,' he said. 'The French have made yet another sortie out of Paris and hard fighting is going on. You cannot be allowed to pass through a battlefield. When the fighting has died down, then we will see what can be done for you, though you may not find the French so amenable to your request. They have something of a mania about Prussian spies, I understand, and they may suspect your motives for entering the city, and mine for promoting your cause.'

Since there was no help for it, Janus waited with such patience as he could muster. What he saw of the fighting filled him with horror. The sufferings of the wounded were terrible, not least because of the appalling weather which froze them to the ground in their own congealed blood. He visited some of the French wounded who were being cared for in German hospitals by the Sisters of Mercy and what he learned from them about conditions in Paris drove away what little sleep he had been able to take since his arrival.

Christmas came and went. Janus spent it with a party of English journalists, but their conviviality grated on him and he excused himself early. He was full of unease. Something about the size of the guns he had seen being brought up to the German lines alarmed him by their implications of enormous power. His fears were not in vain; two days later the bombardment of Paris began.

He applied, with all the politeness he could bring himself to use, to one of the Crown Prince's aides-de-camp for news of his application to enter Paris and the vagueness of the reply he received filled him with foreboding. He continued to wait, the noise of the guns thundering in his head, until he grew reckless from impatience. He went up with some of his newly-acquired journalist friends to observe the action at close quarters and looked thoughtfully at the dismal area which had been covered by the fighting.

'Have any of you made any attempt to get into Paris?' he asked with studied carelessness.

'Not much point,' his companion replied. 'Once in, you can't get out, and the methods of sending news out are primitive, to say the least. I dare say the Prussians have tried to put one or two scouts in, but I don't know how successful they have been.'

'If one were to join a stretcher party . . . ' Janus said slowly.

'And switch to the other side?' The reporter shot him a shrewd glance. 'How well do you speak French?'

'Well enough to make myself understood,' Janus said. 'Not well enough to pass for a Frenchman.'

'You'd be shot,' the reporter said, abandoning all pretence that they were discussing a hypothetical case. 'I wouldn't try it if I were you.'

It took rather more than that to dissuade Janus Chilcote from attempting something on which he had set his heart. That night, before the moon came up, he slipped away and began picking his way across the disputed territory between the outposts of the French and German commands. The air was freezing and the ice crackled in the puddles beneath his feet. The ground, churned up by the passage of feet and vehicles, and pitted by shell holes, was not easy to cover, still less to cover with stealth. His efforts to move silently were constantly frustrated by the broken ground, frozen into deep ruts, beneath his feet. A rough shelter loomed ahead of him. He heard voices and froze into immobility. A German sentry came out and began flapping his arms across his chest in an effort to get warm. He turned away and Janus moved forward again, one slow step at a time, his eyes fixed on the dark hulk of the heavily-coated figure showing vaguely against the night sky.

His preoccupation with the sentry was his downfall. His foot slipped on a patch of ice and, with a noise which sounded in his own ears like a stampede by a herd of elephants, he fell forward, headlong into a hole which seemed to open up beneath him. There was a flurry of activity above him. The sentry shouted a hoarse question and, after the briefest of pauses, Janus called back to him. He shouted that he was a friend, but he doubted whether the man understood him: certainly the hands which helped him out of his muddy pit were far from friendly. He was hauled into the shelter and two suspicious Teutons fired a series of guttural questions at him. His unintelligible replies did nothing to allay their suspicions, but he managed to make them understand that he was English and not French, and he gathered that they had decided to hold him prisoner until the arrival of their officer on his rounds.

It was a long wait. Janus toyed with the idea of making a dash for it out of the shelter, but for all the apparent carelessness with which the two soldiers stood guard over him, they were professionals and well trained, and he had no doubt that they would shoot him without compunction if he attempted to escape. The officer arrived at last, a smart young man who spoke a reasonable amount of English. Fuming inwardly, Janus revealed his identity. He judged that the young officer would be more impressed by a show of high-handedness than by any note of regret and so he adopted a haughty tone, spoke of his recent audience with the Crown Prince and demanded to be taken immediately out of this filthy hovel and restored to his own apartment in Versailles. It was galling to be sent back under the escort of his two captors, but once his identity had been confirmed he was allowed to return to his lodging with the ominous warning that he would be required to account for his actions later in the day.

He stumbled up the stairs, worn out with fatigue and the frustrations of the night, and his reporter friend, awakened by the sound of loud German voices below his window, came out to the landing, sleepy and yawning, to see what was happening.

He snapped awake when he saw Janus. 'You tried to get through the German lines and failed,' he guessed. 'I had my suspicions when I realised you hadn't returned to Versailles. More fool you, my lord. I warned you what would happen. You can think yourself lucky not to have been killed.'

'Go to the devil!' Janus snarled.

The other man, inured to insults, took no notice. He glanced down at Janus's feet and said in sudden concern: 'Are you hurt? You're bleeding!'

'No, I'm not hurt,' Janus said impatiently. 'My feet are wet, that's all.'

They both looked down at the light-coloured wooden floor beneath his feet. Behind him a trail of red footprints mounted the stairs and advanced along the corridor.

'The puddles were iced over. I broke through the ice as I walked and trod in what I took for water,' Janus said.

The other man nodded. 'Pools of blood and melted snow, with a crust of ice. I've seen them myself.'

With a spasm of disgust about his mouth, Janus knelt down and tried to undo the laces of his boots with stiff, cold fingers. The other man darted into his own room and came back with a knife in his hand. 'For God's sake, man, cut them! And when you've got them off come into my room and I'll give you a jigger of brandy to warm you up.'

Lord Chilcote had need of brandy inside him to sustain him through the brief interview he was granted with the Crown Prince later that morning.

'You have betrayed my trust, my lord,' the Prince said. 'I treated you as a friend of his Royal Highness; I promised you that everything possible would be done to help you to find your wife. Could you not be patient?'

Janus, cleaned up and carefully shaven, but grey-faced and red-eyed from sleeplessness, raised his head. 'Listen,' he said. In the distance the constant thud of the guns had begun again. The eyes of the two men met. 'My wife is inside that town you are shelling,' Janus said. 'Was it really necessary, this bombardment of the civilian population?'

The Crown Prince looked suddenly old and weary. 'You have seen the battle ground, you have visited the hospitals,' he said. 'The present situation cannot go on. Paris has held out beyond all expectation, the loss of life has been frightful. You spoke of the civilian population, but as long as they stand out against us they are all our enemies.'

'Do you really believe that?'

The Prince glanced round. His aide-de-camp was out of earshot. 'I must believe it. How else could I go on?' He got up from his desk. 'You will have to exercise a little more patience, Lord Chilcote. I am sorry to say that the French have refused your request to enter Paris.'

'I suspected as much,' Janus said. 'That is why I . . . '

'Took matters into your own hands? It was a foolish thing to do. You do not deserve it; indeed, you deserve that I should have you shipped back to England forthwith, but I will tell you in confidence that there is every possibility of an armistice soon and then I will see that you are given facilities to enter Paris.'

Again they paused and listened to the crash of the great guns. 'God send it is not too late,' Janus said evenly.

He might have been reassured if he had been able to see the insouciance with which the Parisians treated the bombardment, apparently regarding it more as a curiosity and a topic for conversation than a serious threat to life and limb. The damage was not as great as the Prussians believed, nor was the loss of life as horrifying as Lord Chilcote feared. It was nevertheless an added hazard to moving from one part of the city to another, there were ugly gaps amongst the houses, and everyone had a horrible story to tell of someone who had been blown to pieces, if not before their own eyes, then before the eyes of someone they knew intimately, and sometimes these stories were true.

For Madeleine, with her ingrained fear of falling masonry, harking back to the horror of Henri de Cavaillon's death, the bombardment had a particular terror, which she strove to conceal. Since she never spoke to Richard Anthony of her agonised memories, he saw nothing in the fervour with which she clung to him but an echo of his own passion, and she did not feel able to reveal to her young lover that part of the welcome she extended to him arose from her desperate fear of sleeping alone in case the roof fell in on her. The thought came to her one night that Janus would have known, but then Janus was acquainted with her past history. It was not — it was *not* that he had any special insight which was denied to Richard. She loved Richard, he gave her comfort and warm pleasure, and yet her mind turned to Janus and try as she might she could not wholly dismiss the memory of him.

Richard consistently overworked and she, sharing his labours, was often speechless with fatigue. Although he habitually slept in her bed they often clung together more for the comfort of another human presence and for warmth than because of their need for love. As the days wore on and the fighting continued and the terrible civilian casualties increased, Richard turned to her in frantic bouts of passion which seemed to be the only thing to give him release from the bitter frustration which consumed him in the face of his helplessness to stop the senseless slaughter. She submitted to all his demands, readily and lovingly, but she sometimes wondered whether he realised how he exhausted her. She was very patient with him, knowing that he found no fault in her, that everything she did was perfect in his eyes. She laughed at him sometimes for his blatant worship, but it made her a little uneasy. She was not perfect, not the goddess he believed her to be, but full of human frailty, as Janus had known full well. It was when thoughts like that occurred to her that she pulled down a shutter on her thoughts. Janus, that distant, cold and indifferent figure, belonged to the past; Richard was the future.

He spoke of that future to her one day as she lay in his arms, a little hesitantly, since it involved the difficult question of a divorce from her husband.

'Would you marry me, if you were free?' he asked.

'Would you ask me?' Madeleine countered.

'You bet I would! Madeleine, it would be a terrible ordeal for you, I know, but could you bear to go through a divorce for me? You do have divorce in Britain, don't you?'

'It is difficult, but it can be arranged,' Madeleine said. 'A husband can divorce his wife for adultery, but not the other way round.'

'Would Lord Chilcote . . . '

'With alacrity, I imagine,' Madeleine said.

'Unless it offended his pride. I don't know. Oh, Richard, let us survive this terrible war first and then think about the future!' She put her arms round his neck, pulled his head down and began to kiss him, and in the wild delight she invoked in him he overlooked the fact that she had not replied to his question, but Madeleine knew that she had avoided giving him an answer and she was ashamed of her evasion. It was unfair, it was wrong, to use him in this way; to accept his love and think of another man. She had the curious thought that she was like a woman who submitted dutifully to the embraces of her husband while dreaming of her absent lover, which was absurd when it was Richard who was her lover, and Richard who was offering her the chance of a new life away from the European scene which held so many regrets for her.

She treated him with a new gentleness after this conversation. He noticed it and believed that it was because she considered herself his future wife, and he was happy, in spite of the discomforts of their life. Food was now a major problem, but it was his great pride that because of the provisions he was able to draw from the American Embassy he could at least spare her from the worst effects of hunger, and although they had some strange meals they never actually descended to eating the rats which some people claimed to find palatable, nor was he ever conscious of having eaten a cat or a dog. He used his influence to obtain a cut or two of some of the less exotic zoo animals when they were slaughtered, but nothing he could do could secure a regular supply of milk for the little Véronique, and he could only be thankful that she was no younger; he had seen some sad cases of malnutrition amongst the babies.

Their supply of wood began to run low, and still the terrible cold continued. The Government appealed to the people not to take matters into their own hands, chopping down such trees as remained standing and raiding woodyards, and promised to make supplies available. Since they could not keep the stove burning for more than two or three days longer with the wood stacked in the cellar, Madeleine undertook to fetch a fresh supply one day towards the end of January. She set out, dressed in one of Richard's coats, with a woollen scarf tied over her head, and pulling a handcart — a fine costume and a fine occupation for the elegant Lady Chilcote, she thought to herself with a sardonic smile as she tucked her hair away beneath the grey woollen scarf.

She had chosen her time carefully in the hope of avoiding the worst hours of the daily bombardment, although she was not really sure whether it was worse to be caught out in the street by the whining shells or to sit indoors enduring the fear of being trapped. It was on these days when she was not on duty at the hospital that she found her nerves frayed by the constant anticipation of being hit; when she was occupied by the immediate life and death struggle of the hospital tents she could forget her own safety. It was unfortunate that the visit to the woodyard took far longer than she had anticipated, nor did she find there the spirit of helpfulness which normally characterised the Parisians faced by a young and pretty woman struggling to perform a task too heavy for her. The mood was one of sullen apathy and people watched indifferently while she loaded her cart with roughly-cut logs, more intent on securing their own share than in giving her any assistance. The woman next to her said, without any preliminary, 'Have you heard? They're talking of us giving in.'

Madeleine stared at her. 'You mean . . . capitulation?' she asked, as if it were something which had never crossed her mind before.

The man behind her joined in. 'An armistice, so they say. We're beaten, or at least the politicians are: the people would have carried on.'

'Would they?' the first woman asked. 'Speak for yourself! I'm tired of seeing my children go without food and I want my man back. I don't know whether he's dead or alive; he might have frozen to death at the barricades for all I know, let alone got a Prussian bullet through him.'

'You've had it hard, mother,' the man said. 'There's some have had a soft time of it. There'll be changes made once we've got rid of the Germans, I can tell you.'

The woman gave a harsh laugh. 'One of those Reds, are you? I'll tell you something, *mon vieux*; it don't make a mite of difference to me who's got the power at the top; it's people like me and mine who always get the hard end of the bargain!'

Madeleine finished loading her pile of logs and left them to what promised to become a heated political argument, reflecting that it was as well that they had become so absorbed in one another since, no matter what their political opinions, they would both have been bitterly offended to see the joy with which she had received the news of a possible armistice. To her it meant relese. Her footsteps slowed as she realised that it also meant that she would have to reach a decision about her future. Richard or Janus? Or would the choice be made for her if Janus threw her over? What would she do if he refused either to receive her back as his wife or to release her to marry Richard? What ever protestations Richard might make, it would clearly be impossible for her to go back to America with him and live as his wife without marrying him. She would not starve, whatever happened; sheer stiff-necked pride would prevent Janus from allowing his wife to want for the necessities of life, but it would be just like him to give her a lavish allowance and refuse to see her again. Was she even sure which of them she wanted? Dear Richard, who seemed so young, not only in years but also in experience, such a fine person and deeply and truly in love with her; or Janus — what good could she find to say about Janus?

She was so absorbed in her thoughts that the renewal of the bombardment took her by surprise. She was suddenly jolted out of her reverie by the sound of a shell passing overhead and a dull crump as it landed. She shrank back into a doorway, but although she felt the shock of the explosion there was no visible damage in the street along which she was dragging her cart. She was no more than ten minutes from home, even at the pace she was able to walk with the heavy load of wood. With a fearful look at the iron grey sky she continued, making as much progress as she could without upsetting the pile of logs. Another explosion shook the ground beneath her feet, but that had been further away and she took courage, telling herself that the gunners were aiming at a different section of the town.

She was within sight of her destination when she heard the next shell overhead. Through the archway of the apartment house she could see Véronique playing in the courtyard, a comical little figure wrapped up in an old shawl belonging to Madame Soubise, crossed over her chest and tied behind, with the long fringe dragging on the ground as she skipped over the cobbles. She saw Madeleine and waved, calling to her in her sweet, high voice. The shell landed, a direct hit on the far side of the building at right angles to the section where Madeleine and Richard lived.

For one second Madeleine stood frozen to the spot and then she began to run, not away but towards her private hell, where the walls swayed and fell and bricks and stones collapsed with a noise like thunder in a cloud of ancient dust, straight to the spot where Henri de Cavaillon's child stood, deafened and bewildered, her small face blank with incomprehension. She reached the small, soft body and swept it up into her arms, but it was

333

too láte to escape. Huddling the child beneath her own body for protection, Madeleine flung herself to the ground. Something struck her a stunning blow on the head. She felt herself going down, down, down into a bottomless pit, with a roaring noise in her ears which masked the sound of mocking laughter, and a vision of dreadful, clutching hands reaching from the grave to pull her into the abyss.

15

Janus heard the news that the armistice had been declared from an unexpected quarter. On the 31st January one of the journalists with whom he had had some contact came up to him in the street.

'Archibald Forbes of the *Daily News*,' he introduced himself abruptly. 'I hear you've been trying to get into Paris? The armistice is official and I'm off to see what news I can gather. You've got a horse, haven't you?'

'Yes,' Janus agreed.

'Good, so have I, which gives me an advantage over most of my fellow scribes. Do you want to come with me? With any luck, we'll be amongst the first in.'

'Does this mean that I'm to have my name plastered all over the Press?' Janus asked drily.

'It might be worth a line or two,' Mr. Forbes said. 'Touching reunion of sporting peer with his wife. So much else to write about that it might not survive the editor. Coming?'

'Indeed I am,' Janus said. 'I have sat around so long inactive I am beginning to rot.'

They approached the city cautiously, but apart from a brush with a party of half-drunken National Guards who had to be satisfied that they were Englishmen and not Prussians, their advent caused remarkably little interest. The streets were quiet, with few people about, and those who saw them pass looked at them with dull, lack-lustre eyes, not even curious about them. Indeed, once they had penetrated the outskirts of the city there was nothing to distinguish Lord Chilcote and his companion from anyone else except a certain air of wellbeing which was noticeably absent amongst the survivors of the siege.

'Things aren't as chaotic as I had imagined,' Mr. Forbes said. 'Everything seems so quiet.'

'Beaten,' Janus said. 'These are people who know they have been defeated and for the moment they are dulled by the effect of the blow to their pride. They will be terrible when they wake up again.'

'You could be right. Have you noticed the number of funerals we have seen, just in this short ride?'

'The last one which passed us was the sixth,' Janus said. 'I have noticed.' He pulled up his horse. 'I am making for somewhere called the Allée Racine,' he said. 'I am grateful for your company, but I would just as soon find my wife on my own.'

'As you wish,' Mr. Forbes agreed. 'I will come with you at least part of the way; it seems to be an area which has felt the effect of the bombardment and I might get some useful copy.'

Lord Chilcote's lips tightened, but he said nothing. He was anxious now to shake off the company of the journalist and to make his own way to his meeting with Madeleine, and they parted at the next street corner.

Janus dismounted and beckoned to a small boy, who seized the proferred money eagerly and undertook to lead the strange gentleman to the address he was seeking and to hold his horse while he was inside, which, if Lord Chilcote had but known it, would have been a sure guarantee of the rapid disappearance of the horse in the direction of the nearest slaughterhouse a few days earlier.

The child let him up a narrow street and then stopped in shocked surprise. 'But it is the house which has been blown up, m'sieur!' he said in horror.

With his eyes on the ruined shell of the building in which he had hoped to find Madeleine, Janus asked in his careful French, 'Was anyone killed, do you know?'

'Three people — the concierge, and a woman and a man — and there were people hurt, too.'

He looked up anxiously into Lord Chilcote's face. 'There are still people living in the part of the house which has not fallen down,' he volunteered.

Janus tossed him the reins. 'I'll go in and see what I can find out,' he said.

Inside, he found the remaining tenants, too poor or too apathetic to move away from the remains of their home, only too eager to supply him with details of the disaster which had struck them. With a patience which did not normally distinguish him he disentangled their garbled versions of what had happened and eventually arrived at the crux of the matter as far as he was concerned — Madeleine's survival.

'Oh, yes, the beautiful young Englishwoman!' one of the tenants exclaimed. 'Alas, monsieur, she was one of the victims of this barbarity.'

Janus stood like a rock. 'Killed?' he asked.

'No, no! But wounded, stunned, crushed beneath the bricks and mortar. The American doctor took her away, and the child also — the little granddaughter of Madame Soubise. Madame Soubise was killed, poor soul.'

Janus wasted no time on regrets for Madame Soubise. 'Where did the American doctor take them?' he asked, but that was more than they could tell him. He managed to get Richard Anthony's name out of them, and armed with this he made his way to the American Embassy. He was received with slightly weary courtesy which warmed to real interest when his identity was known. Lady Chilcote was known to them, her work in the American Ambulance had been invaluable; that she should have been struck down so near the end of hostilities was tragic. Janus, assimilating this without betraying his surprise at the news that Madeleine had apparently become a valued nurse since he last saw her, asked to be told her present whereabouts.

'Dr. Anthony has her under his own personal care,' he was assured. A tiny flicker of consciousness betrayed the fact that the degree of young Richard Anthony's concern for his beautiful neighbour had not gone unremarked, but nothing was actually known about their relationship; they had lived so much out of the way that their secret had not been revealed to Richard's interested countrymen. 'He has taken a suite for her at a hotel not a stone's throw from here. You will find her there.' There was a brief pause and then his informant added conscientiously, 'Not in very good case, I'm afraid.'

'In danger?'

'Not that — at least not to the best of my knowledge and belief — but there were head injuries and I know Dr. Anthony has been very concerned about her condition.'

He got no more than the curtest word of thanks. Once again Janus set off and this time he succeeded in tracking down his wife. He sent up his name and was asked politely to give himself the trouble of mounting to the second floor. Richard Anthony met him at the door, doing his best to conceal the shock he had suffered on being told that Madeleine's absent husband was in Paris. He studied him surreptitiously. Madeleine had said so little about him that Richard was taken by surprise by this tall, harsh-faced man with the piercing dark eyes, who looked at him in a way which made Richard instantly suspect that he knew all about Richard's relations with his wife. He was both younger and more formidable than Richard had believed. Somehow he had unconsciously formed the idea that Madeleine's husband was an elderly and feeble character who allowed his wife to carry out risky projects, such as coming over to France to rescue children in wartime, while he sat at home in comfort. Lord Chilcote's forceful personality and athletic frame came as a shock, disrupting the comfortable picture he had built up and making him someone to be reckoned with in the struggle that was undoubtedly to come over Madeleine's future. He could not like him, that was certain, but he had to admit that the man betrayed a decent anxiety as he asked about his wife.

'Lady Chilcote has suffered severe concussion, she has multiple bruises and two cracked ribs,' Richard Anthony said.

'Has she recovered consciousness?'

'Briefly, but at the moment she has sunk back into what I am afraid must be called a coma.' He hesitated and then said, 'I don't believe there is any lasting damage to the brain, but naturally there must be cause for anxiety.'

'A typical doctor's answer,' Janus Chilcote said. 'You don't know what is the matter, but you give me leave to worry. Thank you!'

Richard's eyes flashed, but he restrained the angry retort that sprang to his lips.

'I would like to see her,' Lord Chilcote said.

Again Richard hesitated, but much as he would have liked to have refused him entrance, he could hardly keep his patient's husband out of her sickroom. 'Only for a minute or two,' he said.

He stood aside and let Janus go in, but he did not leave him alone with Madeleine. Janus looked down at the white face of his unconscious wife. It was thinner than it had been when he last saw her and the white bandage which covered her head gave her a strangely austere look.

'We had to cut off her beautiful hair,' Richard said, and something about the way he spoke made Lord Chilcote give him a thoughtful look.

'How long will she remain like this?' he asked.

'I wish I knew,' Richard answered honestly. 'These cases are always a little unaccountable, of course, but I had hoped to see a change in her before this. As I told you, she roused up quite quickly after she had been dug out and brought here and I believed that the concussion was not severe. She seemed to be quite rational for a brief minute and then some memory seemed to come back to her which made her try to start up as if in horror. I spoke her name, trying to reassure her, but she turned her head away and closed her eyes and sank back into the state you see her in now.'

'You say she had to be dug out?'

'Yes, she and the little girl, Véronique Soubise, were buried beneath the rubble when the walls of the house collapsed. Véronique was sheltered by Madeleine and received little injury, it was Madeleine . . . ' he caught himself up ' . . . Lady Chilcote, who received the main weight of the collapsed wall on her body. Strangely enough, her injuries might have been much worse if she had not run forward so resolutely to save Véronique. Madame Soubise was killed by the heavy coping stone from the roof; only part of the lower wall fell down and it was made up of dry old bricks which fragmented in the explosion. Lady Chilcote and Véronique were partly sheltered by the parapet of an old well which stood in the middle of the courtyard and we were able to shovel the debris away in a matter of minutes.'

'You were there?'

'Yes.' Richard looked down involuntarily at his hands, still bruised and cut where he had used them in a frantic effort to reach Madeleine and Véronique before it was too late.

'I was in our . . . in my apartment. One of the windows blew in with the force of the explosion, but there was no other damage. I rushed in from another room to see what happened and I was just in time to see . . . '

To see the front of the building to his left crack and shiver and begin to tumble; to see the tiny, frightened child in the courtyard, and then the slender, quick-running figure of the woman who was the dearest thing in the world to him, skimming over the ground with her arms outstretched like a low-flying bird; to see the beautiful, protective curve of her body as she gathered the child underneath her and sheltered her from the menace that threatened the small life; and then they had both disappeared. It was a moment that returned again and again to haunt him. He could not describe it to Madeleine's husband. He passed a trembling, scarred hand over his face, and again the other man looked at him with penetrating attention.

'My wife had a terrible experience just over a year ago, when she saw a man buried alive,' Lord Chilcote said in his abrupt way. 'It preyed on her mind. To suffer a similar experience herself would be particularly terrible to her, to such an extent that I would be afraid of its effect on her sanity.'

'She never told me that,' Richard murmured.

'You have known her for such a short time,' Lord Chilcote pointed out, and noted with malicious satisfaction that he had made the other man wince.

'What you tell me makes her courage all the more remarkable,' Richard said. 'She was outside the courtyard when the shell exploded. She deliberately ran in, straight under the collapsing wall, to save little Véronique Soubise.'

A little smile played about Lord Chilcote's lips. 'Yes, she would do that,' he said. Again he glanced at the young doctor with narrowed eyes. 'The man who died was Véronique's father,' he added softly.

There was a short silence while Richard digested the unwelcome realisation that there were vast areas of shared experience between Madeleine and her husband of which he was ignorant, but Lord Chilcote was speaking again and he had to collect his thoughts to answer him.

'Should she be roused?' he was asking.

'My own knowledge of these cases is limited,' Richard Anthony admitted honestly. 'But I have consulted my Chief Surgeon and his opinion is that the attempt should be made. In fact . . . ' he broke off, unwilling to admit that he had been unable to make any contact with Madeleine's unconscious mind.

'You have tried and failed,' Lord Chilcote

said with his maddening percipience. He moved back to stand by the side of the bed and looked down at his wife's still form with an unreadable expression on his face. 'May I try to reach her?'

The doctor in Richard Anthony struggled with the lover. 'Yes,' he said at last and the effort it cost him was perfectly visible to the other man.

Lord Chilcote sat down by the side of the bed and took Madeleine's hands in a firm clasp. 'Madeleine,' he said in a commanding voice. 'Madeleine, look at me.' The still figure on the bed did not move. 'Madeleine, it's Janus. Open your eyes. You know that you are safe with me.'

The heavy eyelids fluttered; her hand moved under his. Slowly her head turned on the pillow and her eyes opened, blinking as she tried to focus. Her tongue moved over her lips. 'Janus?' she said.

'Yes. Come along, wake up! You have been asleep long enough.'

Again she licked her dry lips. 'The child?' she asked in a faint whisper.

'The child is safe.'

A singularly sweet smile just touched her mouth. 'God has forgiven me,' she said.

'I dare say. Are you thirsty?'

'Yes.'

Richard Anthony came forward, a feeding cup in his hand, and Janus moved away to allow him to hold it to her lips.

'Richard!' Madeleine said. 'Dear Richard!'

It was some comfort that she had recognised him and spoken with obvious affection, but what he had witnessed between her and her husband made him suddenly aware that there might be more difficulty in undoing this marriage than he had anticipated when the whole world had seemed to consist of only Madeleine and himself. A curious uneasiness invaded him. It was not possible that he might lose Madeleine; not now, not to this strange, hard man who had betrayed so little emotion even when she had roused herself to speak to him. With a mixture of bravado and trepidation he resolved to bring the state of his feelings out into the open far sooner than he had intended.

As soon as he and Lord Chilcote had left Madeleine to the care of a nursing sister, Richard said briefly, 'I feel I must tell you, my lord, that I have come to be extremely attached to Lady Chilcote.'

'In love with her, are you?' Janus asked. 'How did you come to know her?'

'We lived . . . we both had lodgings at the apartment house which was shelled,' Richard Anthony said. 'You are right, I am in love with her. I am not ashamed to admit it. If she were free . . . if she were ever to become free,' he added carefully, 'I would be honoured to marry her.'

'And Madeleine?'

Richard hesitated, chivalrously unwilling to commit Madeleine irrevocably without her knowledge. 'I hope . . . I believe that she loves me,' he said.

'I see.' Lord Chilcote's face told him nothing. 'I have no idea whether she still loves me. Probably not. It seems that we shall have to possess our souls in patience until she is well enough to decide between us.'

He departed abruptly, leaving Richard's mind in a state of turmoil. At one moment, when Madeleine had returned from her twilight world at her husband's command, it had seemed to Richard that she must be lost to him, and yet how could she love this unfeeling man who refused to allow himself even to appear surprised on hearing that his wife was probably in love with another man? Had he understood that they had actually been lovers? Richard believed that he had, and yet it seemed that he did not care. If that was the way of the British aristocracy then Richard was ready to believe all the stories he had heard of its decadence. It did not occur to him that his distaste for Lord Chilcote's moral turpitude assorted ill with his own desire to marry a divorced member of that same aristocracy, nor that it was an attitude which might at a later date cause conflict between him and Madeleine if she chose to live with him in a small town in America.

She gained a little strength each day, her bruises began to fade and her cracked ribs to heal. Janus visited her, but only once a day, and since he never requested that the watchful sister should leave him alone with his wife, no controversial subjects were raised. It was Richard who spent more time with her, although he was still required at the military hospital and was not as free as he would have liked to be.

She was promoted to a few stumbling steps out of bed, as far as a chaise-longue by the fire, carefully wrapped in a blanket to keep her warm. Richard was with her, congratulating her on this significant improvement, when a large, flat box was delivered to her. Inside was a gift from Janus, a long, loose dressing-gown in blue quilted silk, light, warm and exquisitely made.

Richard, regretting that he had not thought of this for himself, said jealously, 'I wonder where he found it?'

'If there is any fine lingerie to be had in Paris, Janus would be sure to know where to find it,' Madeleine said, with just the tiniest thread of amusement in her voice. She was, indeed, fighting a wild desire to burst out laughing at this typical, extravagant, yet eminently practical gesture.

'Lord Chilcote seems to be more considerate than I had been giving him credit for.'

'Considerate? No, I wouldn't call him that,' Madeleine said. 'But given to odd, almost inexplicable acts of kindness, sudden flashes of understanding — yes, that is Janus.'

She looked suddenly exhausted and Richard hurriedly abandoned a subject which was obviously beyond her strength to discuss at that time.

She was wearing the dressing-gown the next time Janus visited her. 'You look more like yourself,' he remarked.

'It's a long time since I wore anything so fine,' Madeleine said, smoothing the silk with hands which during her illness had begun to lose the roughness they had acquired while she was doing manual work.

She saw that he was watching her with a smile and she could not keep back the answering gleam of amusement. 'The Rue de la Paix is bent on making a little profit out of the victors,' Lord Chilcote said blandly. 'All sorts of treasures are being brought out of hiding — if you know the right shops.'

It was the first time Véronique had been allowed to visit her and now she drew the child forward. 'This is Jeanne's daughter,' she said. 'Curtsey to Lord Chilcote, *chérie*.'

Véronique made a very creditable curtsey and looked up for applause. Janus's eyes crinkled in amusement. 'Charming,' he said. 'A little fairy.'

Madeleine signalled for the nursing sister to take the child away. 'I have engaged a nurse to look after her,' she said. 'But I have to tell you that I have no money to pay her wages.'

'So I am to pay, I suppose? Very well.'

'I even sold my betrothal ring,' Madeleine said.

'It is of no importance. I will get it back for you — if you want it.'

Since this came too near to the unspoken question between them, Madeleine did not reply. Janus watched her in silence for a moment and then, taking advantage of the sister's absence, he said abruptly, 'Jeanne made me believe that the child was yours.'

Madeleine's eyes flew to his face. 'But that

would have been impossible!' she exclaimed.

Janus shrugged. 'A jealous man can be made to believe anything.'

'Especially when it is told to him by his mistress,' Madeleine said, with a bitterness she could not conceal.

'Jeanne was hardly my mistress — not in the sense you mean,' Janus said evenly. 'She came to my room — of her own volition — once and once only. If you and I had not quarrelled earlier in the evening, if I had not been in a lather of jealousy over that young Frenchman — what was his name?'

'I have forgotten.'

'You've forgotten! How ironical! Well, whatever he was called, I had seen you in his arms and I was ready to take any steps to wipe out the memory.'

'You didn't apparently see me hit him with my fan?'

'No. All I saw was that you gave him your hands to kiss and looked me boldly in the face as if nothing had happened. I was ripe to fall into Jeanne's hands after that. Why the devil did you take her into your employ, Madeleine?'

'Pity,' Madeleine said. 'Guilt. I had so much and she had so little. Henri de Cavaillon threw her over when he discovered that she was having a child. The same thing might so easily have happened to me. The life she was leading . . . I felt I had a duty to rescue her from that. She asked me to give her a chance to rehabilitate herself as my maid and I agreed, mistakenly I suppose.'

'Certainly mistakenly. What Jeanne was looking for was revenge. She's dead by the way.'

'Poor Jeanne.' For a moment Madeleine paused to consider that ill-fated, misspent life. 'That means Véronique has no-one left,' she said. 'I feel responsible for her, Janus.'

'We'll make some suitable arrangement for Véronique — whatever happens,' Janus promised. 'Your young doctor seems very attached to her, too.'

Again the difficult question of Madeleine's position between the two men hovered in the air, and again he let it go. He got up. 'I shall come to visit you tomorrow,' he said. 'I can see you are tired now.'

He moved away and the thought came to her that never once since he had come to Paris had he offered her the slightest caress. She was not sure whether she was glad or sorry. If he had attempted to kiss her in front of Richard it would have been an acute embarrassment, and yet the fact that he had not so much as touched her argued that he either guessed about her involvement with Richard or else that he had grown indifferent to her during their long separation.

'Did you think of me at all in all those long weeks while I was missing?' she asked abruptly before he could reach the door.

'Of course,' he said, looking back over his shoulder. 'Incessantly.' The sardonic, self-mocking smile she recollected from the past was back on his lips. 'I had to take quite drastic steps to drive you out of my thoughts. I don't think I very often went sober to bed.'

'Nor alone either, I presume,' Madeleine asked.

The smile deepened. 'As to that, I will make no admissions, except that I found other women astonishingly tedious after you, Madeleine. I did my best to break my neck on the hunting field, I lost a vast amount of money at the gaming tables — in fact, I pursued a classic course of ruin and dissipation.'

'Why didn't you make any attempt to get me out of France?' she asked.

'I did,' Janus said. 'At least, I did once I had had your letter — which was considerably delayed — and realised that you had not abandoned me to go and seek your own love child.' He paused to consider his frantic efforts to gain entrance to Paris. 'I really went to quite a lot of trouble.' He glanced back at her, looking so much more like her former self in her elegant silk dressing-gown, in spite of the disfigurement of her shorn head. 'I wonder whether it was worth it?' he said and left her to consider his meaning with as much patience as she could muster until their next meeting.

Before she saw her husband again Madeleine had received an enquiry about her health from a quarter which surprised her very much indeed. She heard about it first by way of a whispered consultation between the hotel manager and her nurse.

'What is it?' Madeleine asked.

Soeur Clarice turned, her placid face betraying

neither surprise nor the hostility the manager had shown. 'The Crown Prince of Prussia has sent an officer to enquire about you,' she said.

'The Crown Prince of Prussia!' Madeleine exclaimed. 'You can't be serious!'

'I assure you, miladi,' the hotel manager said. 'His equerry is below, waiting for a reply.'

Madeleine gave a faint, distasteful grimace. 'He can hardly believe that his interest is welcome to me, in the circumstances,' she said. 'I cannot understand it. How did he know I was in Paris?' Again she frowned. 'I think I would like to see this equerry.'

'As you wish, miladi,' the manager murmured.

If she had but known it, the carefully correct attitude of the young officer who was ushered into her room concealed an equally burning curiosity to see this woman who had inspired her husband to an act of folly which was well known to all the Crown Prince's staff. He gave a stiff, heel-clicking bow and delivered himself of his message in excellent English.

'I am flattered by the Crown Prince's interest,' Madeleine said, with an irony which was wasted on the young officer. 'How does it happen that he is aware of my presence in Paris and my unfortunate injury?'

'Lord Chilcote has had more than one audience with the Prince,' the equerry said, trying not to show his surprise that it should be necessary for him to tell her this. He smiled. 'Including an interview at which I regret to say that it was necessary for the Prince to reprove him for most irregular conduct.'

'What did he do?'

'He attempted to cross between our lines and those of the French on foot and alone at night. He was extremely lucky not to have been shot.'

'Was he so impatient to enter Paris?'

'It would seem so — and who can blame him?' He hesitated and then said with a slight awkwardness he had not displayed before, 'I am commanded to convey to you the very great regret of the German High Command that you should have sustained injury in this war in which you were not a participant.'

He got no more in response to this than a slight movement of the head which Janus would have recognised as Madeleine at her most haughty. The bitter weeks she had suffered in the siege weighed too heavily on her to be lightly dismissed in response to a few words of regret, but after a struggle she managed to say, 'Please thank his Highness for his kind enquiry and inform him that I am making excellent progress.'

The interview was at an end and the young officer departed, deeply impressed by the beauty discernible in spite of her sufferings and by the freezing courtesy which had dismissed him and his enquiry as if she had been royalty itself, while Madeleine, beside herself with the anger she had suppressed, picked up one of her cushions and hurled it to the other side of the room.

'How dare he send to enquire about me — just because I am English and the wife of a peer of the realm! No word of regret about anyone else, you'll notice! What about poor old Madame Soubise? What about the other men, women and children who died?'

'They were French, miladi,' Soeur Clarice said with unshaken calm. She picked up the cushion and replaced it behind Madeleine's back. 'It is a sign of grace that the Prince should be concerned about you. You must pray for his charity to increase.'

It was two days before Madeleine was able to share her indignation with the person she held responsible for the visit, and as she might have guessed Janus looked only mildly surprised when she told him about it.

'He struck me as being a decent chap,' he said. 'And a humanitarian.'

'A Prussian humanitarian!'

'Certainly. The bombardment of Paris troubled him greatly. I felt almost sorry for him.'

'You appear to have become quite friendly with him. I'm told you were received by him several times.'

'Twice.'

'Is it true that you tried to get into Paris without permission from either side?'

She waited for his answer with a coolness which concealed her inner impatience. Of all the things she had known him to do, this seemed the most unlikely, and the debate in her mind about his motives for this foolhardy action had kept her awake for hours.

Janus failed to meet her eyes. He shrugged. 'I told you I went to quite a lot of trouble. Letters from the Prince of Wales and an interview with his brother-in-law having failed, I took the matter into my own hands. As you may remember, I have a somewhat impatient nature.'

'Why did you do it?'

'Remorse, my dear — not a thing I suffer from very often. It was borne in on me that I had really been very remiss in not taking steps to remove you to safety somewhat earlier. Once I had realised that my suspicions of you were founded on nothing more substantial than Jeanne's fantasies I felt obliged to move a mountain or two to reach you. With a singular lack of success, you will observe.'

It was not an answer that entirely satisfied Madeleine, but all she said, going off at a tangent, was 'Why didn't you visit me yesterday?'

'I was making arrangements for our return to England. If you intend coming back with me, that is. On the whole I would recommend it. France is rapidly falling into a state of anarchy. You will be safer in England.'

The moment had come which she could no longer avoid. 'There is something I ought to tell you before we leave Paris,' Madeleine said resolutely.

'I think I can guess what it is. Young Anthony has said that if you were free he would marry you.' A slight, cynical smile touched his lips. 'He is too much of a gentleman to suggest the possibility of a divorce, but I imagine that is what he had in mind, rather than my own untimely demise.' There was a brief silence which Madeleine made no attempt to break. 'Do I have grounds for divorce?'

'Yes.'

Again that slight smile. 'You are too honest — as usual. Do you want me to divorce you?'

'Would you?'

He moved away from her and went to look out of the window. 'If that was what you wanted,' he said in a carefully even voice.

'It would cause a great scandal.'

Janus shrugged. 'You would not have to live with it. You, I presume, would be in the New World and I doubt whether a brief scandal in London Society would count for much in America. As for me — my life has been one long scandal. I shall survive.'

'You have every right to discard me,' Madeleine said in a low voice. 'I have not behaved well. I have been unfaithful. At the first temptation, I fell — I, who had condemned you for one lapse.'

'The circumstances were exceptional. Living constantly in the presence of death one clutches at anything which enhances life.'

'You understand that?'

'Yes.'

'And you could forgive me?'

'If it comes to a question of forgiveness, Madeleine, the scales are weighted heavily in your favour. You have a great deal to forgive me.'

'It seems I have a choice, then? Divorce, or . . . ?'

'To return to me as my wife.'

'I had not expected that.' She looked curiously at his rigid back. 'I must make it clear to you that I am not admitting to one isolated act. I lived with Richard for weeks, in some ways more intimately than I ever did with you. My attachment to him goes very deep.'

'You can spare me the details,' he said in a voice that was less well-controlled than it had been.

'No, it has to be brought out into the open. You would have to live with that knowledge if I came back to you. I am not sure you could bear it.'

He half turned towards her and then averted his head again. 'I know you well enough to understand that if you chose to become my wife again it could only be because you loved me better than you loved him. In those circumstances, I would not find it difficult to forgive anything you had done.'

'Do you want me back, Janus?'

'Yes.' Again his voice was not quite steady. 'On any terms, any conditions you care to name.' He turned to face her and she saw the pain in his eyes. 'I love you more than I ever believed possible. I — who swore never to let any woman have such power over me!' He took a deep, steadying breath. 'I even love you enough to let you go, if that is what you want. Why not? Your young American is a fine man and he loves you at least as much as I do; you could make a new life for yourself. The imagination quails slightly at the thought of your impact on a small American town, but no doubt with your well-developed social sense you could adapt yourself to their ideas. I gather he is not without money, he could support you in style.'

'A divorced woman to become the wife of a doctor?'

The door opened and Richard Anthony came in. He glanced from one to the other of them, sensing that he had interrupted an important and intimate discussion, and then realisation of the words he had half heard as he came through the door penetrated his mind and he took an impulsive step forward. 'Divorce?' he said.

'I have told my husband that you and I were lovers during the siege.'

His face flushed and he shot a quick glance at Janus, but Madeleine went on smoothly, 'And he has offered to divorce me in order to enable me to marry you — if that is what you want.'

'Want? It's my dream of heaven come true! And look, there'd be no need to worry about my profession. It was always Dad's intention to set me up in a clinic of my own when I'd got enough experience behind me. Once we've got him on our side — and when he's set eyes on you I've got no fears on that score — my position would be unassailable, and yours too.'

He held out his hands and Madeleine put both of hers into his strong warm clasp. 'A new life, my darling!' he murmured, his face alight with happiness.

'A new life,' Madeleine agreed, but her hands slipped away from his as she spoke.

'Your choice is made?' Janus asked. His voice

was harsh and Richard, seeing the look on his face, took an instinctive step nearer to Madeleine as if to protect her.

'There was never any real doubt about it,' Madeleine said. She turned to Richard again. 'Richard, you have been my dear companion during times more dreadful than I had ever imagined possible. You have been my comfort, my strong support; I honour and respect you; I even love you. But I shall stay with my husband.'

He stared at her, his face rigid with shock, misery dawning in his eyes as he recognised the irrevocable nature of her decision. It was Janus who said, in a voice hoarse with strain, 'Why?'

She turned her head and looked at him with a smile in her eyes. 'Be quiet,' she said. 'I will explain myself to you when we are alone.'

She turned back to Richard, with compassion and regret for the hurt she had dealt him.

'Nothing will make you change your mind?' he asked, knowing that the question was useless.

'Nothing.' She took one of his hands in hers and raised it gently to her lips. He stood for a moment, his head bent, and then he turned and left the room without another word. Madeleine sat looking at the closed door until, behind her, Janus repeated his question, 'Why?'

She turned to face him. 'Richard Anthony is everything you said of him — fine, and honourable, and true — but you and I . . . we are one flesh, one mind. You understand me as Richard would never understand me. I had no hesitation in telling you that he had been my lover and you were hurt, but not shocked. Richard was shocked — did you see? — because I had told you.' She shook her head with a slight smile. 'To Richard I am a figure of high romance, a fairy princess he discovered amongst the ruins of an ancient city, but you know me for the woman I am, and love me in spite of my faults.'

He had not moved from the window. 'And can you love me, in spite of *my* faults?'

Her answer brought him to her in two swift strides. 'You are the other half of my very soul.'

He caught her up in his arms and, looking up into his face, she saw that his eyes were wet, the first time for many squandered years that Janus Chilcote had wept for any cause. He kissed her with all the force of his pent up passion and wild relief, until Madeleine drew back and murmured with a note of laughter in her voice, 'I am supposed to be an invalid.'

'My poor love, how I do abuse you! Come and sit down.' He settled her on the *chaise longue* once more, and sat down beside her, his eyes anxiously scrutinising her face. 'I am as selfish as ever,' he said remorsefully. 'You mustn't expect me to reform overnight, dear girl.' His voice broke and he bent over her hands. 'Oh, Madeleine, the relief of knowing that I am not going to lose you!'

She looked down at his bent head with its dark, ruffled hair and the tide of love which rose in her was so strong that it was difficult to speak.

'When you said you wanted a new life, I thought you were going to leave me,' Janus said.

'I do want a new life,' Madeleine said. 'And I mean to have it. I can't go back to the way I lived before, shut out of every aspect of your life except your bed. You must share more than that with me, Janus.'

'I will,' he promised.

'As for me, you told me once that I must allow myself to be forgiven, and you were right. We must both turn our backs on the past and start again.'

'A new life,' he repeated. 'We'll put this dark night of foolish misunderstanding behind us and start out together in a fresh, bright day.'

THE END

Other titles in the Charnwood Library Series:

LEGACIES
Janet Dailey

The sequel to THE PROUD AND THE FREE. It is twenty years since the feud within his family began, but Lije Stuart, son of the Cherokee chief The Blade, had never forgotten the killing of his grandfather. Now, a promising legal career beckons, and also the love of his childhood sweetheart, Diane Parmalee, the daughter of a US Army officer. Yet as it reawakens, their love is beset by the beginning of civil war.

'L' IS FOR LAWLESS
Sue Grafton

World War II fighter pilot Johnny Lee had died and his grandson was trying to claim military funeral benefits, but none of the authorities have any record of Fighter J. Lee. Was the old man once a US spy? When PI Kinsey Millhone is asked to straighten things out, she finds herself pursued by a psychopath bearing a forty-year-old grudge . . .

BLOOD LINES
Ruth Rendell

This is a collection of long and short stories by Ruth Rendell that will linger in the mind.

THE SUN IN GLORY
Harriet Hudson

When industrialist William Potts sets himself to build a flying machine, his adopted daughter, Rosie, works through the years as his mechanic. In 1906 Pegasus is almost ready, and onto the scene comes Jake Smith, a man who has as deep a love of the air as Rosie herself. But Jake sparks off a deadly rivalry, and the triumph of flight twists into tragedy.

A WOMAN SCORNED
M. R. O'Donnell

Five years after the tragedy that ruined her fifteenth birthday, Judith Carty returns to Castle Moore and resumes her flirtation with its heir, Rick Bellingham. The tragic events of the past forge a special bond between the young couple, but there are those who have a vested interest in the failure of the romance.

PLAINER STILL
Catherine Cookson

Following the success of her previous collection of essays and poems, LET ME MAKE MYSELF PLAIN, Catherine Cookson has compiled a further selection of thoughts, recollections, and observations on life — and death — together with another collection of the poems she prefers to describe as 'prose on short lines'.

THE LOST WORLD
Michael Crichton

The successor to JURASSIC PARK. It is now six years since the secret disaster of Jurassic Park, when that extraordinary dream of science and imagination came to a crashing end — the dinosaurs destroyed, and the park dismantled. There are rumours that something has survived . . .

MORNING, NOON & NIGHT
Sidney Sheldon

When Harry Stanford, one of the wealthiest men in the world, mysteriously drowns, it sets off a chain of events that reverberates around the globe. At the family gathering following the funeral, a beautiful young woman appears, claiming to be Harry's daughter. Is she genuine, or is she an impostor?

FACING THE MUSIC
Jayne Torvill and Christopher Dean

The world's most successful and popular skating couple tell their own story, from their working-class childhoods in Nottingham to world stardom. Finally, they describe how they created their own show, FACE THE MUSIC, with a superb corps of international ice dancers.

ORANGES AND LEMONS
Jeanne Whitmee
When Shirley Rayner is evacuated from London's East End, she finds herself billeted with the theatre's most romantic couple, Tony and Leonie Darrent. She becomes firm friends with their daughter, Imogen, and the two girls dream of making their names on the stage. But they have forgotten the very different backgrounds from which they come.

HALF HIDDEN
Emma Blair
Holly Morgan, a nurse in a hospital on Nazi-occupied Jersey, falls in love with a young German doctor, Peter Schmidt, and is racked by guilt. Can their love survive the future together or will the war destroy all their hopes and dreams?

THE GREAT TRAIN ROBBERY
Michael Crichton
In Victorian London, where lavish wealth and appalling poverty exist side by side, one man navigates both worlds with ease. Rich, handsome and ingenious, Edward Pierce preys on the most prominent of the well-to-do as he cunningly orchestrates the crime of his century.

THIS CHILD IS MINE
Henry Denker

Lori Adams, a young, unmarried actress, gives up her baby boy for adoption with great reluctance. She feels that she and the baby's father, Brett, are not in a position to provide their child with all he deserves. But when, two years later, life has improved dramatically for Lori and Brett, they want their child returned . . .

THE LOST DAUGHTERS
Jeanne Whitmee

At school, Cathy and Rosalind have one thing in common: each is the child of a single parent. For them both, the transition to adulthood is far from easy — until their unexpected reunion. Working together, the two friends take a bold step that will help them to become independent women.

THE DEVIL YOU KNOW
Josephine Cox

When Sonny Fareham overhears a private conversation between her lover and his wife, she realises she is in great danger. Shocked and afraid, she flees to the north of England to make a new life — but never far away is the one person who wants to destroy everything that she now holds dear.

A LETHAL INVOLVEMENT
Clive Egleton

When Captain Simon Oakham of the Royal Army pay Corps goes A.W.O.L. immediately after a suspicious interview with the security service, Peter Ashton is asked to track him down. The key to it all is an embittered woman whose unsuspecting knowledge of a lethal involvement makes her especially vulnerable.

THE WAY WE WERE
Marie Joseph

This is a collection of some of Marie Joseph's most outstanding short stories, and is the companion volume to WHEN LOVE WAS LIKE THAT. With compassion, insight and humour, these stories explore the themes of love — its hopes, joys, disappointments and reconciliations.

EXTREME DENIAL
David Morrell

When CIA agent Stephen Decker is sent on a sensitive mission to Italy, his partner is Brian McKittrick, the incompetent and embittered son of the former chairman of the National Security Council. Disobeying orders throughout the mission, McKittrick makes one final mistake: sleeping with the enemy.

THE WOOD BEYOND
Reginald Hill

Seeing the wood for the trees is a problem shared by Andy Dalziel and Edgar Wield, the latter in his investigations into bones found at a pharmaceutical research centre, and the former in his dangerous involvement with animal rights activist Amanda Marvell.

RAGE OF THE INNOCENT
Frederick E. Smith

The first of a trilogy.

Young Harry Miles clashes with Michael Chadwick, son of a wealthy landowner, and sows the seeds of a lifetime's conflict. When the 1914 – 18 war breaks out, Harry is driven into volunteering and finds himself under Chadwick's command. Taking his revenge, Chadwick makes Harry a machine gunner . . .

MOTHER OF GOD
David Ambrose

Tessa Lambert has just created the first viable artificial intelligence programme — a discovery so controversial that she must keep it a secret even from her colleagues at Oxford University. But soon there is to be a hacker stalking her on the Internet: a serial killer who is about to give her invention its own terrifying and completely malevolent life . . .

THE ANDROMEDA STRAIN
Michael Crichton

When *Project Scoop* sends satellites into outerspace to 'collect organisms and dust for study', one of them crashes into the town of Piedmont, Arizona. Soon after, all but two of the inhabitants are found dead from a strange disease. The scientists must trace what is causing the horrifying virus before it spreads . . .

TO WAR WITH WHITAKER
Countess of Ranfurly

When World War II broke out, Dan Ranfurly was dispatched to the Middle East with his faithful valet, Whitaker. These are the diaries of his young wife, Hermione, who, defying the War Office, raced off in hot pursuit of her husband. When Dan was taken prisoner, Hermione vowed never to return home until they were reunited.

IN PRESENCE OF MY FOES
Frederick E. Smith

Sequel to RAGE OF THE INNOCENT. Harry Miles is now recovered from his war wounds, but a mysterious and compelling urge drives him back to the Front. He faces the menace of Michael Chadwick, his commanding officer and life-long rival, and the fearsome German offensive of March 1918.

YEARS OF THE FURY
Frederick E. Smith
The third volume of the trilogy which began with RAGE OF THE INNOCENT and continued with IN PRESENCE OF MY FOES.
The First World War has ended and, with Harry Miles back from France, he and Mary are hoping to settle down to their married life at last. But they have not taken account of their two unrelenting enemies.

FAMILY TREES
Kate Alexander
Catherine Carew fills her life with good works and is a pillar of the community. But in her distant university days she was a very different person. One night's indiscretion leaves her with a burden of guilt and regret that overshadows her later years — until a stranger appears on her doorstep . . .

INDIAN SUMMER
James Mitchell
Mixed blood courses through Veronica Higgins' veins, resulting in an exotic beauty. But to the expatriates in India at the height of the British Raj she is just another 'bloody chee-chee'. When her Aunt Poppy falls in love with an English industrialist, the three set off for his homeland. The arrival of one of England's richest men with two exquisitely beautiful women causes a flurry of excitement . . .

VANISHING POINT
Morris West

When Carl Strassberger, the son of an old New York banking family, renounces his position in the business to become an artist, his place is taken by his brother-in-law, Larry Lucas. But when Larry disappears, Carl must put himself at risk as he investigates those who live 'on the dangerous edge of things'.

THE RUNAWAY
John Grisham

In Biloxi, Mississippi, a landmark trial begins routinely, then swerves mysteriously off course. The jury is behaving strangely, and at least one juror is convinced that he is being watched. Is the jury somehow being manipulated or even controlled? If so, by whom? And, more importantly, why?

SHADOWS OF THE PAST
Palma Harcourt

When Christopher Grayson, a young Oxford don, decides to trace his family history, he learns that during the Second World War the de Mourvilles were condemned as Nazi sympathisers. Even worse, his grandfather was accused of crimes against humanity. But someone is on Christopher's trail, willing to kill in order to keep a tragic secret.

YEAR OF THE TIGER
Jack Higgins

When Paul Chavasse looks out of his window on a November evening, he is unaware that the figure standing opposite knows a great deal about his past. Back in 1961, Chavasse — now chief of a little-known section of British Intelligence — had been captured by the Chinese. When he had at last escaped he knew that he could be taking with him the means of his betrayal.

THAT CAMDEN SUMMER
LaVyrle Spencer

It is 1916 and Roberta Jewett has returned to the town where she was raised. But in Camden, Maine, a woman divorced is a woman shunned. Only Gabriel Farley treats her with respect. Although the chemistry between them is undeniable, they fight it. Then, a brutal act of violence forces them to aknowledge the powerful feelings that have grown between them.

PASSIONATE TIMES
Emma Blair

When Corporal Reith Douglas was injured during the Second World War, he lost his memory. But once he returns to his wife, Irene, in Glasgow, he gradually recalls the joy of his early married life, and the pain he suffered when Irene declared her love for a renowned villain. Little does he realise that he could well recapture the passionate times of his past.

NOT JUST A SOLDIER'S WAR
Betty Burton
For Lu Wilmott, the call to Spain is irresistible. Signing up as a driver, she breaks the last link with her past and becomes Eve. Her work takes her close to figures of many nationalities, but it is the country and its people in the struggle against Franco that have the greatest effect on her.

THE WITCH OF EXMOOR
Margaret Drabble
The Palmer family and their children are coming to the end of an enjoyable meal. As usual, their conversation is brought back to their eccentric mother, Frieda, who has abandoned them and gone off to live alone on Exmoor. She has always been a monster mother with a mysterious past. What is she plotting against them now?

LEWIN'S MEAD
E. V. Thompson
The sequel to the bestselling novel BECKY When artist Fergus Vincent forsakes the Bristol slums of Lewin's Mead he leaves behind him Becky, the street urchin whom he loved and married. After Becky is struck down in a cholera epidemic, she is cared for by Simon McAllister, a blind musician. But she never gives up hope that one day Fergus will return.

ENDPEACE
Jon Cleary

When Detective Inspector Scobie Malone's host, the wealthy Sydney newspaper magnate Sir Harry Huxwood, is shot dead in his own bed, it is Malone's job to name the killer. He uncovers the stuff of headlines, including a family dogfight over millions of dollars.

TO THE HILT
Dick Francis

Artist Alexander Kinloch's peaceful existence on a remote Scottish mountain is shattered when he returns home one day to find a group of strangers waiting for him. The days that follow contain more danger than he could ever have imagined.

WISH LIST
Fern Michaels

Hollywood actress Ariel Hart has become tired of the empty glamour, so she returns to the place where she was once truly happy — where she was plain Aggie Bixby, in love with a dark-eyed boy named Felix. Then she comes across wealthy rancher Lex Sanders, and there is something familiar about those smouldering eyes . . .

FOR I HAVE SINNED
M. R. O'Donnell
In 1913, on Salome McKenna's seventh birthday, her family emigrates from Ireland to the Cape. Too late they discover that, tragically, they have left her behind. Marion Culham-Browne takes Salome under her wing, intending to arrange her later passage to the Cape. But her resolution fades as her love for the little girl flourishes.

A TIME FOR US
Josephine Cox
Lucy Nolan's happiness is complete when she is made the junior partner of a successful garden centre. But she is prepared to give up everything when Jack Hanson asks her to marry him — even if it means living abroad where Jack has been offered an exciting business opportunity. Then tragedy strikes . . .

SHADOW BABY
Margaret Forster
Evie and Shona have only one thing in common: both were abandoned as babies by their mothers. Different times, different circumstances, but the two girls grow up sharing the same obsession. Each sets out to stalk and then haunt her natural mother . . .

'M' IS FOR MALICE
Sue Grafton

'M' is for the Malek family: four sons now nearing middle age who stand to inherit a fortune — four very different men, linked only by blood and money. Eighteen years ago, one of them — angry and troubled — went missing. 'M' is for Millhone, hired to trace him. And 'M' is for murder . . .

THE MAN WHO LISTENS TO HORSES
Monty Roberts

This is the life story of a man whose unique methods reveal the depth of communication that is possible between man and horse. According to Monty, anyone can learn the language of the horse and anyone can learn Monty's 'join up' methods. In this book he tells you how.

CALL FOR FIRE
Captain Chris Craig

This is a first-hand account of fighting in the Falklands and the Gulf campaigns by the only British senior officer who commanded in both of these major wars.